Honour Among Thieves

David Chandler was born in Pittsburgh, Pennsylvania, in 1971. He attended Penn State and received an MFA in creative writing. In his alter-ego as David Wellington, he writes critically acclaimed and popular horror novels and was one of the co-authors of the *New York Times* bestseller *Marvel Zombies Return*. *The Ancient Blades Trilogy* is his first fantasy series.

By David Chandler

The Ancient Blades Trilogy

DEN OF THIEVES
A THIEF IN THE NIGHT
HONOUR AMONG THIEVES

Honour Among Thieves

Book Three of
The Ancient Blades Trilogy

DAVID CHANDLER

HARPER
Voyager

HarperVoyager
An imprint of HarperCollins*Publishers*
77–85 Fulham Palace Road,
Hammersmith, London W6 8JB

www.harpercollins.co.uk

This paperback edition 2011
1

First published in Great Britain by HarperVoyager in 2011

A catalogue record for this book is
available from the British Library

ISBN: 978 0 00 738415 0

Typeset by Palimpsest Book Production Limited,
Falkirk, Stirlingshire

Printed and bound in Great Britain by
Clays Ltd, St Ives plc

For J.R.R.T. and G.R.R.M., the Epic Overlords.

ACKNOWLEDGMENTS

O warrior, hear now, the song of praises:
'Twas ALEX LENCICKI, son of John, who beat the war drum;
RUSSELL GALEN, who hath launched one thousand ships, gathered us to arms;
DIANA GILL honed raw iron into sharpened blades;
and WILL HINTON put us in formation to do battle.

Lacking these stalwarts, and a host of brave battlers besides, the tale would ne'er be told.

David Wellington
New York City, 2011

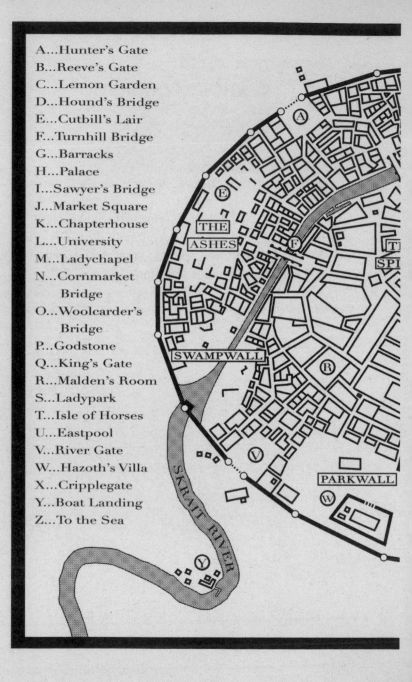

THE FREE CITY OF NESS

PROLOGUE

The Free City of Ness was known around the world as a hotbed of thievery, and one man alone was responsible for that reputation. Cutbill, master of that city's guild of thieves, controlled almost every aspect of clandestine commerce within its walls—from extortion to pickpocketing, from blackmail to shoplifting he oversaw a great empire of crime. His fingers were in far more pies than anyone even realized, and his ambitions far greater than simple acquisition of wealth—and far broader-reaching than the affairs of just one city. His interests lay in every corner of the globe and his spies were everywhere.

As a result he received a fair volume of mail every day.

In his office under the streets of Ness he went through this pile of correspondence with the aid of only one assistant. Lockjaw, an elderly thief with a legendary reputation was always there when Cutbill opened his letters. There were two reasons why Lockjaw held this privileged responsibility—for one, Lockjaw was famous for his discretion. He'd received his sobriquet for the fact he never revealed a secret. The other reason was that he'd never learned to read.

It was Lockjaw's duty to receive the correspondence, usually from messengers who stuck around only long enough to get paid, and to comment on each message as Cutbill told him its contents. If Lockjaw wondered why such a clever man wanted his untutored opinion, he never asked.

"Interesting," Cutbill said, holding a piece of parchment up to the light. "This is from the dwarven kingdom. It seems they've invented a new machine up there. Some kind of winepress that churns out books instead of vintage."

The old thief scowled. "That right? Do they come out soaking wet?"

"I imagine that would be a defect in the process," Cutbill agreed. "Still. If it works, it could produce books at a fraction of the cost a copyist charges now."

"Bad news, then," Lockjaw said.

"Oh?"

"Books is expensive," the thief explained. "There's good money in stealing 'em. If they go cheap all of a sudden we'd be out of a profitable racket."

Cutbill nodded and put the letter aside, taking up another. "It'll probably come to nothing, this book press." He slit open the letter in his hand with a knife and scanned its contents. "News from our friend in the north. It looks like Maelfing will be at war with Skilfing by next summer. Over fishing rights, of course."

"That lot in the northern kingdoms is always fighting about something," Lockjaw pointed out. "You'd figure they'd have sorted everything out by now."

"The king of Skrae certainly hopes they never do," Cutbill told him. "As long as they keep at each other's throats, our northern border will remain secure. Pass me that packet, will you?"

The letter in question was written on a scroll of vellum wrapped in thin leather. Cutbill broke its seal and spread it out across his desk, peering at it from only a few inches away. "This is from our man in the high pass of the Whitewall Mountains."

"What could possibly happen in a desolated place like that?" Lockjaw asked.

"Nothing, nothing at all," Cutbill said. He looked up at the thief. "I pay my man there to make sure it stays that way. He read some more, and opened his mouth to make another comment—and then closed it again, his teeth clicking together. "Oh," he said.

Lockjaw held his peace and waited to hear what Cutbill had found.

The master of the guild of thieves, however, was unforthcoming. He rolled the scroll back up and shoved the whole thing in a charcoal brazier used to keep the office warm. Soon the scroll had caught flame and in a moment it was nothing but ashes.

Lockjaw raised an eyebrow, but said nothing.

Whatever was on that scroll clearly wasn't meant to be shared, even with Cutbill's most trusted associate. Which meant it had to be pretty important, Lockjaw figured. More so than who was stealing from whom or where the bodies were buried.

Cutbill went over to his ledger—the master account of all his dealings, and one of the most secret books on the continent. It contained every detail of all the crime that took place in Ness, as well as many things no one had ever heard of outside of this room. He opened it to a page near the back, then laid his knife across one of the pages, perhaps to keep it from fluttering out of place. Lockjaw noticed that this page was different from the others. Those were filled with columns of neat figures, endless rows of numbers. This page only held a single block of text, like a short message.

"Old man," Cutbill said, then, "could you do me a favor and pour me a cup of wine? My throat feels suddenly raw."

Cutbill had never asked for such a thing before. The man had enough enemies in the world that he made a point of always pouring his own wine—or having someone taste it before him. Lockjaw wondered what had changed, but he shrugged and did as he was told. He was getting paid for his time. He went to a table over by the door and poured a generous cup, then turned around again to hand it to his boss.

Except Cutbill wasn't there anymore.

That in itself wasn't so surprising. There were dozens of secret passages in Cutbill's lair, and only the guildmaster knew them all or where they led. Nor was it surprising that Cutbill would leave the room so abruptly. Cautious to a nicety, he always kept his movements secret.

No, what was surprising was that he didn't come back. He had effectively vanished from the face of the world.

Day after day Lockjaw—and the rest of Ness's thieves— waited for his return. No sign of him was found, nor any message received. Cutbill's operation began to falter in his absence—thieves stopped paying their dues to the guild, citizens under Cutbill's protection were suddenly vulnerable to theft, what coin did come in piled up uncounted and was spent on frivolous expenditures. Half of these excesses were committed in the belief that Cutbill, who had always run a tight ship, would be so offended he would have to come back just to put things in order.

But Cutbill left no trace, wherever he'd traveled.

It was quite a while before anyone thought to check the ledger, and the message Cutbill had so carefully marked.

PART 1

UNDER THE FLAG OF PARLEY

CHAPTER ONE

On the far side of the Whitewall mountains, in the grass-lands of the barbarians, in the mead tent of the Great Chieftain, fires raged and drink was passed from hand to hand, yet not a word was spoken. The gathered housemen of the Great Chieftain were too busy to gossip and sing as was their wont, too busy watching two men compete at an ancient ritual. Massive they were, as big as bears, and their muscles stood out from their arms and legs like the wood of dryland trees. They stood either side of a pit of blazing coals, each clutching hard to one end of a panther's hide. On one side, Torki, the champion of the Great Chieftain, victor of a thou-sand such contests. On the other side stood Mörget, whose lips were pulled back in a manic grin, the lower half of his face painted red in the traditional colors of a berserker, though he was a full chieftain now, leader of many clans.

Heaving, straining, gasping for breath in the fumes of the coals, the two struggled, each trying to pull the other into the coals. Every man and woman in the longhouse, every berserker and reaver of the Great Chieftain, every wife and thrall of the gathered warriors, watched in hushed expectation, each of them alone with their private thoughts, their desperate hopes.

There was only one who dared to speak freely, for such was always his right. Hurlind, the Great Chieftain's scold, was full of wine and laughter. "You're slipping, Mörg's Get! Pull as you might, he's dragging you. Why not let go, and save yourself from the fire? This is not a game for striplings!"

"Silence," Mörget hissed, from between clenched teeth.

Yet his grin was faltering, for it was true. Torki's grasp on the panther hide was like the grip of great tree roots on the earth. His arms were locked at the elbows and with the full power of his body, trained and toughened by the hard life of the steppes, he was pulling as inexorably as the ocean tide. Mörget slid toward the coals a fraction of an inch at a time, no matter how he dug his toes into the grit on the floor.

At the mead bench closest to the fire a reaver of the Great Chieftain placed a sack of gold on the table and nudged his neighbor, a chieftain of great honor. He pointed at Torki and the chieftain nodded, then put his own money next to the reaver's—though as he did so he glanced slyly at the Great Chieftain in his place of honor at the far end of the table. Perhaps he worried that his overlord might take it askance—after all, Mörget was the Great Chieftain's son.

The Great Chieftain did not see the wager, however. His eyes never moved from the contest. Mörg, the man who had made a nation of these people, the man who had seen every land in the world and plundered every coast, father of multitudes, slayer of dragons, Mörg the Great was ancient by the reckoning of the east. Forty-five winters had ground at his bones. Only a little silver ran through the gold of his wild beard, however, and no sign of dotage showed in his glinting eyes. He reached without looking for a haunch of roasted meat. Tearing a generous piece free, he held it down toward the mangy dog at his feet. The dog always ate first. It roused itself from sleep just long enough to swallow the gobbet. When it was done, Mörg fed himself, grease slicking down his chin and the front of his fur robes.

A great deal relied on which combatant let go of the hide first. The destiny of the entire eastern people, the lives of countless warriors were at stake—and a debt of honor nearly two centuries old. No onlooker could have said which of the warriors, his son or his champion, Mörg favored.

Torki never made a sound. He did not appear to move at all—he might have been a marble statue. He had the marks of a reaver, black crosses tattooed on the shaved skin behind his ears. One for every season of pillaging he'd undertaken in the hills to the north. Enough crosses that they ran down the back of his neck. Not a drop of sweat had showed yet on his brow.

Mörget shifted his stance a hair's breadth and was nearly

pulled into the fire. His teeth gnashed at the air as he fought to regain his posture.

Nearby his sister, herself a chieftess of many clans, stood ready with a flagon of wine mulled with sweet gale. Mörgain, as was widely known, hated her brother—had done since infancy. No matter how hard she fought to prove herself, no matter what glory she won in battle, Mörget had always overshadowed her accomplishments. Letting him win this contest now would be bitter as ashes in her mouth. Nor did she need to play the passive spectator here. She could end it in a moment by splashing wine across the boards at Mörget's feet. He would be unable to hold his ground on the slippery boards, and Torki would win for a certainty.

"Sister," Mörget howled, "set down that wine. Do you not thirst for western blood, instead?"

Mörg raised one eyebrow, perhaps very much interested in learning the answer to that question.

The chieftess laughed bitterly, and spat between Mörget's feet. But then she hurled her flagon at the wall, where it burst harmlessly, well clear of the contest. "I've tasted blood. I'd rather have the westerners alive, as my thralls."

"And you shall, as many of them as you desire," Mörget told her, his words bitten off before they left his mouth.

"And steel? Will you give me dwarven steel, better than the iron my warriors wear now?"

"All that they can carry! Now, aid me!"

"I shall," Mörgain said. "I'll pray for your success!"

That was enough to break the general silence, though only long enough for the gathered warriors to laugh uproariously and slap each other on the back. The shadow of a smile even crossed Torki's lips. In the east the clans had a saying: *pray with your back turned, so that at least your enemies won't see your weakness.* The clans worshipped only Death, and beseeching Her aid was rarely a good idea.

"Did you hear that, Torki?" Hurlind the scold asked. "The Mother of us all pulls against you now. Better redouble your grip!"

The champion's lips split open to show his teeth. It was the first sign of emotion he'd given since the contest began.

And yet it was like some witch's spell had been broken. Perhaps Death—or some darker fate—did smile on Mörget then. For suddenly his arms flexed as if he'd found some strength he'd forgotten he had. He leaned back, putting his weight into the pull.

Torki's smile melted all at once. His left foot shifted an inch on the boards. It was not necessarily a fatal slip. Given a moment's grace he could have recovered, locking his knees and reinforcing his strength.

Yet Mörget did not give him that moment. Everyone knew that Mörget, for all his size and strength, was faster than a wildcat. He seized the opportunity and hauled Torki toward him until the balance was broken and the champion toppled, sprawling face first on the coals. Torki screamed as the fire bit into his skin. He leapt out of the pit, releasing the panther skin and grabbing a mead jug to pour honey wine on his burns.

The longhouse erupted in cheers and shouts. Hurlind led a tune of victory and bravery against all odds, an old kenning every man and woman in the longhouse knew. Even Mörgain joined in the refrain, Mörgain of whom it was said her iron ever did her singing for her.

In the chaos, in the tumult, Mörget went to his father's chair and knelt before him. In his hands he held his prize, the singed pelt. Orange coals still flecked its curling fur.

"Great Chieftain," Mörget said, addressing the older man as a warrior, not as a parent, "You hold sway over the hundred clans. They wait for your instructions. For ten years now you have kept them from each other's throats. You have made peace in a land that only knew war."

Ten years, aye, in which no clan had feuded with another. Ten years without warfare, ten years of prosperity. For many of those gathered, ten years of boredom. Mörg had united the clans by being stronger than any man who opposed him, and by giving the chieftains that which they desired. Instead of making war on each other, as they had since time imme- morial, the clans had worked together to hunt such game as the steppes provided and to raid the villages of the hillfolk in the north. Yet now there were murmurs in the camps that what every warrior wanted was not ten more years of peace but a new chance to test their mettle. Mörget had been instrumental in starting those murmurs but he had only fed a fire that was already kindled by restlessness. Eastern men, eastern chieftains, could not sit all day in their tents forever and dream of past victories. Eventually they needed to kill something, or they went mad.

Mörg the Great, Mörg the Wise, had pushed them perhaps as far as he could. As he turned his head to look around at his chieftains, how many eyes did he meet that burned with this new desire for war? Now that the mountains lay open to them, how long could he hold them back?

"All good things," Mörg said, looking down at his son again, "should come to an end, it seems. Just as they say in Old Hrush. You've won the right to make your say. Tell me, Mörget, what you wish."

"Only to stand by your side when we march through this new pass into the west, and crush the decadent kingdom of Skrae beneath our feet."

"You lead many clans, chieftain. And I am not your king. You do not require my permission to raid the west."

It was true. It was law. Mörg was the Great Chieftain, but he ruled only by the consent of the clans. "I have the right, aye, to raid the west. But I don't wish just to scare a few villagers and take their sheep," Mörget explained. "For two hundred years that's all we've done, ever since the Skraelings sealed off the mountain passes. Now there is a new pass. Once, long before any of us were born, our warriors spoke not of raiding but of conquest. Of far greater glories. I wish, Great Chieftain, to make war. To take every mile of Skrae for our people, as has always been their destiny!"

Alone in that place, Mörg carried iron, in the form of a sword at his belt. All other weapons had been stacked outside, for no warrior would dare bring a blade into the house of the Great Chieftain. Should he desire it, if his wishes countered those of his son, Mörg could draw his sword and strike down Mörget this instant. No man there would gainsay him for it.

They called him Mörg the Wise, sometimes, when they wished to flatter him. Behind his back, they called him Mörg the Merciful, which was a great slander among the people of the east. If he struck the blow now, perhaps those whispering tongues would be silenced. Or perhaps they would only grow into a chorus.

The chieftains wanted this. They had made Mörget their spokesman, and sent him here tonight to gain this audience.

And Mörg was no king, to thwart the will of his people for his own whims. That was the way of the decadent west. Here in the east men ruled through respect, or through fear, but always honestly—because the men who served them believed in them. Mörg was no stronger than the chieftains he'd united. He lived and died by their sufferance. If he did not give them what they wanted, they had their own recourse—they could replace him. And that could only be done over his dead body. Great Chieftains ruled for life, so murder was the sole method of their impeachment.

On his knees, Mörget stared up at his father with eyes as clear and blue as a mountain stream. Eyes that never blinked.

Mörg must decide, now. There was no discussion to be had, no council to call. He alone must make this decision. Every eye watched his face. Even Hurlind had fallen silent, waiting to hear what he would say.

"You," Mörg said, rising and pointing at a thrall standing by the door. "Fetch boughs of wet myrtle, and throw them on the fire. Let them make a great smoke, that all will see, and thereby know. Tomorrow we march through the mountains to the west. Tomorrow we make war!"

CHAPTER TWO

There was a mountain, and then there was no mountain. It had been called Cloudblade, for the way its sharp summit had once cut through the sky, and it had possessed a long and storied history. It stood at the eastern frontier of the kingdom of Skrae, tallest of the Whitewall Range. Beneath it, in centuries long gone, the dwarves had built a city they called the Place of Long Shadows. Later on, elves— the last of their kind—had moved into that hollow below the world. For eight hundred years they had hidden there, unknown to the humans above.

Then five fools from the west came along and ruined everything.

Cythera climbed up a high pile of rubble, picking her footholds carefully, testing each rock with her hands to make sure it was stable before she put her weight on it. She was sweating by the time she reached the top. There she could see the new valley that lay where Cloudblade once stood. It ran as wide as a road right through the Whitewall, and a constant chill wind coursed over the endless field of stones like a river of air. Over there to the east lay the great steppes where the barbarians ruled. Behind her, to the west, lay Skrae, the country of her birth.

"How many years did Cloudblade stand? When we first saw it, I would have thought it could last forever," Malden said, coming up behind her.

She turned and saw the thief leaping from one rock to another as nimbly as a goat. She couldn't help but smile at the ease with which he moved. He was a small man, and skinny as an alley cat, but he had an effortless grace that always made her gasp.

"Cloudblade stood longer than you can imagine," Cythera said. She was the daughter of a witch and thus privy to some of the secrets of the universe. She knew if she tried to explain to Malden just how long an eon was his eyes would simply glaze over. Which was not to say he was a simpleton. He was bright enough in his own way, if reckless. "Here," she said, and held out a hand. He took it, holding her fingers as delicately as he might a bundle of flowers. When he had climbed up beside her he kissed her fingertips, one after another.

"Don't," she said, though her heart wasn't in it. She wanted to embrace him, to drag him down behind these rocks and

. . . well. She had to be careful now, at least for a while. She took her hand back and turned to face the west. Down there below the foothills of the Whitewall she could still see the column of elves as they made their way toward a distant forest. They were on foot but they moved quickly, desperate to reach any shelter from the blue sky. They found the broad stretch of the heavens terrifying, for none of them had ever seen it before. "Do you think they'll make it?" she asked. The forest they headed for was only the first stop on a long journey.

"Their ancestors ruled this land before we came along and took it from them," Malden pointed out. "They're tougher than they look. And they have Slag to guide them."

Cythera nodded. She'd been sad to see the dwarf go, but the elfin queen wouldn't have followed anyone else.

"Croy will ride ahead of them for a while, to make sure they aren't spotted," Malden added. If any human authorities saw there were elves abroad in the kingdom again it could only end in bloodshed. There was a reason the elves had hidden so long under Cloudblade. "He told me he won't be back until tomorrow dawn." Malden's eyebrows lifted in what he must have thought was a suggestive leer. "It's just the two of us left here now. I'm supposed to look after you while he's away."

He moved closer and reached out one hand to touch the small of her back.

For the second time she shied away, despite what she might have preferred. "We need to talk," she said. "I'm still betrothed to Croy." That had been the whole point of this adventure. The whole reason she'd left the Free City of Ness. Croy—Sir Croy—had made her promise to marry him. She'd demurred and evaded him as long as she could, but eventually the appointed day had come. At the last minute she had decided she needed to see some of the world first, before he took her to his castle and she had to spend the rest of her life birthing his heirs. She hadn't expected Malden to come along—frankly, he'd been a temptation she was trying to escape. Life, it seemed, could never be simple. "I made a promise to him—a legally binding promise."

The expression on his face shifted through a complicated

series of emotions. Everything from hope to fear to deep confusion. But then his eyes narrowed and he nodded sagely. "I see."

"You do?"

Malden dropped his hand to his side. "Down below the mountain, when you thought I was going to die—when we thought we were all going to die—you told me you loved me. Sometimes people in dangerous situations will say things that they wouldn't, otherwise."

"You think me so inconstant?" she asked, hurt despite her better judgment.

"I'm trying to be noble," he told her, in that frank way he sometimes had. Another endearing quality—a man who could speak honestly to a woman was as rare, in Cythera's experience, as a hen with teeth. "I'm trying to give you an opportunity to change your mind."

She smiled at him. His love for her came without conditions. He would never want to take away her freedom. It was why she had come to love him back. "Croy won't be back before dawn, you said." She looked up and saw the sun was still well above the horizon. "We have all that time?"

Later, in the dark of a night with no moon, he kissed the sweat from her cooling body, while she simply tried to get her breath back. She knew she was playing a dangerous game but she couldn't help herself. "Do you still think I want to change my mind?"

"You frightened me with all that talk of betrothals," he said.

"As I meant to."

He drew back a little. In the dark she couldn't read his face. "Tell me you'll break your promise to him. Tell me you love me. Please."

"I do," she said, and there was no part of her that disagreed. "And I will. But you know it can't be so easy. From the moment I tell Croy about us he'll be determined to kill you."

"You think I'm afraid of him?"

"I think you should be." Croy had trained all his life in the military arts. He would be one of the most dangerous men in the world if he wasn't bound by an iron code of honor. Which in itself was the problem. "He won't want to do it. He thinks of you as his best friend. Honor will require it, though. And you know how he is about anything that touches his honor."

"Let him try me! I can't stand the idea of you marrying him. Not anymore," Malden protested.

"I'll tell him everything. I'll renounce the betrothal and beg his forgiveness," Cythera said, rearing up to kiss his cheeks and chin. "I swear it. But Malden—I'll only do it when we're back in Ness. And when I'm sure you have a generous head start."

CHAPTER THREE

A t dawn—as promised—Croy returned, looking a little tousled after riding in the woods all night. He was all blond hair and muscles and stupid grins but Malden did his best not to hate the man. After all, Croy had already lost the game for Cythera's heart—he just didn't know it yet.

The three of them returned to the abandoned hill fort where they'd left their horses and their prisoner. Balint the dwarf looked angry enough to spit blood, but they'd kept her bound and gagged so she couldn't get into mischief. They threw her over the back of Croy's saddle and headed out, toward Helstrow. Balint was the last errand they had to run before they could finally head back to Ness.

Riding west toward the king's fortress proved far less tedious than the voyage east had been. Back then they'd had to ford the river Strow at one of its wilder bends but now they could approach the fortress directly. The sun had not even reached its apex by the time they saw Helstrow's towers rising above the rolling hills.

Malden was thrilled by the prospect of returning to civilization, but just outside the gates Croy called a stop. The riders stood their horses in the road so they could watch a field full of archers lift bows all at once and take aim.

Bowstrings twanged and a hundred arrows lifted into the sky, the thin shafts spinning and tumbling, some clattering together in mid-air. Others flew true and arced downward to slam into a pile of rusted armor on the far edge of the field. Their wicked points cut through the old iron as easily as through parchment and lodged in the earth below.

Watching from a safe distance atop his horse, Malden jerked back in surprise.

"What are they doing?" he asked.

"Practicing, I think," Sir Croy replied, bringing his rounsey up level with Malden's jennet. "There was a time when every male peasant in the kingdom was expected to know how to draw a bow and hit a target at one hundred yards. The law required them to practice for an hour every day, to keep their arms strong and their eyes true."

The line of peasants—villein farmers, Malden judged, by their russet tunics and the close-fitting cowls they wore— each nocked another arrow and drew back on their strings. A serjeant in leather jack and a kettle helmet shouted an order, and once more the bowmen let fly.

Most of the arrows landed well short of the target. One, knocked off course in mid-air, came directly for Malden. He flinched, but its momentum was already spent and it landed twenty yards from his horse's feet. The jennet didn't even look up.

Cythera shielded her eyes with one hand and looked at the pile of armor. Only a handful of arrows had reached the target. "They're . . . not very good."

Croy shrugged. "The law requiring them to practice every day was repealed a long time ago. Before these men were born, in fact. Most of them have probably never seen a bow before. And no archer hits the mark on his first try."

"Why did they stop the practice?" Cythera asked.

"No reason to keep it up. In the early days, Skrae was always at war with one enemy or another—first the elves, then with upstarts who would seize the crown. Skrae always prevailed. The Northern Kingdoms were beaten into submission, turned against each other until now they only fight amongst themselves. The barbarians were forced back across the mountains, sealed behind the two mountain passes. Now there are no enemies left to fight. Skrae hasn't gone to war in a hundred years. There's been no more than a border skirmish in the last ten," Croy explained. "The king's grandfather saw no need to keep a cadre of trained bowmen around. The peasantry were better used by spending that extra hour a day in the fields, feeding a growing populace."

Malden frowned. All that was probably true, but he could guess another reason. He'd seen what the longbows did to the armor when they actually struck home. No knight in shiny coat of plate would ever really be safe with such weapons arrayed against him, not if the aim of the archer was skillful. He imagined the king had been more afraid of an insurrection of highly trained peasants than a foreign invader.

So why was the practice being resumed? This wasn't some bit of makework to keep idle peasants from getting into trouble—the training was in deadly earnest. When they'd shot a dozen arrows each, the hundred men standing on the field were replaced by a fresh hundred, with more waiting to take their turn. Clearly every villein in the environs of Helstrow was to be given a chance to learn this skill.

Something was up.

As the three riders headed up the perfectly straight road toward the fortress of the king, they passed through the village where the prospective bowmen had their houses. The three on horseback drew more than the usual stares. Women leaned out of the doors of their cottages, distaffs and kitchen knives still in their hands, to get a good look at the riders. A reeve carrying the white wooden baton of his station leaned on the signpost of a tavern and watched them with wide eyes. Children dashed out of the street as they approached.

These people were afraid, Malden saw. Afraid someone was going to come along at any moment and take away the pittance they had, the tiny scrap of safety and wealth they'd managed to accumulate. Even the village blacksmith closed the shutters of his shop as they drew near, though the heat inside his forge made the autumn air shimmer.

What had them so scared?

Of course, they might just have been surprised to see Balint roped and secured atop Croy's palfrey. It wasn't every day you saw a dwarf trussed up like a bird in a roasting pan.

Balint would draw stares in any human village. Dwarves were a rare enough sight outside the big cities, and female dwarves almost unheard of—most of their women remained in the north, in the dwarven kingdom, while their men traveled south into Skrae to make their fortunes. This one stood out on her own merits, too. Balint was accounted a great beauty among her people, but then dwarves had a different notion of loveliness than humans. Balint stood just under four feet tall and was as skinny as a starveling dog. Her hair stuck out from her head in thick braids that looked like the spikes of a morningstar. Her eyebrows met above her nose in a thick tangle of coarse dark hairs and there was a sparser growth of hair on her upper lip. Her eyes were squeezed down to dark beads, the lids pressed tight. As a nocturnal creature she found the sun unbearable.

Even if she'd been more pleasing to the eye, she still would have drawn attention by how she was bound. Once dwarves and humans had been vicious enemies, but a treaty between their two kingdoms had changed that long ago. Now by law no human could touch a dwarf in an offensive manner—not unless the human wanted to be tortured to death. The dwarves had proved too useful as allies to risk the peace between them and humankind. They were too valuable to the king, as they were the only ones who knew the secret of making good steel for weapons and armor and a thousand other uses. That a dwarf should be tied up and brought to justice like a common criminal was unthinkable.

Yet Balint was a criminal, and a particularly vile one. The same treaty that ended the war between dwarves and humans included another law, one that said no dwarf was allowed to use a weapon inside the borders of Skrae. Not even in self-defense, not even one they'd made with their own hands. Balint had broken that law without compunction or remorse. Sir Croy had been quite adamant that she be brought to Helstrow and made to account for her crimes. In all likelihood she would be banished from Skrae—and maybe even exiled by her own people. Where she would go at that point was not to be guessed.

Malden liked it not, even though he was the first person Balint had assaulted. She'd struck him across the face with a wrench with clear intent to kill him and he wanted revenge badly enough. Yet he was a thief by trade, a flounter of the law himself. He lived by a certain code of dishonesty, and the first rule in that code was that you didn't betray another criminal to the authorities, ever, under any circumstances.

She had turned Malden into a snitch. And for that, he would never forgive her. What if word of it got out? His reputation would be dashed on the rocks of gossip.

He tried not to think about it. Ahead of them lay the first gate of the fortress, a massive affair of stone and iron that towered over every house in the village. Guards in studded leather cloaks stood there blocking the way with halberds. High above, amidst the battlements of the gate house, a pot of boiling oil was prepared to spill down hot death on anyone who attacked the guards. A dozen loopholes in the gatehouse wall hid crossbowmen ready to pick off anyone who even dared approach.

"I had expected a friendlier reception," Croy called out, as the guards refused to stand aside to let him pass. "Though of course, I'm not flying my colors today. Perhaps you don't recognize me. I have been gone for a long time. I," he said, placing one leather-gauntleted hand on his breast, "am Sir Croy, a knight of the realm. With me are Cythera, daughter of Coruth the Witch, and Malden, a—well—a—"

"His squire," Malden announced, patting the sword tied to his saddle. He couldn't very well announce himself as Malden the Thief here, not and expect to pass the gate. More than once Croy had offered him the position of squire, and though Malden could imagine few things he'd less rather do for a living—collecting dead bodies for mass graves, perhaps—it was a simple enough ruse.

"Yes. He's my squire," Croy said, and it barely sounded at all like a lie coming out of the knight's mouth.

"Bit old for it, ain't 'e?" one of the guards asked, studying Malden with a yellow eye. But the guards weren't there to challenge subjects of Skrae. They were waiting for something else. "That dwarf ye got," the guard went on. "Is she—"

"An oathbreaker. I've come to present her for the king's justice."

There was a great deal of murmuring and surprise at that, but the guards stood back and the portcullis was raised. The three of them—plus one disgruntled dwarf—passed through without further incident.

CHAPTER FOUR

On a map the fortress of Helstrow would have resembled an egg cracked open and let to spread across the top of a table. Its center, its yolk, was the inner bailey—the center of all power in Skrae. Inside a stout wall lay the homes and offices of all the court, as well as the keep and the king's palace. The buildings there stood tall and crammed close together, some so near that a man could reach out of a window and shake his neighbor's hand. The white of the egg—the outer bailey, which had its own wall—sprawled in all directions. The houses and workshops and churches there weren't as tall or as densely packed, yet twenty times as many people lived there, commoners for the most part, all the servants and tradesmen and merchants who fed and clothed and tended to the highborn folk of the court. Malden tried to imagine the place in his head, to secure his first look at it so that he could start to assemble a mental map of the place.

Once they were through the gate, into the outer bailey, any thought of orienting himself was forgotten. The three riders and the dwarf were funneled into a narrow street that curled away ahead of them into a marketplace of countless stalls and small shops. Half-timbered houses loomed over it all, their upper stories leaning out over the streets to shadow the ground level. Malden was thrust immediately into a chaos of color and life, wholly unlike the placid farm country they'd traveled in for so long. His senses were assaulted and for a while all he could do was stare and try to get their bearings.

Smoke from braziers and open fires sent gray tendrils seeking through the crowded, close streets. The horses picked their way through ordure and startled a covey of pigs who went scurrying down a dark alley. Malden wheeled his jennet to the side as a merchant in a russet jerkin went chasing after the pigs with a stick. He nearly knocked over a noble lady, fat and scrubbed pink, as she was carried past in a litter, a pomander of lilies held close under her nose. Malden could barely hear himself think. Everywhere there were the cries of barkers and hawkers, beckoning those with a little coin toward stalls where could be purchased roast meats, fresh apples, fine fabrics, measures of barley or flour or ink or parchment or wine.

"Ah," Malden said, sighing deeply. "Civilization! It's good to be back."

Cythera laughed. "You didn't enjoy your time out in the countryside? All the fresh air? The green hills and the quiet of the forest?"

"You mean the endless rain and the constant itching from insect bites?" Malden asked. "You ask if I enjoyed sleeping on the cold ground with a rock for my pillow, or perhaps eating meat cooked on an open fire—burned on one side, half-raw still on the other? No, a place like this is where I belong."

It was true. Malden had spent his entire life until recently in the Free City of Ness, a hundred miles west of here. He'd grown up in twisting cobbled alleys like these. He knew the rhythms of city life, knew where he stood in a crowd. His recent adventures in the wilderness had left him saddle sore and weary. To be back in a city—any city—was a great relief. It would not be long before they left again, and headed back into the farmlands, but he planned on enjoying this brief respite in a place that felt familiar.

The riders made their way carefully through the crowd, headed deep into the maze of streets. The going was slow and they had to stop and wait many times as traffic surged across their path. At one point Croy's horse pulled up short and Malden's jennet obediently fell into line. Malden wasn't ready for the stop and he crashed forward across his horse's neck. He had only just recently learned to ride, and was far from proficient at it yet. He saw why Croy had halted, though, and was glad the jennet was wiser than he. A procession of lepers was winding its way through the street ahead. They were covered head to toe with cloth, as the law demanded, and carried wooden clappers that they flapped before them in a mournful rhythm. Croy tossed a gold royal to their leader, who caught it with unthinking ease and hid it away instantly. The hand that had emerged from the leper's robe had only three fingers, and Malden was glad he could not see the rest of the man.

When the lepers were past Croy got them started again, but they didn't go much farther. He took them down a lane that curled up toward the wall of the inner bailey and ended in the wide, muddy yard of an inn. There a stable boy took their horses, and welcomed them with honeyed words.

As Malden slid down off the jennet's back, he groaned for his aching muscles and his bowed legs. He'd never gotten used to riding and he was glad to be on his own feet again, even if he felt decidedly unsteady. The whole world still seemed to rock with the swaying gait of the jennet.

All the same, he was surprised by their destination. He had not expected them to spend the night in Helstrow. He would welcome a night in a real bed stuffed with straw, true, but he was more interested in getting to Ness as quickly as possible. He and Cythera would never be alone together again until they were back home, after all. "An inn?" he asked. "Must we spend the night here? I thought we had only to turn Balint over to the local constable and then be on our way again."

Croy leaned backwards, stretching the muscles of his back. "We need to make sure she receives justice from the king's own chief magistrate. It may be many days before we can gain audience with him."

"Days? How many days?" Malden demanded. "Two? Three? As many as a sennight?"

Cythera reached over and brushed road dust off his shoulders. She gave him a knowing look. "Are you in such a hurry to return to Ness? What's there, waiting for you?"

Malden said nothing, and kept his face carefully still. She was teasing him—after all, she knew exactly why he longed to be back in Ness, where all secrets could be revealed. Yet he had another good reason to return home as quickly as possible. He could not help but reach up to the front of his jerkin and touch a piece of parchment folded carefully and held next to his heart. The others did not need to know what was written there, or the betrayal it tokened. The message on the parchment must remain his alone, for now.

CHAPTER FIVE

Inside the common room of the inn, food and wine was brought to them before they'd even asked for it. Malden was sure they'd be charged for it whether they wanted it or not, so he ate greedily of the cold meat and fresh bread he was served, and drank his first cup of wine down before it touched the table. Riding had left him with a deep thirst.

Croy lifted Balint up onto a chair and let her sit upright, though he left her hands bound. The innkeeper stared but said nothing as Cythera drew the gag away and held a pewter cup toward the dwarf's mouth.

Balint stared at the cup as if it held poison. "Aren't you all going to take turns spitting in it first, before I drink? Not that I could tell the difference, not with human wine. I'll bet it tastes like something you drained from a boil off one of those lepers' arses."

There was a reason they had kept her gagged.

Cythera started to take the cup away, but Balint's head snaked forward and she grabbed at its rim with her lips. She sucked deeply at the drink, then leaned back and belched. "I'll take some of that food, now."

Malden frowned at her but he broke off a crust of bread and held it so she could take bites from it. "If you bite my fingers," he told the dwarf, "I'll pick you up by your feet and shake you until we get the wine back."

Something like grudging respect lit up Balint's eye as she chewed. Curses and oaths were all the dwarves knew of poetry. They competed with each other for who could be more vulgar or rude, and counted a good obscenity as a fine jest. Clearly Malden had scored a point with her.

Cythera didn't seem to see it that way. "Be more kind," she said, "please. Balint may be guilty of much, but she still deserves some respect."

"Ask the elves how much," Malden said.

"The elves," Croy said, shaking his head. "That makes me think—when we meet the magistrate, what do we tell him of the elves?"

"If he's to know of her crimes," Malden pointed out, "we'll need to say something. After all, it was their city Balint toppled—nearly killing all of them in the process, not to mention us."

"Once the king knows the elves are at large in his kingdom, though, I shudder to think what he'll do. Send his knights to round them up, surely, and then—no. No, I won't even think of that." Cythera put her head in her hands. "Can we not just tell him that the elves all perished when Cloudblade fell?"

"And get me cooked for mass murder?" Balint said, her eyes wide. "You know that's a lie. The elves survived. Most of them, anyway."

"A blessing you had no hand in achieving," Croy said. "You did not seem to care if they did all die, when you toppled Cloudblade."

Malden shook his head. "It matters little. Our king has no authority to have you hanged. The worst he can do is send you north," he pointed out, "which he's bound to do anyway, no matter how many of them you killed. So it doesn't matter what crimes we heap upon you, since the punishment will be the same."

"I'll take my lumps for what I did. I acted in the interest of *my* king, that's all," Balint insisted. When the humans didn't relent and free her on the spot, she shrank within her ropes. "It's been a long ride and I need to make water," she said, then, looking away from their faces. "Which of you brave young men wants to pull down my breeches for me?"

Croy recoiled in disgust. That was what Balint had wanted, of course. She smiled broadly and tried to catch Malden's eye.

It was Cythera who responded, however. "I'll take her to the privy," she said, rising from her seat. Once standing, however, she let out a gasp.

Malden spun around in his chair and saw a pair of men coming toward them, pushing their way through the common room. They were not dressed in the cloaks-of-eyes the city watch of Ness wore, but he knew immediately they were men of the law. Each wore a jerkin of leather jack with steel plates sewn to the elbows and shoulders, and each of them had a weapon in his hand. They had gold crowns painted on their cloaks as insignia of office.

Even without their uniforms he would have recognized them as lawmen, just from the smug looks on their faces. They were bigger than anyone else in the room and that look said they knew it. Their rough features and tiny eyes marked them as men who wouldn't back down from a fight, as well. Malden had spent his whole life learning how to recognize such signs—and learning how to avoid the men who showed them.

"Good sirs," Croy said, rising and spreading his arms wide in welcome. "I thank you for coming. We'd planned on bringing her to the keep directly, but perhaps you can save us the journey."

One of the kingsmen—the one who still had most of his teeth—stared down at the dwarf and frowned. "What's this?"

"Nobody said nothin' 'bout a dwarf girl," the other one said, looking at his comrade. A bad scar crossed his neck, just one side of his windpipe.

"This," Croy said, "is Balint, late of the service of the dwarven envoy at Redweir. She's broken her oath, and—"

"We didn't come for a dwarf," the first one, the toothy one, told Croy.

Malden slowly pushed his chair back from the table. He tried not to make a sound as its legs dragged across the floorboards. So occupied, he failed to notice that he was backing up into a wall. When the back of his head struck the plaster, he looked to either side, searching for windows he might jump out of. He found none.

The scarred one spoke next, saying exactly what Malden expected—and dreaded—to hear. "We're here," he announced, "for yer thief."

Malden jumped up onto his chair. He looked up toward the rafters and saw they were too high to reach, at least ten feet above his head. The two kingsmen had by reflex moved to flank the table on either side, blocking off his escape that way, as well.

"Hold," Croy said, rising to his feet. "What's the meaning of this?"

"He was spotted comin' in through the gate today under false identity. Somebody knew his face, and passed along the particulars. Now we're to take him in."

Malden had thought he would be safe here. Though he was well known in Ness he was a stranger in Helstrow. He'd assumed no one here had so much as heard of him.

That foolishness had made him lax, made him forget his usual caution.

Cursing himself, he tried to decide which way to run. Normally when he entered a public building like this he would take a moment to memorize all the exits. This time he'd been so tired from the day's riding he hadn't bothered.

"But what's the charge?" Cythera demanded.

Toothy looked at Scar, who looked back at him, as if they couldn't decide between the two of them which one should answer. "Suspicion of bein' a thief," Toothy said, finally. "Now, which one of ye is called Malden?"

Balint began to laugh. Croy started to turn to look at Malden, giving him away.

Malden dropped his hand to his belt, where his bodkin used to be. It hadn't been a good knife, really, but it had been his. Now it was gone—and in its place was a sword. A sword that should never have been his, a sword Croy had given him under false trust. A sword, more to the point, that he'd never learned how to use.

"Look out, Halbert—he's got a cutter," Scar said.

"Hand it over, boy," Toothy—Halbert—said.

"What, this thing?" Malden asked. Then he drew the sword from its scabbard and let it taste the air. "It's harmless."

The sword had a name. It was called Acidtongue. The name came from the fact that while the blade looked like an old piece of iron, pitted and scored by age, it was in fact quite magical—on contact with the air, it secreted a powerful foaming acid that could burn through just about anything.

In olden times when demons walked the land, the sword had been made to fight against them. It was one of the seven Ancient Blades, brother to the one Croy wore at his own belt, and it had magic woven into its very metal. It could sear through demonic flesh that would resist normal iron weapons and cut through even the thickest armored shell or matted, brimstone-stinking fur. Malden knew from personal experience it worked just fine on more worldly substances as well.

With both hands on the hilt, Malden brought the blade around in a tight arc. The blade passed through the middle of a pewter tankard as if it were made of smoke. The top half of the tankard fell to the table with a clink—even as the wine it had contained splashed out across the table in a hissing wave.

Halbert and Scar both jumped back as if he'd thrown a snake at them. They also jumped a little to the side—Halbert to the left, Scar to the right.

Malden split the difference and dashed between the two of them, headed straight for the door.

CHAPTER SIX

Bursting out into the sunlight, Malden turned his head wildly from side to side, looking for any avenue of escape. His foot slipped on a pile of horse droppings and he slid wildly for a long second before he got his feet under him again. Scar and Halbert were already emerging from the inn's door when he finally spotted his next move.

A low wall ran along one side of the innyard, a pile of unmortared stone attached to the side of the stables. It sloped gently upward toward the thatched roof of the stables and to one as fleet as Malden it was as good as a staircase. He danced up the rocks, hearing them tumble and crash as Scar tried to follow him. It was hard to be light-footed when you were covered in armor.

Malden grabbed a double handful of thatch and hauled himself up onto the roof. From there he looked out on a sea of rooftops belonging to the half-timbered houses he'd seen on the way to the inn. Most had slate shingles—which were hard to run on, as they tended to crack and shift under one's feet. Far to his left, though he could see the lead-lined roof of a church.

If he could reach the church he could make some real speed. He jumped across a narrow alley to the top of the house nearest the inn and landed on his feet on the sloping roof. He'd come down hard on his left ankle but Malden merely switched his weight to his right foot and kept running. He heard the watchmen shouting for him to halt, but paid no mind. He'd yet to meet a watchman anywhere who could run along roof ridges as nimbly as he.

He was wise enough, however, to know he wasn't free yet. As he jumped to the next roof he passed over an alley choked with workmen and beggars—and two more kingsmen, who gestured upward with their weapons as he passed. Up ahead he could see a public square where women were gathered around a well, washing clothes. More kingsmen were stationed there.

By Sadu's eight index fingers, Malden swore, how many men had they sent for him? But then he saw other figures mixed in with the kingsmen. Smaller men, wearing no armor—their hands tied together before them. They had bruised faces and some were limping. They looked broken, and Malden understood.

The local watch wasn't just after one thief who had entered the gate under false pretenses. They were sweeping up every criminal they could find. He had seen it happen before, in Ness, when the Burgrave of that city wanted to convince the populace of the grip he held on the streets. There was no better way to show one's passion for law and order than rounding up a dozen thieves and hanging them all together in the market square.

He'd stumbled right into a mess, coming to Helstrow when he did. What an ignominious way to end his career. He hated to think he'd be brought down by something so crass.

Malden had no intention of being taken by the law, especially by the law of a town where he'd never actually committed a crime. He knew exactly what he would have to do, and having a plan put him a little more at his ease. For a while he would have to abandon his friends. He would have to find a cheap hostelry where he could lie low for a few days, then meet up again with Croy and Cythera once their business was done. He could join up with them after they'd dropped Balint off in front of a magistrate, when they were ready to leave again. Croy would probably urge him to turn himself in, but Cythera would smooth things over and the three of them could make a discrete exit from Helstrow fortress. If things got too hot in the meantime he could always climb over the wall and hide among the peasants outside.

But first he had to actually get away. Looking back, toward the inn, he saw that Scar and Halbert had procured a ladder and were even at that moment preparing to come up and catch him.

Had this been Ness, Malden would have known instantly which way to turn. He would have known some blind alley where he could lose his pursuers, or where the nearest bridge might be found so he could leap into the river, or he would remember the location of a root cellar where no one would ever think to look for him. But this was Helstrow, which he knew not at all.

The church he'd been running toward was out of the question. It fronted on the square where the kingsmen were gathering their catch. So he turned instead and headed north, toward the wall that separated the outer and inner baileys. It was the highest point he could see, and he always felt safest up in the air.

Leaping to a thatched roof he tucked and rolled, knowing the tight-packed straw would offer only spongy, uncertain footing. Spitting dry husks from his mouth he started running toward the rough stones of the wall—and then stopped in his tracks.

Up on the wall, between the crenellations, he saw royal guards in white cloaks looking down at him. One of them had a crossbow and was busy cranking at its windlass. In a moment the weapon would be ready to fire.

Crossbow bolts were designed to penetrate steel armor and pierce the vitals beneath. At this range, the shot would probably skewer Malden—who wore no armor at all—like a roasting chicken.

Backpedaling in horror, Malden dashed to the far side of the roof and grabbed its edge. He swung down toward the street and let go to drop the last few feet. He landed in the stall of a costermonger, amidst barrels of apples and pears.

The merchant shrieked and pointed at him.

"Good sir, I beg you, be still!" Malden said, leaning out of the entrance to the stall and looking up and down the street. "The kingsmen are after me, and—"

"Thief! Thief!" the coster howled. He plucked up a handful of plums and threw them at Malden with great force. Sticky juice splattered Malden's cloak and the side of his face.

Holding up one arm to protect his eyes, Malden ran out of the shop and into a street full of marketers. They turned as one at the sound of the costermonger's shout and stared at Malden with terrified eyes.

"Murder!" the fruit merchant shouted. "Fire!" The man would say anything, it seemed, to get the blood of the crowd up.

Malden had made a bad miscalculation. Had he dropped into a similar stall in Ness, he would have received a far warmer welcome. The coster would have shoved him under a blanket where he could hide until the coast was clear. But Ness was a Free City, where it was a point of civic pride that no one trusted their rulers. Here, in Helstrow, every man was a vassal of the king—his property, in all but name. And Malden knew from bitter experience that slaves often feared their masters more than they loved freedom.

"Thief! Fire! Guards!" the cry went up, from every lip in the street. A dozen fingers pointed accusingly at Malden, while shopkeepers rang bells and clanged pots together to add to the hue and cry.

"Damn you all for traitors," Malden spat, and hurried down the street as women pelted him with eggs and rotten vegetables and children grabbed at his cloak to try to trip him. He thrust his arm across his eyes to save himself from being blinded by the shower of filth and ran as fast as he dared on the trash-slick cobblestones.

But just as suddenly as it started, the cry ceased. Malden was left in silence, unmolested. Had he escaped the throng? He'd taken no more than a dozen steps away from them, yet—

He lowered his arm, and saw a knight in armor come striding toward him, sword in hand.

CHAPTER SEVEN

The marketers all fled or pressed into the doors of shops where they could watch from something like safety. Malden was alone with his enemy in a wide open street, alone and very short on options.

The knight clanked as he walked. He wore a full coat of plate that covered him from head to toe. Even his joints were protected by chain mail. The visor of his helmet was down and Malden could see nothing of his face.

Such armor, Malden knew, had an effect on the mind of the man who wore it. It made him believe himself to be invulnerable. Which was true, for all practical purposes—no iron sword could slash through that steel. Spear blades and bill hooks would simply clash off the armor, at worst denting its shiny plates. Protected thus, men tended to think that their safety meant they were blessed by the gods, and that whatever they chose to do was also blessed.

Such armor was a license for cruelty and rapine.

Yet there were weapons that could pierce that protective shell. The bodkin Malden had once carried was designed to pierce even steel, if driven with enough force and good aim. Battle axes were designed to smash through armor by sheer momentum. An arrow from a longbow, as Malden had seen, could cut through it like paper.

And then there was Acidtongue, the sword at Malden's belt. If he could strike one solid blow with it, the sword could cut the knight in half.

Yet that might be the stupidest thing Malden ever did. Atop the plate, the knight wore a long white tabard that hung down to his knees. Painted on the cloth was a golden crown. This wasn't a knight errant like Croy, but a knight in full estate, a champion of the king of Skrae. Most likely he was the captain of the watch, superior in rank to all the Scars and Halberts in Helstrow.

If Malden got lucky and cut the man down, he would be pursued unto the ends of the world. You did not kill a nobleman and get away with it, not ever.

He could, of course, run away. The knight seemed agile enough even weighed down with so much steel, but Malden would undoubtedly be fleeter and the chase would not go far. He turned around, intending to do this very thing, only to find he had hesitated a moment too long.

Coming down the street from the other direction, a pack of kingsmen were advancing on him steadily. Their weapons were all pointed straight at his belly. They held their ground, not advancing with any kind of speed—clearly they intended to let the knight handle him. Yet there was no chance of getting past that wall of blades. Malden's only possible escape was to get past the knight.

Malden wasn't the type to pray, even in extremity, but he called on Sadu then. Sadu the bloodgod, the leveler, who brought justice to all men in the end, even knights and nobility. Then he drew his magic sword, and wished he'd bothered to learn how to swing it correctly. Or at least to hold it properly. Acid dripped from the eroded blade and spat where it struck the dusty cobbles.

The knight swore, his voice echoing inside his helmet. "By the Lady! Where'd you get that treasure, son? Did you steal it from Sir Bikker?"

Malden's eyes narrowed. How could the knight know who had first owned Acidtongue? "Bikker is dead," he said.

"But yours wasn't the hand that slew him, I warrant. You're no Ancient Blade."

For the first time Malden looked on the knight's own sword. No jewels decorated the pommel, and the quillions were of plain iron, though well polished. The blade was not even particularly long. Yet vapor lifted from its flat to spin in the air, and patterns of frost crackled in its fuller.

"Do you recognize my sword?" the knight asked.

"Judging by the fact I'm still in one piece, I think it's fair to say I haven't made its acquaintance."

The knight laughed. "This is Chillbrand," he said. "You'd know that, if Acidtongue was rightfully yours. No Ancient Blade is handed down to a new wielder until he's been trained by the man who wielded it before him. He's taught its proper use, and about the history and powers of all seven. None of us would ever let one of the swords fall into the hands of one who didn't appreciate their traditions."

"I'm still being trained," Malden said, which was true enough.

The knight shook his head, though. "If you don't know Chillbrand, you have no right to bear Acidtongue. I must assume you stole it from Bikker—or looted it from his dead body. Put the sword back in its sheath, now, and lay it gently on the ground. That's a good boy."

Malden's lips pulled back from his teeth and he roared as he ran at the knight. He brought Acidtongue up high over his shoulder—vitriol pattered and burned holes through his cloak—and then swung it down hard.

The knight laughed, and easily batted Acidtongue away with Chillbrand.

"It's not a quarterstaff, son," the knight said, taking two steps to Malden's right, forcing Malden to whirl around to face him again. "Don't swing it around like a stick. That's a waste of its strength. Cut with it. Like you'd chop the head off a fish."

"You'd teach me to fight, even as I'm trying to kill you?" Malden asked.

"Judging by your skill it'll take you quite a while to do

that," the knight responded. "I have to find some way to pass the time."

Malden seethed with rage. He tried a stroke he'd seen Croy make a dozen times—*feint quickly to the left, then shift all your weight to your right side and on the follow-through, bring the blade around to—*

Iron clanged on iron. Chillbrand slid down Acidtongue's blade and its point was suddenly at Malden's throat, while Acidtongue was thrust harmlessly to one side.

"A swordsman," the knight told Malden, "trains every day of his life. He sustains himself on wholesome food, to build up his strength. You're puny, boy. You've gone to bed hungry one too many times. You're quick on your feet, I'll give you that, but the muscles in your arm are soft as cheese. I can feel it."

"Will you insult me to death? Stop toying with me!"

"When two knights meet, swords in hand, they call it a conversation, because of the way the steel sounds its joy, back and forth. But you'd know that, too, if—"

Without warning, Malden brought Acidtongue around with his weight behind it, intending to run it straight through the knight's body. Acidtongue flickered in the air it moved so quickly. Yet the knight was as ready for the blow as if he'd read Malden's mind. Chillbrand came down from overhead and turned Acidtongue to the side like earth off the blade of a plow.

"Cut me down or let me pass!" Malden shrieked.

"If you insist," the knight said.

Yet he would not even grant Malden the mercy of a quick death. Instead he just lunged forward and slapped Malden across the forehead with the flat of his blade.

Ice crystals grew and burst inside Malden's brain, exploding his thoughts and freezing his senses. He felt every shred of warmth sucked from his body, drawn into the freezing sword. He started to shake and his teeth clacked together like the wooden clappers of the lepers he'd seen. His body convulsed with the cold and suddenly he could not control his fingers, and Acidtongue fell from his hand to bounce off the cobblestones.

Desperately Malden tried to wrap his arms around himself, to stamp his feet—anything to get warm. His body had rebelled against him, and he could not stop shaking.

It was the work of a moment for the kingsmen behind him to grab him up, and bind him, and haul him away. He could offer no resistance at all.

CHAPTER EIGHT

When Malden burst out of the inn, Cythera leapt to her feet fully intending to follow him. People pressed in on every side though and she just could not match the thief's speed or nimbleness. Still she tried to push her way through the crowd—until Croy grabbed her arm and dragged her back.

"If they have a warrant for his arrest," Croy said, "we must—"

"He's our friend," Cythera said, staring daggers at the knight errant. "I'm going after him!"

"If you must, then at least let's do it the right way. We'll speak to the proper authorities, and find out why they want him and how he can be freed. Just let me settle up our bill here, and—"

She stared at him with wild eyes. "I'll go alone. You keep an eye on Balint." She twisted her arm out of his grip and ducked under the elbow of the taverner, who had come to see what all the fuss was about. The people in the inn drew back when they saw the look in her face.

She would not lose Malden. Not now, when she'd just realized how she felt about him. That fate should take him away from her now was unacceptable.

Outside of the inn she sought wildly through the crowded streets, having no idea where she should look for Malden first. She knew he would likely have taken to the rooftops but she wasn't as nimble and couldn't follow him that way. When she heard the hue and cry go up, though, she knew to head in the direction of the shouting—and raced around a corner just in time to see Malden struck down. She called out his name in horror but couldn't move from the spot, paralyzed in terror. She thought for certain he was dead, his head caved in by the blow, but instead he merely collapsed to the street, quaking like a man in the grip of a terrible seizure.

She wanted to run forward, to grab him up and take him away, to rescue him. But the square was full of kingsmen and the armored knight stood watchful and ready. There was no way she could help Malden now, not directly. There must be something she could do, though, something to—

"Daughter. You have been gone too long."

Cythera's jaw dropped. "Mother?"

Creeping dread made every muscle in her back ripple and tense. Slowly she turned around, expecting to see Coruth the witch standing in the alley behind her.

Instead there was a boy there, a little peasant boy with a dirty face. And several hundred birds.

Rooks, starlings, pigeons and doves all stood on the cobbles, or perched on the timbers of the houses on either side. More of them came down to land around the boy as Cythera watched. Some fluttered down to land on his shoulders, others to perch atop his head. The birds were all staring at her.

The boy, in way of contrast, looked at nothing. His eyes were unfocused and looked like they might roll up into their sockets. His arms hung loose at his sides and the muscles of his face were all slack, so that he slurred his words as he spoke to her again.

"You are required in Ness. You must come home immediately."

Cythera knew what was happening. That didn't make it any less unsettling. Her mother had set her spirit loose upon the ether, let it drift with the movements of birds, as was her wont. It allowed her to see things hidden from human eyes and to keep a watch on the entire kingdom of Skrae at once. Yet birds could not convey proper messages—their beaks and tongues were ill-formed for human speech. So Coruth must have overridden the boy's consciousness with her own. It was a cruel thing to do and Cythera knew Coruth would only have turned to such magic if she had no other choice.

"Malden's in trouble, mother. You and I both owe him a great debt—I can't go anywhere until he's safe. I just watched him get struck by an Ancient Blade."

"Chillbrand," the boy said. He did not nod. Coruth was controlling only enough of his functions to speak with. That was the difference between witchcraft and sorcery, sometimes. A sorcerer would have taken the boy over completely—and left him mindless and half-dead when the sorcerer was done with him. "One of the seven. Strange. I can see them all now, all seven of the swords. They are coming together, as if drawn by a magnet."

"The swords are coming to Helstrow?" Cythera asked, intrigued despite herself.

"For a brief while. Hmm. This could be trouble. The future is not entirely clear right now. What is clear is that you must return to Ness. We must speak, you and I. Great events are unfolding. Some we care about will be brought low, while others are lifted to the heights. What was solid and eternal will become mutable. Malden . . . did you say Malden was in trouble? But that's impossible. He has—he will—"

The boy's lips pressed tightly together, and one of his hands twitched. Coruth was losing control of him.

"Mother? Mother, what are you talking about?" Cythera demanded. Coruth could see the underpinnings of reality, she could even glimpse the future, but often what she saw was so cryptic even she could make no sense of it. Cythera understood maybe one part in ten of what Coruth told her of those visions. "Mother, please. I need to know more—if this will effect Malden, or Croy, I need to know!"

But Coruth had released the boy. His eyes slowly focused and his face regained something like normal muscle tone. Cythera knelt down to put her hands on his shoulders and help him retūrn to full control of his body by stroking his forehead and rubbing his back. "Mistress," he said, and blinked his eyes rapidly. "Mistress, I beg your pardon—I must'a come runnin' down here and bumped you, and scattered me wits for a moment. I—I—where am I? I was s'posed to do somethin', but I can't rightly recall what. I can't remember much, tell the truth. My head aches somethin' awful."

"You were supposed to give me a message. You did just fine." Cythera took a farthing from her purse and pressed it into his hand. "You do look like you've had a shock. Best run home now and lie down."

The boy took the coin and headed off, scattering the birds that bobbed and scampered around the alley. Cythera hoped he would do as she'd said—the spell he'd been under would leave him drained and scattered for days, and she would hate to find out he'd come to some mischief just for helping Coruth.

Slowly she rose to her feet again. She would return to the inn and find Croy. The knight-errant was Malden's only hope, now. Before she headed back, though, she waited until one of the birds was turned away from her. Then she darted forward and grabbed it with both hands. It was a pigeon with iridescent wings and it was not so frightened as it should have been. That meant some piece of Coruth's mind was still inside its head. "Mother," she whispered to the bird, "you could have been more helpful. I got your message but all you've achieved is to scare me a bit. If you have any idea what I'm supposed to do now, I'd love to hear it."

The bird struggled in her hands, and she released it. Without even looking at her it took to the air and flew away.

CHAPTER NINE

They dragged Malden through the gate to the inner bailey, then up a hill to the keep. No one spoke to him, and he was still too blasted with cold to ask any questions. When they arrived inside the thick stone walls of the keep he expected to be thrown into an oubliette and forgotten. He had, after all, threatened a knight of the king. Instead, however, he was taken into a spacious feasting hall where an iron collar was locked around his throat and then chained to a staple in one wall. The hall was already full of men, mostly young, mostly with the scrawny, shifty-eyed look of dire poverty. Malden thought he recognized a few of the faces—he had seen them being rounded up in the square. These, it seemed, were his people. Thieves and beggars, the seedy underbelly of Helstrovian society. Not that this knowledge was likely to help him—they didn't know him from the Emperor of the South. Nor was he in any shape to introduce himself. He could barely keep his teeth from breaking, they chattered so much.

For a great while, Malden curled himself about his stomach and just shivered. He felt like all of winter's chill had gathered in his bones. He felt his heart racing, booming in his chest. His fingers turned bright red as if they had been frostbitten. A fire burned in a hearth at one side of the hall, and he longed and dreamed of going to it, of shoving his hands directly into the flames, simply for the warmth he would feel before his flesh singed and burnt. Luckily the chain around his neck kept him from doing so.

In time, the supernatural chill withdrew from his bones. He doubted he would ever truly feel warm again, but his teeth stopped knocking together so much.

Blowing warm breath on his fingers, he struggled to sit

up and look around. Nothing had changed over the last hour, save that more men had been brought into the hall. Very few of them were talking to each other. Mostly they sat in dull silence and stared at things that weren't there. They came and chained up a man next to Malden, a middle-aged starveling whose eyes were quite mad. He stared at Malden without speaking until Malden turned to the man on his other side.

"You," Malden said, to the surly fellow. He needed information and no other source provided itself. "What did they get you for, then?"

"What's it to ye?"

"I'm a scholar of justice," Malden told him.

That elicited a brief laugh, though little humor. "They never said why. Just grabbed me up outta me bed. Mind, I suppose I deserve to be here more'n some."

"You're a thief, then?" Malden asked. The other bridled so he held up his hands for peace. "I'm in the trade myself," he explained, "and will say as much to any man who asks."

"Alright, then. Call me a thief, if ye like."

Malden nodded eagerly. Then he ran his hands across the rushes on the floor. As expected there was a thick layer of dust underneath. He cleared some rushes away, then drew in the dust with his finger, sketching a heart transfixed by a key.

The other thief stared down at the image. Malden knew right away that the man recognized the symbol—he knew it for the mark of Cutbill, the master of the thieves' guild in Ness. He had worried that the symbol might not be known in Helstrow.

The other thief slid one foot through the drawing, obliterating it before anyone else could see. "You're *his* man?" he asked.

Malden nodded.

"We got our own boss here, though I shan't say his name out loud, not in this place. You can have what they call me, though, which is Velmont."

"Malden."

The two of them clasped hands, but only for a moment. The thief made a point of looking away as he spoke out of the side of his mouth. "Now maybe *my* boss has heard o' *your* boss. Maybe they's even friends. Well, men of business will come together, eh, and find ways to help each other out, from time to time. Still, I don't know what you're after, showing me that."

Malden frowned. "Just a bit of knowledge, really. The watch here—the kingsmen—are rounding up every scofflaw in town, it seems. I've never seen such a complete sweep before. Unless you tell me this is a common occurrence in Helstrow—"

"It ain't."

"—then I can only wonder why they're being so thorough. There must be a hundred men in this room. And why here? This looks like a banquet hall, not a dungeon. The only reason to put us here is if the gaol is already full. And that means there must be plenty more of us stashed in other places, too. Maybe hundreds of men. Surely the king doesn't intend to hang us all. He wouldn't need to slaughter so many just to improve public morale."

Velmont scratched himself. "It started just a few days ago. Folks that'd been in the game far longer'n me—folks that shoulda been untouchable, like—got scooped up in the middle o' the night. Then they started raiding the gambling houses and the brothels at dawn." He shrugged. "No one tells us anything, o' course. We're just peasants, what do we need t'know? But 'twas at the same time, that all the honest men in town got taken outside the wall to learn how to shoot a bow." The thief shook his head. "You just in town today? Your accent says you're from Ness, is that right?"

Malden assented with a nod.

"You picked a lousy time to come see Helstrow, friend. Now, I don't think we're to be killed. No, not as such. But I've been wondering 'bout what they're up to meself, and there's only one conclusion I can draw. Conscription."

"They're going to press us into military service?"

"Give us a choice, like." Velmont smiled wickedly. "The noose or the army. Well, I know my answer already."

"I suppose we all do. That must be what they're counting on. By law they can't force freemen to fight for the king—"

"But a prisoner's another story, aye."

Conjecture was all Velmont had to go on, but what he said made sense to Malden. Why the king wanted an army now, of all times, Malden had no idea. The two thieves discussed various theories for some time, without coming to any further useful ideas.

They were still talking when the sun went down and darkness filled the hall. The only light they had came from the fire in the hearth. All around them men laid down as best they could and curled themselves in sleep. Those who still spoke softly amongst themselves all seemed to agree that they were to be kept in the banquet hall overnight at the very least. So when someone entered the hall with a lantern and started shining it in the faces of the imprisoned, everyone sat up and looked. Velmont and Malden fell silent and tried to look as if they'd never spoken to one another. They were in enough trouble as it was and didn't need to be accused of conspiracy.

The lantern moved up and down the hall. The guards never spoke, just played their light over each face and then moved on, clearly not finding what they sought. As the guard with the lantern came closer, Malden somehow knew they were coming for him. When the light hit his face, he refused to blink. The guard beckoned to someone else—a kingsman—who came rushing up out of the darkness. Then the guard pointed one accusing finger at Malden. "Him."

CHAPTER TEN

"This way, sir knight, milady," the castellan said, and ushered them inside a low-ceilinged room. "Please wait here until you are officially presented."

"What are we waiting for?" Cythera asked. "I don't understand. We wanted to talk to the magistrate, so we could find out where our friend is being held."

"I was bidden only to bring you here, where you may await your audience," the castellan told her. Then he stepped backward out into the hall and closed the door behind him.

Croy stared at the doors, wondering exactly what was going on. Why had they been brought here, of all places? Why now?

Cythera turned to him and asked, "This doesn't look like a law court. Where are we?"

The knight cleared his throat. "The privy council chamber. This is where the king consults his closest advisors."

"And—our audience? Who have we been summoned to see? One of those advisors?"

Croy could barely speak for the emotion he felt. This room—this very room. "I don't know why we were brought here," he said at last.

Cythera sighed deeply and went to sit down. It had been a very long day for her, Croy thought. They'd had to run from office to office in the inner bailey, looking for anyone who might tell them where Malden might be, or who might take charge of Balint so they didn't have to keep looking after her. They had at least succeeded in the latter goal. They had been allowed to turn the dwarf prisoner over to the king's equerry, of all people—the official in charge of the royal stables. It seemed there was nowhere else in the inner bailey that wasn't already full of prisoners.

No one could tell them anything about Malden. But after they had approached the keep, where they were told some prisoners were being held, the castellan himself had come looking for them, and he had brought them here.

Here. To this room.

Croy had been inside the privy council chamber before, many times. There had been a time he had stood in this room every day. The Ancient Blades had been forged to slay demons, but by the time Croy received Ghostcutter from his father there had been too few demons left to justify having five knights just for that purpose. Instead the bearers of the Blades had been commissioned to be the personal bodyguards of the king—the previous king, Ulfram IV.

It was in this room that Ulfram IV had died. A villainous councilor had slipped poison into his mutton. The Ancient Blades had caught the councilor before he could escape but it was already too late. It was also in this room that his son, Ulfram V, current sovereign of Skrae, had blamed the bodyguards for his father's death, and stripped them of their commission. He would have done far more to them, if he'd been able to prove they had anything to do with the assassination, but everyone knew the sacred honor of the Blades. All he could do was send them forth from Helstrow in disgrace.

Croy remembered that day very well. It had been the worst day of his life. In some ways he would have preferred to have been hanged rather than face that shame. That was the day he became a knight errant—a servant without a master.

He had never expected to enter this room again.

He looked around him and saw how little had changed. The shields hanging on the walls were a bit rustier than they had been. The upholstery on the chairs that lined the walls had been changed from red to green, that was all, really. Then he spotted the one significant change.

A tapestry map covered one wall of the chamber, a cunning depiction of the natural and political features of Skrae picked out in minute embroidery of silken floss. The Whitewall—the mountain range that formed Skrae's eastern border—had been stitched from thread of silver, and it glittered in the firelight. Except for one dull patch.

Croy approached the map and looked more closely. It was as he expected. Someone had used the point of a knife to pick out all the threads that had made up the image of Cloudblade, the kingdom's tallest mountain. Which only made sense, since the mountain wasn't there any more.

Croy blushed to think of the part he'd had in that.

"Croy," Cythera said, turning to him to speak in a hurried whisper, "I don't know what we're doing here. But I'm certain that once it's done we should leave Helstrow as soon as possible. My mother sent me a message today, telling me to come home."

"She sent a message here? How did the messenger find you?"

"She didn't send me a letter," Cythera pointed out. "She has other methods of getting her point across. It doesn't matter how it was done. She said that things were about to change, that all seven of the Ancient Blades were coming here. She said many things I didn't understand. We need to find Malden as soon as possible and—"

She stopped because there was a knock on the door, and then two prisoners were brought inside. Balint and Malden, both of them in chains. Croy rushed toward Malden's side, intending to ask his friend what had happened, but he was not given time. The same guard who brought in the prisoners had an announcement to make.

"All bow for His Majesty Ulfram Taer, Fifth of that Name!"

It was to be a royal audience, then. They had been brought here to wait for the king himself. It made no sense. Yet Croy knew exactly what to do. He drew his sword and held it before him with the point on the floor, then knelt behind it. He lowered his head as far as it would go.

"Oh, do stand up, Croy," the king said. "And put that thing away before you scratch up the floorboards."

CHAPTER ELEVEN

Ulfram V was a year younger than Croy, but the strain of ruling a nation had aged him prematurely. The hair on his chin had turned gray since the last time the two had seen each other, and a constant diet of rich foods had swollen his belly. It was held almost in check now by a steel breastplate and gorget that he wore over his state robes.

When Croy saw the king's armor, he knew at once the explanation for many of the strange things he'd seen since coming to Helstrow. The king of Skrae only wore such protection in times of war.

"My liege," Croy said, "I beseech your mercy, and honor your rank, for—"

"Shut up," the king said, in a tone that could not be argued with. "I told you never to come back here, didn't I? Don't bother answering. I know I did. But here you are. I could have you hanged, right now. Unfortunately for me, however, it turns out I have need of you, Croy. So I'm going to let you live."

Croy said nothing, only lowered his head further.

"I have very little time for this audience, so we'll dispense with formal salutations, I think," the king told him. "I seem to recall that when I took away your commission, you said some pointlessly devout thing about never forgetting your vows anyway. Is that right?"

"It is," Croy said, and dropped to one knee again. "The vow I made to you is a sacred bond. I swore it on the name of the Lady, and to break that promise would cost me my utter soul. I will forever be your vassal, your majesty."

The king sighed and waved for Croy to stand again. "Very well. As of now you're reinstated as one of my knights. I suppose you'll want a ceremony for that or something, but I don't care. You'll report immediately to Sir Hew at the gatehouse. He'll give you your orders. You may leave me now—I have these others to account for."

"Majesty," Croy said. He almost knelt again, but thought better of it. "I came here for a reason. It's of these two prisoners I wished to speak."

The king had started to turn away, to address Balint. Now he stopped and for a long moment he stood in silence, a confused expression on his face. "I beg your pardon? *You* wished to speak to *me?*" he asked. He seemed more surprised than angry. "You have been errant a long time, knight.

Perhaps you've forgotten that a vassal does not speak to the king unless he is bidden."

Croy lowered his head. "Your forgiveness, Majesty. Yet you must know of the crimes of this dwarf, and the innocence of this man. Justice demands that I speak."

The king crossed over to one of the chairs against the wall and sat down. It was a chair like any other in the room, but by virtue of Ulfram V's presence, it legally became a throne at that moment. Croy knelt before it.

"Just make haste," the king said. "I'm quite busy at the moment."

Croy kept his head bowed. "This dwarf is an oathbreaker. I'll bear witness to the fact, in any court you decree. She is a murderer and a despoiler. A . . . poisoner," he added. Ever since his father's death, the king had been especially frightened of poisoners. It was cruel of Croy to even speak the word in this room, but it was the truth, and it needed to be aired. "She took up arms against humans and . . . others. She laid waste to an entire city, by deceit, by design, and by use of weapons."

Ulfram turned to look at the dwarf. "Is this true?" he asked.

"Every fucking word of it," Balint told the king. She rolled her eyes. "Do your worst, and send me on my way. I've an itch on my buttocks I can't scratch, not with my hands tied like this."

"Another pointless delay!" the king screeched. Pressing his fingertips against his temples, he called out to his servants in the hall. "Fetch a scribe! Have him bring parchment and ink. And someone unchain her. What is your name, dwarf?"

"Balint."

Croy glared at her. "When addressing the king, you will call him, 'your majesty', or—"

"Or not. I certainly don't care," Ulfram said. Croy's shoulders tensed. He'd always thought kings should be slightly aloof, detached at least from the lesser folk they governed. Ulfram V clearly thought otherwise—he'd always disdained the careful phrases of court etiquette and spoke plainly as a peasant. That was his right, of course—the king could speak how he chose to whom he chose. If Croy found it unseemly that was his own problem.

"It seems I'm to be merciful today," the king said. "Believe me, it's not by choice. Any other day if you came here under these accusations I'd exile you on the spot. I have very little patience for those who won't do as they're told."

Balint said nothing. Her face was a mask of nonchalance, though Croy could see her bound hands were trembling.

"Tell me," Ulfram said. "Can you repair a broken ballista?"

"Any dwarf could do that," Balint assured him.

The king nodded. "And you laid waste to a city. That's what Croy said. He does tend to exaggerate, but you don't deny the charge. So you know how to conduct a siege. Do you know how to defend cities, too, or is it just destroying them you're good at?"

"I'm trained in all manner of siegecraft," Balint said. "I can work either side."

"Sometimes the Lady drops Her blessings right in our laps." The king reached down and put a hand on the dwarf's shoulder. "I'm going to give you a pardon for all crimes you may have committed in the past," he told her.

Croy's jaw fell.

"I assume that will earn me some gratitude. Perhaps," the king went on, "you'll consent to come work for me. I am in desperate need of sappers and engineers. Are we agreed?"

"Do I have to kiss your royal fucking codpiece or something to seal the deal?" Balint asked.

The king studied her carefully, then raised one eyebrow. "No."

"Then I'm all yours."

"Your majesty!" Croy objected. "I—I can't believe that—"

But then he stopped. He couldn't finish that thought out loud. He wasn't a knight errant anymore. He had lost certain freedoms the moment he was recommissioned. Questioning the king's word was one of them. "I beg your pardon, Majesty. I will be silent now."

"That'll be a nice change of pace," the king told him. "Very good. Milady Balint, you'll report to the keep. Sir Goris is the master of the armory there—tell him I want a full inventory of every trebuchet, battering ram and mantlet in our possession, and how many more of the same can be constructed in short order. Goris is a fool of parts. He knows the difference between a besagew and a rerebrace, but I'm not sure he can tell his hundreds from his thousands, so double check every number he gives you. We'll have much to discuss later, so stay close by."

Balint bowed low and said, "Your majesty."

"One thing," the king said, before dismissing her. "Sir Croy may be an idiot but all the same if he says someone's not to be trusted he's probably right. Serve me well and we'll forget about your indiscretions. Betray me and I'll send you back to the dwarven kingdom sealed up in a barrel like salt pork. Do you understand?"

Balint nodded agreeably. Then she marched out of the room with her chin up. She couldn't resist giving an evil snicker as she walked past Croy.

"Now, this one—your name is Malden, is that right? And you're a thief?"

"My name is Malden, your majesty," Malden said, glancing over at Croy and Cythera. He pleaded silently with his eyes.

Yet what could Croy do? If he tried to free Malden now, he'd be breaking his promise to the king. And that was unthinkable.

"Sir Hew took you into custody this morning. Ordinarily he would have sent you to the magistrates, but he told me there was something special about your case, and of course, my time is valued so little around here that he insisted I judge you personally. Apparently you were in possession, at the time of your arrest, of one of the famous swords. The blasted Ancient Blades."

"The one called Acidtongue, highness," Malden confirmed.

"A rather valuable piece of iron." The king frowned. His eye took in Malden's cheap cloak, the lack of flesh on his bones. "Look, lad, it's clear that you stole the blade. You're no more a swordsman than I'm a fishwife. So I'll give you the same choice I plan on giving every criminal and vagrant in this city. You can go back to the gaol and wait until I have time to hang you properly. Or—if you prefer—I can enlist you in my army as a foot soldier, and you can earn forgiveness through military service. Assuming you survive."

"Begging your majesty's pardon, I like neither of those options," Malden said.

"No, I don't suppose you would. But that's what I'm offering."

"To a guilty man, yes. But I am innocent. I did not steal the sword. It was given to me freely by its rightful owner— Sir Croy."

Every eye in the room turned to stare at the knight.

CHAPTER TWELVE

"Is this true, Croy?" the king demanded. "Did you—in fact—make a gift of a priceless and irreplaceable, aye, a magical sword . . . to what is clearly a piece of gutter trash from the most base dungpit in Ness?"

Croy was still on his knees. It was not appropriate to drop prostrate before the king, but he considered it. "It is true," he said.

The king frowned. "I was under the impression that you already had an Ancient Blade. Yes, I see it there on your belt—Ghostcutter, I believe. Hmm. The last time I saw Acidtongue, it was in the possession of Sir Bikker. Wasn't it?"

"Sir Bikker is dead, Majesty," Croy said. He had to

swallow thickly before he could go on. "I slew him in a duel of honor. With his dying breath he gave Acidtongue to me, and bade me find another to wield it. That is the way of our order, that we each choose our successors. And I chose this man—Malden—as the next to wield Acidtongue."

"There weren't any better candidates available? I have a nephew, for instance, who is absolutely useless at organizing his farms, but who loves nothing better than to whack away at the quintain all day with a wooden sword. He reminds me of you quite a bit, Croy. His head's just as full of fancies and notions of honor and chivalry." The king sighed. "Absolutely bloody useless. You can't give Acidtongue to him?"

Croy couldn't just say no. One did not gainsay the king. Yet he certainly could not say yes, either. He knew the nephew in question. Like every knight in the kingdom, he was distantly related to the king himself, and the nephew was his second cousin, once or twice removed. He couldn't remember which. The boy had always struck him as a simpleton. Then there was the fact that Croy had already given the sword to Malden. Once an Ancient Blade passed to its next wielder, it could not be taken back. The only way that could happen was if Croy decided Malden had broken his vows as an Ancient Blade. Then Croy would be required to kill Malden to secure the blade. The king might demand he do just that (and Croy would be required to comply), but even there was a problem. There had been no time for Croy to train Malden as an Ancient Blade—and thus Malden had never taken the sacred vows. He couldn't very well be said to have broken them since he had never even heard them spoken, much less repeated them.

There had to be a way to convince the king that Croy had made the right choice. "Your majesty, Malden may be lowborn, but his heart is strong. He is a natural wonder at footwork and quickness. I believed that with a few years of proper training and a strict physical regimen, he could be made into a swordsman."

Malden's chains rattled. Croy looked over and saw the thief pointing at his own face. He mouthed the word, "Me?" as if he couldn't believe it. Yet surely, when Croy had given

him the sword, Malden must have understood that this was
to be his destiny. Surely . . .

The king rose from his chair and strode briskly across
the room. Going to the door, he waved one hand into the
hallway. In a moment Sir Hew came in, carrying Acidtongue
in its special glass-lined scabbard.

"You heard something of this?" the king asked.

"Yes, your majesty. I heard all. And I'll swear all of it
is true. I've never known Croy to lie, not even to save his
own skin. Much less that of a street rat like this Malden.
The boy is a weakling, but he's quick on his feet as a tomcat.
As for his heart, Croy would be the best judge."

The king pulled wearily at his beard. "Fine, fine, give
the boy his sword. Unchain him. Then the three of you go
stand against that wall. If I'm to be beset by three Ancient
Blades at once, at least they can make themselves useful."

It was done quickly. When they were against the wall,
Croy and Hew grasped forearms with great fondness. It had
been a long time since they'd seen each other. "You wear
the king's crown on your chest," Croy said, looking down
at Hew's tabard. "I am so glad to see you, old friend—yet
not a little surprised!"

Hew shrugged. "After we were disbanded I tried being
a knight errant for a while, just like you. Running about the
countryside slaying goblins and brigands, burning sorcerers
at the stake, you know. All the usual thing. I found, however,
that I couldn't take being my own master. So I came back
here last year and begged for my old job back. His Majesty
took pity on me and let me captain his watch. Now the
worst thing I face most days is a starveling who's snatched
a loaf of bread, but I have honor, true honor."

"I am so glad to hear it," Croy said. A tear had formed
in the corner of his eye.

"Me too," Malden said. Croy hadn't even realized he was
standing there.

Sir Hew turned to look at the thief with disdain. "You're
not one of us yet, boy. Not just because you hold a sword.
Don't forget that."

Malden laughed. "I'm just glad to not be hanged. But

take a lesson from this, sir knight, and mark it well—not every street rat is what he seems to be."

Hew bridled and looked as if he was about to say something sharp in return, but his imprecation was cut short when the king cleared his throat. Remembering their instructions the three men lined up against the wall, Malden trying to ape the posture of the two knights.

"One last order of business," the king said, "and then we can move on. Who's she?"

The king had turned and pointed at Cythera.

"Your majesty," Cythera said, and made a proper curtsey. "I am Cythera, daughter of Coruth. With Croy and Malden I brought Balint to you so that—"

The king waved on hand in dismissal. "You should have stopped at 'daughter of Coruth'. So you're a witch?"

"Not exactly."

The king gripped the bridge of his nose. "Can you do anything . . . witch-like?"

Cythera blushed. Then she put her hands in front of her, a few inches apart. Bright sparks burst between them.

The king nodded eagerly. "Good, good—keep doing that! It's almost impressive. Now, you four—your job in the next few minutes is to stand there, looking menacing. That is all. I don't want you to speak. I don't want you to move at all. Just look dangerous. Can you do that?"

"Certainly, Majesty," Croy said, "but for what purpose?"

"I have a guest I need to entertain." It was the only explanation the king would give. He hurried to the door again and nodded to someone outside. "Send her in, now. I haven't got all day." Then he hurried back inside and took a seat in one of the room's chairs.

A herald in bright green livery strode into the room and made an elaborate flourishing bow. "Your majesty," he announced, "I must present the lady Mörgain, princess of the eastern steppes!"

The woman who came through the door wore very little other than a cloak of wolf fur. She stood taller than anyone in the room and broader through the shoulders than anyone but Croy or Hew. Her face was painted to look as if the flesh had been stripped from her skull, and her hair was hacked short and stuck out in wild bunches. If she was the daughter of Mörg the Wise then that made her the brother of Mörget, whom Croy had once called brother. Mörget was dead now, a fact that made him secretly breathe easier—he had no desire to test his prowess in a fight against Mörget. But by the look of her Mörgain would be nearly as deadly.

In her hand she held an iron axe, and she brought it round in a powerful swing that struck the herald in the small of the back. The small man went flying and crashed against the side of the hearth.

"No man calls me princess," Mörgain said.

CHAPTER THIRTEEN

Instantly Ghostcutter came to Croy's hand. Beside him he saw Chillbrand appear in Sir Hew's grip. Croy glanced over at Malden and nodded at the thief's belt. Malden made a rather clumsy draw of it, but he got Acidtongue into the air.

Cythera drew her hands apart, and light jumped between her fingers.

Yet even before Croy could take a step toward the barbarian, Mörgain had drawn her own sword and dropped into a defensive crouch. The sight of the blade was enough to make even a disciplined knight take pause.

Croy had seen longer swords, but never any so massive. It was longer than Ghostcutter by a good six inches and the blade was broader than his palm. The sword had no quillions, nor needed any, for the blade was far wider than the grip, and only tapered near its point. It looked not so much like a sword as a grotesquely large kitchen knife. The iron

had a perfect fibrous grain that spoke of master craftsman-
ship, but no matter how well balanced it might be Croy
knew most men would never have been able to hold its
weight in both hands.

Mörgain held it in one of her own, and the muscles in
her bare arm showed little strain.

Sir Hew spoke the name that echoed inside Croy's own
skull.

"That's Fangbreaker."

Fangbreaker—one of the seven Ancient Blades. Made
eight hundred years ago, at the same time as Ghostcutter,
or Chillbrand, or Acidtongue, and sworn as they were to
slay demons and defend humanity. Fangbreaker and another
Ancient Blade called Dawnbringer had been lost to the
people of Skrae centuries before in the final terrible battle
they'd fought against the barbarians—the battle that had
pushed the horde back beyond the Whitewall. The knights
who wielded the blades perished in the fighting up in the
mountains, and their swords were lost to Skrae. It had long
been conjectured that they had ended up in the hands of the
barbarians. Croy had confirmed the truth of that—he had
seen Dawnbringer in the hand of Mörget, and now Mörgain
held Fangbreaker. He wondered if Mörgain was as untrustworthy—and as unworthy of carrying an Ancient Blade—as
her brother.

Maybe it was time to take the sword back for Skrae. He
lunged forward, bringing Ghostcutter up from a low quarter.
Mörgain moved faster than Croy expected and swept down
with Fangbreaker so the two swords rang and grated along
each others' edge. Croy sensed Sir Hew coming up from
behind him on his left, his weak side. Together they could
make short work of this defiler—

Except that just then the king called, "Hold! Hold, all of
you."

Croy leapt back and shot a quick glance toward his liege.
Ulfram V was crouching by the hearth, one hand pressed
against the neck of the fallen herald.

"This man's not dead. Just stunned. I will not have blood
shed in my privy chamber. Not in this room, where my

father died. And you, Malden—put that blasted thing away. You're spilling acid on my good parquet floor."

Croy kept his eyes on Mörgain. Her painted face showed nothing, though her eyes were on fire with bloodlust. If he or Hew wanted to continue the conversation, she would be happy to oblige, he was certain.

"Stop. Put away your weapons. All of you!" Ulfram demanded again.

Croy met Mörgain's eyes, then slowly nodded. She nodded in return. They both sheathed their swords at the same time. Croy knew he could count on Sir Hew to do the same.

"As long as you do not use that filthy word again," Mörgain announced, "I will remain at peace. I am no princess. Princesses are vain, idle things, good only for sitting in towers waiting to be married off to the richest man their fathers can find. I am a chieftess of the eastern clans. Thousands of men obey my command."

The king stood up to his full height. The king might be overly familiar with his inferiors and he might fail to understand the value of the Ancient Blades, but Croy knew that Ulfram V did not lack for courage. "You're in my land, now. I don't see these thousands of men in this room. You've already given me offense. Did you come all this way to insult me? It's a long voyage from the eastern steppes."

"Not anymore," Mörgain said, and smiled to show her teeth. Matched with the painted teeth on her lips, they looked like vicious fangs. "I rode here, driving my horse to the point of death by exhaustion. It took me two days. My clansmen are coming on foot. It will take them a little longer. But only a little."

"So it's true, what my scouts have told me," Ulfram said, his voice hollow. "When Cloudblade fell, it cleared a new pass through the mountains."

"One near as flat as the plains of my birth," Mörgain agreed.

"And you'll cross that pass to invade Skrae. For conquest."

"As is our right. We are stronger than you. We've always been stronger than you," Mörgain said, "and the strong should rule the weak. For centuries now you've hidden behind those mountains, just as you hide behind the walls of your cities. It seems even mountains can fall. Where will you hide now, little king?"

Ulfram bristled but he was enough of a statesman not to rise to an obvious taunt. Mörgain might be bigger than him but he didn't have to fight her himself. "This is an act of aggression. A bald-faced move of conquest."

Mörgain shrugged. "I am to let you know we were provoked." She reached inside her wolf-fur cloak and took out something round and coated in tar. She turned it around and Croy saw it had a face on one side. A human head, hacked off and preserved in gruesome fashion.

It was enough to churn his guts. Even worse, he recognized the face. It belonged to a holy man who had once lived in an old fort just west of the Whitewall. Herward was his name, and he was one of the gentlest souls Croy had ever met.

"This one crossed the new pass a week ago. He came to where we were camped for the autumn and spread lies amongst my people. The Great Chieftain of the clans considers this an act of invasion on the part of Skrae."

"Herward? An invader?" Croy cried out in disbelief. "He was a devotee of the Lady! Perhaps he was not entirely sane." In fact the hermit had been driven mad by visions and black mead. Still—"He was no threat to you."

"He spread lies," Mörgain said again. "He spoke of a god called the Lady. He demanded we give her our worship. In the east we have only one deity—Death, mother of us all. We will not be converted to your decadent religion."

The king went and took the head from her. He looked down into the distorted features. "This is base rationalization and you know it, Mörgain. One crazed preacher is not an invasion force."

"I have come for two reasons only," Mörgain said, "and they are both now achieved. I came to give you warning, for among my people, only base cowards attack without warning. We are coming. You have been warned."

"And the other reason?" Ulfram asked.

"To prove I have more courage in my heart than any man."

The king nodded sadly. "I imagine you must. Because you would make an excellent hostage. I could seize you right now and force your clansmen to return to their steppes in exchange for your safety."

Mörgain laughed.

Croy knew that laugh. He'd heard a deeper, slightly louder version before. Mörget had laughed like that. It was the laugh of one who found violent death to be the ultimate jest.

"Any man who touches me will die. Perhaps some man will kill me, or even take me alive," she said. "But he will still die. I will be avenged, even if it takes fifty thousand warriors. If it takes every clan of the east, their bodies piled up outside these walls to make siege towers. If it takes the last drop of blood in the last vein of my people, the man who touches me will die. Now. Dare you take me hostage?"

Croy turned to watch the king's face. There was no fear there. He refused to be intimidated—or at least he refused to let Mörgain see that her threats had worked. Croy felt a certain pride at that. This was the man he served.

"Not when I have a better use for you. Go from here in peace," Ulfram said, "and take word to your Great Chieftain. I'll meet with him under the flag of parley, in a place and time of his choosing. Go. I will not stay you. Frankly I don't want you in my home another second."

CHAPTER FOURTEEN

After Mörgain left, no one spoke for some while. Croy grew uneasy, standing against the wall with his hand on his sword hilt. The king, his liege, was clearly distressed—Ulfram sat in his chair, chin in hand, deep in thought.

"It's far worse than I thought," the king said, at last. "I thought they would give us a chance to pay tribute in exchange for peace." He shook his head. "Croy—Sir Croy. You were there. You saw the mountain come down. How wide is this pass? How many men can march abreast through it?"

Croy's brow furrowed as he considered that. "When the mountain fell, it wreaked terrible damage on the surrounding land. The pass is perhaps a quarter of a mile across."

"That big? That big!" Ulfram got up and ran to the door. He waved outside and Croy heard footsteps in the hall. "My scouts told me it was passable, but they forgot to mention it was wide enough to march an entire army through. Incompetence everywhere! A hole that big in my kingdom. The barbarians will flood through. There'll be no stopping them."

"Your majesty," Sir Hew said. "I suspect you knew this was coming."

The king looked up at his Captain of the Guard. "I knew they were massing the clans just east of the mountains, yes."

"Already you've begun the process of conscription. We'll have an army ready before they arrive," Hew went on.

"An untrained rabble," Ulfram told him. He waved one hand in frustration. "And only a few real knights to lead them."

"We could send to the northern kingdoms, to hire more soldiers." The kingdoms of Skilfing, Ryving, Maelfing and Anfald were constantly at war with each other, and in times of peace they hired their soldiers out as mercenaries.

"Already done," the king said. "Skilfing has promised to come to our aid as soon as they're finished making their own war on Maelfing. They won't arrive for many weeks, though—and the barbarians are only days away."

"What of the Old Empire?" Croy asked.

The king shook his head. The first settlers of Skrae had been exiles from the continent across the southern sea, a land ruled for thousands of years by a grand imperial court. "I sent an envoy as soon as I heard about the new pass, of course," Ulfram said, "but the Emperor there has no love for us, not even after all this time. And I wouldn't trust him if he did send us troops. They'd probably beat the barbarians, then stick around to conquer us as well. No, we'll have to rely on the army we have. But we've had too much peace, for too long! Barely any man in Skrae remembers how to lift a sword. We're fat and soft. The barbarians—if they're anything like her—will run roughshod over us."

One by one, the king's councilors filed in from the hall. The exchequer, the seneschal, the chancellor, the Duke of Greenmarsh, the Archpriest of the Lady, many more Croy had never met. The Baron of Easthull nodded in a friendly way to Croy, but was quickly drawn into conversation with a man who wore the golden chain of the keeper of the royal seals. These were the most powerful men in Skrae—and unlike their king they all looked terrified.

A table was brought in and maps unfurled across its surface. Croy was asked a thousand questions, very few of which he could answer, but he did his best. Cythera had a few more answers, but she lacked any military training and couldn't speak to strategy. Yet the need for information seemed endless. Even Malden was interrogated about what he'd seen of the land near Cloudblade's ruin.

Everyone crowded around the maps, working out where the invasion would come from. "The forest—here—will slow them down a bit, but we can expect at most ten days' grace before they reach the river Strow," Sir Hew said.

"If we could only hold them off until winter," the king said, wringing his hands. "Just a few months. No army can march properly through a bank of snow. They'd have to either make camp where we could harry them, or, more likely, withdraw into the mountains and wait for spring. By then we could fortify the pass and seal them back where they belong."

"There might be a way to slow them at least," Croy suggested. "Here," he said, pointing to the map, quite near where the new pass lay, "there is an old fort. It's where we met Herward. It's half in ruins, but the walls still stand. My liege, give me five hundred men, and I'll hold it for a month, though it cost me my life."

The king stared at the map. Then he took a step back from the table and shook his head. "No," he told Croy.

"I beg you, Majesty! Allow me this chance to prove my honor."

"I said no, Sir Croy. Your five hundred would be overrun, eventually. Every man of them slain, and still you wouldn't buy us enough time. I can't sacrifice that many on a noble gesture. No, we will make our defense here, at Helstrow."

Sir Hew cleared his throat but the king shot him a piercing glance. "I have spoken," he announced.

Silence fell across the room.

"When word of this gets out, everyone in the outer bailey will try to flee. I can't allow that. Seal the gates of the outer bailey—all of them. No man will leave Helstrow, not until I bid it," Ulfram declared. "Redouble our efforts to conscript the population. I want every soul within these walls dedicated to preparing for the attack. As for you three Ancient Blades—go now, and make yourselves useful. Train as many of the rabble as you can. My councilors and I have a great deal of work to do, and you're wasting our time."

Croy's cheeks burned. His heart raced in his chest. He bowed deep and said, "My liege." Then he nodded at Cythera and Malden and hurried them out of the chamber.

It was not until they were beyond the gates of the palace that any of them spoke again. It was Cythera who spoke first. "I can't believe he just let Balint go like that—after all she did!"

"We cannot gainsay him," Croy told her. "He is the Lady's appointed sovereign, and his word is law."

"He's a man. And any man can be a fool," Malden insisted.

Croy's blood surged to hear the slander, but he knew better than to take Malden's words too seriously. The thief didn't understand what he was talking about. "He's a king, and that's all that matters. It is his right to do as he sees fit, for all our sake."

"Not mine. I know nothing of war," Malden admitted, "but he's making a mistake, isn't he? Sir Hew seemed to think your strategy could have worked. It could have kept the barbarians bottled up. Instead he's going to just let them march up to his gate so he can have a nice chat with *their* king. Or whatever it is they have instead of a king. He's going to talk to them, when all they want is to destroy us."

Croy's honor wouldn't allow him to agree. But he knew enough of military history to say, "If the barbarians come through the pass unhindered, they'll have time before the first snow falls to establish a strong foothold inside Skrae's borders. Once they're here, it'll be a hard thing to drive them out again."

The thief placed a hand on Croy's shoulder. Croy could feel Malden's fingers shaking. "I—I'm not good enough with this sword to fight in battle," he said. "I can't stay here. I can't stand beside you."

Croy closed his eyes. Cowardly words, but truthful ones. "No, Malden, you can't. Which is why you're leaving Helstrow tonight—and you're taking Cythera with you."

CHAPTER FIFTEEN

After darkness fell, Malden and Croy headed back into the outer bailey. The air was crisp with autumn's chill, but Helstrow's streets were full of people heading this way and that, as if they didn't know where to go but didn't dare go to their homes. The kingsmen were out in force, hauling away anyone they could find who could be legally conscripted. Even the slightest offense was enough to get a man arrested that night. Public drunkenness, failure to keep a pig off the street—things that were commonplaces in peace time had become hanging offenses, it seemed. Nor were the women of Helstrow left unaccosted. They were herded toward churches and public houses, where they would be put to work making bandages and bowstrings.

Malden still wore his old green cloak, but Croy had put on a tabard with the colors of the king, green and gold, and the people they passed gave them a wide berth. The swords on their hips probably made room for them as well.

The two of them passed a bloody-handed preacher standing on the lip of a well, shouting for all who would hear it the old religion of the bloodgod—heresy in a fortress-town dedicated to the Lady. More than a few young men had stopped to listen, perhaps thinking Sadu could save them from the coming barbarians. When the crowd saw Croy's colors, though, they ran off into the night.

"They'd do better putting their faith in the king," Croy said, through clenched teeth. He found the piglet the holy man had sacrificed hidden in the well's bucket. He tossed it angrily into the street.

"They're terrified," Malden told him. He could sympathize. "They'll turn to anything that offers some hope." He looked ahead into the dark street, lit only by the moon. "Is it much farther now?"

"The conscripts you want are being held in a churchyard by the outer wall," Croy told him. "It's only a few streets from here. Once you find these men—"

"It's better if you don't know what I'll do after that," Malden told him. "We'll part ways as soon as they're freed."

Croy nodded. "Malden," he said, "this may be the last time I have a chance to talk to you about . . . something that has been troubling me."

Malden tensed, wondering what the knight was talking about. Was he going to change his mind now, and demand that Malden stay and help with the defense of Helstrow?

"There is no time for Cythera and I to be wed before you leave," Croy went on, looking away from Malden's face. "I have her promise, but . . . Malden. I've never doubted your friendship. Yet I saw something, under Cloudblade. Something I cannot explain."

Malden's heart stopped beating for a moment. "You saw her kiss me."

Croy couldn't seem to speak.

This might be the moment, Malden thought, when he tells me he's going to have to kill me. He considered which way he would run.

But Croy lived by a code of honor. And that meant he had to give a man a chance to defend himself. "Why did she do it?" he asked.

The thief licked his lips. What he said next was going to have to be very carefully worded. Cythera had said she would tell Croy everything when they returned to Ness. Implicit in that was that he shouldn't tell Croy himself. He couldn't tell Croy that he and Cythera loved each other. That the betrothal between the knight and Cythera was already broken.

There was good reason for that silence. Still, Malden burned to have it all out in the open. It would make life so much simpler. In all likelihood, it would also make *his* life much shorter. Yet he found he couldn't quite lie. "Allow me to explain. At that moment—the moment of that kiss—I was moments from certain death. The assassin, Prestwicke, was going to kill me. I was a condemned man and I had no hope of survival. I begged her for that kiss, as the last request of a dying man. In such a case, what woman could refuse?"

Croy's eyes were wide and his face had turned bright red. He was embarrassed, Malden realized, to even have to ask. If another man had caught Malden kissing his betrothed, a lesser man than Croy he doubted that explanation would have sufficed. Yet Malden saw other emotions in Croy's face. Gratitude. Relief. Croy had wanted so badly for there to be a simple, innocent explanation that he probably would have accepted anything Malden said. Anything other than the full truth.

"Surely you don't doubt her constancy," Malden insisted. "Her honor—"

"Her honor is my honor, and I would die to defend it. And you're right, she could not refuse you in a moment like that. She is such a compassionate woman. You see why I love her? Do you understand the strength of my feelings?"

"I think I do," Malden said, softly.

"But that very quality I love makes her vulnerable. Men can be schemers. They can take advantage of woman's gentler nature, and women aren't always wise enough to resist their charms."

Not for the first time Malden remembered that Croy had never spent much time around women. Malden, who had been raised by harlots, thought he might know the female mind a little better. He also knew just how well women could resist men's charms—when they chose to. He decided not to share this knowledge, just then.

"Someone else, someone with a less noble heart than yours, Malden, might have taken advantage of that situation. They might have asked for more than a kiss. If she were in a situation where she had to compromise herself, she might question the promise she made to me."

"Put these thoughts from your mind! Croy, you have enough to worry about!"

Croy shook his head. "I need to ask your aid, Malden, and please, don't refuse this. I need you to watch her. Make sure she stays safe. And . . . and pure. I—" Croy let out a little gasp. His fists were clenched before him. "I would die, my soul would shrivel, if I ever learned she did not love me any longer. It would pain me more than arrows through my vitals, Malden!"

"I swear this, Croy," he said. "No new lover will come near her. I won't so much as let her be alone with any man but me."

There were tears in Croy's eyes when he grasped Malden in a crushing embrace. "You are my friend, after all. I doubted it sometimes—but you are my true friend."

"Put all your trust in me," Malden told him. And for the first time in his life, he felt the pangs of conscience for deceiving someone. But he knew he would feel pangs of another sort—the sort one feels with two feet of steel shoved through one's belly—should Croy ever learn the truth.

CHAPTER SIXTEEN

He made a point of saying no more until they reached the churchyard.

It was a gloomy place for men to sleep, even thieves. Yet the conscripts would have been disconsolate even if they'd been billeted in the courtly homes of the inner bailey. To a man they looked beaten and exhausted. While Malden had been brought to his audience with the king, these men had spent the day training. Shouting serjeants had put them through endless paces, teaching them the basics of how to use a bill hook as a weapon or how to march and even run in heavy leather harness. The reward for all that hard work was that now they were chained together in groups of six so they could not run away, given a bowl of thin pottage each to eat, and then utterly ignored by their captors.

Malden supposed it was better than being hanged in a public square. He wondered how many of the groaning men would agree. Well, at least for one of them the future held a little more promise. He scanned the crowd among the graves until he found Velmont, his friend from his own previous confinement.

"That one," he told Croy.

They approached the chained men and Velmont looked up with half a smile when he saw Malden. Then he glanced down at the sword on Malden's belt and his face fell. Malden realized he must be wondering if the man he'd spoken to while chained up in the banquet hall had in fact been an informer for the kingsmen. He had to admit to himself that if their positions were reversed he would have a hard time of trusting Velmont. "Just keep quiet, and this will go well for you," he whispered.

"You had me good, didn't you?" Velmont asked, ignoring

what Malden had said. "All that talk o' being brothers in the trade."

"Be of good cheer, Velmont," Malden told the man. "I'm not here to do you any harm."

"You're no thief, are you?" Velmont asked. He spat into the weeds between two graves. "What is it you want now, more o' our secrets?"

"These others with you—are they part of your crew?" Malden asked.

"You want me to start giving up names? You'll have to beat 'em out of me."

"Listen to my proposal before you reject it," Malden told him. He put his hand on the iron collar fastened around Velmont's neck, but the thief jerked away from him. "I'm going to free you, you fool!"

"Oh, aye, free me from me mortal station, I'd reckon. With all I told ye . . . I gave out plenty enough to end up swingin' from a rope."

Croy bent to study the chains holding Velmont, and drew his belt knife to break the lock. Malden looked up and saw they'd been observed. The guards set to watch the conscripts had been huddled around a fire near the church, but now a serjeant in a rusted kettle hat came running toward them. He had a green and yellow ribbon wound around the brim of his helmet, and a thick truncheon in his hand.

"Saving your grace, sir knight," the man said, addressing Croy, "but may I ask exactly what you think you're doing here?"

Malden's hand dropped toward the hilt of Acidtongue, but Croy stepped in front of him and leaned close to the serjeant's face. "The king's work," he said. His voice was hard—harder than Malden had ever heard it before. "I've been sent on this fool's errand by Sir Hew himself, the Captain of the Guard. I want it done quickly so I can get back to more important things. Now, release these men."

"But—they're criminals!" the serjeant protested.

"They're wanted at the keep for a special detail. We need laborers to oil and clean every piece of iron in the armory before morning. Of course, if you'd prefer, I can take you and your men instead."

Malden's jaw dropped. He'd never heard Croy talk to anyone with such an air of command—or threat. Nor had he ever heard Croy lie. He would have thought the knight incapable of dissembling. It seemed the knight had hidden depths.

The serjeant shook his head hurriedly. "No, no sir. I'll fetch the keys."

In short order Velmont and the five men he'd been chained with were free. The serjeant offered to bind their hands. "I don't think that's necessary," Croy told him. "The two of us are armed well enough to control a half dozen dogs like this."

"As you'd have it, sir," the serjeant said. When he was dismissed he went gratefully back to his fire, glad to have escaped Croy's attention. There would be no more trouble from that quarter.

Malden and Croy led the six conscripts down an alley and around a corner before they spoke again. Croy clasped Malden's hands and said, "It's done. I'll make sure Cythera is waiting for you at the inn, with full packs and some food. Malden, if the war goes poorly, or I am killed—"

"We'll meet again," Malden told him. "Get back before Sir Hew wonders where you've been."

Croy nodded. "Lady speed you on your path," he said, and hurried off into the night. Malden watched him go for a moment, then turned around to face the conscripts.

Before he could say a word to Velmont, however, a hand reached across his front and slipped the buckle of his belt. Acidtongue fell to the cobbles and Malden, too surprised to think clearly, bent to retrieve it.

A stone came down on the back of his head, hard enough to send his brains spinning.

CHAPTER SEVENTEEN

Cythera stood by the window in their room at the inn, watching the street through a narrow gap in the shutters. It was near midnight, but the fortress city still rumbled with activity, and a fair amount of traffic still moved through the narrow lanes. Groups of men—soldiers, or simply men who had gathered together for security—hurried this way and that on errands, their heads down, their voices low, showing few lights. All of Helstrow was terrified of what was coming.

Coruth had tried to warn her of this, she was sure. Of the coming invasion and the war that would follow. Cythera tried to remember the words the boy had spoken in the alley, words sent across a hundred miles. Surely this was what Coruth had meant. The swords coming together, men brought low or carried to high station. What else could it mean?

A knock at the door startled her. She hurried across the room and reached for the latch, but hesitated before opening. Croy had been quite clear in his instructions, and for once she'd agreed with him. They could not be too careful now. The king was unwilling to let anyone leave Helstrow, whether or not they could fight. If his agents found out that Cythera planned to escape they would try to stop her. She did not call out to ask who was at the door, only waited a moment, her nerves jangling.

A second knock came after a short pause. And then a third right away. That was the signal.

She opened the door and saw Croy there. He pushed past her into the room without speaking. He held a pair of heavy packs which he set down on the bed. "It's done," he whispered. "I can't stay long."

She nodded, understanding. The less said the better. No

one in Helstrow was sleeping now, and it was impossible to know who might hear them.

Croy lifted one hand as if he might touch her cheek. Instead his fingers moved to her lips. She blinked, unsure of what he was trying to communicate. "I'll come to Ness as soon as I can," he whispered. "If I can."

Cythera closed her eyes. If he lived through the invasion, he meant.

Cythera didn't know if she'd ever truly loved Croy. When he'd asked for her hand in marriage it had seemed like a way to escape her father. Later it had sounded like a grand adventure. Now she knew she could never be happy as his wife, that only Malden could give her life she wanted.

Yet she had never doubted Croy's love, or his kindness. He had been so good to her and her mother—she owed him far more than she could repay. And here she was, betraying him. She opened her mouth, absolutely convinced she had to tell him the truth. She would tell him everything about Malden. She would beg his forgiveness. It was the right thing to do.

"Don't speak," he told her. "Just listen. When we meet again we'll get married, right away. I won't worry about the banns, or about all the formalities and niceties. I'll take you to the Ladychapel in whatever clothes we're wearing, day or night. If we must we'll wake the priests and force them to perform the ceremony. I'll kneel with you before the altar there and take your hand and it will be done. It will be forever."

She had to tell him. It was unthinkable cruelty not to.

"I can see it in my mind's eye, even now. The candles. The golden cornucopia above the altar. I can smell the incense. Yes," he said, and he leaned forward to rest his forehead against hers. "Yes. That image is going to get me through anything that's to come. I don't care about the bloodshed. I don't care about the danger. I will see only your face as you give yourself to me. As I give myself to you."

"Croy," she managed to say, though her voice cracked. "There's something—"

He wasn't finished, though. "I had a teacher once, a fencing master, who told me there were only two ways to ride into battle. You could go in expecting to die, but wanting to die honorably, and the Lady would favor you and you would live. Or you could go to war with a reason to survive, a reason to keep going—and the Lady would make sure you were victorious. He said the latter was always better. I'm going to fight for you, Cythera. I'm going to fight to make sure I get that moment in the Ladychapel."

"You," she said. "You should know that . . . you should . . ."

The words were there in her throat. She could no more have conjured them forth, though, than she could fly to the moon. She opened her eyes to look at him. Perhaps that would help her summon up the strength to do what was right.

There were tears on his cheeks, but he was smiling.

If she told him now she would destroy him. It was wrong to keep this secret all the same. She still felt that way. It would have taken a saint to say the words, though, and Cythera knew she was no saint. So she did what a witch would do instead. What her mother would do.

"You'll be a hero then," she told him. "You'll be a champion of Skrae. What woman could resist that?"

He laughed, a sound of happiness in that dark hour. He kissed her on the cheek, and he left her there. Hurried back out into the night, to do what he must.

When he was gone she shivered for a while, though she was not cold. Then she went back to the window to continue her vigil—this time, waiting for Malden to come and take her away.

CHAPTER EIGHTEEN

Malden never actually lost consciousness, but between the pain in his head and the fact that he was shoved through the dark streets by a group of angry men who beat him every time he faltered, he had little idea where he was taken. He saw torches and doorways pass by, now he was looking down at cobblestones, now up at an empty, cold sky. He was bounced down a flight of stairs and thrown onto a surface of packed earth in a place that smelled of old mildew. He was turned on his side and he saw a wall of stone, criss-crossed with the glittering tracks of snails.

And then a bucket of stagnant water was dumped across his face, and he fought and spluttered and shouted as he desperately tried to sit up. The wooden bucket bounced off his shoulder and he drew back in fresh pain.

But suddenly he could think clearly again. He could hear many men grumbling all around him, and see them silhouetted against a fire at the far side of the room.

He could hear their voices just fine.

"Slit his throat. Bury him down here, aye. But what of his fuckin' sword? Can't sell that, any fence'd known it for a Ancient Blade, jus' lookin' at it. And then we'd have every bleedin' kingsman in town down here, wantin' to ask questions and crack heads."

"I say we cut off his fingers and toes, 'til he tells us who he really is."

"And I say—and my word is law, yeah?—I say, we don't got much time 'til that knight comes lookin' for him. So we settle this now, we do it quiet, and we all find someplace else to be 'til it blows o'er."

There were more grumbling protests, but the voices never grew too loud. And then a man with a knife no longer than his thumb came toward Malden, his free hand out to grab the thief's hair and pull his head back. The size of the knife was not reassuring. They were going to cut his throat. It didn't take a very big knife to slash a man's windpipe.

Malden scuttled backwards, until his back hit a wall. He was out of options. "Don't you lot practice the ancient custom of sanctuary?" he demanded.

The man with the knife stopped where he was.

A much bigger man, with a head as bald and round as the moon, came stomping forward. "What're you talkin' about?" he demanded.

"I'm assuming that Velmont brought me to the local guild of thieves. I very much hope I'm not mistaken. In Ness, where Cutbill runs the guild, we practice the custom of sanctuary. Any thief, no matter where he's from, can demand the right to hide out in one of our safe houses, and he cannot be denied. As long as his dues are paid up."

The man with the knife turned to face the bald one. In silhouette, Malden could tell it was Velmont who'd been about to slit his throat.

"He's speakin' true, boss," Velmont said.

"Aye, save for one thing. Sanctuary's for thieves. And you ain't no thief, kingsman. Now be quiet while we murther you."

"Velmont," Malden insisted, "tell them. You and I spoke of many things this morning. Things only a thief would know. And tonight, after I'd engineered my own escape, I came back for you. If all I wanted was to make trouble for you, why would I loose your chains? Why would I be so stupid as to put myself in your power? I'm no kingsman! I'm just a thief, like you."

Velmont lowered his knife hand, but he didn't back off. "I saw that man you were with. For a thief, you've got some pretty funny friends."

"I tricked that knight into helping me," Malden told him. "I stole that sword and everyone just assumed I was one of them." That made a certain degree of sense. No man in Skrae who fell below the class of freeholder was allowed by law to even touch a sword. Wearing one on your hip would automatically convince a lot of people you were of a certain social level, and deserving of a certain level of trust. "It was a long shot, but it was my only chance of getting out of the fortress alive."

"But e'en then, why would some blasted knight help the likes o' you?" the boss inquired.

"Because he wanted someone to smuggle his betrothed out of here, before the fighting starts. A woman named Cythera."

The thieves looked at each other skeptically. There was some grumbling, but the boss cut it off with a gesture.

"A woman, I might add," Malden went on, "who I've already swived."

Laughter erupted amongst the gathered thieves of Helstrow. The boss tried to silence it but every thief enjoyed a good jest at the expense of a landed knight. By besmirching Cythera's honor—though not by lying—Malden had just scored a point with the crew.

He needed to win over their leader, though. The boss went to one corner of the room where a thickly recessed window was set into the wall very close to the ceiling. They must be in a cellar, Malden realized. Probably beneath a tavern or a gambling hall. The boss stared up through the window as if expecting to see a kingsman staring back down at him. Then he hobbled back over to Malden. Malden saw that the man had a wooden leg. It would be difficult to convince a man like that to take a journey of a hundred miles on foot. Yet that was exactly what he needed to do.

"I need to get out of here. Tonight, with the woman. I'll pay handsomely to anyone who can help me with that," Malden said, softly.

Malden knew that in Ness the possibility of money changing hands never failed to get a thief's attention. The Helstrovian crew seemed no different.

"The walls are sealed," Malden went on. "And I'm a stranger here. I don't know the secret ways of this place. But the man who does could be very rich once I'm free."

"Mayhap I know a way out," Velmont said.

"Shut it, Vellie!" the boss thundered. "I'll hear no more o'—"

"Ye'll hear what I have to say, by the bloodgod's guts," Velmont shot back. "If there's silver to be had—or at very least, the promise o' silver—I'm listening."

Malden nodded. He had no money to give these thieves, not now. But at least they'd stopped talking of slitting his throat. It also sounded like there was still a chance at escape. He'd hoped for this—that Velmont or his organization would have some secret route out of the fortress. "I'm glad to hear it. Maybe it's good for you, as well. Maybe you should come with me when I leave. By tomorrow it'll be too late. Every one of you will be conscripted. Forced to fight. And believe me—you don't want to face what's coming for you. The barbarians are only ten days from the river, and coming fast."

"Barbarians?" one of the thieves asked, and suddenly the clamor in the cellar made Malden's ears hurt. He realized with a start that the thieves had no idea why their king was girding for war. Most likely no one had bothered to inform the populace of the news from the east. "How many of 'em? Are they on horseback? I've heard they got witches that can curdle a man's blood with one nasty look!"

"There's still time for all of us to flee. It must be tonight, though. If we do it now, we're refugees. If we do it tomorrow we're deserters, and they hang deserters," Malden pointed out.

"Why don't you just tell me where your lady's at," the boss asked Malden. "I'll make sure she gets where she oughta be, eh?"

"Do you think me such a fool? I leave with her—and any of you that want to come. Any of you who want to live through the next fortnight, that is." Malden shook his head. "The barbarians are fearsome enemies. Some of them paint their faces red, to show they've drunk human blood. Their women paint their faces like skulls, because they say it's the only way to get the men to kiss them. Come with me, now, and we'll travel together to Ness. There Cutbill will grant you more than sanctuary. He'll make you full members in our guild. He'll shower you with gold."

Malden was barely aware of everything he was saying and all the promises he'd made. He would have said anything to get the thieves on his side.

"Listen, boss," Velmont said, "I think he's tellin' the truth—"

"I didn't ask for your opinion, Vellie," the boss told the thief. "It's my decision to make. And I say we stay put."

The crowd of thieves fell silent. Dead silent. Malden felt the blood in his veins jumping as his heart sped in his chest.

"I lived right here me whole life, and I ain't runnin' now," the boss said. "War's good for our kind. They send all the kingsmen out to fight, and leave us here, alone with all the pickin's. No, we're not leavin'. And if he won't tell me where this lady is, and this knight's pile o' gold, I'll find 'em me own way. Now. I believe I told you once already. Cut 'im."

Velmont looked down at the knife in his hand.

"Sorry 'bout this, but it's hard times," he said.

Malden flattened himself against the wall. There was no escape.

Then Velmont took a step to the side—and slashed his knife across the throat of his boss. Blood flew from the wound and misted the far wall, as bright as the snail tracks there. The boss clutched at his neck but made no sound whatsoever as he collapsed. The other thieves drew back in terror, pressing themselves up against the far wall. They didn't shout or make a peep of surprise or fear, though. These were men who'd seen murder before, men who knew when to keep silent. For a while the only noise in the cellar was the drumming of the boss's wooden leg on the earthen floor. Eventually that, too, stopped.

Velmont turned to face his fellow thieves, gory knife still in hand. "He was a good boss, in 'is way, but he was gonna get us all killed. I'm sidin' with the fella that wants to save our skins. Any man of you have a problem with that?" he demanded.

His question evoked more silence.

"Good." He put his knife away. Then he bent down to offer Malden a hand up. "Now. Let's talk about how I expect to get us all out o' Helstrow, without marchin' us through the front door."

CHAPTER NINETEEN

The bridge across the river Strow began and ended within the walls of the outer bailey. No one crossed the river without the king's approval—at least, not from above.

Underneath the bridge a complicated sparwork of stone beams held up the road surface. An agile man unafraid of heights could cross from one end to the other without having to climb up top.

Malden had both those qualities. It didn't bother him in the slightest to hang from his hands by a stringcourse of granite, thirty feet above the foaming waters of the river. Velmont and his crew took their time about it, but managed to make the crossing without slipping. Yet when Cythera began to climb across, she made it a third of the way and then stopped, clinging hard to a stone pillar, her eyes clenched tightly shut.

Malden looked up. He could hear horses drawing heavy loads across the timber surface of the bridge. It creaked and rattled under the strain. He swung back over to where Cythera waited and put an arm around her back. Slowly, unwillingly, she opened her eyes and looked at him.

"This is your stock in trade, isn't it?" she asked him, in a very small voice. "I thought I would be fine. I've been on rooftops before, climbed towers—"

"This is different. I understand," Malden said, in a soothing voice. He looked across the underside of the bridge and saw Velmont staring back at him. The Helstrovian thief made a pushing motion with both hands.

Malden tried not to take offense at the notion. They were, in fact, pressed for time. Dawn was only an hour away and they needed to be outside the walls by then, outside and well clear of the eyes of Helstrow's kingsmen.

"Take it slowly. Don't look down," Malden said.

"I can't move my arms. They won't let go," Cythera told him.

Malden fought down the impatience and fear in his heart. He thought of what he should say. He couldn't very well carry Cythera across. Perhaps he should coax her on like a stubborn mule, or a frightened child, or—

—no. This was Cythera. She was no blushing virgin, afraid of specters in the privy and spiders in the basin.

"You are the daughter of a sorcerer and a witch," Malden said.

"I can't magic my way over there!" Cythera shouted at him. Her voice was nearly lost, all the same, in the rushing of the water. She looked down. "If I fall from here, how far do you think my body will be carried before the current before I wash up on some distant bank, my lips blue, my eyes cloudy, my bones shattered by rocks?"

"You are the daughter of the witch Coruth," Malden said again. He was sure he was on the right track. "You went willingly into the Vincularium. You fought demons and elves and undead things there. This," he said, carefully, "is a very sturdy bridge. Stonemasons work tirelessly to keep it from falling down. Now. Come with me. I expect you to follow my every step."

Then he turned away and jumped to a ledge of stone no more than three feet away. With one hand on a beam for support, he used the other to gesture for her to follow.

And she did.

Moving carefully, one step at a time, they swung across the beams, jumping where necessary, walking sideways on thin ledges, always moving forward so momentum helped carry them along.

Cythera did not fall.

At the far side, a thick pipe stuck out from under the bridge. It drained the dungeons and cellars of the keep into the river. An iron grate covered its end, but Velmont already had that unlocked and pulled back on its hinges. Inside they had to crawl a ways before coming to a wider space. It was so dark inside Malden felt the blackness pressing against his eyeballs. He reached back, and Cythera took his hand.

This was the perfect place for a betrayal. If Velmont wanted to kill him, it could be done with no trouble at all.

Instead the Helstrovian made fire and lit a torch. Malden saw that they had come to a junction of many pipes, some no wider than his fist, some high enough to walk through. "Smugglers use this route all the time," Velmont explained, gesturing at one wall. Hundreds of marks and sigils decorated the bricks, names and columns of numbers scratched into the niter-thickened stone of the walls. It looked like whole generations of thieves had been through this way. "There's an outflow pipe what fetches up at the base of the outermost wall, just o'er here." He pointed down a broad pipe that led away into darkness. Malden started to lead Cythera toward its mouth, but just then Velmont grabbed his shoulder and spun him around.

"Your Cutbill," Velmont said, "had better come through for me and mine. I ain't leavin' behind e'erything I ever knew, just to end a beggar in some pisspot o' a free city."

Malden nodded, but said nothing.

It was not long after that they pushed open another iron grate and stepped out into moonlight. Above Malden's head the wall of Helstrow stretched high. He was outside that wall, out in the country beyond the king's fortress. Free.

Looking up he could make out lights among the battlements. There were guards up there, keeping watch. They'd crossed an important barrier, but this was no time for exultation. Not yet.

Velmont extinguished his torch and gestured for Malden to keep moving. The outflow pipe emptied in a narrow ditch that ran straight away from the fortress-town. Malden didn't look back until they were a quarter mile away. Then he looked to see lights burning in the keep and palace. He looked to see the sealed gates of Helstrow, and the empty villages that stood outside each portal. No lights there—the people who lived in those villages had all been herded inside the walls— either for their own safety, or so they could be conscripted.

He saw Velmont looking back, too. He wondered if Velmont had ever in his life been beyond that wall before. It could be a terrifying experience, first setting foot in a countryside of which you knew nothing. Malden should know—until his recent adventure, he'd spent every day of his life in Ness, and the first time he'd left he'd felt like he'd been picked up by a great wind and thrown out into the middle of the sea. He'd never quite gotten used to country life. "In a few months," Malden told the Helstrovian thief, "the war will be won. You'll return richer than when you left—and you'll like Helstrow all the more for the money you bring back."

"Assumin' your barbarians don't stink my city up too much, after they turn it into one o' their tent camps." Velmont's face contorted through a variety of emotions. "There's a piece of me, not a big 'un, mind, but a piece—wishes I could stay to see what's goin' to happen."

"You want to remain here and fight for your home?" Malden asked, a little surprised. Thieves as a rule were not known for their patriotic sentiment.

"Nah," Velmont said, with a chuckle. "I kinda wanna stay and watch it burn."

CHAPTER TWENTY

In the king's own chapel in the keep at Helstrow, Croy knelt before the altar of the Lady, hands clasped in supplication. He did not see the burning censers set all around him by the acolytes, or smell the pungent incense they contained. He did not see the golden cornucopia that hung on the wall before him. He saw nothing but the Lady in his mind's eye, a woman of supernal radiance clothed all in green and white. His ears heard nothing but the whispered prayers that came from his lips, faint rustlings barely recognizable as sounds after a night without wine or even milk to sustain him.

He did not hear the clank of Sir Hew's armor as the Captain of the Guard entered the royal chapel, nor the polite clearing of Sir Hew's throat. Nor even his own name, spoken in hushed tones, as Hew tried to get his attention.

It was not until Hew's hand fell on his shoulder that his vigil was broken.

"It's dawn, Croy," Hew said, not unkindly. "You've been here long enough."

Croy blinked and looked up. He saw everything, heard all. His senses felt tuned to an agonizing pitch.

Slowly he shifted on his knees. Brought one leg up and put his foot on the floor. His knee joint popped and clamored in pain. Every part of his body was stiff as he rose carefully to his feet.

There had been a time when he could kneel in vigil for days on end, and leap to his feet when he was done, without so much as a groan or an ache. There had also been a time when he could meditate on the Lady for just as long—and not see Cythera's face when he looked into his goddess' eyes.

"I'm getting old," he said to Hew, with a weak smile.

The Captain of the Guard clapped him on the shoulders. "Knights so rarely do. Ancient blades even less often. Take it as the Lady's blessing that she let you live this long." Hew steered him toward the chapel's door. "Don't complain overmuch, man. We have a full day ahead of us, and I don't want to catch you napping. Where's your squire—what was his name, Malden?"

"He should be here attending me. Perhaps asleep in one of the pews," Croy said, looking around as if he expected to see the thief at once. "That's odd. I don't see him here anywhere."

Hew raised one eyebrow. "I knew that boy was no good. If he's run off—with an Ancient Blade on his belt . . . I'll have the guard look for him. Damn my eyes. He won't get far."

"Make no curse or oath in this place," Croy chided.

Hew laughed as he led Croy out of the chapel and down toward the armory in the cellar of the keep. They passed down a long stair, their weapons and armor clattering in the enclosed space. "The same old Croy, I see. Most devout of us all—and the most trusting. Are you sure this Malden is worth your faith?"

"He's a good man. I've seen true honor in him, though he denies it if he's asked."

Hew scowled. "If I find him down by the gates trying to bribe his way out, I won't ask your permission before I have him beaten. What were you thinking, giving Acidtongue to that boy?"

"He saved my life, and my honor, which I value more," Croy told Hew. He needed to change the subject. If Hew found out he'd sent Malden away, there could be real trouble. "What work do you have for me today?"

"I want you fitted for a proper suit of armor." Hew slapped Croy's ribs. "What are you wearing, a brigantine? That's infantry stuff." He pushed open a door at the end of a dim hallway and gestured for Croy to go through. "Here, meet Groomwich, our armorer. He's a dab hand with a hammer and tongs, no matter what he looks like."

The armorer bowed low as the knights entered his domain. He had the permanently blackened skin of a metalsmith, save on the left half of his face which was a horrid expanse of burnt tissue, white and rugged in the light of his forge.

"Get this one in a proper coat of plate," Hew commanded. "And ready another suit, for a boy the same height but about half his size. You stay here, Croy. I'll go roust out Malden. After you're done here you need to go down to the archery butts and say some inspiring words to the new recruits. That's what the king feels we Ancient Blades are best employed at—rousing speeches."

Croy frowned. "He's never had faith in our strength of arms. Not since our father died. I worry he won't use us to best advantage."

"Well, I suppose our time will come soon enough, to show him what we can do."

Hew left him, then. The silent armorer got to work right away, fitting various pieces of steel to Croy's body. The work required Croy to stand perfectly still for long stretches of time, and wasn't that different from the vigil he'd just completed. As each piece was measured and marked, Groomwich would hammer it into the right shape and size. He never said a word. In the heat of the armory, Croy soon found himself falling asleep, rising only when he was called upon to stand and be measured again.

It must have been hours later when Hew came back, his face red with anger, to say that Malden was nowhere to be found—nor Cythera. How they had escaped the fortress of Helstrow was a complete mystery, but Hew did not hesitate a moment to blame Croy for what he considered a crime of the first magnitude: Malden had taken Acidtongue with him.

"The thrice-damned barbarians already have two of the seven," Hew said, spittle leaping from his teeth. "Now some frightened boy has another—Croy, how could you let this happen? How could you give such a treasure to someone so clearly untrustworthy? If it were anyone else, I'd have you drawn and broken as a traitor. If it was anyone else I'd think you were trying to undermine us! But I know you too well, Croy. I know you'd never be capable of such folly. If only you had as much brains as you do honor!"

Croy stood there and listened with a contrite expression. After a while he heard none of the words. He stopped hearing the endless pounding of Groomwich's hammer, and no longer felt the heat of the forge on his skin.

In his mind's eye he only saw the Lady, dressed in green and white. And wearing Cythera's face.

CHAPTER TWENTY-ONE

The day after the gates of Helstrow were sealed, the town moved quickly to a war footing. Wagons full of men streamed toward Helstrow from a hundred villages. Croy and Hew stood on horses near the main gate, watching as each new consignment was checked in and sent to be armed and trained. These were farmers, men—boys—who had never been more than a mile outside their homes. They all had the same goggle-eyed expression as they first took in the colors and chaos of Helstrow. They'd never seen a town before, but even if they had, they couldn't have been prepared. The outer bailey was packed now from side to side with humanity, every house a billet and every tavern an arsenal. Men in formation marched everywhere through the streets, while serjeants in kettle hats screamed orders at them and beat those who failed to keep in line.

The few dwarves who hadn't packed up and fled for their own kingdom in the north were working day and night to make weapons and rudimentary armor. They worked side by side with human blacksmiths and the night rang with hammer blows and was lit by great gusts of sparks shooting out of the chimney of every forge. Fires broke out constantly, but at least there were plenty of men ready to hold buckets of water and sand. The iron flowed, and piece by piece the city was armed— with bill hooks, halberds, axes and swords. With lances and flails and maces with grotesquely flanged heads. With leather jack, and ring mail, and chain hauberks, and coats of plate.

On the third day Sir Rory rode up to the gates, and beat on them with the pommel of Crowsbill to be let in, and another Ancient Blade took the king's colors. Sir Rory was the oldest of their order, running a little to fat, and he rode with his wife and six children all on horses behind him. He brought a company of volunteers, as well, which the king was happy to receive. Anyone who actually chose to fight for Skrae was automatically commissioned as a serjeant and given the best pick of the weapons.

"They'll fight to their last breath," Rory promised, as his men marched up toward the keep in a semblance of good order. "Though perhaps not well."

Croy clasped the old knight's vambrace and said, "Well met, my friend. Any word of Sir Orne?"

Rory drew his fingers through his thick mustache. "Last

I heard, he was up north, hunting some centuries-old sorcerer. I'm sure he'll hear the call."

Croy hoped so. Orne had more military experience than any of them—after Ulfram V had discharged them all, Orne had gone north where there was always fighting to be done. Endless skirmishes with the hill people there had turned the knight into a master strategist—something Helstrow needed more than iron or steel.

"There are only four of us now, I hear, for Bikker's dead, and Acidtongue's in unknown hands," Sir Rory said, and made the sign of the Lady on his breast. "Against two."

"I'm not so worried about the barbarians holding Dawnbringer and Fangbreaker," Hew insisted. "They haven't had our training. They never took our vows. And one of them's a girl!"

"You saw Mörgain, though," Croy told him.

"She's a woman. I don't care how big she is, no woman has the stomach to cut a man from crop to crupper."

Croy wished he could share the sentiment. He'd met more than a few woman warriors in his time, and they'd been fierce enough. Woman who chose to take up swords had to constantly prove themselves, and it made them more driven and more dangerous than any man. And Mörgain had seemed altogether too much like her brother, Mörget—the strongest and most dangerous fighter Croy had ever known.

"The Lady will sustain us," he said, more for his own sake than the others.

On the sixth day Balint showed herself in the courtyard before the keep. Croy had managed to avoid her so far but that evening, as she wheeled a train of ballistae out of the armory cellars, a great cheer went up from the people and the Ancient Blades had to be on hand to do her honor.

The dwarf rode high on the bolt of one of her great contraptions as it was pushed through the streets, kicking her legs and waving a wrench in the air. The war machines were dragged by conscripts down through the gate into the outer bailey, and then across the Strow bridge, where half the city waited to cheer them on. The king showed himself at a balcony atop the palace while his heralds waved pennons and sounded great trumpets. As Balint came even with the knights on their horses, she gave Croy a long and triumphant look.

"When they see my babies here," she told him, "the barbarians will turn around and run so fast we'll send bolts straight up their arseholes."

"I have no doubt of it, dwarf," Croy said, his mouth tasting of gall and vinegar. "You have shown yourself a genius at shooting men in the back."

Balint crowed in joy—she loved a good taunt, whether she was giving it or receiving it—and rode on toward the eastern gate, where she placed the giant crossbows high atop the wall.

On the eighth day the conscripts tried to revolt. A rumor had been going about that only one man in two would be armed with iron when the battle came, and the rest would be given nothing but shields, their lives to be thrown away blunting the barbarians' first charge.

"Who told them any of them were going to get shields?" Rory asked, his voice little more than a whisper. From atop the wall of the outer bailey, the Ancient Blades watched the conscripts strive against their serjeants, pushing the shouting officers up against the wall.

"We should be down there imposing order," Croy said, through gritted teeth.

"You heard the king. He has a better way," Sir Hew told him.

And the king, in fact, did. Making no show of aggression, he appeared before the crowd at the head of a train of mules, each pulling the largest a giant hogshead of ale. Bungs were thrown open and foaming brown liquor streamed into the streets. The conscripts forgot the serjeants immediately, lest the ale go to waste.

In the morning not many of them felt like renewing their rebellion. It was the quietest morning Croy could remember since the gates were sealed. He was able to walk the wall nearly halfway around the town without hearing a curse or a profanity uttered. Not much work got done, either, but at least Helstrow was at peace.

When he reached the northernmost point on the wall, he

lingered, and looked out across the rolling farmland toward the distant northern forests. But it wasn't until the ninth day that Sir Orne finally appeared, standing his horse in a field half a mile away, Bloodquaffer held high over his head. The sword's edges looked fuzzy in the distance, as if it were glowing with its own light. For hours he stood like that, the horse's head lowering occasionally to graze on field stubble.

When the sun set Orne lowered the weapon, then slid from his saddle to kneel on the earth. He left the horse behind and crawled the rest of the way on his knees.

It was an act of devotion to the Lady. No one dared rush out to help him or speed his way. It wasn't until well after midnight that he was brought inside the walls of the fortress.

Croy was there to receive him. As Hew helped the knight to his feet, Croy tried to take Orne's free hand in hearty embrace—only to be rebuffed after a very short clasping of wrists.

"Do not take offense, I beg you," Orne told Croy. The knight was the youngest of the four, yet his dark eyes hid an old and unhealed pain. "It's for your own sake I am so cold. I do not wish to pass on my curse."

"Curse?" Hew demanded. "We heard you were chasing a sorcerer up north. Did you get the bastard?"

"I did," Orne said. He looked as if he would gladly have said no more. Croy and Hew stared at him until he relented. "With his last breath, though, he laughed in my face. And told me how I am to die."

None of them missed what the knight was not saying. If he was this afraid to come to Helstrow, it could only mean one thing. The sorcerer's dying prophecy must have told Orne that he would die here, inside the fortress.

Hew looked to Croy with eerie dread in his eyes. Croy shook his head. "You came," he said, bowing to Orne. "That's what's important."

"I took a vow," Orne told him. "I took a vow."

They took him to a bed, and posted a guard on his door—not for Orne's own sake, but to keep away the curious, who heard the knight screaming in his sleep, and wished to hear the prophetic words he could not speak while wakeful.

On the tenth day after the gates were sealed, the barbarians arrived.

CHAPTER TWENTY-TWO

Malden put his hand on Acidtongue's hilt, but kept the sword in its sheath. It was a ridiculous weapon for a thief to use—once drawn, it began to foam and spit, and its acid dripped on everything and made a hissing noise. Noise that could be Malden's downfall.

Moving by nothing but starlight, he came around the corner of the milehouse and looked out into its dooryard. He saw nothing—no movement, save a wisp of old smoke that trailed away through the weeds.

By law, a milehouse stood every ten miles on the road from Helstrow to the Free City of Ness, and was required to stay open to common traffic at all hours. They were places where weary travelers could spend the night, or buy new horses, or simply choke down the dust of the road with a tankard of cheap ale. Malden and his crew had passed most of them by on their way since they had no desire to be seen. This one, however, had drawn the thief's interest, because it had been burned to the ground.

The stone walls still stood but the roof had collapsed inward. The stables were empty and there was no sign of human life anywhere nearby.

Perhaps it would have been wiser to pass this milehouse by as well, but Malden didn't like what he saw. He thought it might augur trouble for them further down the road, and he wanted information.

Velmont had laughed and said he was welcome to go and check it out—alone.

Moving with the silence of a hunting cat, Malden dashed into the shadows below the milehouse's empty doorway. Inside he smelled ash and burnt hair. The stars winked on a pool of water in the center of what had been the common room. Maybe the proprietors had tried to put out the fire, or maybe it was only rainwater that had collected since the roof fell in.

Malden slipped inside, keeping close to the soot-blackened walls. He heard nothing, sensed no movement in the place. But he liked to be careful.

A spot of the floor had been cleared of ash and debris. A pile of clay bottles stood to one side of the remains of a campfire. Bits of rag had been gathered together to make crude bedding. So someone had been there since the fire. Malden chanced detection by slinking out into the light, just enough to pick up one of the bottles and sniff at its mouth. He smelled old, sour wine. The bottle had been emptied down to the lees.

Then someone moaned in the dark, and Acidtongue flashed out of its scabbard.

"No, I beg you, not again," a woman croaked.

She was covered in soot that hid her nakedness. Her hair might have been blonde once but was so smeared with ashes it looked white. Only her eyes reflected light as she held one hand up, trying to fend him away.

"I'm a friend," Malden whispered to her. "Are you alone here?"

"Friend? What friend have I?"

He saw her lips were badly chapped and her tongue dry and white. Searching through the debris, Malden turned up a bottle that had survived the cataclysm—and whatever had come afterwards. He dug out the cork with his belt knife and brought the bottle to her lips.

She sucked greedily at it like an infant at the teat.

"What's your name?"

She only stared at him, still lost in terror.

"Alright," Malden said. "I don't need to know it. There were others here, earlier," he went on, looking back at the pile of empty bottles. "I'm guessing they weren't paying guests. Bandits?"

She nodded, careful not to take her eyes off of him. "Six of them. Some of them came back for seconds."

Malden took off his cloak and draped it over her body.

"After the recruiting serjeants came, and took away all the men, there was no one but me to run the place. The law demands we stay open," she told Malden.

"They conscripted your . . . husband?"

"My father, and all my brothers. They came through taking every man they could find. All the farmers from the local manor, all the villagers. Most women fled to wherever they had family or friends to shelter them. I had no one. I knew it wasn't safe, but . . . 'tis the law. And I thought every man was gone, so what was there to fear? But it seems a few stayed behind. The sort that would refuse the call. There were six of them, still, six who kept their freedom. And I was all alone here."

Malden closed his eyes in horror.

"Do what you must to me," the woman said, her voice a resigned whisper. "Just please . . . I'm hurt. I'm hurt down there and I don't think I can anymore . . ."

Malden strode out into the dooryard, wanting to spit with anger. He stood in the brightest spot before the door and waved one arm in the air. Soon Cythera and Velmont's crew joined him. He only wanted Cythera. "There's a woman in there who doesn't need to see another male face for a long time. Can you try to comfort her?"

"Of course," Cythera told him. She hurried inside.

He turned next to Velmont. "From now on, we stay off the roads. This whole county has been stripped of able-bodied men. That doesn't mean the recruiters aren't still looking. Worse, there are bandits afoot."

Velmont shrugged. "That's the way of it, in a war. Just lads havin' a bit o' fun while they can. And you shouldn't get your blood up, seein' as you're about one peg up from them as did this."

Malden's face burned as he stared at his fellow thief. "I take money from fat merchants and fools who don't know to keep their hands on their purses. But I don't hurt anyone, not if I can help it, and I never—*never*—harm a woman. If you're working for me, now, you'll follow the same code."

"Do I, now? Do I work for you? Or for meself?"

"You'd better decide soon," Malden told him. Careful of his fingers, he put Acidtongue back in its sheath.

CHAPTER TWENTY-THREE

The woman from the milehouse turned out to be a homely girl of sixteen named Gerta. Once Cythera had seen to her hurts and washed the soot from her hair, she was able to rise and walk under her own power. Malden was glad for that. He didn't know what he would have done, had she been unable to care for herself.

Gerta was happy to travel with them—the thought of staying behind all alone visibly terrified her. After a while Velmont tried to talk her up, telling her how pretty her hair was, offering her his manly protection. Malden put a stop to that right away.

The next night they found a holdfast on the grounds of an abandoned manor. Not much to it, just four stone walls and a locked door, but it offered more safety than the thatch-roofed cottages they'd seen along the way. A score or so of women from the local villages had sealed themselves inside. They wouldn't open up for Malden or his crew, but they agreed to take Gerta in once all the men had gone away. Cythera stayed with Gerta to make sure the women kept their promise, then rejoined Malden and his crew as they headed south, away from the road.

Getting off the highway slowed them down considerably, but they spent all that day without seeing another living soul. They crossed through stubbled fields turning into patches of mud, well out of sight of any village or manor house.

Cythera stopped, once, to pick up a stray shaft of wheat that had been trampled into an irrigation ditch. "We won't starve this winter, at least," she said.

Malden pursed his lips. "How's that?"

Cythera sighed and dropped the stem to flutter on the air. "The wheat's all been taken in, probably milled by now, too. It's harvest time. If this war had begun in mid-summer, and all the farmers pulled away from their labor, the wheat would have been left to rot on the ground." She shook her head dolefully. "I've read of wars in the north where more men died of starvation and disease than ever could have been slain by steel. I worry what will come in the spring, if this war drags on—there will be no one here to plow or plant."

Malden had never really thought about where the food he ate came from. Grain appeared at the gates of Ness twice a year, and was somehow turned into bread. Livestock were driven through the streets to great slaughterhouses, and steaks and cuts came out to be sold in the shops of butchers on market days. It all went on without his knowledge or labor, and so he'd assumed it always would continue the same way.

He had gone hungry many times, of course, but only for lack of coin—not because there was no food to be had. The idea of reversing that situation, of having plenty of coin but no grain to spend it on, made him feel a bit queasy. He could hardly raise his own food—that was a skill he'd never learned, nor wanted to. How many citizens of the Free City had the secret of it? How many of them would starve before they learned how it was done?

"That's a problem for a future worry," he told Cythera, because he didn't like to think on what Ness would be like if there was no food in it. "Right now we need to make our rendezvous. We're already a day late."

They made camp that night in a deserted barn. They

dared make no fire, but the walls kept some of the wind out. Malden made sure Cythera was awake enough to stand guard—he would never leave her sleeping alone with Velmont and his thieves around. Near midnight he slipped back out into the cold.

A mile away, at a place where two roads crossed, stood an ancient gallows. It had been built on the site of an old and desecrated shrine of the bloodgod. Once the Lady's church had taken over this land, it had been turned into a place of punishment.

Normally no thief in his right—if superstitious—mind would get within a half mile of the place. Even Malden found it nigh unbearable to listen to the crosstree creak above his head. Hanging was the penalty for thievery, and he had lived his whole life expecting to end suspended from such a beam. In that flat land, however, it was the most convenient landmark available. Malden lit a single candle that guttered in the night breeze, and sat down to wait.

Nothing moved in the cloud shadows. Nothing stirred. He heard an owl hoot from miles away, a low, mournful sound almost lost under the noise of his own breathing.

He waited.

He took the scrap of parchment out of his tunic and unfolded it against his leg. In the light of the candle he could just make out the words, and the symbol at the bottom of the page—a kind of signature.

"What's that, lad?" Slag asked, stepping into the light.

Slag stood no more than four feet tall. He was as thin as a rail, and as pale as moonlight on snow. His dark beard stuck out in wild profusion and his keen eyes glimmered in the candlelight, but in the dark his clothing made him nearly invisible so his face seemed to float in the light. He might have been a specter of vengeance, bound to the place where he'd been killed.

For Malden, he was a sight for sore eyes.

The thief rushed to his old friend and embraced him warmly. He hadn't seen the dwarf since they split up outside the ruins of the Vincularium. Not since before he'd gone to Helstrow.

"A love letter from your leman?" Slag asked, tapping the parchment.

"Not exactly," Malden said, hurriedly folding it up again.

"I thought not. I saw you pull it off of Prestwicke's body, way back," Slag said. "I've been wondering about it since."

Malden shook his head. He wouldn't speak of the parchment, not yet. Not until he had a proper measure of Slag's loyalties. "How are the elves?" he asked, instead.

"Squared away, neat as nails in a fucking drawer," Slag told him. "I took 'em up to the Green Barrens, where at least they'll have trees for company, and bade 'em to be fruitful but keep their heads down. The desolation of that place, and their natural mistrustfulness, will make sure the humans never know they're there." The dwarf sighed deeply. "Though they threatened to follow after me, and would not sit still, not 'til I promised Aethil I'd come back for her. She's still besotted with me."

Malden laughed, though he kept his voice low. "Maybe she just likes short men." Aethil, the queen of the elves, had been given a powerful love potion that would make her give her heart to the first man she saw. Unfortunately for everyone involved, that had been Slag. According to Cythera—who knew about such things—the effects were permanent.

The fact that the elves and the dwarves were bitter ancestral enemies had made no difference. The last time Malden had seen them together, Aethil was still under the impression that Slag was just a very short human.

"But enough of my love life," Slag said. "Tell me about the paper. Have we got fucking secrets between us now?"

Malden glanced down at the creased parchment in his hand. He'd hoped to distract Slag, but dwarves had keen and penetrating minds and he knew Slag wouldn't give up until he'd learned the truth. "It's a contract for an execution. Mine. It just describes me, gives information on my favorite haunts in Ness. There's no price named, but considering that Prestwicke crossed an entire kingdom to fulfill it, I can assume the bounty was high."

"Is it signed?" Slag asked.

Malden frowned as he unfolded the parchment. "In a

fashion," he said. He held the paper where Slag could see it. At the bottom of the page was a crude sketch of a heart, transfixed by a key.

Slag's eyes went wide.

"The boss sent an assassin after you?" Slag asked.

Malden watched the dwarf's eyes. Slag was a fellow employee of Cutbill. Malden wasn't sure if he'd made the right decision showing Cutbill's mark to the dwarf.

"But for fuck's sake, why? You're one of his best earners."

"Maybe that's reason enough. Maybe he was worried I was too good at my job, and that made me a threat."

"To Cutbill? Hardly. I'm sorry, lad, but you're no kind of match for that villainous bastard." Slag pulled at his beard. "I can't figure this at all."

"I was never supposed to see this. I was just supposed to die. Cutbill doesn't know I have it."

"What'll you do now that you know?" the dwarf asked, quite carefully. "If you plan to move against him you'd better do it quick. He's smarter than you. If he gets any idea you're coming for him it'll be over before you can fucking blink."

Malden stood up slowly. If Slag decided that his allegiance to Cutbill was worth fighting over, this conversation could end very badly. "Slag, I need to know——"

The dwarf waved away his concerns with one hand. "Cutbill's my employer. You're my friend. Dwarves count those things different. I don't know how humans rate them."

Malden nodded carefully. It was a kind of reassurance, and it would have to do. He could never hurt Slag, he knew that much. They'd been through too much together.

"You're still headed to Ness?" Slag asked.

Malden filled him in quickly on the barbarian invasion. Slag had already known some of the information.

"Aye, sounds like Ness is the safest place in the storm of shit. When we get there, I don't want to know what you have planned," Slag told Malden. "Maybe you're not going to do anything. Just play along like you never saw that parchment. Maybe you're going to forget the whole fucking thing. That would be pretty smart. Smarter than most humans

I've known. Maybe you're going to try for something else. Don't tell me, and I can't tell anyone else, alright?"

"I think we have a deal," Malden told him.

CHAPTER TWENTY-FOUR

Croy's rounsey whickered and bucked as he climbed onto its back. "Gentle, there," he soothed, and rubbed the horse's neck. It wasn't used to his weight in full armor. Neither was he, for that matter. He was already sweating under the quilted gambeson he wore next to his skin. With the hauberk of chain over that and the whole covered with his full coat of plate he thought he might broil in the warm sunlight.

A serjeant handed him up his great helm, which he tucked under his arm. Finally he was given his shield—painted black and silver, Ghostcutter's colors, and thus Croy's as well. He goaded the rounsey over to where the others were assembling. Sir Orne already had his helmet on and Croy was glad for it, as he had no wish to see the knight's doomed eyes. Sir Hew had been ready for an hour and looked impatient to make a start.

Sir Rory's children polished his greaves and cuisses with rags, while his wife, up on a stepladder, fed him morsels of chicken. "That's enough, woman," he said at last, and rode away from his family. Together the four Ancient Blades made their way down to the eastern gate.

And there they sat, staring at the lowered portcullis for the better part of another hour while they waited for the king.

They said little in that time. The horses stamped and were shushed. The men-at-arms gathered around the gate leaned on the hafts of their bill hooks and made quiet jokes with each other to ease the tension.

When the king came on his massive destrier, he came alone save for his herald, who carried his banner. The gold and green snapped in a stiff breeze as the gate was drawn open.

"None of you speak, no matter what the provocation," Ulfram V instructed. Someone handed him his crown, a massive piece of gold worked with emeralds. He put it on his head and adjusted its level while he spoke. "This is to be a parley between myself and the Great Chieftain. Do not draw your weapons unless I give direct command. Do not make any sudden movements, and do not—under any circumstances—offer me counsel. You are here to be my honor guard, and nothing else."

"Of course, your majesty," Sir Hew said.

Croy spurred his horse forward to keep pace with the king's enormous warhorse. As he passed through the gate he lifted his helm over the chain hood of his hauberk. The eye slits narrowed his vision to only what was directly in front of him. Once outside the gate, he had to turn his head from side to side, just to see all the forces arrayed against them.

Ten thousand barbarians had come through the pass. They'd been sighted that morning, marching without any sign of lines or formation. Nor had they formed up since. They stood like a great rabble of giants on the grassy field east of Helstrow. Only a very few of their number sat on horses, and nowhere did Croy see any sign of organized archers, nor any siege machines. Ten thousand foot soldiers against a fortress—it made no sense to Croy's classically trained military mind. Where, even, were the serjeants, where the drummers, where the flags? Many of the barbarians had tired of waiting on foot and had sat down in the sward. Some had started up games of dice or bones.

At the head of this—army, for lack of a better word—a line of firepits had been dug and fed great blocks of peat. Around the fires, the biggest of the barbarians danced wildly, throwing their arms up to the sky at random intervals, stomping down the grass with their massive feet. The dancers all wore the same markings Croy had seen on Mörget's face—everything below their eyes was painted a bright, blood red.

Alone among the barbarians, these dancers didn't look up as the king of Skrae came riding toward them.

As the royal party closed the distance to the firepits, only one barbarian stirred. A man who had been in the throes of a dice game slowly stood up. He looked older than the rest. His hair was longer than most—the barbarians cropped their hair, or shaved their heads entirely, and this one had a mop of gold and silver atop his head, as well as a full beard. He also stood out a bit for the fact that no visible part of him was painted. He was dressed in furs no finer than the others wore, however, nor was he possessed of any jewelry or harness. He had a single broadsword strapped to his back and when he rose a mongrel dog stood up beside him and trotted along at his heels.

A second man got up from where he'd been lying in the grass, drinking wine. This one looked more like the others—his hair was cut very short and he had a mocking smile painted over his own lips. He followed the golden-haired oldster past the firepits and up to a point just far enough from the walls of Helstrow to be out of longbow range. The two men—and one dog—raised no banners or flags, nor did they call out.

Ulfram's herald raced forward on his horse and shouted down some words to the two barbarians. The golden-haired one nodded and then looked up and beckoned to the king of Skrae with one arm. There was a warm smile on his face.

The king approached warily. Hew brought his horse close to Croy's. "I half think we're being made sport of," he whispered.

"It's just their way," Croy returned, just as softly. "East of the mountains they treat their inferiors like equals. There are few divisions between the classes."

"But how do they know their proper place, then?" Hew asked. "Are they even men, like us? Or some hairless kind of ape? They're big enough for me to believe it."

"They're men. Don't underestimate them," Croy told his friend.

Hew turned his helm from side to side as if he were counting the vast number of the horde. "No fear in that."

CHAPTER TWENTY-FIVE

The king walked his horse up to where the two barbarians stood. The four Ancient Blades kept close position behind him.

It was Ulfram's herald who spoke first. "Hail and well met under the banner of parley! King Ulfram, fifth of the name, lord of Skrae, master of the fortress of Helstrow, protector of the people, favored of the Lady—"

"Owner of a very nice horse," the barbarian with the painted smile said. "Can I have it?"

His golden-haired companion chuckled.

Ulfram's herald went white with rage, but he finished his announcement. "River warden of the Strow and the Skrait, lord protector of the dwarven kingdom—may I present to you the Great Chieftain Mörg of the eastern steppes?"

"Ha! Don't forget me!" the barbarian with the painted smile insisted. "Hurlind the scold! Ah, is it my turn to speak? This fellow went on so long I completely forgot my lines. Oh great Mörg the Wise, this is . . . some king or other, I believe you heard his recommends already."

Mörg laughed openly. "Aye, I did. And well met, I say." He shot out one hand to clasp the king's.

"And the dog, Skari, what is it, the fifteenth of that name?" the scold went on.

The dog looked up on hearing its name, then flopped down on its side in the grass and panted.

"You dare introduce your dog to the king of Skrae?" Ulfram's herald said, his face turning purple now.

"He's not my dog," Mörg said. "Sometimes I feed him, that's all. More than once, when I was starving, he fed me. Sometimes I think I'm *his* man."

Ulfram's herald began to complain again, but the king stopped him with a gesture. "That will do, I think. Ride back to the gate now, and tell them I've been met with the required civility. Go on, man."

The herald glared down at the barbarians one last time before he left. Ulfram sighed deeply once he was gone and then dismounted so he could face Mörg man to man. "I'll choose not to take offense at the jests and boasts," the king said. "It is my understanding your man there—your scold— is trained to taunt and provoke, rather than to offer your own thoughts."

"He's not my man," Mörg said. He waved behind him, toward the rabble. "None of these are. They let me talk for them, that's all. That's what a chieftain does. A Great Chieftain just talks for a lot of them."

"But you are invested with the power to make terms, today?" the king asked.

"I am. Should we sit? This might take a while."

"I'd rather not soil my robes of state," Ulfram said.

"As you wish."

Ulfram nodded gratefully. "I understand you believe you were invaded first, by one Herward, a lone, insane religious hermit. Who you slaughtered without trial."

Mörg waved a hand in front of his face, as if dismissing a fly.

"To show my contrition for this grave offense," Ulfram said, "I am willing to offer you tribute—one hundred chests of gold coin. Once the exchange is made, I will expect you to lead your people back through the new pass to your own lands."

Mörg sighed. "I already have a lot of gold."

Croy could see Ulfram trembling. The crown rattled on the king's head.

"What I'm really looking for is land," Mörg went on.

"We have plenty of that, too, in the east, but it's no good for farming. My people need to eat. I've spent my life trying to convince them there's more to life than just looting and pillaging, but when I can't grow good wheat, it's hard to get the point across. Now, personally, I'd prefer to avoid bloodshed today. I don't like watching men die."

"I'm glad to hear it," Ulfram said, softly.

"Unfortunately, that makes me a rarity among my people."

The scold laughed. "For us, the sound of dying men screaming their last is sweet music! We love the ring of iron on iron. Some like to drink hot blood, and others—"

Mörg punched the scold in the side of his jaw. His fist was like a hammer's head, and it sent Hurlind sprawling into the grass, clutching his face as if his bones were broken.

Instantly Croy's hand dropped to his sword hilt. It was all he could do not to draw Ghostcutter and race forward to cut down the golden-haired barbarian. But he had his orders.

"Sorry," Mörg said. "He annoys even me, sometimes. As I was saying—the clans want to go to war. It's what they love best. I might be able to convince them to let you live. But they'll want something good in return."

"Such as?" Ulfram inquired.

"A grant of all the land east of the river Strow, and every one living there now as our thralls."

Croy couldn't help but gasp. That was a third of the entire kingdom.

CHAPTER TWENTY-SIX

The king of Skrae spluttered in rage. Croy didn't blame him.

"Thralls," Ulfram finally managed to spit out. "You want thousands of my subject reduced to thralldom. To slavery."

Mörg shrugged. "I need people to teach us how to plant, and how to tend crops."

"We know already how to reap," Hurlind the scold said, still rubbing his jaw.

"Anyway," Mörg went on, "thralldom's not that bad. Our laws say a thrall has the same rights as a chieftain, and he can even buy his freedom if he works hard for twenty years or so. You have villeinage here in Skrae, yes? Tell me something—if a reeve beats a villein for some offense, what happens to the villein if he fights back?"

Ulfram glanced back at his knights as if expecting them to explain to him why he was being questioned on the finer points of the feudal system. "He'd be placed under arrest, of course, and tried for assault. Most likely he'd be hanged, as an example to others."

"I thought so. Yes," Mörg said, nodding. "I'd much rather be a thrall. If a thrall's master beats him too severely, and he breaks his master's neck, most of us would cheer."

"We do love a good avenging," Hurlind affirmed.

Mörg smiled. "I imagine more than a few of your villeins would prefer thralldom if they had the choice."

"They don't," Ulfram pronounced. "The people of Skrae will never be sold as slaves. Only the Lady can assign a man to his station—that lies outside my power. So the answer is no. I will not grant you that land, nor give you my subjects in tribute. If that means war, then so be it."

"I was afraid you'd say that." Mörg stretched his arms over his head and arched his back. "Well, I gave it my best shot."

Ulfram sneered at the barbarian. "Did you really expect me to take what you offered, or was this just another naked ruse to justify mass slaughter?"

"Actually," Mörg told him, "it was mostly a play for time. It takes a while for the berserkers to get good and hot." He turned and looked toward the firepits, where the wild dancers gyrated at a frenzied pitch. He threw them a simple hand signal, and they all stopped on the instant, freezing in place.

One by one the red-painted men started trembling. Even from a distance Croy could see how they shook. Their teeth chattered in their heads and their eyes waxed red with blood. It looked like they were suffering from some kind of mass apoplectic fit.

"Your majesty," Sir Hew said, his voice taut as a bowstring.

"I told you not to speak," Ulfram snarled at the knight.

The berserkers picked up axes and shields from where they lay on the grass. Their faces were as red now as the paint across their mouths. One of them started gnawing on the wooden rim of his shield as if he would take a bite out of it.

"Forgive me, liege," Sir Hew said, "but get on your damned horse right now!"

The king was not blind. He jumped up into his saddle. Yet before he turned the horse back toward Helstrow, he glowered down at Mörg. "You dare to sully the sacred rite of parley," he said. "No violence offered, no treachery brooked!"

Mörg laughed. "That's your custom, not ours. Ours is to cheat every way we can. We win a lot more battles, our way."

Sir Hew dashed forward and kicked at the haunches of the king's horse. Croy didn't need further provocation to wheel his rounsey about and get it moving.

"Guard me," the king shouted. "On me, all of you!"

The Ancient Blades moved swiftly to box him in, even as the berserkers started to howl and chase them on foot. They ran far faster than any man should, their axes waving high over their heads, their shields bashing forward at thin air.

"The gate! Open the gate!" Sir Rory called. Up ahead Croy could see soldiers desperately trying to get the gate open before their king reached it.

"The ballistae!" Croy shouted. Up on the battlements above the gate, the giant crossbows were slowly cranked to tension. "Shoot over our heads—do it now!"

The horses thundered toward the gate, throwing up great clods of earth as their hooves pounded at the soil. The gate was still a hundred yards away.

The berserkers were gaining on them. And behind the running men, ten thousand barbarians were rising to their feet, their weapons already in their hands.

A ballista fired with a twang like the world's longest lute string snapping in the middle of a chord, and an iron bolt six feet long flashed over the top of Croy's great helm. It passed through one berserker, leaving a hole in his chest big enough to put a fist through. It impaled the man behind him, too, before plowing deep into the earth without a sound.

The first berserker died before he hit the ground, his axe slashing again and again at the yellow grass. The second berserker, the one who had been impaled, took longer about it. Incredibly, as Croy watched over his shoulder, he saw the berserker try to pull himself forward, attempting to drag himself off of the ballista bolt that transfixed him.

Step by excruciating step, the berserker forced himself forward. There was no pain written on his face at all. Had he made himself totally insensate with his wild dancing? The berserker took another step—and pulled himself free. The ballista bolt thrummed as it came clear from his back.

The berserker laughed—and then died, as blood erupted like a fountain from his wound.

Behind him fifty more of them were still coming.

"The gate! Open the gate!" the king screamed, and Croy looked forward to see that the gate was in fact open—but the portcullis behind it was still lowered.

CHAPTER TWENTY-SEVEN

Behind the portcullis, soldiers shouted at one another and men ran back and forth as they tried desperately to get

the gate open again. It was designed to be dropped in a
hurry, to fall its full length in a split second, but as a result
it took far too long to raise again. Men working at a pair
of windlasses had to strain and strive to lift its massive
weight inch by inch. Croy jumped down from his horse just
as the iron bars began to lift—but slowly, so slowly it was
like watching death come creeping. Croy yanked off his
gauntlets, then grabbed the bars with his bare hands and
heaved at them, trying to help the soldiers manning the
windlass behind the gate.

"Your majesty!" Sir Hew shouted. Croy turned to look—
and saw a flight of arrows, dark in the air.

He'd seen so few bows among the barbarians that he'd
assumed they disdained their use. But now a hundred arrows
or more were hurtling toward him.

Sir Hew grabbed the king off his horse just in time. He
pulled the monarch down behind the destrier's flanks, just
as the arrows struck home. A dozen points clattered against
Croy's armored back, bouncing off harmlessly, but the horses
screamed and some of them bolted.

And still the berserkers were coming, howling, cutting
themselves with their own weapons to add bright streamers
of blood to their already red faces.

"Your king is in peril," Croy shouted through the bars
of the portcullis. The wicked spear points at the bottom of
the gate were only a few inches off the ground.

Sir Rory drew Crowsbill and strode out toward the
berserkers. The fat old knight struck left and right as the
first of the manic barbarians came upon him. The blade
looked like a normal sword until it struck, when its metal
flowed and curved like quicksilver, reshaping itself even as
Rory swung it about. Crowsbill twisted like a snake as it
sought out their vital organs, guided by magic to always
strike the most tender spot, just as a crow on a battlefield
will pluck at the liver and lights of a dead man. The
berserkers showed no sign of fear or pain as the blade curled
again and again toward their bellies, their hearts—but one
by one they went down. Sir Orne rushed to help, drawing
Bloodquaffer from its broad sheath. The blade looked fuzzy

even close up, but nasty all the same. Its two edges were viciously serrated—and the teeth of the serrations were themselves serrated, and those serrations as well, and those, until the serrations were too small to see with the naked eye. When it struck even the lightest of slashing blows, it cut down to the bone and its wounds bled violently. Orne had learned to use his Blade to maximal advantage, whirling about reaching only for the fastest, most shallow cuts. Light as they were Bloodquaffer's strokes always sheared flesh down to the bone. Blood hung in the air all around Orne like a red fog as veins burst open and arteries pumped blood out onto the grass.

The berserkers didn't stop coming, though. They seemed wholly ignorant of the numbers of their dead that piled up before the gate under the constant attacks of Rory and Orne. The berserkers ran pell-mell right into the teeth of the fight and they struck with an inhuman savagery, driven by their trance to strength and speed no normal man could match. The heavy armor that Orne and Rory wore turned away most of their axe blows, but one cleaved right through Rory's left pauldron and bit deep into the flesh below. His arm went limp and he dropped his shield—even as Orne stepped in to cover his friend's left with his own shield, and took a barbarian's head off with a backhanded slash from Bloodquaffer.

"Get the king through—get him inside," Sir Hew shouted into Croy's ear. Croy looked down and saw the portcullis had lifted a hand's breadth from the ground. "Shove him in there, if you must."

Croy grabbed Ulfram's robes of state and pulled the king to him. The man was unconscious. It looked like an arrow had struck him a glancing blow on the temple. His crown was gone, lost somewhere out on the field. Croy had no time to find it. As the portcullis lifted another jerking inch, Croy picked up the king and stuffed him through the opening. The points of the bars tore at Ulfram's silks, but Croy could only hope they hadn't snagged his royal skin as well.

Once the king was past the bars, soldiers on the other side grabbed him and pulled him through the rest of the way, then lifted him off the ground and carried him off.

"Now, you," Hew told Croy. Hew started to draw Chillbrand.

"No," Croy told him, putting a hand on Hew's wrist. "He's in no state to give orders. You're in command now—you go through next."

Hew didn't waste time arguing. He dropped to his belly and crawled through the gap, the points of the portcullis shrieking against the steel on his back.

Croy rushed to Rory's side just as the old knight began to droop. He propped Rory up while Orne defended him from axe blows, and shouted into Rory's great helm, "You go next, brother."

Rory nodded gratefully and hurried to clamber under the bars.

Bloodquaffer came down in a wild slashing stroke that cut a berserker's face in half. Another barbarian replaced the dead man, and it was all Croy could do to bring Ghostcutter up and parry a whistling axe blade. The berserker lunged forward and Croy was suddenly face to face with his foe. He saw the wildness in the red eyes, the exultant rage in the red-painted face. Spinning around, Ghostcutter an extension of his arm as he whipped it up and in, he gutted the man, but even that wasn't enough. The axe came up again like the berserker was chopping wood.

Before it could cut down into Croy's neck, Bloodquaffer took off the berserker's arm. Orne bashed out with his shield and broke another barbarian's nose.

"Orne! Is this what the sorcerer foretold? Is this your time?" Croy demanded.

Orne twisted at the waist and Bloodquaffer slid across the ribcage of a berserker. Blood jetted from the wound and bathed both knights.

"Not yet," Orne said.

"Then get inside—until we're both through, they can't lower the portcullis again," Croy insisted. He brought his shield around and pushed Orne back, toward the gate. He did not look to see if Orne obeyed his command or not—a dozen berserkers were right there in front of Croy, and he had to duck and weave to avoid being cut to pieces.

One of the barbarians threw his shield at Croy. It bounced

pointlessly off Croy's legs. Croy kicked it upwards with one foot so it tripped up two of the berserkers, then he lunged outward with Ghostcutter and stabbed a barbarian in the throat. Yanking his blade free, he swept it through the crowd, cutting ears and eyes and noses. Normal men, men who could feel pain, would have danced backwards from such an attack, terrified of being maimed. The berserkers didn't even flinch.

A man could be the ultimate warrior—he could be a consummate knight—and still that wave of unwashed barbarian flesh would crash down on him eventually. Croy knew he must retreat or be slaughtered where he stood.

An axe came down where Croy had been a moment before. He bashed out with his shield, not caring if he connected or not, then threw himself backwards and rolled under the bars of the portcullis.

On the far side he jumped to his feet just as three berserkers came crawling after him, their heads and arms already through the gap.

"Now," Croy shouted, "drop it now!"

A block was knocked free from where it held a windlass, and a chain rattled as the portcullis came crashing down. Its points impaled all three berserkers, but still they tried to drag themselves forward, still they tried to fight.

Croy left them to die, and went running to find Hew.

CHAPTER TWENTY-EIGHT

Berserkers crashed up against the gate, straining and howling as they tried to bend the bars of the portcullis with their bare hands. Croy was afraid they just might do it, even though those bars were solid iron two inches thick.

High above his head he heard the ballistae twanging and jumping. They were too slow—barely able to get four shots off in a minute. "Archers!" he shouted. "Get longbowmen up there—drive the host back." He glanced at the berserkers at the gate. "And men with pikestaffs. Clear the gate!"

Sir Hew was a dozen yards away, bellowing his own orders at a huddle of serjeants in leather jack. When Croy came running toward him, the knight dismissed the serjeants and shook his head. "Most of the men are still in their billets, and will be until someone comes to collect them. We weren't ready—didn't expect the attack until tomorrow's dawning."

"No time for cursing fate now," Croy said. "We need to—"

An arrow came down from straight above and knocked Chillbrand out of Hew's hand. Croy looked up—it was as if the arrow had been dropped from the clouds.

A hundred more of them appeared as he watched.

"They're lobbing arrows over the wall, in the hopes of hitting anyone defending the gate," Croy said, as the shafts twisted down toward him. He ducked down and threw his shield over his head. The arrows struck him like wooden raindrops, with about as much effect. He started to laugh, thinking the barbarians had wasted their ammunition. Then he looked up and saw a soldier in canvas jack standing before him. The man looked deeply confused by the three arrows that had transfixed his chest. The soldier took a step toward Croy and started screaming.

Croy grabbed the man and laid him down on the side of the road, out of the way of trampling feet. Not that it mattered. The soldier was dead before Croy set him down. All around, other soldiers were screaming or running willy-nilly, trying to get out of the barrage.

Up on the wall one of the ballistae slumped over on its side. Its master fell from the battlements, an arrow through one of his eyes. Balint watched him fall, then screamed for a replacement. "One that can fucking aim properly!" she added.

"Archers!" Croy shouted again. "Where are our archers?" He heard a great crash and a noise like a bell falling from its tower. He looked up and saw the barbarians had a battering ram in the shape of a giant iron skull and they were slamming it again and again against the portcullis.

"Hew," Croy shouted.

"I know it, brother. Back! Everyone get back—retreat to the inner bailey. We can't hold the gate. Retreat! Sound the retreat!"

Sir Orne was suddenly at Croy's elbow. "The king? What of him?"

Croy could only shake his head. He didn't know where the king had been taken.

"He can't be lost yet. I am certain he'll outlive me, anyway," Orne said. "Help Sir Rory—he looks like he can barely stand."

The oldest of the Ancient Blades had slumped against a wall not ten feet away. Crowsbill dangled from his gauntleted hand as if he might drop it at any moment. Croy took it from him and put it in its sheath on Rory's belt.

"Thank you, brother," Rory said. He slurred the words as if he were drunk. Croy checked his wound and saw gore clotted and thick under the gap in his steel armor. What kind of man could cut through steel plate and chain mail with an iron axe? The berserkers must be stronger than giants when they entered their trance.

"How is it?" Rory asked. For a moment his face showed no courage at all, just the desperate fear of a man who knows he will die soon. Then his lips pressed together under his mustache. "It doesn't feel too bad," he blustered.

Croy nodded slowly. Even if Rory survived, even if the wound didn't fester, he'd never use his arm again. "It's just your left arm," he said, knowing what Rory needed to hear. "You can still wield your Blade."

"Hah!" Rory said, and tried to laugh. Mostly he just wheezed. "We'll show 'em yet, won't we, Croy, we'll—"

He was interrupted by a sudden blare of noise. Trumpets sounding the retreat—but there was no need. A crowd of soldiers was already rushing up the high street toward the inner bailey, many of them throwing away their weapons as they ran.

"Cowards!" Sir Rory said, spitting up blood.

"Villeins, most of them," Croy observed. Conscripts. Until ten days ago, for such men even holding a weapon was a crime. Now in less than a fortnight they'd been told they would have to take up arms in defense of their king. They hadn't been given enough training. They had never fought before. "They're scared."

"We should hang every last one of the rotters," Rory insisted.

Croy said nothing but started to head up the high street himself, one shoulder under Rory's good arm. He didn't get more than twenty feet before Hew grabbed his sword hand.

"Croy, the king—"

Croy shook his head. "No one seems to know where he is."

"We must find him. He could be under the feet of this mob. He could be wounded and dying even now."

Croy grimaced at the thought. "I'll find him. You take Rory and get to the keep. Orne! Orne, are you here?"

The doomed knight came running.

"Orne," Croy said, "we need to find the king."

Orne sighed. "Yes, we do."

Hew grabbed the side of Croy's helm and pulled it around so they were looking in each other's eyes. "Get him to safety. At any cost. That's my command."

"And I shall obey," Croy said. Then he broke away and started running.

Panicked men were everywhere. Only a handful still carried their weapons. Some had even torn off their canvas jack and their kettle hats, perhaps thinking they would not be slaughtered if they didn't look like soldiers. Croy tried to grab a few of them and tell them to get to the keep, that the only safety available lay there, but none of them listened. They were crowding into cellars or the upper floors of houses, barricading themselves in as if a few pieces of furniture or a locked door could keep out the barbarians.

It was tough going to move through the fortress-town against the flow of that crowd. Once Orne had to draw

Bloodquaffer and wave it over his head to force the fleeing men to make room.

Before they had covered a half dozen streets, they heard a rumbling groan and a shriek of tearing metal, and knew the portcullis had fallen. The barbarians had entered Helstrow.

"How long do you think Hew can hold the keep?" Orne asked.

"I don't know," Croy said, between clenched teeth. He stepped out of the way of a cart full of men still holding their bill hooks. The men looked scared but they hadn't deserted yet, so maybe they were headed for the fighting. "There's food in the keep for months, and barrels of arrows, and the smithies . . . but this isn't a siege. It's a direct assault. If Hew gets enough men inside and locks the gates before the barbarians get to him, maybe a few days."

"What of the queen, and their children?"

Croy pushed his way through a knot of soldiers on their knees, begging the bloodgod for help. "They were sent to Greenmarsh days ago. You," he shouted, and grabbed one of the praying men. "Did the king come through here?"

The man wouldn't stop praying until Croy shook him. "I'll ask again. Have you seen the king?"

"He's not with you, sir knight?" the man asked, and his face dissolved in blubbering terror.

Croy pushed the wretch away and started to storm off when a woman leaned out of a window above his head and shouted for his attention.

"They went down there," she said, and pointed to a narrow lane between two houses.

"Milady," Croy said, "you have my thanks."

"I'm no lady! But if you'd repay me, tell me—what should we do? I have six children up here and they want to know what all the noise is."

Croy looked back toward the eastern gate, where he knew the fighting would be hot and desperate. For the moment at least his view was blocked by the intervening houses, but any minute now the berserkers would come flooding through this street, destroying everything in their path, murdering every man, woman and child they met. He looked up again at the woman in the window and thought of what advice he could possibly give her.

"Please, sir knight. For my children's sake?"

He closed his eyes and looked down. "Get to the keep, if you can. Stick as close to the western wall as possible—if you see anyone bloodied or screaming, run away. I'll pray for you, goodwife."

She slammed the shutters of the window closed without another word.

Croy and Orne hurried down the lane she'd indicated and saw a serjeant with an arrow sticking out of his back. He was breathing heavily and looked as pale as a sheet, but he waved them over when he saw them.

The serjeant led them down into a root cellar, where the king lay on a bed of sack cloth. His eyes were closed and there was a bad bruise on his left temple. "Hasn't . . . woken since I . . . brought him here," the serjeant gasped.

Sir Orne grabbed the arrow in the man's back and twisted it free, then shoved a piece of cloth into the wound. The serjeant winced until tears came from his eyes, but he would not cry out.

"You're a good man," Croy said, and put a hand on the serjeant's shoulder.

"Get him . . . to Sir Hew . . . he'll . . ." The serjeant said no more. He sat down on the close-packed earth of the floor and just stared at the ceiling.

Croy ran back up to the street and sought about until he found what he wanted—a pair of bill hooks with long enough hafts. With these and a bed sheet from an abandoned house, he made a litter that he and Orne could carry between them. They put the king on it and started to carry him up the stairs. "Come with us," Croy said to the wounded serjeant.

But the man was dead, his eyes rolled back up into their sockets. Croy closed his eyelids, then went back to his burden.

CHAPTER TWENTY-NINE

"Where do we take him?" Orne asked, when they were back in the street. "The keep? Or the western gate?"

Croy tried to think. He must keep the king alive, at any cost—that was Hew's order. But where did safety lie? It was impossible to say without better information.

Lady, he prayed silently, *give me a sign.*

He got it—though he would gladly have taken her silence instead.

A berserker came howling down the street toward him. The man was naked and covered in wounds—shallow cuts across his face and chest, deep gashes in his legs. He held an axe in either hand.

Perhaps the berserker hadn't even seen them in his fury—he didn't turn to engage them, instead looking as if he would run right past the two knights in his fury. Croy whipped Ghostcutter from its sheath and cut the barbarian's throat without resistance. The berserker fell, but behind him, perhaps only a street away, Croy could hear more of them whooping and laughing for the joy of battle.

The choice was made for them. There was no way they could reach the keep, not if they had to hack their way through Mörg's entire army to get there. Instead they must make for the gate and leave Helstrow behind. Croy and Orne picked up the litter and hurried as fast as they could for the western gate. It wasn't far, only a dozen streets or so, but in full armor and carrying the king they made slow going of it.

Before they'd covered half the distance, the barbarians had spotted them. A great howl went up and the knights had to duck down a side passage or be overrun.

Taking a winding route, trying to stay ahead of their

pursuers, they covered the distance somehow. Croy was past rational thought at that point—he was only aware of his feet, and of the sounds of murder and butchery all around him. He had to do everything in his power to save the king. That was his duty. If he was cut down before he reached the gate, the Lady could ask no more of him. But he would not stop. He would not consider the possibility of hiding or of not taking another step.

When the gate appeared before him, he realized he had a new problem. It was sealed. As it had been for ten days.

"Put him down over there," Croy said, and when it was done he went to the massive bar that held the iron gates closed. There was no portcullis on this side, but the wooden doors closing the gate were made of massive planks of age-hardened wood reinforced with thick metal fittings. The bar of the gate was a rod of iron thicker than his wrist. "Help me," he said.

"No," Orne told Croy. "You have to get it open yourself."

Croy turned around in a rage, but then he saw Bloodquaffer in Orne's hand—and a crowd of barbarians in the street behind him. Orne ran to meet the invaders, his Ancient Blade whistling as it swooped around and around in the air.

This was it, then. This was the foretold moment—the moment Orne was to die.

Croy decided he would make that death mean something, at any cost. Struggling with the iron bar, he put all his muscles into moving it until he felt something tear in his back. The bar came loose from its brackets and crashed to the ground with a noise so loud it jarred Croy's bones. He pushed hard on the gate until it started to swing open.

Only then did he look back.

Orne was lost in the melee, but he could see Bloodquaffer rise and fall and slash and spin. Never had Croy seen a man fight so desperately, never had he watched a sword move so fast. Heads, arms, fingers bounced and spun in the air as Bloodquaffer took its due. But with every barbarian that the sword cut down, a dozen axe blows came at Orne, while spears jabbed at him through every opening and arrows seemed to float on air above him. The barbarians didn't seem to care if they struck or killed their own numbers in the confusion, only that they took down the doomed knight. Blood pooled between the cobblestones and ran in the gutters, but they fought on.

Croy longed to go and help his friend—but he dared not. He bent to pick up the king and throw his sleeping form over one shoulder.

It was then he heard a booming, horrible laugh that he knew all too well. Striding through the crowd of barbarians, Mörget came to challenge Orne.

"No," Croy said, staggering under the weight of the king.

No, it could not be. Mörget could not still be alive. He'd been under Cloudblade when it fell. It had been Mörget's own hand that set off the explosion which leveled the mountain. Not even Mörget could have survived that.

Yet here he was.

Mörget—the biggest man Croy had ever seen. The fiercest warrior he'd ever known. The son of Mörg, and himself a chieftain of many barbarian clans. Mörget's face was painted half red like those of the berserkers, but he was more dangerous than any of those insensate warriors.

Croy had called Mörget brother, once. They had fought together against a demon, and Croy had marveled at the strength in Mörget's massive arms and the sheer delight Mörget took in hacking and slashing and killing. Mörget had terrified Croy even when they'd been on the same side.

But Mörget had betrayed Croy—he had betrayed everyone who went into the mountain with him. Even before the barbarians declared war on Skrae, Croy and Mörget had become sworn enemies. If he'd thought Mörget still lived, Croy would have been honor bound to do nothing until he had tracked down Mörget and slain him in single combat. Slain him and taken from his treacherous hands the sword called Dawnbringer.

Mörget waded into the fight, an axe in one hand, the self-same Ancient Blade in the other. The throng of barbarians drew back and Croy saw Orne in the sudden clearing. The knight had lost half the armor from his left arm and his helm had been torn from his head. His face was perfectly calm and resigned to his fate.

He brought Bloodquaffer up, ready to parry Mörget's axe stroke.

Mörget was as big as a horse and his arm was like a tree trunk. The axe came round in an unstoppable arc, a blow as fast and inescapable as an avalanche.

Orne took the perfect stance and gripped Bloodquaffer's hilt in both hands. He braced himself in perfect form. How many times had he stood like that, ready to take a blow that could have killed a normal man? Orne was a knight and an Ancient Blade. A warrior of incomparable skill.

He could no more have stopped the axe blow than he could have held back the ocean at high tide. The axe would have cut him in half if that had been Mörget's intention. Instead, it cut right through Bloodquaffer's blade.

The end of the serrated sword spun in the air for a moment, then dropped to clatter in the street. Orne was left holding a hilt and a foot of severed iron.

Impossible, Croy thought. Swords could be broken, of course. A strong enough man could shatter even dwarven steel, and Mörget was the strongest man Croy had ever seen. Yet—Bloodquaffer was no ordinary sword. The Ancient Blades were eight hundred years old. They had been forged by the greatest smiths of their day using techniques long lost to modern metalcrafters. They had been imbued with potent magics and blessed by priests of both the Bloodgod and the Lady, back when the people of Skrae worshipped them both equally. The swords were sacred, and they were supposed to be eternal. In all those centuries, none of them had ever been broken. Yet Croy saw it with his own eyes. Bloodquaffer shattered as easily as a piece of poorly forged iron, and with it eight hundred years of tradition.

It was like the world had come to an end.

It was like everything Croy had ever known had proved wrong.

Even Mörget looked surprised at what had happened. But he did not slow in his attack. The axe smashed against the cobblestones, carried onward by its inexorable momentum, but now Mörget's sword arm swung around, his own Ancient Blade held straight outward in a perfect form.

Orne did not flinch as Dawnbringer's chopping stroke took off his head.

His time, at last. As had been foreseen.

Croy longed to howl out in injustice, to call to Mörget to try his hand and his axe against Ghostcutter next. He burned with the need to avenge Orne's death and strike down Mörget as his vows required. Every particle of his being and every shred of his soul needed that, needed to see the battle through.

Yet he had taken a vow, another vow he could never break. He must save the king, no matter what he personally desired. His battle with Mörget would have to wait.

Croy did not waste another moment. He hurried through the open gate and pushed it quietly closed behind him. If the barbarians had seen him, they would come howling for his blood next. They would give chase.

They would kill him, and the king.

He could do nothing but keep running.

He tried to be quiet, willed himself not to be seen, as he hurried down the road to the west, outside of Helstrow's walls. He did not stop until he reached a copse of trees well outside the fortress-town's precincts, a place where he thought he might hide long enough to catch his breath. He laid the king down in a sward of soft grass, and looked back the way he'd come, his eyes unblinking.

Looming above the walls of Helstrow, he could see the keep and the palace. Both of them were burning.

PART 2

THE SLEEPING KING

INTERLUDE

There was a place in the Free City of Ness where drovers brought their sheep to pasture while they waited to be taken to market. A pleasant common of green in the midst of a boisterous and noisy city. It was not particularly safe at night (no place in Ness truly was), yet for its idyllic calm it had become somewhat fashionable, and some of the richest men of Ness built villas on its edges, pleasure palaces where they could get away from the endless flow and ebb of commerce.

In the middle of this sward there stood a wide swath of rubble and burnt timbers that no one had ever fully cleared away. It marked where the grandest of those houses once stood. Everything of even remote value had been gleaned from the spot, but no one wanted to build anew there and even the sheep gave it a wide berth.

It had been the house of Hazoth, the sorcerer. It was the place where that great man had been dragged down into the pit by his own enslaved demons. It was also the place where Cythera had been born, and where Coruth the witch had been imprisoned for many, many years.

Coruth was probably the first person to set foot inside its ruins since the night it came down. It had never occurred to her to do so before—she had been glad enough to get away from the place—but sometimes a witch had to go where others feared to tread.

That day she looked mostly like an old and bent woman, because that was how she felt most of the time and no one was watching so she didn't have to take the trouble to appear as an imposing figure. Her robes were black and shapeless and unremarkable. Her iron-colored hair was bound back with a bit of cheap ribbon. She walked with a measured step that suggested some of her great age, though she retained enough vanity not to use a walking stick.

It was not difficult to find the place where Hazoth died. The very ground there had cracked open to admit him, and while the earth had smoothed itself over, finding its own level, not even weeds would ever grow there again. She paced out the patch of utterly barren ground to find its center, then sat down on the dirt and let the sun warm her for a while before she did anything else.

"She's your daughter too," Coruth said, finally. Hazoth couldn't hear her, of course. He was dead. But some things needed to be said even if there was no one there to hear them. "You were a terrible man, a right bastard, frankly. One of the worst. But it was your seed that put her in my womb, and I figure you have a right to know what's going to become of her. It isn't pretty."

A soft breeze stirred the grass at the edge of the barren patch. Each individual blade fluttered, rubbing against its neighbors. A cricket looking for a meal approached the place where Coruth sat, then reconsidered and turned away. No human being was in sight—and definitely not in earshot.

"She's going to learn magic, one way or another. She'll gain the kind of power you and I work with, maybe even more. I'm going to have to train her. It's the only chance she's got. And you, of all people, know what that means. I've seen her future and it can go one of two ways. Normally when I see the future, I know it's bound to happen. That there's no changing it. I do my best to look surprised when it comes to pass. And being a witch, well, that means when I see something unpropitious, something I don't like, it's just too bad. More times than not I have to go along and help make it happen anyway. This time, though, I see two possibilities. One is she becomes like me. A witch. Old and alone and bitter, but the world is better for it. The other chance is she becomes a sorcerer like you, and every horror of the pit can't match what happens next. I can't let that come to pass. There's still time for her to pick which path she'll walk. Do you know how rare that is? How infrequently I get this chance to make the future a better place?"

A cloud passed briefly across the sun, one of those thin insubstantial clouds that can't block out all the light. A chill breeze ruffled her clothes, but soon enough the cloud passed by and the sun returned. Coruth tilted her head back and let the heat sink into her face.

"It's going to cost me. Especially now, when I'm needed for other things. I don't suppose you care, but Helstrow fell today to the barbarians. I'm going to have far more work than I can handle. As if that's something new."

In the distance she could hear a cowbell chiming, as a herd of animals was brought down to the common.

"Sod this," she said. "I'm getting stiff, sitting here talking to you. I just thought you had a right to know about Cythera. A father should know these things."

It hurt her old joints to stand up, but she did it without making too much noise. She started away from the barren patch of earth, intending to head home and begin her preparations. But then she glanced around slyly to make sure no one was watching, and headed back.

The patch of dirt was the closest thing Hazoth had to a grave. She hitched up her skirt and pissed all over it, cackling the whole time. And then she went home.

CHAPTER THIRTY

Helstrow burned for days. The barbarians were too busy celebrating to notice. A great carousing went on in whatever houses remained spared by the flames, an orgy of drinking and debauchery. Out in the streets men of Skrae hung by their necks from every eave and standard, or lay stinking and bloody on the cobbles. Inside the houses berserkers danced and reavers gambled for the spoils of war, while drunken thralls made sport in the elegant mansions, stealing what they could carry, smashing anything too big to be moved.

Of all that horde, one man stayed sober on the night of the victory—Mörget, now called Mountainslayer, who never touched spirits. Nor did he exult or crow in victory. Instead he roamed the alleys and lanes of Helstrow, looking for something he could not find.

This place, this fortress city, belonged to him and his people now. As it should be. As it always should have been. Mörget knew the story of this land, having heard it repeated by scolds since he was just a boy.

Once Mörget's people and the people of Skrae had been cut from the same cloth. When they first arrived on this continent, fleeing from the decadence and bureaucracy of the Old Empire, they had all been warriors, every man among them as proud and fierce as Mörget's berserkers and reavers. They had lived as nomadic hunters and raiders. Over time, though, the weaker among them had banded together to form villages and holdfasts and eventually permanent cities. They had built high walls to keep out those who were too strong and wild to live in any structure more permanent than a tent. Eventually the city people united against the nomads. A great war was fought and the wanderers, the warriors, had been too small in number to resist. They had been pushed back to the east, where they could not endanger the city folk. Eventually they'd been pushed right over the Whitewall range. A wall higher than anything their cities could boast.

For two hundred years the clans of the east had been penned in, kept locked behind those mountains by the men of Skrae. Once Mörget's people had been great warriors— soldiers, generals, slayers of elves and ogres. For far too long they'd been reduced to raiding the sheep of the hillfolk north of their Steppes or at best picking away at the edges of Skilfing in the northern kingdoms. It had kept them sharp, forcing them to keep their arms strong and their fighting skills honed. But it had made them bitter as well because they knew their true destiny was to rule, to smash open every wall and plunder the treasures inside.

Now that destiny was coming to fruition. And yet . . .

Mörget had believed it would make him happy to stand here, to walk these streets he'd conquered. He'd thought he would feel some kind of fulfillment now his life's grand task was underway. He would take the west back for the strong, for the righteous, for those who worshipped only Mother Death.

So why, then, did he wander aimlessly, feeling empty, feeling like he was still only part of what he should become?

For anyone else it would have been reckless to wander those ways alone. Mörgain and her spearmaidens roamed the rooftops with bows. Their faces were all painted to resemble the visage of their goddess Death, and they acted as Her servants in the world that night, finishing off those few soldiers of Skrae who had not surrendered and who thought to hide in dark and small places. Time and again as Mörget turned down a new street his thoughts were interrupted by the sudden twang of a bowstring and a desperate cry. Mörgain's clanswomen were drunk on black mead, that most befuddling of brews, and Mörget wondered if they even saw half the targets they fired at or if they chased as many phantoms as real enemies. More than once they drew on him but he had only to stare upwards, his red-painted face fixed in a scowl, and strings were eased, arrows un-nocked.

He came at one point to the Halls of Justice, the last public building in the fortress-town untouched by fire. Inside he heard Hurlind the scold recounting the day's battle, embellishing the tale with many a jest and pointed observation on the quality and quantity of Skrae's collective manhood. Mörget almost passed by, but as he glanced in toward the light and merriment he saw something he could not ignore.

His father sat on a stone bench, surrounded by half-dressed barbarian women as drunk as he was. The masterless dog was curled up on Mörg's lap, kicking one leg in sleep. Berserkers had passed out on the marble floor in heaps. As the first to the gate, the first to storm the city and brave its defenders, these men had been given the honor of feasting with the Great Chieftain, yet none of them had managed to stay awake long enough to enjoy it. The fury they brought to battle was not without a price to be paid later, a torporous exhaustion that could last for days. Mörget had been one of them once and he understood, so as he stormed into the chamber of justice he did not trod on his brethren but stepped over their snoring bodies.

Hurlind was bowing low as Mörget came upon him from behind. The scold had a velvet pillow in his hands, upon which lay the crown of Skrae. Mörget knew it had been recovered after the battle of the eastern gate, picked up from where it fell in the grass. The crown had been crushed in on one side and a few of its emeralds were missing, but someone had polished it to a high luster.

And now Mörg, Great Chieftain of the eastern clans, was reaching for it.

Mörget struck Hurlind across the back of the neck with one massive fist and drove him to the floor. The crown went flying to spin in circles in a corner of the room.

Mörg frowned at his son. From behind a column, Torki, Mörg's champion, loomed into the firelight, a great-axe in his hand.

Mörget sneered at the burned face of the giant champion. He'd beaten him once, and could do it again. If challenged were offered, Mörget was ready to accept.

But it seemed Mörg had received the message his son meant to send. That crown was not for the Great Chieftain. No man of the eastern steppes could ever call himself king— that was the law. The Great Chieftain only spoke for the men under them. He did not rule them.

Besides, the battle might be over but the war was just beginning. Helstrow had been taken and sacked, but Helstrow was not all of Skrae. Nor was it certain the true owner of that crown dead. Most of the clans believed the king had perished in the fighting, but until Ulfram V's body was found, Mörget would not believe it.

Mörg stared down into his son's eyes as if mistrusting the fire there, the fire that would not let Mörget rest, even in triumph. The fire that had always separated father from son and kept them understanding one another. Mörg had never respected that fire. *You put it there*, Mörget wanted to say, but this was not a time for words. Eventually the Great Chieftain waved away his son, and Torki took a step back. Mörget spat on the floor near Hurlind's face and went back out into the night.

He spent a while by the eastern gate, digging bodies out of the rubble. Even after the portcullis came down, the gate had not been wide enough to admit the barbarian horde en masse, so much of the stonework had been pulled down— while defenders still thronged its battlements. There were plenty of corpses to find.

None of them belonged to the king.

Howling with frustration, Mörget picked up stones and threw them into the night, not caring what he struck. He trampled on the king's banner, dropped here by a sniveling herald.

There will be other days, he told himself. *Other battles. The clans will not be satisfied for long by this blood. They will want more, and I will give it to them, in the name of our mother Death. I will make this country bleed until it runs white.*

He sat down on the pile of fallen masonry and took from his belt the only souvenirs he'd kept from the day's spoils. A hilt, its corresponding blade broken off at a jagged edge, and six inches of another blade from a sword older than history. Bloodquaffer and Crowsbill, or what was left of them.

He'd been surprised as anyone when the swords had shattered. The axe he carried was of the finest dwarven steel, he knew—he'd stolen it himself from an abandoned dwarven city. The mirror-bright face of its blade was streaked with wavy shadows and in a certain light the axe looked iridescent. It was a fine weapon, though not magical in any way.

Yet it had sheared through two Ancient Blades without stopping. Mörget had long believed the seven swords to be indestructible. Everyone believed that—it was an article of faith. Yet here he had the proof that even magic swords were mortal.

Knowing that, he could only wonder one thing.

*Will I truly find an enemy here in Skrae, the enemy I've
sought so long? The enemy who will be more precious than
any lover—the enemy who can challenge me, and make me
sweat, because I do not know I can beat him?*

He had conquered every foe he'd met east of the mountains. He had pushed so hard to come west because he
thought he would find there what he sought. But if even the
legendary Ancient Blades of Skrae were so easily brought low—

His reverie came to an instant stop when he heard a moan
rise up from the pile of corpses. A survivor—one he had
not found in his frantic search, one his sister had not discovered as she haunted the dead city.

Mörget leapt down from his perch on the rubble and
kicked bricks and bits of scorched mortar away from the
source of the sound. Then he reached down with one massive
hand and lifted his prize free of the debris.

"You," he said, the first word he'd spoken all night.

"Are you going to kiss me now, or stick me on a spit
and roast me alive?" Balint the dwarf asked. She must have
fallen here when the gate collapsed, staying with her ballista
crews until the fatal moment. "Either way, I need a change
of breeches first."

CHAPTER THIRTY-ONE

Just outside the gates of Ness a recruiting serjeant had been
broken on a wheel and hung up on a pole. The man's
kettle hat had been nailed to his head so it wouldn't fall
off, and so that anyone passing by would recognize his
occupation. Then his legs and arms had been broken in
several places so his limbs could be woven through the

spokes of the wagon wheel, and then the wheel had been lifted high in the air so all could see.

Malden just hoped that he'd already been dead beforehand.

The message this grisly execution sent was clear. Recruiters had swept through all the counties and baronies around Ness, calling up every man who could fight for Skrae. Ness had refused that call. As a Free City it technically owed no obligation to the king—he could not conscript Ness's citizens, nor could he demand they pay taxes to fund his campaigns. Clearly at least one serjeant had been foolish enough to think the people of Ness were patriots all the same.

It was that independent streak that had birthed Malden and made him who he was, that unique Nessian truculence in the face of authority. Still, he doubted the serjeant deserved such treatment. Surely the Burgrave who ruled Ness could just have had the man tarred and feathered and sent on his way.

But of course Malden knew it had probably been the Burgrave himself who ordered the death of the serjeant. Ommen Tarness, the current Burgrave, was fiercely independent of nature. He answered only and directly to the king, and even then he excelled in sticking to the exact letter of the city's charter. Tarness saw the Free City as his own personal fiefdom, and he would not have looked kindly on any attempt to recruit from among his people.

"Poor bugger," Slag said.

Cythera didn't even look at the dead man. Her eyes were on the city walls. "Home," she said, with some weary measure of relief and hope. Malden took her hand, not caring who saw it. Their journey from Helstrow had been an endless round of nights spent slogging through muddy fields and long days hiding in abandoned barns when they saw signs that bandits were about. Velmont and his crew had given them numbers, and a certain degree of security, but Malden hadn't been willing to chance an encounter with desperate men.

Funny, that. It wasn't so long ago he'd considered himself as desperate as they came.

"It'll be good to get back to my workshop in Cutbill's lair," Slag said, rubbing dust out of his eyes.

"Aye, Cutbill should be glad to see us," Malden said.

The dwarf shot him a meaningful look. Malden chose to ignore it.

The city gate was manned by a single guard, a lame old watchman in a shabby undyed cloak embroidered with a pattern of eyes. That made him a watchman, one of the bailiff's enforcers of public order. Normally the watch didn't stand gate duty. Malden worried the oldster might recognize him but the guard took one look at the sword on the thief's hip and waved him through.

The street beyond the gate was empty. Normally it would have been thronged with hawkers and beggars, hoping to make some coin from any newly arrived travelers. Malden couldn't remember the last time he'd seen this street—or any street in Ness for that matter—when it wasn't crammed with people. "Where is everyone?" Malden asked.

The watchman laughed. "Gone to ground if they're smart, or run as far and as fast as their feet could carry 'em. You haven't heard there's war coming?"

Malden bit his lip. "We heard rumors, I suppose."

"Where are you coming from, if I may ask?" the guard said, giving Malden a second look. Malden shouldn't have asked any questions, he realized. "I've been told to expect refugees from Helstrow. You're dusty enough for a refugee, I suppose."

"We're late of Redweir," Malden lied, unsure what the guard's orders might be regarding such refugees. Most likely he'd been told to drive them away—no city wanted new immigrants in time of war. Refugees were extra mouths to feed who would come with nothing but the clothes on their backs. "We've come to do business with Guthrun Whiteclay, the master of the potter's guild."

The guard snorted. "Fare well with that, then, for he's not here. Him and most of the burgesses've already run for it. Some to the west, some as far as the Empire, I hear tell. Is that a dwarf you've got with you? They were the first to go—high-tailed it for their own kingdom days before we even knew there was barbarians coming. Nobody knows why."

"Because we're smarter than you humans," Slag pointed out.

"Well, that's what they say. And yet, you're here, little fella."

Slag was discrete enough not to react to the barb.

"Whiteclay wouldn't just have abandoned his business altogether. He must have left some agent inside," Malden said, trying to get the conversation back on track. "I'll need to speak with him, then."

"More luck to you, if you do find someone to do business with. Get on inside."

"My thanks," Malden told him, and headed through the open gate.

He found his city changed enormously since he'd left. Oh, the buildings were the same, the streets just as winding and close and full of filth as he remembered. Yet every shop's sign, every standard in the street, every gable of every house had been strewn with hawthorn branches—that tree most sacred to the Lady, for it wore her colors. It seemed like every door had been hung with a hawthorn wreath.

And yet there was no one about to appreciate all this decoration. It wasn't just the street by the gate. Every street in Ness was empty. Occasionally Malden would spy someone through a window, or hear footsteps echoing in a side street, but otherwise the city might have been abandoned, deserted—silent. Or nearly so.

"Do you hear that music?" Cythera asked.

Once she said it, he did hear it—the high strains of a fife and the dull, slow beating of a drum. "Sounds like it's coming from up on Castle Hill."

Ness had been built on a massive hill, constructed in concentric zones around the Burgrave's palace. Market Square was up top, surrounded by the Spires—the district of temples, public buildings, and the university. Malden led his crew up the Cornmarket Bridge, intending to investigate the music and see where all the people had gone. Weary as they were, Velmont and his thieves followed close behind. They had never been here before and most likely just didn't want to get lost.

It was a long walk up a steep slope, but the cobblestones

were so familiar under Malden's soft leather shoes that he didn't feel the fatigue of climbing. Slag grumbled but Cythera kept drawing ahead, as if impatient for Malden to get to the top. When they reached the side of the counting house, just outside Market Square, Malden stopped them all and just stood there, staring.

An army had formed in the Square, perhaps a thousand men in tabards of russet and green. No two of them seemed to carry the same weapons or wear the same sort of armor, but they marched around the edges of the Square in scrupulous order, their feet moving to the beat of the drum. Some of them carried flags with the coat of arms of Ness, while others held campaign banners so old and decayed they frayed visibly as Malden watched.

He'd seen those campaign banners before. They had hung in a secret chamber inside the Burgrave's palace. They were the souvenirs of Juring Tarness, the first Burgrave of the city, a general who had helped found the kingdom of Skrae eight hundred years ago. Ommen Tarness, the current Burgrave, was Juring's direct descendant.

"Ye men, will you come, and heed the call?" someone asked, in a high, clear voice. Malden looked up with a start and saw an old man with one leg come hobbling toward him on a crutch. There was a sprig of hawthorn pinned to his tunic. "Skrae has need, for this is a dark hour. But the Free Army will show these barbarians a thing or two yet!" The cripple held out sprigs just like the one he wore.

Malden looked again at the soldiers in the Square. He thought he recognized some of them. Joiners, cobblers, redsmiths, ropewalkers—men from a hundred other occupations. These were the good solid citizenry of Ness alright, men who had worked the city's many trades when last he'd seen them. Men who grumbled about the Burgrave's policies and taxes, and spoke open treason against him in taverns and gaming houses. Men who thought of government as an evil rarely necessary but somehow inescapable. Now they were soldiers, recruits—could it be, volunteers?

"What happens if we say no?" Malden asked.

The cripple looked as if he'd bitten into a lemon. "Well,

that's your right, of course. As citizens you cannot be forced
to serve. But you look able-bodied to me. Why would you
turn down this opportunity? You'll get to see the kingdom,
and the pay's better than anything the guilds offer. Look
how many of your neighbors have joined up already! See
how dashing they look. And don't forget—every good girl
loves a soldier. Isn't that right, mistress?"

Cythera shook her head in disbelief. "Malden," she said,
ignoring the cripple, "they're not bewitched. I would see it
if a spell had been cast over them. Beyond that, I have no
explanation for this. I should go and talk to my mother."

Malden grasped her hand and looked deep into her eyes.
"Be safe," he said, "I don't like the look of this. Come," he
told Slag and Velmont. "Let's go find Cutbill. Maybe he
knows what's going on."

CHAPTER THIRTY-TWO

Cythera found her mother down in Swampwall, where
the river Skrait entered the walls of Ness. The district
flooded every spring, so no one lived there—and because
it was so eerily deserted in the midst of the thronging city
it had gained an evil reputation. Supposedly it was full of
spirits and deadly wildlife and places where the ground had
subsided and would suck a man down to his death before
he had time to call for help. In fact it would have been a
pleasant, tranquil place if not for all the stinging insects.
Whole city blocks there had been abandoned to sprawling
vegetation, interrupted only by a broken bit of wall or the
sunken foundations of some ancient house.

Coruth came there quite often to collect herbs and

simples. When Cythera spied her mother, Coruth was bent over a reddish plant gathering flower petals. She had a basket tucked under one arm already full to the brim with bryony, dittany and rue.

"You came," Coruth said, without looking up. "I thought perhaps you had ignored my summons. I hope your journey here was uneventful."

"I spent a week dodging bandits and comforting girls who had been abused by men and worrying always that some barbarian would find us and kill us all while we slept. I huddled in burnt-out barns by day and clutched myself for warmth at night," Cythera said. "I was terrified and miserable the entire time. I don't know if you're aware of this, but there's a war on. And now I return to find Ness all but deserted. Mother, what is going on? What have you seen?"

The witch straightened up and smiled at her daughter. "Oh, terrible things. But then I always do. The problem with seeing the future is the same as the problem with seeing the past. So much of it is bloody and brutal. Today, though, the sun is shining and the leaves are changing color. It's good to see you."

Cythera felt her jaw drop. She couldn't remember the last time her mother had spoken to her with tenderness. Coruth was not a particularly warm sort. She was a witch, after all, and witches had to maintain a fearful aspect. "I've missed you, myself," Cythera replied.

"I've always loved this part of the work," Coruth said, and bent to pluck the spiky leaves of a plant so small that anyone else would have passed it by. "So nice to be out in the fresh air, close to green and growing things. Do you know this one?"

"Calendula," Cythera said, nodding at the plant. "The flower gives it away."

"Quite so," Coruth said. "It's good for reducing a fever. Very useful. What about this?"

She pointed at a wild tangle of grass growing around the base of an ancient signpost. Cythera took a moment to think. Most grasses looked exactly alike, but they had wildly different uses and virtues. "Fountain grass," she said, finally.

"Very good. And why would I want to gather it?" Coruth asked.

Cythera shook her head. She knew she was being tested—this wasn't the first time she and Coruth had played this particular game—but this had to be a trick. "It has no uses that I'm aware of."

"Really?" Coruth asked.

Cythera bit her lower lip and tried to recall. This had to be a trick question. "Yes. I'm certain. Absolutely useless."

"Unless I wished to thatch the roof of a house. Or feed a sheep," Coruth pointed out. "It has a pleasant smell, too, so I might mix it with the rushes I lay on my floor. To a man being hunted by enemy soldiers fountain grass might be very useful. It might mean the difference between life and death, because it grows tall enough to hide him from view."

Cythera sighed. "I meant it had no use in magic."

Coruth laughed. It barely sounded like a cackle at all. "I thought I'd taught you better than that. Magic isn't all about casting spells. Now, help your old mother out with your young eyes. Do you see any poppies around here? If we're going to have wounded men stacked in heaps, and we will, very soon, we'll need something to ease their pain."

Cythera cast around her looking for the red flowers but couldn't see any. This was another test, but she didn't know whether she should keep looking until she found the poppies or if she was supposed to announce there weren't any. Then she caught sight of a particular purple flower she knew all too well and gasped.

"Did you find some?" Coruth asked.

"No—no, just—look here. Mandrake."

The witch and her daughter bent low over the plant, which grew very close to the ground. Its fleshly leaves spread out around the purple flowers and shaded the ground below. Mandrake was one of the rarest of plants, and also one of the most useful to a witch. Every part of it was deadly poison, but if properly diluted and prepared it could work a hundred different charms.

"An excellent find," Coruth agreed. "And at a time when I have a need for its roots." She began to reach for the plant.

"Mother, no!"

"Something wrong?" Coruth asked.

"Everyone knows about mandrake. The roots are like little men, and when they're drawn from the earth they die. But they don't go alone. They scream in their agony, and anyone who hears that cry will perish with them."

"Oh?" Coruth asked. "Yet surely there must be a way to harvest them."

Ah. So this was the real test. Cythera nodded. "You feed a little dog until it will follow you anywhere. Then you tie its tail to the stalk of the mandrake, and run away. The dog will try to come after you, and in the process it will pull the root free. The dog dies but you have your treasure."

"What an absolutely horrible thing to do," Coruth said. She clucked her tongue. "No dog deserves to die like that."

Cythera steeled herself. "Witches can't always be kind. Sometimes they must be ruthless, for the greater good. A witch is beyond common notions of good and evil, but not beyond true morality. She must know when doing a little evil will prevent great suffering later. And she must be willing to take on that weight."

"I see you've actually heard some of the things I tried to teach you," Coruth said. "Yes. You've even memorized some of them. I suppose that's a good start."

"I see now why you wanted me to return to Ness," Cythera said. Her blood felt as cold and greasy as river water in midwinter. "You want to train me to follow in your footsteps. To become a witch."

There had been a time when Cythera had begged her mother to do just that. When she had thought that having that power would be the only way to be free, to live her own life, instead of just becoming some man's wife. Coruth had refused her, back then, and Cythera had been mortified because she thought Coruth was telling her she wasn't good enough. She'd been so distressed she ran right into Croy's arms.

Now—now when she'd finally found love with Malden, love that wasn't the same thing as iron chains around her neck. Now when she had a reason to want to be a normal woman, now—only now—Coruth seemed to have changed her mind.

"Yes," Coruth said. "You have it. Though you don't know why, yet."

Cythera lowered her head. "Because Ness is going to need as many witches as it can get. That's right, isn't it? The barbarians will come here. They'll try to take the city. And we need to fight back."

"That isn't it at all, actually," Coruth said.

"Mother," Cythera said, drawing herself up to her full height. "You do me great honor by offering to train me. I'm not sure that I want this, however. I—"

"I wasn't asking if you wanted it," Coruth said, not even looking up.

Cythera held herself very stiff, as if she could make this moment pass her by if she just held perfectly still.

"You wanted the power I offer you once. You wanted the power of witchcraft, so you could be free. As so few women in this world ever get to be. You were wrong in thinking that it would give you freedom—a witch is never free. So I denied you."

"I don't claim to understand what you mean," Cythera said. "I only know that a witch can't marry. She can't even take a lover. Mother, I've found something with Malden, something that—"

Coruth's voice as she interrupted was hollow and free of inflection. Cythera knew that voice well. "You will have your chance to be his lover. You will be happy with him, for a short while. And then you will do something so horrible that you will never be able to look him in the eye again."

Cythera's jaw dropped.

That was the voice that Coruth used when she made prophecy.

"You've seen something," she whispered. "You've seen my future. Will you tell me what it is that you see me do?"

"No," Coruth said, in a more natural tone.

"But—something horrible? So horrible that . . . Mother! What am I going to do?"

"You're going to train to become a witch, because it is the only way you can avoid what is to come. I've seen enough to know that. Now. May we stop pretending that you have a choice? That what you want actually matters?"

Cythera wanted to cry. She wanted to wail, and run away, and go as far from Ness as she could get. She balled her hands into fists. Clamped her eyes shut. Finally, she nodded.

"Good. Let's get started with your training, shall we? Lesson the first." Coruth's hand shot forward and grabbed her wrist. It felt like the claws of a demon were digging into her flesh. Cythera cried out but the pressure only increased. She could never have broken that grip—not even Croy could have resisted as Coruth forced Cythera's hand down to the soil, forced her fingers to lock around the stem of the mandrake plant.

"Mother? No!" Cythera screamed.

"Pull," Coruth said. And their two hands, locked together, dragged the mandrake root free of the ground. Cythera tried to cover one of her ears with her free hand, thinking to block out even a little of the deadly sound, the death throes of the root, which were always fatal, always deadly to anyone who dared to—

The root came free of the ground without so much as a squeak.

It looked nothing at all like a man, either, not really. Cythera had been expecting a tiny homunculus with staring dead eyes and little fangs. Instead it looked like a root vegetable, brown and fibrous, bifurcated at one end to give the barest suggestion of legs.

"But—"

"Lesson the first," Coruth said, "is this. *Think*. Always, always *think*. Have you ever seen a plant that had lungs or a throat? The mandrake root can't scream. Even if it could, what sound could possibly kill someone? At worst such a scream might give you a headache, and there's plenty of willow bark around here to help with that."

"But every authority agrees," Cythera said, when she had assured herself she was not dead. "Maybe this isn't true mandrake, maybe you're just trying to make a point, a point about . . . about . . ."

"That's real mandrake, alright. Don't believe everything you're told. Half the old stories about our art are just that—stories. Stories made up to scare off the uninitiated. It would be too dangerous to allow just anyone to play around with mandrake, so we made up this silly story about screaming roots to keep their grubby little hands off of it. Here. Take this basket. We need a round dozen of those roots for what I have in mind."

CHAPTER THIRTY-THREE

After Cythera went to find her mother, Malden led Slag and the crew of thieves downhill, through the district of smithies and work yards known locally as the Smoke. Normally that name was self-evident—the chimneys of a thousand forges and the fuming tanner's vats cloaked the streets in an eternal pall of foul smoke. Today the air was almost breathable. With the exception of the blacksmiths, whose shops were crowded with men churning out arms and armor, work had ground to a halt.

"That's—that's fucking disgusting," Slag said, when they passed by a pewterer's that had been deserted and locked up tight. He placed his thin hands against the workshop's brick chimney. "Ice cold, when it should be too hot to touch. They've let their fires go out—you never do that! Do you know how long it takes to get a furnace going from a cold start?"

"Every shop along this way's closed," Velmont observed. "The masters must've fled, and the 'prentices gone to join up wi' that piebald army we saw." A wicked smile crossed the thief's face. "That makes fer a prime looting opportunity, now, don't it? I think I might like it here in Ness, Malden."

Malden kept his own counsel. They descended farther through the Stink. When he was in town Malden lived in this part of the city, in a little room above a waxchandler's. His room was always warm in the winter from the great vats of molten wax directly beneath him and the idea of sleeping in his own bed that night was appealing. However he could not raise his landlord or any of the workers there no matter how much he hallooed or pounded on the doors.

At least the Stink was not as deserted as the Smoke had been. There were still plenty of women around, going about their business as they always had—hanging washing on lines that ran above the streets, grinding meal to make bread, carting home their shopping. The women looked wary at the sight of men, but said nothing. There were oldsters and cripples about, too, far more than Malden expected, and very young children played everywhere or ran errands for their mothers. Without any men around they seemed far more numerous than they'd ever been before.

His face was a mask of quiet confusion by the time they reached the bottom of the city, down by Westwall. Down there lay the Ashes, a region of houses that had burned down in the Seven Day Fire before Malden was born. The district had been so badly impoverished before the fire that the houses had never been rebuilt. Weeds sprouted now between the cobbles, looking bedraggled by autumn's coolth, and land-slides of charred debris filled most of the alleys. One expected the Ashes to be deserted, and it certainly was—but there was something here as well that felt slightly off to Malden. When he realized what it was, he began to worry in earnest.

He didn't feel like he was being watched.

The Ashes were home to Cutbill's headquarters, but also to a gang of wholly non-innocent urchins, orphan children who had gathered together for safety and made concord with the guild of thieves for mutual protection. Normally they served as ever-vigilant guardians. They stood ready to kill anyone who came too close without Cutbill's approval.

Normally, if you knew where to look, you could see the glint of small eyes in every razed stub of a house, or see children watching you unblinking from the exposed rafters of the district's fallen churches. Normally Malden knew they were about long before he saw them.

This day he felt completely alone in the Ashes.

Surely the Burgrave would not have recruited the feral children? Most of them were too young, no matter how good they might be with their makeshift weapons.

When he reached Cutbill's lair without being challenged, Malden knew to be on his best guard. When he entered the fire-ravaged inn that topped the lair, he was no longer surprised to find it empty. A plain wooden coffin sat in the middle of the blackened floor, but no one sat atop it.

"There should be three old men here," Malden explained for Velmont's benefit. "Loophole, 'Levenfingers, and Lockjaw. The elders of our guild. I like this not."

Slag stood well back as Malden opened the trap door that led down into the lair. Nothing escaped from underneath however, save for a puff of stale air. Malden went down first, bidding the others to stay up top until he was sure it was safe.

Below lay the common room where Cutbill's legions normally disported themselves between jobs. Malden had never seen the room empty before. Always—at any hour of day or night—there had been a dice game here, while Cutbill's latest enforcer or bodyguard watched the door. Now the room was empty and silent. Perhaps, he thought, the Burgrave had taken the present crisis as an excuse to finally break and disperse the guild of thieves. Maybe he'd sent his troops down here to kill Cutbill and all his workers. Yet there was no sign of a struggle. The rich tapestries on the walls were untouched, the stolen furniture was all in its proper place. Fresh tapers even stood in the cressets, only waiting to be lit. Malden struck flint and let a little light into the place but that just served to make it seem spookier.

Tentatively, knowing better from past experience, Malden approached the door to Cutbill's office unbidden. No one popped their head out to offer him welcome or to warn him off. He checked carefully to see if the door was booby-trapped, but found no sign.

He pushed gently, and the door opened. It wasn't even locked.

Malden pressed further into the office, expecting to find darkness and abandonment. At least in this he was mistaken.

Candles burned inside. He saw the big desk that Cutbill never used, and the stool where the master of the guild of thieves was always perched. It was empty now. Cutbill's ledger lay on its stand. That book recorded every transaction of the guild—including the names of every thief who had failed Cutbill and been slain for their mistakes. It would never have been left behind if the thieves had deserted this place, and if the Burgrave had raided it he would certainly have confiscated the ledger as evidence against Cutbill.

No, Cutbill would never have let that book out of his sight. It was his life's work, and he spent every day scribbling figures on its wide vellum pages. Yet Cutbill himself was nowhere to be seen, which was itself a wonder. As far as Malden knew, the guildmaster never left this room.

The place was not, however, empty. At first glance Malden's eye ran completely over the old man sitting behind the desk, and failed to even register his presence. Then Lockjaw lifted a hand in greeting, and Malden jumped.

"Welcome home, lad," the oldster said. His voice was thin, starved by many years of earning his sobriquet. Lockjaw knew many secrets but had earned them by keeping them close. He was famous for never betraying a confidence . . . until the maximum profit could be made by divulging it.

"Old friend, well met," Malden said, and bowed to his elder. He had learned a great deal from this man and loved him dearly. "Is Cutbill available?" Perhaps he had simply stepped out to use the privy. Or maybe he was sleeping.

"Gone," Lockjaw said.

"Gone? Just gone?"

"Like every man in the city who could afford to flee, aye."

Malden could scarcely credit it. Cutbill would never leave Ness . . . but then, he'd never known Lockjaw to actually lie. He was a master at the half-truth, but he never lied. "And his bodyguard, Tyburn? What of the other thieves?"

Lockjaw shrugged. "Most of 'em joined up already."

Malden nodded carefully. "They went to join the Burgrave, you mean. That madness seems to have spread through the city like a fever. But then, tell me, who's in charge down here? Have you taken Cutbill's place?"

Lockjaw favored him with a very short chuckle. More of a "ha." "Me, lad? Not a chance."

"But—someone must be holding the reins."

"Aye, Cutbill's most trusted man's been given mastery of the place."

Malden frowned. He could think of no one that Cutbill actually trusted. "Most trusted" in this case could only mean the one Cutbill least expected to betray his interests. "Now who would that be?" Malden asked.

"You, lad. He left it all to you, to await your return."

CHAPTER THIRTY-FOUR

"That's ridiculous," Malden said. How could he be Cutbill's most trusted man? More to the point—why had Cutbill even expected him to return here? Cutbill had sent an assassin to kill Malden. It had very nearly worked.

"Let me get the others," Lockjaw said. He looked as if saying so much already had thoroughly tired him out. Ducking behind a tapestry on one wall, he emerged a few moments later leading Loophole and 'Levenfingers. The other two oldsters looked bleary-eyed, as if they'd been sleeping.

"Oh, lad, you're a welcome vision," Loophole said, and embraced Malden fondly. Malden had no reservations returning the warmth. 'Levenfingers patted him on the back and was all smiles.

"Cutbill was one of the first to leave the City, back before any of us had heard there was barbarians coming. Things have been hard here, with no one leading us," 'Levenfingers told Malden. "Every day a few more men grew tired of waiting and just left, and we couldn't stop 'em. We might have fled ourselves, had we anywhere else to go. We've been taking turns sitting watch, waiting for you. I never doubted you'd be back, not me. I'm sure you'll have things whipped into shape in no time at all."

"Surely," Malden said, wishing he had any idea how he was supposed to make that happen. "Listen, fellows, I've been away a long while. I was at Helstrow, almost until the barbarians arrived—but I've had no news since then. What's been happening?"

The oldsters looked at each other as if they didn't want to answer. "Helstrow's fallen," 'Levenfingers said.

"Sacked," Lockjaw agreed.

"The fortress is in the enemy's hands, and the king, they say, is dead."

Malden's jaw dropped. Croy had been there, helping to lead the troops. Whatever else he thought of the knight, Malden had always believed Croy to be a master of things military. If Helstrow had fallen that meant Croy had failed, and that was nearly unthinkable. "I assumed it would still be under siege—"

"Taken by base treachery," Loophole said, looking less outraged than grudgingly respectful. If a master thief wanted to take a city, he wouldn't use force of arms, of course. He would steal the place out from under its current owners. It sounded like the barbarians had much the same idea. "The people enslaved, the army there broken and routed. The news came a sennight ago, just when the Burgrave started raising his own troops."

"I saw them marching in Market Square," Malden said.

'Levenfingers nodded sagely. "And that's just the latest batch. Many more—many thousands of 'em—are already encamped along the river Skrait. Ready to engage the enemy, should he tend this way."

"I have trouble believing the people of Ness would jump so quick to the defense of the crown," Malden said. "I know these people! A more corrupt, self-serving rabble you'd never find."

"At first, it was hard for the Burgrave to inspire anyone to patriotism, true. But then the rich folk all started running like dogs," Loophole said. "About the time the fortress fell. They must have had better information than us, because most of 'em left in a single night. Took only what they could carry, headed for anywhere they thought they might be safe. It's clear they had no faith in their common man."

"The next morn," 'Levenfingers went on, "the Burgrave declared them all traitors, and as such, their worldly goods was fair game. So he seized their plate and their coin, all their land. Sold everything for gold royals. Then he addressed the people, standing tall on a dais in Market Square. Said a plague had been purged from the city, a plague of faithless cowards. Said only good, honest working men remained. Said they deserved a reward for being true."

"A reward?" Malden asked.

"Gold," Lockjaw answered.

"Every man what signs on with the Burgrave gets a gold royal, and a promise of another for every month he's in the field."

"Aha!" Malden said.

Now he had it. The cripple who tried to recruit him had mentioned good pay. He hadn't mentioned any numbers, though.

He certainly hadn't said anything about gold.

One gold royal was a full year's wages for an untrained laborer in Ness. Even a skilled apprentice in a smithy, or for that matter a master in the guild of gleaners, could expect to see only a handful of the big gold coins in his lifetime. And of course they weren't usually handed out as pay—most commerce in the free city took the form of silver, or copper pennies and farthings. A single gold royal was a small fortune, and the promise of twelve a year was a promise that a man could get rich by fighting.

If there was one way to motivate the people of Ness, one thing sure to get their attention, it was an appeal to their greed. The Burgrave knew his people well, it seemed.

"But such folly!" Malden went on. "How many soldiers does he command, now? If every able-bodied man in the city joined, that would be what, how many? Twenty thousand? There's no possible way he could spend twenty thousand gold royals—a month—for long. He'll bankrupt his own treasury!"

"Some have noticed that," Loophole said, with a shrug. "Some have even lampooned the Burgrave for it, and given pretty speeches to that effect in the squares and the taverns." Another shrug. "Then the royals started appearing in the hands of men who'd never even seen one before. Men whose most marketable skill was leaning against a tavern wall and hoisting a tankard back and forth to their mouths. The gold is real, Malden."

For now, the thief thought. *It'll run out pretty quick at that rate*. But he supposed that wasn't as big a problem as it first seemed. The men of Ness weren't born warriors. If they had to fight the barbarians, most of them would perish in the first wave. The Burgrave would only have to pay the survivors.

That cunning bastard. But maybe that was what it took to be a ruler of men—you had to be a villain just to keep them in line. Malden had never had any use for authority, and had always hated those who called themselves his superiors. He'd met the Burgrave and the man had confirmed all his prejudices.

Yet, still—this was more cynical than any man had a right to be. And that stood at odds with the whole point of raising an army in the first place. "I can't believe that Ommen Tarness loves his king so much that he would spend his own money defending the country," Malden pointed out. "What's he really after?"

Loophole snorted. "He hasn't seen fit to share his motivations with us."

No, Malden thought. He supposed Tarness wouldn't make his plans public. It wasn't the man's style. "I suppose it matters not. Let him get himself and half of Ness killed, if he wants to play at soldiers," Malden said with a sigh. "Anyway. Once he's gone and taken his army with him, that'll just make it easier for us to steal what he leaves behind. It's an ill wave that doesn't wash something up on shore."

CHAPTER THIRTY-FIVE

"Alright," Malden said. "Well, that's got me up to date. Now I imagine I need to think about the future. If I'm running this guild, I'll need to get started. Did Cutbill leave me instructions, at least?" He had never run so much as a card game before. Surely Cutbill wouldn't just assume he knew how to keep a criminal enterprise in motion.

"He said it's all in the ledger," Loophole told Malden.

Malden nodded and went to the lectern, where the infamous book lay open to a half-filled page. He saw columns and columns of numbers, each with a corresponding notation in a tiny, spidery hand. Very few of the notes meant anything to him, but he assumed they represented quantities of money brought in by various thieves, or paid out in bribes or other expenses. It wasn't exactly a manual of instructions. Thinking Cutbill must have left him a message in plainer words, he flipped to the next blank page. And found what he was looking for—though it made him even more confused.

The top of the page was inscribed FOR MALDEN, SHOULD HE RETURN. Those were the only words Malden recognized. The rest were in some bizarre alphabet he'd never encountered before. Or perhaps not in any kind of alphabet at all, but a cipher—for the words were inscribed in circles and triangles and congeries of dots. It looked more like dwarven runes than human writing.

"What do you make of this?" he asked the oldsters, showing them the encoded page.

'Levenfingers looked away. "Well, now, that's really a private matter—"

Loophole nodded eagerly. "None of our business, properly—"

"None of us can read," Lockjaw finished.

"Ah," Malden said. "No, of course not." It was not that common a skill. Malden had learned to read and write because he'd grown up in a brothel that required a book-keeper. Expecting thieves—even learned, wise, and venerable elders like these three—to know the art was expecting too much. "I beg your pardon." He took the page in hand and started to tear it from the book. He hesitated, because this was Cutbill's ledger. In the annals of the thieves of Ness, it was close on being a holy relic.

Still. The page was addressed directly to him. He tore it out and stuffed it into his tunic, right next to Cutbill's signed contract for his assassination.

"I want word sent to every thief in the city who hasn't joined on with the Burgrave yet," Malden told the oldsters. "Have them all meet me tonight. Midnight," he said, because that was a fitting time for a conclave of thieves. He thought for a moment, then added, "At the Godstone."

The oldsters agreed to do as he asked. Once he'd thanked them properly, and handed each a bag of coins for expenses, Malden left the office and went back to the common room. Velmont and his crew had come down already and made themselves at home, lounging on the furniture with their dirty boots. That seemed less acceptable, now that it was technically Malden's furniture.

"Velmont," he said. "You work for me now. Is that a problem?"

"Where's your famous Cutbill?" the Helstrovian thief asked.

"Gone. He left me in charge. I'll ask again, is that a problem?"

Velmont held one hand out, palm upwards.

Malden nodded and took a dozen coins from his purse. After what he'd given the oldsters he had precious little left, but that was the cost of doing business. He laid the silver on Velmont's palm.

"No problem 'tall," the Helstrovian told him.

"Good." Malden looked over and saw Slag was at his workbench, sorting through his tools as if to make sure nothing had been taken. "Slag—show this bunch around.

Find some food for them. I'm sure they're all hungry after traveling so far."

"Sure, lad," Slag said, and rose from his bench. If he was at all surprised that Malden had just taken over the thieves' guild, he showed no sign of it.

I wish I had the same confidence, Malden thought.

He started for the trap door, but Slag stopped him with a look. "Where are you headed?" the dwarf asked. "In case we need you."

Malden thought of telling the dwarf to mind his own business. But he supposed Slag had a point. If the watch broke in and raided the lair in his absence, he would want to know about it, wouldn't he? "I'm going to see the witch Coruth."

"Your prospective mother-in-law," Slag said, with a grin.

That fact hadn't occurred to him. Instead he'd thought that Coruth might be the one person in Ness who could decipher Cutbill's instructions.

CHAPTER THIRTY-SIX

Croy brought the whetstone carefully up the iron edge of his sword. The sound it made grated on his nerves, which were at an especially fine pitch already. It was alright. The irritation would help keep him awake. He hadn't slept in three days.

He brought the whetstone back down to Ghostcutter's hilt. Touched it gently to the iron. Drew it back up toward the point. Ghostcutter required a very special kind of maintenance. The iron blade was cold-forged by an ancient and forgotten process that imbued a certain virtue to the metal. If the blade were ever exposed to high heat—even from the friction of a whetstone—its mystical temper would be lost. It would no longer be so puissant at its original purpose: slaying demons.

Not that any demons had presented themselves lately. At least none of the inhuman variety called up from the pit by mad sorcerers.

There had been a time when seven swords were needed, when demons had roamed the land freely and seven knights had been required to vanquish them. Now they had become rare, as sorcery was slowly being wiped out. Now, more and more often, the Ancient Blades were being turned against human enemies—and even each other.

Was their time passing? Was this the dawning of a new age, when men fought only against men? The elves were all but extinct. Ogres, trolls and goblins were becoming the stuff of mere rumor and campfire tales.

And at Helstrow, Croy himself had seen an Ancient Blade broken.

The swords had been forged with a certain destiny in mind. If that destiny had come to fruition, if they were no longer needed, then perhaps that explained how the impossible had happened. Perhaps it was a sign from the Lady, a warning not to depend on the things of the past.

Or perhaps there was a more worldly reason. The axe Mörget had used to cut through Bloodquaffer had been made of dwarven steel. That metal had not existed eight hundred years ago, when the blades were forged. There was nothing of magic in steel—but it was stronger, more flexible, and held an edge better than even the most arcane iron.

He stared down into the dark flat of Ghostcutter, into the shining mirror of the silver that coated its trailing edge. It was a weapon ill-suited to making war against men with steel armor and modern weapons, perhaps. Yet it was still his soul. That was the credo of the Ancient Blades: *my sword is my soul. It is not my possession. I am its servant. I will perish, but the blade will survive.*

Had Mörget broken Ghostcutter, instead of Bloodquaffer— well. Perhaps it was a mercy that Orne had not survived his blade for more than a moment.

From the battlements of the holdfast on which he sat, Croy could just see Helstrow on the horizon. He could see the tent camps outside the western gate and a hint of movement there. The barbarians had grown bored with the fortress they'd stolen, and were preparing to move on some other hapless target.

Croy brought the whetstone back down to Ghostcutter's hilt. Started its journey back toward the point.

The iron edge was as sharp as he could make it.

The other edge of the sword was coated with silver, good for cutting through curses and sorcerous magic. When the molten silver had been applied to the sword it had been kept just above its melting point, and as a result it had run across the blade like molten candle wax, leaving long runners of bright metal in the fuller and across the flat. The silver didn't require sharpening—that which it cut was not material. Croy inspected the soft silver carefully, though, looking for nicks and dents which might show black iron underneath. These he smoothed over with endless pressure from his own thumb.

On the horizon, a barbarian on a horse went galloping southward, hurrying for the road to Redweir. It made sense that the learned city there would be the next to come under attack. All power in Skrae rested on a stool with three legs: Helstrow, Redweir and Ness, the three largest cities and the kingdom's most defensible walls. Anyone who wished to conquer the kingdom must first break that stability. Cut two of those legs out from under the kingdom and it would topple. Redweir was the obvious choice for the barbarians' next target for another reason as well. If Mörg and his children held Helstrow and Redweir both, they would control the river Strow—and gain the land they had asked for in tribute, and been denied.

Croy prayed that city would be ready for the battle.

He knew it would not.

Still rubbing at the silver with his thumb, Croy climbed off the merlon he'd been using as a seat and went down the stairs into the open space of the holdfast.

The structure was not built to be comfortable. It was

drafty and damp, and there was nothing inside but a floor of packed earth and a few barrels of salted pork. In times long past, the stone structure had stood in the middle of a farming village. The village had moved on, following more fertile soil, but the holdfast remained, its entrance choked with weeds, its walls green and black with perfectly circular patches of lichen. It still served its original purpose, however. It was a place where the local villeins could shelter in case of an attack by bandits or reavers.

It would not have held for an hour against the full force of the barbarian horde. But it was the best Croy had been able to find under the circumstances.

King Ulfram V lay on a pallet of straw, next to a smoky fire. He had not woken, or moved, since Croy brought him there. Yet he breathed still, and when Croy touched the monarch's neck, he felt a dull pulse.

He found a pot and put it over the fire. He made a thin soup, mostly broth with a few carrots and green potatoes chopped in. He put a spoon in the pot, let it cool in the chill air of the holdfast, and then carefully placed it against the king's lips.

Very little of the liquid went into Ulfram's mouth, but the king swallowed reflexively when the warm broth hit the back of his throat. Croy waited a moment, then dipped the spoon in the pot again.

When he decided the king had swallowed enough of the soup, Croy pulled a blanket up around the man's shoulders. He fluffed the wadded-up tunic the king had for a pillow. It was all he could do.

He went back to smoothing the silver edge of his sword.

Eventually, he dozed. He would not have called it sleep. More like a devotional trance, the same hypnotic reverie he fell into during his night-long vigils. He was never totally unaware of his surroundings. His hand's grip never truly relaxed on the hilt of Ghostcutter.

So when someone pounded on the door of the holdfast, he scuttled up to his feet in an instant, sword in hand.

CHAPTER THIRTY-SEVEN

Through the stout oak door, Croy could hear the voices of men outside the holdfast. He could not tell how many of them there were, nor whose men they might be—they could be barbarians, or bandits, or any manner of evil pursuers.

"I can hear a fire crackling in there," one man said, quite close to the door.

"Aye—and I heard clanking armor," another said, fainter.

"So what if there's someone inside?" the first voice argued. "I'm cold, and tired, and hungry. We'll make short work of 'em, and have the place to—"

Croy wrenched the door open and saw a terrified face staring back at him. He grabbed the man by the throat, then pulled him inside and slammed the door behind him before the others could force their way in. He dropped the bar across the door, sealing it again, then whirled around with Ghostcutter's point to face the man he'd drawn in.

The intruder fell backwards to clatter on the floor, his kettle hat sliding down over his eyes. He reached up to move the helmet but Croy batted his hand away with the flat of Ghostcutter.

"Who are you?" Croy demanded.

The man seemed too frightened to answer. He was dressed in canvas jack, with iron plates sewn to his elbows and shoulders. He wore a hanger at his belt—more dagger than sword, but deadly enough. The man made no attempt to reach for his weapon.

Croy placed the point of Ghostcutter against the man's throat. "You wear the harness of a soldier of the king," he said. "If you're true to your coat, you'll find no enemy here."

"G-g-gavin," the man choked out.

"That's your name, Gavin? Where did you serve?"

"At Helstrow, milord," Gavin said. He reached up slowly to adjust the brim of his helmet. Croy allowed it. "You're Sir Croy!"

Croy didn't deny it.

"Milord, I beg you—have mercy. I only sought shelter here!"

"And you would have taken it from me, by force of arms," Croy said, nodding.

Gavin's eyes were wide with fright. "How long have you been in here? Since the battle? You don't know what it's like out there! The barbarians harry the countryside. They kill any man they find, take any woman. They burn villages and ravage good crop land. Any place with a roof over your head, any place safe, is worth fighting for."

"And the king was good enough to give you arms to fight with," Croy said. He tapped the knife at Gavin's belt, then the helmet on the soldier's head. "How many others are with you?"

"Seven. All that's left of my company. Please, milord—just let me go in peace."

Croy stepped away from the man on the floor. He unbarred the door and cracked it open. Beyond he could see men peering back at him. They looked more frightened than Gavin. "You'll come inside one at a time, and drop all your weapons as you enter. At the slightest sign of treachery I'll cut Gavin to pieces. Understood?"

The men outside nodded eagerly.

Croy allowed them to file inside. They were filthy after days of crawling through mud and their pale faces had the haunted eyes of men who'd seen too much bloodshed. They obeyed his instructions, dropping even their belt knives. One had a shield. He made to hold onto it, but Croy smacked it with Ghostcutter so it rang. All of the men jumped at the sound.

"A shield's as good as a mace, in the right hands," he said. "Drop it."

The soldier did as he was told.

"Good," Croy said. "Now. There's soup in that pot. If you're hungry."

Six of them fell on the soup, making cups of their hands in the absence of proper bowls. Only Gavin seemed able to resist. Perhaps because he'd seen something so astonishing he'd forgotten his appetite.

"Sir Croy," he said, after a moment. "Is that—"

"Aye," Croy said, moving to stand over the sleeping form of Ulfram V. "This is your sovereign. You see now why I am so careful about what guests I entertain."

Two of them men at the pot broke away to kneel and make the sign of the Lady on their breasts, the proper form of reverence for men of their station. The rest were too hungry—or not devout enough—to stop their feasting.

"He's wounded," Gavin said, his eyes wide.

"He sleeps. I cannot rouse him. Were any of you apothecaries or herbalists, before you became soldiers?"

The men stared up at him in incomprehension. No, of course they hadn't been healers. Croy's luck wasn't running in that direction, these days. They had probably been farmers, like ninety-nine men out of a hundred in Ulfram's army. Like ninety-nine of every hundred men in Skrae. Farmers conscripted, given a day or two's training, and then armed and put to service before they knew what was happening.

Croy turned away from them. "Eat, Gavin," he commanded. "What was the last food you had?"

"A bit of bread three days ago," the soldier told him. "Thank you, milord."

Croy nodded. While Gavin went to the soup pot, Croy sat down by Ulfram's head. He placed the point of Ghostcutter against the earthen floor and leaned on it, his forehead resting on the pommel. "What news have you of the war?"

One of the men—not Gavin—answered. "War's lost," he said, shaking his head. "The barbarian has all this land for himself, and none dare oppose him."

"I saw them sending riders toward Redweir. Scouts before an invading force," Croy said. "They don't think it's over yet."

The soldier threw up his hands. "I never been to Redweir.

Don't know nobody down there. Why should I care what happens to them?"

Croy closed his eyes for a moment. If he could trust these men, if they could stand watch while he slept—but no. Not yet.

"Has any man seen Sir Hew, or Sir Rory?" he asked.

The soldiers looked at each other as if afraid to answer. "Everyone says they perished in the rout," Gavin answered, between sips of lukewarm soup. "Of course, they say the same of you, milord. And—and your master, there."

"They think him dead?" Croy asked, suddenly looking up. That might actually be the first bit of good news he'd heard. If the general wisdom was that the king had died in the battle, then perhaps the barbarians thought so, too. At the very least that would mean they weren't actively looking for him.

"Good, good," Croy said. "We'll let them think that until we're ready to surprise them with the truth. When we've gathered our men in secret—all those who survived the battle. All those who would stand under the king's banner. There must be others like you, others who fought and were defeated but not destroyed. Others ready to rise again, true men of Skrae, bloodied but not beaten, and when—"

He stopped because he'd caught the men looking at each other again. Like they shared a secret they didn't want to give him.

Croy frowned, but said nothing for a while. He waited until the men had finished eating. Then he asked, quite carefully, "Where was your company posted, during the battle?"

Gavin looked away as he answered. "We were billeted in the western part of town, in an old almshouse. We didn't get word that the battle had been joined, not until the barbarian was already inside the gate."

Croy nodded. "And when word did come, that the fortress was in full distress. Where did your serjeants send you, then?"

Another conspiratorial glance.

Croy knew what their shared silence meant. These men

had not been part of the fighting. They had probably never had a chance to draw their weapons. If they escaped Helstrow before the barbarians took the western gate, then they must have left even before Croy fled with the king over his shoulder.

These men weren't battle-hardened veterans. They were deserters.

"Never mind, don't answer," he said. There were some things he didn't want to know. Like whether Gavin and his men had deserted the fortress unhindered—or whether they'd had to fight and perhaps kill their own serjeants before they were allowed to go. Whether they were craven cowards, or, much worse, traitors.

Either way he knew he would not be sleeping for some time yet. He couldn't leave the king's safety in such hands.

Honor—the vows he'd taken—the principles on which his life was built—all demanded that he bring these men to justice, if they were guilty. That he slay them on the spot. That was the penalty for desertion in every army Croy had heard of.

But the fortunes of war could play havoc with honor, he thought. Fear could do strange things to a man's heart. So he decided to temper his anger with mercy. He would watch Gavin and his crew closely—but he wouldn't slay them in the name of justice, not yet. Not until they'd had another chance to prove themselves.

"The past is the past. You're here, now, and that's what matters," he said. "Here where you can still serve your king. We'll need to make a litter for him, something two men can carry. We won't get far if I have to keep him over my shoulder."

"Milord," Gavin said, carefully, "you aren't thinking of going out *there*," he said, pointing toward the door, "when we've safety and warmth right here?"

"Just as soon as we've all had a chance to rest," Croy told him.

The war wasn't over. Not while Ulfram V still lived.

CHAPTER THIRTY-EIGHT

The river Skrait twisted through Ness, carving its way between Castle Hill and the Royal Ditch before diving straight for Eastpool. There it widened out to make a natural haven for river boats. The land on either side of this harbor, also called Eastpool, was a district of tar-stinking wharves and low shacks. It gave home to the fish market by day and a steady trade in the seedier commodities after dark. It was a natural magnet for thieves, yet Cutbill's charges rarely ventured there alone, since its quays and unpaved lanes were patrolled constantly by rivermen carrying spikes and harpoons—men who did not trust the watch to keep them safe.

In Malden's experience there had been no time of day or night when Eastpool was not crowded with fishwives and burly salters, with sea captains and pirates looking for a place to lie low. Now, though, like all the Free City, it was a desolate wasteland, almost untenanted. He saw a few women gathered around a jug of strong spirits. They were watching the fishing boats that had been pulled up on the banks and turned hull-up to resist the sun. He saw a few confused-looking sailors, just in from far ports of call and unknowing of the war or the game fate was playing with Skrae. Yet in many of the twisty ways he passed through, under the shade of half the shanties in Eastpool, Malden was alone.

He headed down the Ditchside Stair toward the water and there he was able to hire a rowboat from a one-armed man who looked very glad for his custom. Yet when Malden told him where he wished to row to, the boatman scowled and demanded a deposit on guarantee of return.

"I shall be quite welcome there, I assure you. I'm known there, and fondly," Malden told the man, but failed to convince him.

"There's those in this world like their privacy, and Coruth, she don't welcome nobody," the boatman insisted. "Even old friends."

Malden sighed and turned over an extra shilling, which he doubted he would get back even if he returned the boat in perfect condition. The boatman would probably insist the rowboat had been contaminated just by coming in contact with the Isle of Horses.

It mattered little. If Malden was truly master of the guild of thieves now—*ha*, he thought, *it's but some trick Cutbill's playing*, as he'd been thinking all day—then he could afford the surcharge. He leapt into the little boat and grabbed up its oars.

He'd never cared much for rowboats since you couldn't see where you were going when you rowed. Yet this time he was almost glad to be pulling himself backwards across the Skrait's slow current. The Isle of Horses was none too easy on the eyes. It had been named for a calamity long passed, during a very rainy year when the Skrait had swollen and flooded its banks and been far too wild to navigate. Still, ships had tried, for Ness was the richest port in Skrae, and paid well for cargo. One ship had foundered just inside Eastpool, run aground on a shoal. It had sunk with all hands and all its goods aboard, yet somehow a consignment of horses had managed to escape the wreck and make their way onto the only available piece of dry land. Every attempt to retrieve the animals had failed in the foaming water of a bad storm, and for days the people of Eastpool had been forced to listen to the screams of terrified beasts as the water rose and rose, every hour coming a foot closer to washing the island away altogether.

The island had survived, but no one found any trace of the horses when the storm had passed. The locals considered the tiny scrap of land haunted now, and neither landed there nor used it for any purpose. It had been one of the few uninhabited parcels of land inside the city's walls, and that should have made it invaluable as the city's population grew and crowded every available square foot. Yet no one had ever tried to live there—until Coruth had claimed it for her own.

Barely six feet above the water at its highest point, the

Isle of Horses was choked with gorse and bramble. Coruth's house was its only salient feature, a shack made of driftwood from which odd lights were often seen by night, and from which sometimes noises issued that could not be explained. The perfect home for a witch.

Malden pulled at the oars until his boat grated on the rocky beach below the house. Because he had not announced his arrival—he knew no way to contact Coruth save to knock on her door—he stood a while in the boat, letting himself be seen, before he stepped down onto the strand.

When there was no response from the house, he tried calling out, shouting that it was Malden and that he wished to speak with Coruth. That elicited no response, either.

So he jumped down from the boat, onto the pebbled shore, and started walking toward the house.

He'd taken no more than a half dozen steps before a rope, half-buried in the pebbles, shifted under his foot as he trod on it. Instantly he felt the rope shift as it took up tension and he cursed silently. A trap—a trap he should have seen, because this was no magical ward. It was one of the simplest traps he'd ever encountered. The rope stretched away toward a post to which hundreds of cockle shells had been loosely nailed. As the pressure of his foot tightened the rope, it waggled the post and the shells chimed together—a soft, pleasant sound that was lost in the sighing of the wind. Malden had tripped enough alarms in his life to know someone would hear it.

CHAPTER THIRTY-NINE

Walking through the brambles surrounding Coruth's shack was disincitement enough, Malden thought, to keep most intruders away. Yet he now knew there would be other, less passive guardians to deal with. He tried to be on his guard.

Yet when a horse snorted close to his left ear, he still jumped. He wheeled around, half expecting to see some spectral animal gnashing its big ghostly teeth at him, but there was nothing there.

Malden had dealt with the supernatural often enough to respect it, and to avoid it whenever possible. He was willing to give up, to return to his boat and row away, his original purpose thwarted. He would come by at some later date when Coruth was prepared to receive him. However when he tried to retrace his steps toward the shore, he heard a great rumbling thunder of hooves treading the flinty soil, directly between him and his rented boat.

"Alright, witch—show me how to leave, that's all I ask," he said aloud.

The neighing of horses all around him was like laughter.

He could see nothing. The ghosts of horses left no hoof prints in the soil, it seemed. Nor could he smell any animals. Yet whenever he tried to lift a foot, or move his hands, he heard them all about him as if they were pressed very close, ready to stampede and trample him.

If he remained very still, he thought, perhaps he would be safe. Perhaps the ghostly trap was only meant to keep him where he was, until such time as Coruth chose to collect him.

But then he heard the noise of a great charger come running straight toward him, every hoof falling like thunder. He could hear its great infernal breath snorting in and out of its undead lungs, even hear the brasses slapping and ringing on its sides. If he didn't move, if he didn't flee, it would surely run roughshod right over him—

—unless, of course, this was one of those traps that only fooled you into thinking you were in danger, when in fact you were perfectly safe the whole time. Typically such traps were designed to startle you into running away, right into an actual hazard you could have easily avoided.

Malden tried to stand his ground. Yet as the sound of the galloping horse came closer and closer, never deviating in the slightest from its course, clearly intent on his destruction, even Malden's devious brain stopped thinking, and started reacting.

Shouting in his fear, he turned and ran.

Horses were on either side of him, their heavy feet crashing down so fast and so frequently he was certain they would step on him at any moment. He felt their hot breath on his neck, could hear nothing but their whinnying and snorting and the enormous noise of their rhythmic running. He threw his arms over his head for protection and ran he knew not where. If he ended up running right into the cold waters of Eastpool, that was fine. If he was being herded back to his boat, he would give great thanks, if—

—something very solid and very real smacked into his face and nearly broke his nose. When he dared open his eyes again he saw he was standing on the porch of Coruth's shack in the middle of the island. He'd run right into her front door.

He could no longer hear the sound of horses from any direction. The salt wind barely moved through the thorny vegetation behind him. The silence was like deafening laughter, and he felt his cheeks grow hot.

Then the door of the shack opened with a creak. Light and warmth spilled out across him, and then Cythera was standing before him, speaking his name, a look of utter confusion on her face.

He grabbed her up in a feverish embrace and kissed her deeply. She did not resist—not here, where there was no one to see it.

"What are you doing here?" she asked.

He kissed her again.

"Sweet kisses," she laughed, "do not an explanation make."

"Just glad to be alive," he told her. "Your mother's illusory guardians are most compellingly believable."

"The horses?" she asked.

"The horses," he said. "Though—now that I can think again, I have to wonder. Why not something more immediately frightening? Like basilisks, or demons?"

"I seem to remember the first time you sat a horse," Cythera laughed. "You were certainly frightened then!"

Malden smiled. "It wouldn't stop moving. I was certain I would fall."

Cythera laughed again. "If you must know, witchcraft doesn't work that way," she told him, ushering him inside. "Certainly a sorcerer could create the illusion of dragons swooping down, spitting fire, or whatever the sorcerer could imagine to scare away interlopers. Sorcery draws power from the pit and its denizens, but they have to be repaid for their gifts—you've seen the way they distort a sorcerer's soul."

"Not to mention his face," Malden said, thinking of some of the sorcerers he'd met. No natural deformity could match the freakish countenances of wizards. In public, they always wore black veils to hide their features.

"Witches use the power of the world around them. They make subtle changes in what is already there, that's all. This is the Isle of Horses, so horses it must be."

"I see," Malden said, though as usual when someone tried to explain magic to him, he had the creeping suspicion that the parts that seemed to make sense were only glosses on a text far beyond his comprehension. "To actually answer your question," he said, putting matters of philosophy aside, "I've come to see your mother."

"You've met someone else," Cythera said, teasingly. "You want to buy a love spell. Or is it revenge you want—on me for being such a fickle lover?"

He smiled. She wasn't normally this playful. "Neither, my leman. You're the only woman in all Skrae who can catch my eye, and I love your contradictions as much as I love your deeper constancy. But tell me—what's put you in such a good mood?"

Her smile fell for a moment, but then it returned. "Mother's been scrying. Watching the land around Helstrow, specifically."

"A grisly sight to behold, I'm sure," Malden said, thinking of what the barbarians must at that very moment be doing to the farmland around the royal fortress.

"I didn't ask for details. I only wanted to know one thing, and I got the answer I was looking for. Croy still lives."

"Does he?" Malden asked.

"Don't look so dismayed. When he finds out about us he'll be wrathful, but for now he thinks of you as his best friend. Here, sit down. I'll get you a cup of tea. Mother will be out in a moment, once she's finished with her working."

Malden sat down and watched her head through another doorway into what appeared to be a kitchen. The shack was quite different from what he'd expected. He had imagined a cauldron bubbling over a fuming fire of brimstone. Bits of various animals, hacked off and dried and hanging from the ceiling by bits of string. Perhaps bones everywhere, or instead thousands of glass bottles holding weird and unknowable substances. A pile of books with a human skull on top as a paperweight. He would not have thought a stuffed reptile or two would be remiss.

Instead he was sitting in a very tidy, very plain parlor. The chair he sat in and the few other sticks of furniture in the room looked well-made but simple. There was a fire in a hearth but it glowed the cheery orange of normal, healthy, burning wood. There was only one sign that he was in the receiving room of a terrifying witch, and at first glance it seemed wholly innocuous: a bucket sat on a table at the far end of the room. Malden got up and glanced inside it, sure he would find frogs brains or skinned ghosts or the blood of virgins set to congeal—the kinds of things a witch would collect and use in her spells.

Instead the bucket held a half dozen long, pale roots, parsnips perhaps. Maybe Cythera had collected them to make her mother's dinner. Malden was slightly disappointed. Yet when he looked closer he saw the roots were strangely bifurcated, so that each of them seemed to have legs and arms. Indeed, they looked almost like human bodies. One even had a crude mouth and a pair of wrinkles that might have been eyes. Malden started to reach for one of the roots, but before he could touch it he jumped back in terror. He was certain one of those wrinkles had opened—and a blind, milky eye had peered back at him.

Coruth came storming into the room, then, her iron-colored hair flying all around her head. "Whoever you are, it'll mean your life if you touch that!" she screamed.

CHAPTER FORTY

M alden moved out of the way as Coruth swept into
the room, her long dress whirling around her. She
went to the bucket and bent low over it, speaking incantations
he couldn't follow. The words were in no language he knew,
but he swore they sounded more like a mother soothing a
crying baby than a witch invoking dark powers. Malden
pressed himself up against the wall and tried not to move.

"Who are you? Why are you here?" Coruth shrieked,
spinning around to face him. Her eyes didn't focus on his
features, however. They didn't seem focused on anything.

"Coruth, it's me, Malden," he said.

"Malden?" she asked, as if trying to remember the name.
Then, "Malden!" Her eyes snapped to his face and her mouth
curled in a warm smile. She rushed to embrace him with
something like fondness. "So very good of you to come,
my boy. So very good of you to visit an old woman and
her spinster daughter."

"Mother!" Cythera said, from the door. "Malden, please
forgive her. She was very far away there, for a moment."

"Seeing," Coruth agreed. "Far seeing. Dangerous stuff."
Coruth dropped into a chair and put her legs up on a table.
Leaning her head back she exhaled noisily. "You can get
lost so easily, when you're that far from your body. And of
course there's no guarantee you'll like what you find.
Malden," she said, leaning toward him, "how fare you? I
haven't seen you in quite a while."

"I live, which is something I'm always grateful for,"
Malden said with a shrug. "Beyond that, it seems the wheel
of luck turns for us all. Helstrow has fallen, and—"

"Redweir will be next," Coruth announced. Her mouth
tightened into a defensive scowl. "The barbarians move

quickly—that's one of their greatest tricks. They are not hampered by complicated supply lines, for they ravage every land they cross, and provender themselves on the spoils. Each chieftain commands his own clan with great autonomy, so there's no need for companies to sit in garrison waiting for orders from on high." She shook her head. "Redweir will fall. But they won't stop there. They'll turn west. They'll come here."

Malden felt all the blood rush out of his face. "You've . . . seen this? With the second sight?"

"Don't need to," Coruth said, waving one bony hand. "It's just logical. Everyone here knows it's coming. That's why anyone who could has already left." She gave him a shrewd look. "Cutbill, they say, even Cutbill has fled."

Malden was slightly shocked that Coruth even knew Cutbill's name. Yet he supposed a witch might know anyone—and know their business, too, and more than they care for her to. He nodded. "Yes, I learned that just a short while ago myself."

"And with him gone, who will minister to the thieves?" Coruth asked.

Had it been anyone else, Malden would have lied. No need advertising his new position—that was likely to get him killed or arrested. This was Coruth, however. She would see through any falsehood. "As a matter of fact," he told her, "that's why I came to speak with you. He left me in charge."

Coruth's eyes widened and her smile returned. She did not seem surprised that Cutbill would choose Malden as his successor. "Did you hear that, Cythera? He's a guildmaster now! A man of position. You could do a lot worse."

"I take it you know that Cythera and I have . . ." Malden said. Or tried to say.

"I know all, see all," Coruth said, with a twinkle in her eye. "If she wishes to marry you I won't stop her. That's her decision to make."

"Right now, I've decided to see to our supper," Cythera said, and hurried into the kitchen.

For a while Coruth and Malden sat in silence. Eventually the witch took a pouch from her belt and spilled its contents into her hand, what looked like dried fruit. Malden would not have ventured a guess as to what it actually might be. Coruth took one of the desiccated things and tucked it under her tongue.

"You didn't come for advice on love," the witch said, quietly.

Malden took out the page he'd torn from Cutbill's ledger. "No," he said. "I came to ask your help with this. It's some kind of cipher, but I can't make odds or orts of it."

Coruth nodded and studied the paper carefully for a while. Then she brought it to her face and sniffed the paper. Rubbed it between her fingers and listened to the way it squeaked. "No magic to it. Nor would I expect such from Cutbill."

"Why not?"

Coruth smiled. "Because then I could have read it for you as easily as if it were written in plain Skraeling. No, this cipher is meant to be broken the hard way. He meant you to work this out on your own."

"I may not have time for that. I have to meet with his— rather, with my thieves tonight. I need to tell them something, give them some direction. Otherwise they'll think I'm just a puppet, someone to keep the books while Cutbill's gone. If I want them to actually follow my orders, I need them to know I can actually give some."

"Then you have your work cut out for you," Coruth said, handing the page back to Malden. "This message isn't for me, at any rate. He would not have enciphered it had he wished someone else to read it. I can't solve your riddle, Malden. But I can show you how it is to be done, if you like."

"That would be most kind," he said. "I can pay you, of course, for your trouble."

"No, you can't," Coruth said. "I won't take your money. You saved me from eternal imprisonment once Malden, and I will not forget that." Coruth gave him a smile that looked almost matronly. "I may be your mother-in-law some day, as well."

"I won't ask for Cythera's hand as some kind of reward," Malden said. "She'd never love me, not truly, if she thought

I'd bought her somehow." He shook his head. "No, she must decide to take my hand freely."

"Good man. Now," she said, "before Cythera has finished cooking for us—you will stay to eat, won't you?—let's discuss ciphers, and their proper use, and how they can be broken."

CHAPTER FORTY-ONE

When dinner was finished Malden took his leave. He was all smiles and graces, and he even bowed and kissed Coruth's hand to thank her for what she'd taught him. Cythera stood in the doorway of the kitchen and smiled to see her mother turn her head away like a bashful girl. The two of them got along so well.

Cythera imagined a different life, then. One where she never became a witch, but instead became Malden's wife. If she imagined it in the abstract, as just a hypothetical situation, it didn't hurt nearly as much as she'd thought it would.

Malden stood up straight and looked across the room at her, and her heart melted a little when she saw the look in his eyes. He loved her—truly, honestly. He didn't want to lock her away in a tower somewhere and fill her stomach with his babies. He wanted her to be happy.

When he was gone Cythera went and washed the dishes and got things ready for the morning, banking the fire in the hearth and laying out the oats she would cook so she and Coruth could break their fast. Then she walked out into the main room and found her mother sitting at the table. A large book sat before her, though she wasn't reading it. Wasn't even touching it. It didn't look like any book Cythera had seen in her mother's house before. The cover was tooled leather ornamented with skulls and bones, and a small brass lock held it shut.

"What's that?" she asked, because she knew she was supposed to.

Yet Coruth didn't answer right away. "The boy is becoming a good man," she said. "He'll rise higher yet. Looks like he'd be good in bed, too, with those long thin fingers and the way he moves."

"Mother, please, my love life is of no concern to—"

"Don't be squeamish with me, girl. I know you've had him before."

Cythera blushed and turned back toward the kitchen, just wanting to get away. But she knew she wouldn't be allowed to just retire to bed. That book meant something.

"There's little enough sweetness in this life that we can afford not to taste honey for fear of bee stings," Coruth said.

Cythera sighed. "He can't be mine, though. Not if I'm to be a witch."

"Not forever, no. But you have a little time left to spend with him before your initiation. If you throw away that chance you will regret it later." Coruth sounded like she knew that from personal experience. Cythera knew little of her mother's life before Hazoth kidnapped and imprisoned her. She'd never really thought about it before.

"Mother," she said. "What if I simply renounced magic?" She didn't believe it could be that easy. But what if it was?

"It's in your blood. And in your future. Come here."

Cythera had no choice. She went and sat across the table from her mother.

"This book belonged to your father."

Cythera nodded. Yes, that was exactly what it looked like. She remembered Hazoth's library. It had been full of tomes like this—and far stranger and more sinister books as well.

"When his villa came down most of his books were destroyed, but not this one. I saved it and brought it here so it wouldn't fall into the wrong hands. Read it."

"Now? It's getting late."

"Leaf through it, then. Skim it," Coruth ordered. "It's all you'll get of an inheritance from him, after all."

Coruth didn't move or speak any incantations, but the book slid across the table toward her, as if of its own volition. The brass lock clicked and popped open, and the cover lifted and fell back until it was open to the title page:

CHILDREN of the PITTE, or-
The Boke of Fouel Names

Writ by the hand of
Daulben of Myraum

Cythera couldn't help but gasp. She'd heard of this book before. It was a basic treatise on demonology, the first work any prospective sorcerer would have to read. "No witch should look at something like this," she said.

"This isn't part of your training. It's in way of an explanation," Coruth insisted. "Now. Read."

Cythera reached a trembling hand to turn the first page. She looked at the dense block of words there as if they might come to life and jump out at her. But they were just words. She read the opening chapter quickly, barely paying attention to the warnings it contained, much more interested in the promises it made. The author suggested that someone who could call demons up from the pit would possess powers beyond imagining. Demons could fly around the entire world in one night. They could find things that had been lost for centuries. They knew the secrets of anyone who had ever died, and they could slay any enemy without fail. A master— or a mistress—of demons could make themselves rich beyond imagining, they could rule nations, they could possess any lover they chose.

They could marry anyone they chose.

Daulben had been a sorcerer, though not a particularly powerful one—nothing like her father. His words suggested such things as he described must be done with caution, but that they were not truly forbidden. Demons were evil creatures but they could be turned to helping humanity as well.

They could heal the sick, or make crops grow in stultified deserts. They could teach a sorcerer how to do great and compassionate works as easily as they could give them dark secrets. Put that way, sorcery didn't seem so bad. It certainly didn't seem evil in itself.

The rest of the book was full of incantations Cythera didn't dare to read even silently, even to herself. Some of the names the book listed had power even if they were simply thought with the right intention. There were woodcut illustrations of various famous demons as well, which she flipped past as quickly as she dared. Demons were unnatural things and not wholesome to human eyes.

Coruth got up and moved around the room while she read. Though Cythera was barely aware of it, her mother replaced candles as they burned down and stirred the fire when the room grew too cold. It seemed neither of them would sleep that night, as Cythera grew so absorbed in the book she couldn't even look up.

When she reached the end, and closed the cover once more, she found she was so stiff and tired she could barely rise from the chair.

Coruth, on the other hand, had never looked more lively. She came around the table to lean close to Cythera's face. "Seen enough?" she asked. "Tempted yet?"

Cythera blinked and rubbed at her eyes. She had already figured out why Coruth wanted her to read the book. "You said if I was not trained as a witch, I would end up committing some horrible sin. Something unforgivable. This is what you saw, wasn't it? You glimpsed my future and you saw me becoming a sorceress. Like my father."

Coruth nodded. "Yet I also saw it was not writ in stone. There is a chance you can avoid that mistake. You'll need discipline, though. And before you'll truly believe me you'll need the second sight. You'll need to see your own future. Only then can you resist the temptations that are to come."

"I'm your daughter," Cythera insisted. "I don't need to be convinced! I know you see truly." She pushed the book away. "I didn't want to know these things. You forced me to read this."

"You're my daughter, and my responsibility," Coruth said, ignoring her words. "You're Hazoth's daughter as well. You have it within you to gain just as much power as he had. More, perhaps. You could be a great woman."

"I'm going to be a witch," Cythera said. Coruth had been right all along. There couldn't be any other way.

"Witches have power as well," Coruth told her. "All the things the demons can do, all the promises in that book. How many of them do you think I could accomplish, if I set my mind to it, using only witchcraft and abjuring sorcery?"

Cythera knew the answer. She'd never quite believed it, but Coruth had told her many times before.

"None of them," she said.

Coruth snarled. "You think me impotent compared to *him*?"

"No," she said. "But I understand the difference between you. He worked magic to satisfy his desires. To get what he wanted."

"And me?"

"You are a witch, mother. You don't have desires. You have responsibilities. The magic you work isn't to make your life easier, or to gain power. It's to do the bidding of forces larger than you. To do the work of fate and destiny. That's what witchcraft is. Not power to be squandered, but a willingness to surrender. To do what must be done, whether you like it or not."

"You've learned the words," Coruth said, "but I can see in your eyes you think it's nonsense."

"No—no, I—" She stammered to a stop. Changed tack. "I would never perform sorcery, mother. Certainly not now."

"In the court of Ulfram V you were asked to do something 'witch-like'," Coruth said. "You made fire spring between your hands. Oh yes, I saw it. I was watching."

"The king wanted to frighten the barbarian princess, so I performed a little trick that father taught me. That was all. I did what I was told. Wasn't that proper?"

"A witch doesn't take orders from a man. Not even a king. Where do you think that fire came from, girl? Did you think you were doing witchcraft? That was the fire of the pit you played with. When you made it appear, you opened a small fissure between this world and the one below."

"You mean—"

"The pit, indeed."

Cythera trembled in terror. Truly? That was what she'd done? "But—something might have come through!"

Coruth shook her head. "No, the rift you made was too small. This time. Can you convince me you'll never try something like that again? Can you promise me?"

"Mother, I swear it! If I'd known I never would have done it!"

"You say it now. But there will be other temptations. And now that you've read that book you know how the power works. You know how to make even bigger holes between the worlds. Holes big enough for anything to claw its way through."

"I swear, Mother! I swear I won't!"

Coruth drew back as Cythera dropped her head to the table and wept. For a while the witch was silent, and simply stood watching her daughter cry. Then she nodded just once to herself.

"You know what your father was like. I know you remember. He didn't start out that way. There was a time when he was a good man who simply wanted to help others. And he did great things, truly. Over time, as he grew more powerful, he began to see other people as weaker than himself. Well, after all, they were. In time he came to despise them for that weakness. He began to think he was superior to them, not just a great man but some wholly different sort of being, a better being. His power grew, always, and theirs kept diminishing. They grew old and died while he stayed young and strong. That kind of power can't ever make a man a better person. In the end he locked me in a room for years, drawing on my power. He tortured you and used you, Cythera. Neither of us meant more to him than a single page of that book. No human being in this world was his equal, and he would have consigned them all to balefire rather than see one simple whim go unfulfilled. That is what sorcery does to those who use it."

"I remember," Cythera pleaded.

Coruth studied her carefully. "We begin your second lesson tonight. Before dawn it will be finished, and you will be well on your way to becoming a witch. Let me assure you of one thing before we begin. If I ever suspect that you are practicing sorcery, even for a moment—and no matter how pure your intentions—I will kill you on the spot. I will not hesitate a moment."

Cythera stared up at Coruth with wide eyes.

"I'm a witch. And I will do what a witch must," Coruth said. Then she left the room, leaving Cythera alone at the table.

With the book.

Cythera understood why. Coruth could have destroyed the book long ago. She could have thrown it on a fire and been done with it. Yet that wouldn't have made her point utterly clear. Cythera had to be exposed to the temptation. She had to know the kind of power that she could possess, if she only chose to use it.

Power. So much power between those covers. And wasn't that what she had wanted, all along? She had rebelled against the way women were forced to live in her world. She had refused to be someone's wife, because it would mean giving up her own freedom. Her own power to make her own decisions.

The book offered the power to do just that. And so much more.

Which was exactly why she had to choose not to use it.

Coruth had told her—many times—that witchcraft wasn't about making other people do your will. That was exactly what it should never be. A witch could try to convince others that she was right. She could show them the consequences of their actions. But she could never compel someone to do something against their will. Coruth had given her the book because in the end Cythera had to choose for herself.

It was crucial that she renounce that power on her own. And not just because of threats or warnings. Cythera had to come to the realization on her own that she was bound to be a witch, not a sorceress, and that was the right of things.

And it was. It was the right path, to push this book away. To burn it and forget she had ever seen it. It would be an important statement, a meaningful step on her path to initiation as a witch.

She didn't even want to touch the book again. But she picked it up off the table and went to the hearth.

A strange thrill went through her as she stood before the fire. Coruth had seen her practicing sorcery, somewhere in the future. A sorceress could marry anyone she chose. Cythera could have Malden for her own. He would never meet her eye again if she gave in to that temptation, Coruth had said. But with the power of demons at her disposal, Cythera could make him look on her. She could make anyone do what she wanted.

No.

She shivered, her whole body shaking as if she were consumed by frost, though the fire before her burned hot enough to singe the downy hair on her arms. She cast the book into the flames, the flames that could never burn so hot as the pit. She watched the book burn.

I will become a witch, she thought. *There is no other way. Malden—I'm sorry.*

CHAPTER FORTY-TWO

The thieves of Ness gathered just before midnight, when the moon had fallen behind the city wall, and Godstone Square was a bowl of ink. By starlight only they met, many of them staying to thicker shadows still, where even Malden couldn't see their faces.

Those he could see came from every corner of the city,

arriving alone, and they stood alone, not one of them whispering to a friend or an accomplice, none of them with eyes for anything but Malden on his perch.

He stood atop the Godstone, an ancient and desecrated altar deep in the Stink. A standing stone fifteen feet high that was just too big to be moved when the religion of the bloodgod was officially put down. To most of the City's population it had become nothing but one more landmark, but to some it was still an object of great reverence. Malden was more interested in where it was than what it had once been. The city watch rarely traveled that far from Castle Hill.

The people who lived around the square kept their windows shut at night, and could be trusted not to talk—as long as Malden didn't say anything the city watch might pay to hear. So he would name no names tonight, nor address any of the gathered thieves directly. But they would listen, and hear him.

He had not had time to decipher Cutbill's message. He didn't know what orders he'd been given, or what the guildmaster had expected of him. But he was out of time, and he had better think of something quick.

Nearly a hundred men stood below him, looking up. He studied their faces carefully and suddenly realized why Cutbill might have even considered him for this position.

He knew every man in the square. Knew their names, knew their specialties. He knew the difference between the ones in the dark cloaks—burglars and confidence men, good earners but rarely to be trusted—and those in poorer clothes, drab tunics and patched hoods: pickpockets, false beggars, dippers, silk-snatchers, boothalers, thimbleriggers, filchers and smash-and-grab men. Strictly small-time operators, who lived and ate on the pennies and farthings they managed to scrape together. Men for whom the guild was the only authority in their lives, and Cutbill the closest thing to a father any of them had ever had. Those men he could trust—as long as they accepted his ascension.

Many, from both sorts, he had recruited for the guild himself. Some of them still had grudges against him for how that had gone—entry to the guild was often by way of subtle blackmail or coercion. Some he could almost call his friends. He knew which were which, and who would speak against him when the time came.

He knew what these men wanted, and what they feared, and what they were willing to do to get the one and avoid the other.

And he could see, forming already in his mind's eye, the plots and stratagems that would neutralize his enemies and make his friends closer.

And despite the fact that he still didn't know what advice Cutbill had left him, he knew exactly what to say.

"Evening, men," he said, with a grin. "Thanks for dropping by."

Relief passed over many of the faces below like a cloud across the moon. They had been looking for something in Malden's countenance—perhaps simply confidence, or even just good humor—and they'd found it. Cutbill's disappearance must have left them all feeling vulnerable and exposed. Anyone who stepped up now and promised them continuity—that they had not just been hung out and left to dry—would at least get their attention.

"You've heard by now that the boss has scarpered. Gone south, perhaps, in search of better weather. Someone will have told you he chose a replacement before he left. Now, in most honest trade fraternities like the Coopers' Guild or the Bakers' Guild, there's simple rules for a change of leadership. There are practices to follow, formulae to keep. Our kind are different. We don't have that. Generally, when a guild like ours changes hands, there's those who see in it an opportunity to shake things up. Maybe pick a leader closer to their heart's desire, and back his number like in a dice game, laying bets for one man or another to win. That's when guilds like ours tear themselves apart—every man is for himself, at first, but that doesn't last long. Men with common interests form crews for protection from other crews. Crews get together and form gangs. But gangs don't make money. Gangs exist for one real reason, and that's to fight other gangs. You know who always wins in a war like that? The city watch. They just love it when a fraternity like ours turns on itself. Because they're lazy. In a war of gangs, they don't have to go chasing after villains in the night. They just need to come round in the morning and collect the bodies."

Malden watched the faces below carefully. He saw Velmont, at the edge of the crowd, looking away. He saw 'Levenfingers, sitting on a horse trough, nodding as if he'd seen it happen before, many times. The oldster probably had.

"We have a whole other kind of opportunity coming," Malden went on, "if we can just stick together. The Burgrave's about to ride out through Hunter's Gate with half the city trailing along behind him—including every single man of the watch. Oh, I have no doubt he'll leave a few one-legged halberdiers behind to watch his own stash. But we'll have our pick of jobs—empty houses are easy to burgle. Purses are child's play to snatch when there's no watchman eyeing your back. We all stand to make a pretty farthing.

"But only if we work together. That's why the old boss brought us in, remember? It's what he promised us. Work together. Work for each other, and we're all safer. We all get richer than we could on our own. Honor among thieves. The rest of the world thinks that's a joke. A thing that couldn't possibly exist. The old boss knew better. He also knew honor among thieves isn't free. It has to be earned. But where it exists, we're all safer. We're all a little wealthier. And we can all breathe easy."

Malden sat down on the top of the Godstone, his legs dangling in the air. He looked and saw Slag in the middle of the crowd, starting to raise one fist in the air. The dwarf wasn't the only one—but Malden knew that a half-hearted cheer now would hurt his cause more than help it.

He held up his hands for peace. "Don't answer me now. Don't say a word, anybody. Go home now. Or go to the tavern, or a bawdy house, wherever you might normally go at this time of night. I don't want lauds and acclaim—yet. I haven't given you anything yet but words, and we all know what words will buy you. What I want, is a chance to prove everything I just said. Give me that chance. And when the time comes, we'll all cheer together, for what we pulled off—together."

CHAPTER FORTY-THREE

A few murmurs drifted up from the crowd regardless of his plea for silence. Most likely the most vocal would be the naysayers, the rebels, the ones who hated Malden and wanted to take his place. It didn't matter. If he couldn't hear what they were saying clearly, that meant they weren't shouting it. Not yet.

One member at a time, the guild of thieves started filing out of the square. Some of them turned and gave him encouraging nods. Some left without looking back. When they were all gone, Malden started climbing down the Godstone. Though the sides of the obelisk were smooth, runes had been carved into the stone centuries ago and he found handholds enough if he took it slow. When he was six feet off the ground, he jumped the rest of the way and landed on the cobblestones as silent as a cat.

He did not intend to head straight home, though he had nowhere else in particular to go that night. He was certain that at least one spy had been amongst the crowd, someone who would report to the Burgrave what he had said. That was unavoidable. He figured if he went where the Burgrave expected him to go, he might very well arrive to find a watchman with a knife waiting at his door.

He considered a tavern, but knew he was tired enough already and that if he started drinking now he'd be asleep before the hour was out. Instead he decided to head out to the Lemon Garden, a brothel he knew out on Pokekirtle Lane. He longed for the companionship he'd find there. Not the traditional kind of companionship one sought in brothels, of course—Malden never paid for sex. But he'd been raised in a house much like the Lemon Garden, and some of the women there remembered his mother, who'd been a colleague. They would take him in and feed him and give him a soft and—if he asked politely—an empty bed.

He made his way quickly through the streets, headed for the Sawyer's Bridge that would take him down into the Royal Ditch. He kept to the street level rather than the rooftops only because it was darker on the cobbles.

Thus, when he realized he was being followed, he was a little surprised. He couldn't see his pursuer, but he could hear soft footfalls behind him. From more than one set of feet, too.

He frowned in the dark but didn't worry overmuch. He'd spent enough of his life running away from people that he felt confident he could lose this bunch. He ducked down the first alley he could find, a blind turning that emptied into a close—a clutch of houses built so near one another that in places their upper stories met above street level. Normally no one being followed would be so stupid as to enter a close, with only one way out. But Malden knew this particular close, and knew the ivy clutching to the walls of its courtyard was strong enough to hold his weight. He could climb to the roofs and be gone before his pursuers even got to the alley. They had no chance.

Except, of course, if they had a man waiting in the yard of the close, standing by a fire and holding a halberd in his hand. His cloak was embroidered all over with eyes, making him a man of the watch.

Malden backpedaled with all due speed, darting back out of the alley and up the first street that presented itself. The men who were following him started running to catch up. Just ahead, starlight showed Malden an intersection with a high street. Plenty of opportunities for escape there—

But before he could reach it, an elegant carriage pulled to a stop just in front of him. It was drawn by snow white horses and the driver wore fancy livery, though in the dark the colors were hard to make out.

The side door of the carriage opened and a man leaned out into the night. "Malden," he said, "I'd have words with you. Do my men really need to chase you all night?"

Malden swallowed, his throat suddenly tight.

He couldn't see the man's face in the dark, but he recognized the voice—and he certainly recognized the simple golden crown on the man's head. It was Ommen Tarness, the Burgrave of the Free City himself.

CHAPTER FORTY-FOUR

Perhaps there was a second reason why Cutbill had chosen Malden as his successor. Malden did run in certain influential circles. He was well know to be associated with Sir Croy, one of the most glamorous and famous men in Ness. He was rumored to be in league with the witch Coruth, the most powerful practitioner of magic in the city. And a few people knew that he had once performed a vital service for Ommen Tarness, the sole ruler of the Free City.

They probably figured that gave Malden some leverage. That maybe even Tarness owed him a favor. Too bad Tarness didn't see it that way.

Malden would rather have climbed into the carriage of Sadu the bloodgod Himself, and be taken at once down to the pit, than to have words with Ommen Tarness. But he got into the Burgrave's carriage anyway.

It wasn't like he had any choice.

Once the door was closed, the carriage started moving, bouncing wildly on the cobbles even though the driver wasn't pushing his team very hard. Malden grabbed for something to hold onto, but found only brocaded pillows.

"An impressive speech you gave, Malden," Tarness said, looking out the window at the pitch-black streets.

"You were there in the crowd?" Malden asked, knowing the Burgrave had been nowhere near. He considered suggesting that Tarness was the most successful thief Ness had ever known, but that would be impolite.

Tarness didn't answer his question, anyway. "Truly inspiring. Reminded me of me when I was your age."

There were only a handful of people still living who knew that Ommen Tarness was, in fact, an idiot. A near-mindless creature who couldn't dress himself. The man sitting across from Malden was merely a shell of a person. It was the crown that was talking to him. The crown contained the soul of Juring Tarness, the first Burgrave of the Free City. A man who had been dead for eight hundred years, but lived on by possessing his direct descendants. When Juring said Malden reminded him of a younger time, he was speaking of centuries past.

Malden chose not to comment on this fact. The Burgrave had a funny way of repaying people who knew his secret, even the ones who were willing keep it to themselves. It had only been the direct intercession of Cutbill that kept Juring from killing Malden on the spot. And now Cutbill was gone.

"I imagine you expected to see more faces around the Godstone," Juring went on. "There used to be twice that number of thieves in Ness, didn't there? But of course my recruiters don't ask questions when they hand out my gold royals. They take any man with two hands and a head—whether he's a thief or an honest workman. The past is obliterated when one signs on to my glorious campaign. Many, many of your thieves have already taken what I offer. How about you, Malden? Will you take a golden coin, and serve me by strength of arms?"

Malden shoved himself into a corner of the carriage and braced himself with both hands. He was starting to feel nauseous. "You can't afford to pay the men you already have," he said. Perhaps foolishly.

Juring laughed, however. "I have enough gold on hand to recruit. That's all I need for now. But rest assured, my men-at-arms will be paid."

Malden shook his head. "Not at that rate. Not every month. Even when you get this batch killed, the survivors will still bankrupt you. You would need to rob the royal treasury to keep those wages coming."

"You don't think the next king will happily pay to have his country back?"

"No," Malden said, "I don't. And I don't think you're such a f—such an optimist to go to war on the hope that he will." That had been close. He'd almost called the man a fool. That would have been a mistake.

Juring waved one hand in dismissal. "I didn't actually come for you in the middle of the night to discuss my finances."

Malden stared at the Burgrave. What was his secret plan? He must have some notion of where he'd find so much gold. If he defaulted on his promise, and failed to pay even one month's wages, his army would disperse on the spot. They weren't professional soldiers, used to waiting for their pay. They were greedy citizens of Ness, who lived by the credo of cash in hand. "Perhaps you expect to trounce the barbarians, and use the spoils of that victory to keep your army together."

"You think I can beat them quickly enough?" Tarness asked. He sounded as if he was looking for flattery. Well, Juring Tarness had been a great general, in his time. Back before the invention of steel, or plate armor, or the crossbow.

"No, I don't," Malden said.

"Neither do I," the Burgrave said with a sigh. "But enough of this."

Malden looked up at the crown on the Burgrave's head. You weren't supposed to argue with someone wearing such a piece of jewelry. The Lady's teachings said that such people were sacrosanct and infallible. They must be, since She had chosen them by hand. A crown meant—

A crown. Except the thing Tarness wore wasn't a real crown, it was just a coronet. Only kings wore real crowns.

"You didn't start recruiting until you heard the king was dead," Malden said, because he thought he had just pieced it together. "How long will it take for his heir to be elevated?"

Juring squinted at the thief. "Ulfram's only living child—a daughter—is fourteen years old. She can't be made queen for another four years. But what does that have to do with anything?"

"You wouldn't have to beg her for money to pay your troops—if you had her crown on your head already. You aren't putting this army together to drive off the barbarians.

You're going to seize Skrae for your own. Make yourself the new king."

"No! You haven't glimpsed my plan at all!" Juring shouted, and lunged forward to grab Malden by the throat. He did not, however, squeeze hard enough to strangle the thief. "There will be no queen. Nor will any man call himself king. No longer. I built this city, thief. I built it for free men. I will build a nation for free men, now."

Malden's eyes went wide. What could that even mean? The very concept was foreign to him. A country needed a king. That was what he'd been taught since birth. That was the only way he could imagine a country working.

"They'll make me their Lord Protector, because of what I've given them. All those who were once villeins, or worse—all those farmers who have been slaves in all but name their whole lives—will turn to me in gratitude. And they will *allow* me to rule in their name."

Ah, Malden thought. So nothing at all would change, except a few titles.

That made more sense.

CHAPTER FORTY-FIVE

"I have grand plans for the people of Skrae," the Burgrave said. "I will usher in a new age. But first I have to win this war. I need to drive off the barbarians before I can take Helstrow. And that's where you come in."

Malden shook his head. He couldn't speak, not with the Burgrave's hand on his throat.

Apparently, his voice wasn't required. "I need a symbol, Malden. I need something that will inspire my troops. They think of me as Ommen Tarness, a peaceful and rather fat functionary in service to a dead king. Not the kind of man who can save a country, or even govern one. They need to see that I am a warrior."

Malden shrugged. He had no idea what Juring was talking about.

"I need an Ancient Blade. And you have one you aren't using."

This was about Acidtongue? Malden could scarce credit it. "I don't . . . seem . . . to have . . . worn it . . . tonight," he choked out.

The Burgrave released him. Malden fell back amongst the pillows, gasping for breath.

"The seven blades are puissant arms," Juring went on. "But they are more than that. For centuries they have been identified with the greatest warriors of the age. When I wear one at my belt, my men will see me as anointed. A champion of virtue. What do you think of that?"

It sounded like piffle, honestly. Juring Tarness was eight hundred years old, and you couldn't live that long and become a little unstable. Had the soul in the crown finally come unhinged?

And yet—the idea wasn't completely ludicrous. Malden had seen the effect in person, after all. Croy's sword, Ghostcutter, was more than just a blade. When Croy drew it he got a certain respect. People who saw it stopped thinking he was an idiot and started taking him seriously. Of course, that might just be because it enabled him to cut them in half if they laughed at him.

Maybe Tarness did have a point. Maybe someone who people already respected—the man who was the ultimate power in Ness—could go far with an Ancient Blade in his hand. And Malden had never really wanted Acidtongue—Croy had forced it on him and just assumed he would suddenly turn into a noble warrior. Malden had drawn it maybe half a dozen times since then and he'd never actually used it to kill anybody. Certainly he'd never used it to its potential. He was a thief, not a swordsman. He could part with it and not miss it, truly.

Still. Just handing it over felt . . . wrong.

"What are you offering in exchange?" Malden asked.

The Burgrave laughed. "Are you under the impression that I owe you something? I've spared your life. That's all the payment you'll have from me. I don't negotiate with thieves."

"Then perhaps you should find some knight and buy his sword," Malden said. He reached for the handle of the carriage door, intending to leap out into the dark and get away. Before he could touch the handle, however, a flanged mace came crashing down where his hand would have been. Malden was fast enough to pull his fingers back, but he hadn't even seen the blow coming. He hadn't even realized the Burgrave was armed.

"I could simply take the blade. It doesn't properly belong to you," Juring said. His eyes were very calm. Malden was impressed. Normally men who tried to conceal their rage gave themselves away through their eyes. But Juring was in total control.

Malden had never cared for situations where someone else held all the cards. Luckily, he still had one up his sleeve. "The blade is safe. If you kill me, you'll never find it."

He tried not to think about the fact that a man could be tortured for days without killing him.

"I wonder where you hid it," Juring mused. "You have yet to go home to your little room since you returned to Ness, so it can't be under the loose floorboards there. Is it in the Ashes? In some deep part of Cutbill's lair? Or perhaps you put it in Coruth's care, on the Isle of Horses."

Malden frowned. Juring's spies must have been watching him all day, if he knew Malden's itinerary that well. Or perhaps the Burgrave had employed some wizard with a shewstone to track Malden's movements. Perhaps he had seen everything . . .

. . . but no. If that were the case, the Burgrave would already know where Acidtongue was. The sword wasn't guarded or even hidden particularly well—Malden had not thought anyone would want to steal it from him. It wasn't easy to get to, but any reasonably agile person could find it, if they knew where to look.

"I'll be riding out tomorrow morning, at dawn, at the head of my Army of Free Men," Juring said. "You'll present the blade to me then, before I reach the gates."

"And if I don't?"

Juring rapped on the roof of the carriage with his mace. The driver brought his horses to a stop in Market Square, just outside the entrance to the fortified part of Castle Hill. Juring's home. Men with torches came running from the gate—footmen in livery, but also one man in the silk robes of a major functionary. Malden recognized the robes, though not the man who wore them.

"Malden, please allow me to introduce Pritchard Hood," Juring said, as he stepped down from the carriage. "Bailiff of the Free City of Ness."

The bailiff bowed low—to his lord, not to Malden.

The thief studied Hood carefully. The position of bailiff was one of paramount importance in Malden's world. The bailiff was tasked with maintaining civic order, which made him the head of the city watch, and gave him free rein to arrest anyone he saw as a threat to Ness. In many ways the office of bailiff was the antithesis of Cutbill's position. The position Malden now held.

"Pritchard will remain here when I march out," Juring told Malden. "He will be my eye and my hand in my absence. He will assume all my normal powers. Pritchard, this is Malden, the master of the guild of thieves."

"Well met," Malden said, with a warm smile.

The bailiff sneered and looked away.

"Pritchard: as you know, the previous holder of your office, Anselm Vry, had an understanding with Malden's guild. He looked the other way when certain crimes were committed, and made a point of not hanging thieves whose guild dues were paid up. He did this with my tacit approval, for the thieves provided certain services I could not otherwise acquire."

"Our aim is satisfaction," Malden said, wearily. He had an idea he knew where this was going.

"Malden here is going to perform one of those services tomorrow. When he does so, Pritchard, I want to reaffirm my—silent—approval of this most unconventional arrangement. Of course, if he fails to do what I ask, that approval will not be forthcoming. In fact, should he fail me, I want you to arrest thieves of the guild on a distinctly punitive basis. I want them hanging from every gallows in the city. I want you to be tireless in your extermination of such vermin. And I will want you to make it clear, as plainly as you see fit, that this purging will be Malden's fault, and his alone."

"As you wish, milord," Hood said, and bowed again.

"Good night, Malden," Juring said, waving through the open door of the carriage. "My coachman will take you wherever you wish to go. Perhaps you should go home and get some rest. Don't sleep too late, though. I'll see you at dawn."

CHAPTER FORTY-SIX

The sky glowed a deep blue-black that made Malden's head hurt as he began to climb the spire of the Ladychapel, the tallest church in Ness. Lack of sleep was catching up with him. His hands ached as he pulled himself up onto a gargoyle in the shape of a toothy fish. His feet kept slipping on even the widest ledges.

Down below him, in Market Square, the Army of Free Men was forming up. The Burgrave's rotting battle standards snapped in the wind as men with drums signaled their companies to come together. The soldiers formed semi-orderly squares, their weapons leaning on their shoulders. Serjeants in the colors of the Burgrave walked up and down between the formations, flailing at their men with batons to get them into better lines.

Up on Castle Hill, behind the wall, a white horse was

being dressed in steel barding chased with silver. A whole train of sumpter horses laden with chests and barrels were brought around the side of the palace, while two oxen drew a wagon full of clanking iron—armor and weapons, presumably, an abundant panoply for the general who would lead all the men in the square.

As dawn drew near, the men kept coming. The thousand Malden had seen the day before marching in the Square were nothing to the numbers that arrived now. They filled Market Square to bursting, and overflowed into the streets beyond. They formed up in the cloister of the university and on the forecourt of the Ladychapel. They did their best to stand in orderly rows on the Cornmarket Bridge, even as mounted men raced back and forth between Castle Hill and the Spires, carrying messages or delivering loads of weaponry.

Malden found a perch on the steeple and sat down, head in hands, to watch. He still didn't know what he was going to do. As the first red ray of dawn painted the wall of the Burgrave's palace, he scratched his nose, then got to his feet and slipped inside the belfry.

Acidtongue was there, right where he'd left it. Hidden in plain sight of half the city. The swallows that nested up there had avoided it—perhaps birds were more sensitive to dangerous magic than men. There weren't any droppings or curled feathers on the scabbard. Anyone who could climb a ladder could have come up here and just taken it.

Why hadn't the Burgrave just had his thousands of men scour the city for the blade? That would have saved Malden the trouble of deciding. Now he was out of time. He must jump one way or another, and either give the Burgrave what he wanted or defy the man and risk everything.

A sword he didn't need. A sword he barely knew how to use. *Give it away*, he told himself, *and buy a little good will*.

Croy wouldn't like that, of course. To Croy, the Ancient Blades weren't just weapons. Croy considered Ghostcutter to be the manifest form of his own soul. And when he'd given Acidtongue to Malden, he'd assumed the thief would come to feel the same way. Croy had always intended to take Malden under his wing, to teach him the proper use of the sword and make a knight of him.

Malden could imagine few fates he'd relish less. But still . . . to Croy, the Ancient Blades were not commodities to be traded like coins. They *meant* something. And Malden didn't trust the Burgrave, not an inch. This free nation Tarness wanted to build—it was just the same old feudal system with different management. No question about that. The Burgrave could use all the pretty words he liked, but it came down to one thing: he was going to usurp the throne of Skrae. In the process he would start a civil war that would mean unending bloodshed and pain for the people he claimed to represent. And if Malden handed over the sword, he would be helping to make that happen.

But still . . .

Malden had a responsibility to the thieves of the guild, too.

If he didn't do this, Cutbill's men—Malden's men— would be hanged, one by one. That was the threat, and he understood it just fine. Hood, the new bailiff, would wipe the guild off the map. Long before he finished the last one off, though, Malden himself would already be dead. When the other thieves realized what he'd brought down on their heads they would turn on him. His life wouldn't be worth a farthing.

The sun showed half its disc over Eastwall. Orange fire traced the ribbon of the Skrait as it wound through the Free City of Ness. The old stones of the Spires, of the Golden Slope, and of Castle Hill were washed with yellow light.

Down in Market Square, the Burgrave rode out. Under the biggest and brightest of his faded banners, he rode in iron armor painted black with enamel, with silver filigree coating every inch of him, head to toe, in a convoluted floral pattern. Old-fashioned stuff, but that was the point. Ommen Tarness, the current Burgrave, wanted people to associate him with Juring Tarness, the ancient general and founder of the city. Bright red plumes bobbed on his shoulders and helmet, and he carried a lance pointed at the sky.

The assembled men cheered to see him, and together their voices roared like the ocean pounding on the shore.

Tarness had no retinue but the packhorses and wagons that followed after him. He had no knights to protect him, nor any priests to bless every prancing step of his horse. That would be intentional, of course. Supposedly he was just like all the men who followed him—free and equal. Maybe dressed a little better, but really, just one of the boys. It was hard to believe anyone would fall for such nonsense, but then in times of hardship—in times of war—every man clutched at straws.

Tarness stopped his horse and made a very brief speech Malden could not hear. Then he paused a while, and just sat there, looking left and right.

Malden knew what he was looking for.

Time to give it to him.

The decision was made. Malden had to accept it could never really have gone another way. The Burgrave was just too powerful, and too dangerous. Thwarting him would be suicide.

Malden's feelings didn't matter one bit. He had to do this, and he had to do it now. He would give Acidtongue to Tarness and let historians decide if he'd done the right thing.

He paused to let out one long, pained sigh. Then he leaned over and grabbed the hilt of Acidtongue where it lay in the belfry. Tried to pick it up.

The sword wouldn't budge.

Malden stared down at the weapon, confused. The thing was heavy, surely, but he'd lifted it many times before. He tried to pick it up again, with no better luck. Tried to pry it off the floor of the belfry. Heaved and grunted and sweated as he tried to lift it.

Acidtongue might as well have been fused to the belfry floor—or carved out of the stones themselves. It would not, no matter how hard Malden tried, shift even a fraction of an inch from where it lay.

Down in Market Square, the Burgrave made a gesture. Pritchard Hood came running over to take his lord's final orders.

"No," Malden said. "No! You fucking bastard, let go!"
But the sword wouldn't move.

In the Square, Hood nodded in understanding, and then headed back into the walls of Castle Hill. The Burgrave dipped his lance, and there was more cheering, and then almost every able-bodied man in Ness followed him as he trotted downhill toward Hunter's Gate, and glory.

Up in the belfry, Malden kept heaving and shoving and prying at the sword. Eventually, the last soldier cleared Hunter's Gate, and its massive doors were shut behind the army, and bolted, and locked up tight.

And only then—only when it was too late—did Acidtongue move. It came free from the floor in Malden's hand as if it had never been stuck.

"Sorcery!" Malden cursed, fuming with rage.

But even then he knew he was wrong. It wasn't sorcery that had bound the sword where it lay. It had been witchcraft.

CHAPTER FORTY-SEVEN

The air in Coruth's house felt like it had been replaced with thick jelly. Cythera gasped in great breaths of the thick stuff and stared at the candles around her. The flames burned low and greenish, as if they burned not wax but strange vapors. She was too weak to ask why, too weak to do anything but hold her head up as she slumped in a straight-backed chair.

Directly before her she saw her mother's face, framed by its wild iron-grey hair. Coruth's eyes met hers exactly, stare for stare. Then the old witch nodded, just once.

"Good," she said. "You did well."

Cythera struggled to speak. Every muscle in her body felt heavy and weak. What she'd done . . . what they'd done together made no sense to her. She had felt the power moving through the room, like a wind so subtle it could not even stir her hair, and yet so vast and world-engulfing she thought it might pitch all of Ness into the sea.

"Is . . . it . . . always . . ." she gasped. She couldn't finish the thought.

She didn't need to. "It will get easier. You'll learn to work with the natural currents and eddies of the ether, rather than fighting them. That is what a witch does. She works with what is already there. Do you understand?"

Cythera thought she might be starting to get it. And that terrified her.

"Was . . . it . . .?"

"Necessary?" Coruth asked. "You want to know why we thwarted your lover. It does seem strange, doesn't it? I like the boy. I did not choose this to inconvenience him, girl. I am not that petty. Close your eyes."

Cythera felt Coruth's thumbs touch her closed eyelids, felt her mother's fingers digging through her hair to her scalp. Coruth's nails were ragged and they scratched Cythera's skin. "I'm going to give you a vision now, child. Just a little glimpse."

What she saw then made Cythera scream for her mother to stop. War—bloodshed—bodies piled before city walls—fire lancing across battlefields—a sword—always the sword—*the* sword, Acidtongue, the one she'd enchanted just as dawn came up. The sword she'd touched with her own power. She saw the sword in a number of different hands, and knew she was seeing possible futures. She saw Skrae fall. She saw the barbarians driven back, cut to pieces as they screamed for mercy, and Skrae saved. She saw a war that never ended. All the images were superimposed one atop the other, yet she could make each one out distinct and so vivid it had to be real.

The hands that held the sword were all bloody, but Malden's hand—she recognized it instantly—was only flecked with gore, where others were stained so red they could never be washed clean.

"Nothing is necessary," Coruth said. "But some things are more devoutly to be wished for than others. The sword must stay with Malden. No matter what."

"Even if—he doesn't—want it?"

Coruth clucked her tongue. "This is the problem with being able to see the future. You see how little what people want matters. And you watch them make terrible choices, and do things you know they will regret. Malden will have no joy of that sword. But if he does not keep it everyone will suffer."

Cythera understood—though she wasn't sure she wanted to. Being a witch was about making hard choices. Or maybe it was about having no choices at all.

"Even if Malden keeps the sword, though," she said, close to sobbing now. She was certain she would collapse soon, and fall into black, deep sleep. She lacked the energy for anything else, but she could not rest until she knew. "Even if he—keeps it. I saw—I saw multiple futures where he still held it. Which one will come to pass?"

"That's not for me to say. It's up to you."

"Me?"

"There's a reason I demanded you start your training now. Malden will have a role to play in the shape of destiny to come. Yours will be even larger—and darker."

The look on Coruth's face was almost sympathetic, now. Cythera knew why, because she'd seen herself in those glimpses. She'd seen her own fate.

In some of those futures Malden put down the sword and took up a golden ring which he slipped on Cythera's finger. Those futures were already fading, receding as they became less and less probable.

In some—still bright and lucid, still distinctly possible—he turned away from her and they never saw each other again.

And in others just as real to her, he used Acidtongue to strike her down, to slay her, while tears rolled down his cheeks.

CHAPTER FORTY-EIGHT

Mörget whirled his axe through the air and brought it down hard against his makeshift pell—a block of fire-hardened wood driven into the ground. The axe bit deep into the post and he felt the bones of his arm flex and twist with the blow. The pell was already scarred in a hundred places and chunks had been taken out of its sides, revealing pale wood underneath.

He lifted the axe for another stroke.

He had, after all, nothing better to do.

At his back two thousand warriors cooked food or sang old drinking songs or sharpened weapons or gambled or fought amongst themselves. Most of them were drunk. It was the oldest barbarian remedy for boredom. But Mörget never touched ale or mead. He drank milk when he could get it, or water when he must. Unlike most people he never got sick from drinking well water. Whatever fate drove him would not let the flux or an ague bring him low. His abstemiousness made him a rarity among the eastern clans, and added to his fearsome reputation.

But it did mean he had to sit through every boring moment of a warrior's life (of which there were far too many) stone cold sober—and therefore prey to his own dark thoughts.

Two hundred yards away, the walls of Redweir loomed over him, blocking out the morning sun. Whatever architect or engineer had designed this place had done a better job than they did at Helstrow. The bricks of the wall were made of red sandstone, impervious to any weapon the barbarians had brought with them. The city's gates were sealed tight and barred with stout iron that would resist Mörget's battering rams. The defenders inside refused to be drawn out to fight for their city, despite constant taunting and the threat of a protracted siege. Though Mörget had been camped for three days outside the wall, well clear of arrow range, occasionally one of the soldiers inside would still come out on the battlements and fire a volley at them. The barbarians made sport of running out into the no-man's land to collect these missiles and then running back before the archers could nock another arrow. Only one man had been killed, when the defenders had been smart enough to send up two archers at a time.

Mörget's axe came down and chopped a scroll of wood off the side of the pell. His back ached with the effort. He prepared for another blow.

Before he could strike, however, he heard a hollow voice echo up from a hole in the ground near his feet.

"—mud in places I can't wash," the voice grumbled. "Mud so far down my ears it's coming out my arse."

Mörget set down the axe.

Balint and her sappers emerged from the hole, climbing wearily up a ladder to the surface. The dwarf's men were westerners—thralls now, recruited from the great mass of prisoners taken at Helstrow. They looked like their souls hurt worse than their backs. They carried mattocks and picks that they tossed on the grass as if they loathed the very touch of their tools.

"It's done?" Mörget asked.

Balint hauled the end of a rope out of the hole. "I used to live in this city, you know. There's a whole colony of dwarves in there, maybe twenty of 'em, all living together in a palace all their own. This is the only place in Skrae you can get proper dwarven ale before it goes flatter than a spinster's chest."

"Were you successful?" Mörget asked again.

Balint reached up to touch the spiked iron collar around her throat. Mörget had fastened it there himself, after he'd spared her life.

"Aye," she said, softly. She handed him the end of the rope.

Mörget hurried to attach the line to the harness of a team of oxen, big wooly beasts he'd had brought over from the eastern steppes. They could haul away the ocean, he'd been told, if you could find a way to chain it. Their drover lowered his goads and they started stumbling forward.

"You're a bastard, you know that?" Balint asked.

Mörget frowned, unsure of what she meant by that. Marriage was a rare occurrence in the east, and most children were born of passion, not wedlock.

"You know. A son of a bitch," Balint tried.

Mörget shrugged. He knew very little about his mother, actually. "The woman who birthed me was a thrall from the north. When they brought me to her, moments after I came howling into this world, she turned her face away, and then she died."

"After giving birth to a pillock as big as you," Balint said, "I would *want* to die."

"Death is my mother, now," Mörget said. He turned away from this cryptic debate and roared at the drover to redouble his efforts.

The rope Balint had brought him led down into a tunnel she'd been digging for three days. Its far end was attached securely to a series of supports directly under the wall of Redweir. She had so thoroughly excavated down there that the supports were the only thing holding that wall up.

The oxen hauled on the taut rope, digging their feet deep into the reddish soil. The rope creaked. The oxen lowed. If the rope broke—ah—but suddenly, it went slack and the oxen hurried away.

For a moment it seemed the rope had simply snapped, and achieved nothing. Then he began to feel the ground roll under his feet. Very good—it was done.

Mörget turned to face his army. He lifted Dawnbringer over his head and to a man, no matter how drunk they might be, they gathered their weapons and stirred. "Now," he said, as a deep rumbling noise began to sound from the tunnel.

The barbarians screamed and rushed toward the wall. The defenders, jumping up and down in their bewilderment, rushed to the battlements and started drawing their bows. A random volley of arrows swept toward the horde and a few barbarians were knocked down and trampled. Still Mörget's army howled toward the impenetrable wall. They weren't even headed toward one of the gates—just an unbroken stretch of red sandstone brick, as if they meant to dash their heads against it.

Before they reached the wall, it was gone.

It came down in a spectacular cascade of falling masonry and red dust. They swept through a cloud that choked them and brought tears to their eyes. They stormed over a pile of rubble that was still settling.

Of what happened then, numbers speak louder than words.

The garrison at Redweir numbered less than five hundred. Even the best-trained serjeant in that company had been a professional soldier for less than a year, and had held his command position for only a few months. At least a third of the defenders perished in the collapse of the wall.

Inside the town lived five thousand souls—workmen, scholars, children. These defended themselves to the best of their ability with whatever tools and cutlery they could find. None of them had any military training at all.

Against these forces were arrayed two thousand screaming barbarians, each of whom had been fighting since the day he escaped from the womb.

The streets of Redweir, cobbled in the ubiquitous red sandstone, ran bright with blood that day. The town had been built on top of a massive dam with a wide spillway. It would be an exaggeration to say the river Strow ran red as far as the sea—but it was definitely tinged with pink.

The fighting—the slaughter—went on for hours. It would not, truly, stop for days. Mörget led the way down the town's sole high street to the spiritual center of Redweir—its famous library, the largest collection of books and scrolls and manuscripts outside of the Old Empire. Mörget had been there once before, long before Cloudblade fell and the barbarians swept into Skrae. He had come seeking knowledge and had offered violence to no man. At that time he'd been treated as a curiosity, an exotic figure of disdain, because he had come alone.

Now he was feared more than all the demons in the pits.

The massive doors of the library were not built for defense. Mörget's men hewed them down with axes in a matter of minutes.

Inside a monk of the Learned Brethren stood waiting for him. He bore no weapons—such were forbidden to holy brothers—but he raised his hands in a gesture of defiance.

"You must not defile this place!" the monk shrieked. "If you burn this building to the ground, the knowledge of a thousand years will be lost! The works collected here can never be replaced. I warn you, barbarian. It would be a sin of the greatest magnitude."

Mörget laughed his booming, wicked laugh. "Fear not, little man," he said. "My father, the Great Chieftain, has already declared your books sacrosanct. He is a lover of learning, and I am bidden not to harm one page, not to deface one word of your precious collection. We need every book you possess."

The monk slowly lowered his hands. His face trembled with relief.

"We don't need any monks, though," Mörget went on. And then he brought his axe down in a whistling sweep, as he had a million times before.

CHAPTER FORTY-NINE

The bandit camp proved a sorry affair. Two dozen men holed up in a gorge, their weapons piled in a heap by a firepit. Broken bottles and gnawed bones littered the main entrance to the defile, a midden that would foul the only route of escape. High mossy walls of rock stood over the camp, making the screams of the captive women echo and resound.

The leader of the bandits was a big man with the soot-stained face of a former blacksmith. He had a bad scar under one eye that looked especially bright under the grime. He wore a leather vest over his tunic that was studded with iron rivets. Perhaps he thought of this as armor.

His men debauched themselves around the fire, too drunk to notice anything but their sport. They had stolen two women from a nearby village—after slaughtering the elderly menfolk—and brought them here for purposes Croy could guess at, but didn't wish to. The bandits had tied together the women's braids in a complicated knot so they were bound together. It seemed to amuse the bandits to watch the women struggle and pull at each other.

Kneeling atop the rock wall behind the camp, Croy lifted one hand, two fingers outstretched. With his other hand he pointed at the leader of the bandits. Then he dropped both hands.

Nothing happened.

Croy closed his eyes and tried to calm himself. His soldiers had not been properly trained. There had been no time. They probably weren't even watching for his signal. It occurred to him that the men he now led were little better than the bandits they were about to ambush.

He had not been given much choice while recruiting his company. His little band of deserters, Gavin and his men, had been the first and among the best organized. Most of the soldiers he'd found in the farmland around Helstrow had been alone, or working with a single partner, and they'd been near death from starvation or exposure when he found them. A little salt pork had been enough to buy their loyalty.

Croy stood up slowly, careful not to let his knees creak. He turned around and looked for the pair of archers—his entire missile corps—who he had stationed in the branches of a tree that leaned out over the gorge. The two men were chatting quietly, their bows not even strung.

Given six months and the proper equipment, Croy was certain he could turn these men into an effective fighting force. Lacking either of those things, he had to fall back on the last refuge of desperate serjeants everywhere—bullying his men into a pale semblance of proper order. He pulled Ghostcutter from its scabbard and hacked at the tree trunk. The branches shook and a few twigs fell from the upper boughs.

The archers grabbed tight to the tree and stared down at him as if he was mad. Croy stared back up at them in such a way to confirm that impression. Then he slowly repeated his hand signals.

One of the archers nodded, and strung his bow. The other, wanting to be helpful, handed his fellow an arrow from his own quiver.

Croy turned to look back down into the gorge. The leader of the bandits was urinating into the narrow creek that ran through the defile. The arrow took him in the neck, passing through his voicebox before it hit the stone wall behind the dead man and clattered noisily to the ground.

Croy's original order had been to put the arrow between the leader's feet, as a warning. He supposed he shouldn't be overly angry with this result.

The leader slumped forward into the water without making a sound. One of his followers, a gap-toothed bandit in a potter's smock, pointed and laughed. Maybe he thought his chief had passed out from strong drink. It was a dark night, and visibility would be limited away from the fire. Perhaps the bandit couldn't see the blood gushing from either side of the leader's neck. Or maybe he could, and still thought it was funny.

Croy called out, "Seize them!" At the trash-strewn opening to the gorge, his ten biggest men came rushing in with weapons bared. They roared like he'd taught them, a horrifying noise that sent some of the bandits sprawling in terror.

A few of the bandits had the presence of mind to make a dash for their own weapons. Before they could get there, Croy slid down a rope and met them with the point of Ghostcutter.

The bandits surrendered on the spot, kneeling before the Ancient Blade. Their eyes could not have been wider, and their teeth chattered in their heads, even though the fire did a passable job of dispelling the night's chill.

"I am the king's man, and you have broken the king's peace," Croy told them. He sent one of his men to untie the women from each other. "In less chaotic times, I would march you all to the nearest manor and have you tried for

what you did today in the village. You would all be found
wanting and you would all hang."

One of the bandits vomited down the front of his own
shirt. His eyes never stopped watching Croy.

"Right now, however, we are at war. There are rogues
and cutthroats worse even than your sorry selves out there.
I aim to drive them out of Skrae. To that end, I need your
help. If you're with me, come forth and kiss the sword."

Their greasy lips defiled Ghostcutter's blade. Croy's
conscience cringed at what he was doing. But it didn't matter.
A sword could be cleaned with water, or sand, or by wiping
it on a cloth. A kingdom could be cleansed only by the blood
of its brave sons—and for now, this lot would have to do.

CHAPTER FIFTY

Barbarian pickets controlled the road between Helstrow
and Redweir, but at night they were few and far between.
Croy led his rabble over the road under a thin crescent of
moon and hurried them through the fens toward Easthull,
home of the last living member of the king's privy council.

No lights showed on the manor—the windows had all
been covered in sackcloth, and the fires inside kept damped
to minimize the smoke they made. The track that split off
from the main road and headed to the Baron's house had
been carefully covered with autumn leaves so that it could
not be found unless you knew what to look for. On their
way to conquer Redweir, Mörget and his troops had passed
right by all of Greenmarsh without stopping. The Baron
didn't want to give them a reason to come calling on their
way back. Even Croy didn't see the manor house of Easthull

until he was a hundred yards from its low wall. He ignored the gate, chained shut with rusted locks to look like it hadn't been opened in years. Instead he helped his men hop over the wall like they were climbing a stile. Once on the other side, he signaled them to stop in place and make no sound.

A serjeant with a loaded crossbow came out of the dark and studied Croy's face carefully before nodding them in.

They went through the stables, where the last six trained warhorses in Skrae—as far as Croy knew—watched them with suspicious eyes. Once into the great hall, Croy breathed a sigh of relief and told his men to rack their weapons by the door and find something to eat. There was plenty of bread, and great cauldrons of pottage and bacon water. Simple stuff, but nourishing. Croy's best tactic for recruiting was the promise of a full belly, and so far he'd been able to deliver. Time, always the greatest enemy in war, had smiled on him in a small way. The law of Skrae held that the king could not conscript his subjects in autumn until the harvest was in. It had been a close thing, but the fields of Greenmarsh had been emptied of their bounty before the barbarians invaded. Now the Baron had full granaries that would see them through a winter campaign.

His men would not starve to death. It was something.

Croy shrugged off his heavy mantle and left it to dry on a peg by the hearth. Taking up a slice of bread smeared with butter and honey, he headed into the private chambers off the great hall and announced himself to the Baron's herald.

"Milord is still awake, and would receive you," the herald told him, "when you are fed and rested, of course."

"I'm ready now," Croy said, finishing his humble meal. Rested he was not, but then he hadn't slept more than a few hours a night since fleeing Helstrow. He was getting used to fatigue. He headed through the door to the Baron's closet, where the king lay on a camp bed, still unconscious. Ulfram's daughter Bethane knelt by his side, praying for his recovery. She was a good girl, as far as Croy was concerned, though her sheltered youth had left her ill-prepared for the role she now played.

"Is there any change?" Croy asked, as softly as he could.

Bethane shook her head. Rising to her feet she gave him a warm smile and opened her arms. He embraced her fondly.

He had never met her until a week prior, when he had first discovered that Easthull remained untaken. She had been hidden there before the invasion and had been crouching in a back kitchen, surrounded by old men and women armed with rolling pins. They had thought Croy and his recruits were reavers come to raid and pillage them, and Bethane had wept and wailed when he came and knelt before her, thinking he was simply mocking her before he cut her down. Even when he'd proven his bona fides to the Baron, still Bethane had feared Croy—he smelled of death, no matter how he smiled. Yet time had passed since then, and the fortunes of war make fondness grow even in hearts that cannot afford to be gentle.

"Was there any more fighting?" Bethane asked. "How many men do you bring tonight? Did you get close enough to see how Helstrow fares? Is there any news of my mother?"

Croy smiled and stroked the girl's hair. A month ago, Bethane's greatest concern in life had been with what color ribbons the ladies of the court should use to tie their sleeves. She was learning very quickly. He answered her questions as best he could, leaving out no details. She would be queen some day, and perhaps soon, if her father's condition did not improve. She deserved to hear everything. "I recruited another crew of bandits. Rougher than the usual sort I bring in, but they'll serve. After that we set an ambuscade for some of Mörg's farther-reaching scouts. I took two of them, though one of my men lost an arm and probably won't survive. Helstrow seems unchanged. The fires there have all been put out, at least. Your mother . . . remains unaccounted for."

When Helstrow was first threatened, Ulfram's wife had headed to Greenmarsh by a different route than the princess. The intention had been to make sure at least one of them got through. There had been no word from the queen since. Perhaps she had heard that the king was dead, and had gone into hiding.

It was something to hope for, anyway.

The inner door of the closet opened and Baron Easthull entered carrying a taper. He beckoned for Croy to step into his withdrawing chamber. Croy knelt quickly before Bethane and kissed her hand, but she bade him to go and join the baron. He knew she would not follow—she rarely left her father's side these days.

The withdrawing chamber was a small room filled with simple furniture, a place where in better days guests would come after dining to sit and talk over a bottle of brandy. Now its wide tables were littered with maps and written reports, a great hoard of words for the Baron to pore over while Croy went out every night looking for more men. From this room the only legitimate authority in Skrae was organized. It bore no comparison to the privy chamber in Helstrow, but it served.

"It's good of you to comfort the princess," the Baron said. He was a thin man with very bushy eyebrows, and he dressed always in linen. He had never, to Croy's knowledge, swung a sword in his life, though he always wore one at his belt. Yet when Croy had shown up in his dooryard, haggard and bramble-torn and lugging a wounded king, the Baron had taken him in, and for that Croy owed him much gratitude. "She talks of nothing but your exploits, you know."

"It helps keep her mind off her father's condition," Croy suggested.

"Hmm. Interesting. I've seen how you are at court, Croy. You're a true gallant, aren't you? I've seen you walk past a coterie of fair ladies, all of them endeavoring to catch your eye, and never a single one does." The Baron giggled. "If you were a less virtuous man, you'd have a passel of bastards by now, and no one in the kingdom would look askance at it. You might do well, in this case," the Baron went on, choosing his words carefully, "to be warmer. My physick tells me the king will not awaken. That his body is wasting away. Before you know it, you could be the royal consort, and all it would cost you is a few encouraging words. Maybe a gentle caress now and again."

Croy blushed and looked away. "She's a girl of fourteen!"

The Baron giggled again. "Her mother married Ulfram when she was twelve and he was thirty. Oh, don't look so scandalized. Such marriages are common at court, and they're not nearly as venal as you might think. They say Ulfram didn't lay a hand on the current queen until her breasts had swollen and her hips were round enough."

"This is immaterial. I . . . have a lady of my own, though she's far away," Croy insisted. "I would never betray her affections."

"Yes, yes, fine. I wish I had a son at hand, that's all, or perhaps that I wasn't already married myself. Someone needs to woo Bethane. She can't possibly rule the kingdom herself—and it wouldn't hurt our cause if we had a strong king ready to put in place."

In gentler days Croy might have thought such talk smacked of treason. But he knew the baron was simply being realistic. High principles were in shorter supply now than even proper arms and armor.

The Baron brought a fist down hard on his table and made the cutlery there jump. "But we came together tonight to talk of manly things, not the affairs of princesses. We are here to discuss swords and blood and war."

"Indeed," Croy said, glad for the change in subject.

CHAPTER FIFTY-ONE

The Baron sighed and looked down at his maps and reports. "Redweir has collapsed, as we expected. Mörget used sappers—a strange tactic for a barbarian, but it works. The town is invested and most of its populace is dead, according to my spies." The Baron unrolled a map and held it down on the table with a goblet and a jeweled dagger. "Two thousand men are inside its walls, under Mörget's direct leadership."

"I've seen what he's capable of now," Croy said. "He's

proved an effective leader of men. I didn't expect that when I first met him."

"Leading barbarians is easy. You point them in the direction of defenseless women and untapped kegs of ale. They run after those things like a mule after a wormy apple. Here," the Baron said, and tapped at a point on the map, on the road just north of Redweir. "Here, we have reports of messengers heading back to Helstrow. It will take them two days to get there, even if they push their horses to death. By tomorrow dusk, they'll likely be this far." He pointed again, at a spot quite close to Easthull.

"You wish me to ambush them, milord?"

"Of course. If Mörg doesn't hear from his son in a few days, he'll wonder what went wrong. He'll send another contingent of troops to investigate. Not too many—a few hundred. Those are numbers we can oppose."

Croy nodded, thinking. It would be a costly battle. For all his tireless efforts at recruiting he'd found precious few men. He could marshal perhaps three hundred bandits and deserters and farmers who'd been missed in the original conscription. Against even a hundred well-trained, well-armed barbarians, he still could not guarantee a victory. The cost in blood would be staggering. "Perhaps," he said. "But it will alert Mörg to our presence here. So far we've stayed below his notice—the worst we've done to harry him could be written off as the work of bandit raiders and a few soldiers still fighting on their own."

"That can't last forever. Someone will see your face and tell Mörg that an Ancient Blade is still at large. When that does happen we need to capitalize on his surprise—and how it will invigorate the villeins. Better, I think, that we take the battle to him now. We need a victory, Croy. A victory to show the barbarian he is not invulnerable."

Croy took a deep breath. A victory—a small victory—might give Mörg reason to pause. It might concern him. But a major victory could shake him to his core. Give him enough of a fright to send him back east, across the mountains, and forget about Skrae for a while. One decisive stroke, made at the perfect moment, could turn everything around.

He knew Easthull didn't see it that way. The Baron could only imagine the war stretching on for years, a bitter back and forth of sieges and counter-sieges as the barbarian moved west, a mile at a time. He was afraid, and Croy didn't blame him. Croy's plan involved major risk, in the short term. Still, he knew he was right.

"This is the wrong time," Croy said. "In a month I can double our forces, even treble them. I can send runners to the western fiefs and manors. I can recruit men from as far as Ness. And I can train them, teach them how to hold their ground. Then, when Mörget withdraws from Redweir, I can meet him on the road before he can regroup with his father at Helstrow."

"Out of the question. He has two thousand men."

"He'll need to leave a garrison at Redweir. That might cut his force in half. And we'll never have another chance like this to catch one of the main chieftains by surprise. If we strike now, even if we win, Mörg will strike back. He'll scour all of Greenmarsh looking for us. We'll be forced to disperse again—and we won't be able to regroup before winter."

"Hmm," Easthull said, smoothing his map with one hand. "I see you've been giving this some thought, Croy." He walked over to the narrow window at the back of the withdrawing chamber, perhaps forgetting it was covered with cloth to keep any light from escaping. "Militarily, perhaps, your plan makes good sense."

"I'm . . . glad to hear you say that," Croy said, cautiously optimistic.

"Politically, of course, it's too large a gamble. You've been away from the court for too long, old friend. Even when you were there you never learned the art of statecraft. If we have a victory now, so soon after Mörg's initial success, we show him that we speak his language. He'll treat with us, then. He'll come and make parley with me and we'll come to some agreement. Perhaps we'll have to let him keep some of our land, and give over some of our peasants into his thralldom. Perhaps he'll want tribute of gold." The Baron shrugged. "Let him have these things. The majority of Skrae will be free of this shadow. Then slowly, over time, we can negotiate for a return of what is ours."

Croy's blood surged in his veins. "That's . . . folly."

The Baron turned to look at him. "I beg your pardon?"

It was an insult. He was calling Easthull a fool. Duels were fought over such lapses of polite speech. Yet Croy could not stand here and listen to such drivel. Mörg would never negotiate with them now. They were down on their backs, with their bellies in the air. Mörg had them right where he wanted them. When dealing with barbarians, you didn't try to talk to them. Bribing them was no use, either. Ulfram V had proven that, and paid for it dearly. You responded to their force with force—and you had better be sure you could back up your feints. "Your pardon, milord. But this plan of yours—"

"I have decided on it. I await only your making it so."

The dimly lit room was tinged with red in Croy's vision. "I think you are forgetting something, Easthull. I'm the one who recruited our troops. I'm the one who commands them."

"And I believe you are forgetting something, *Croy*." The Baron thumped the table again. "You are a knight, and I am a baron."

Croy could feel his hand moving toward Ghostcutter's hilt. He forced it to stay by his side.

"The Lady put me in this station for a reason," Easthull went on. "Because I am a man who can see the larger picture. She made you a knight to ride about on chargers and lop the heads off of *my* enemies."

"I serve the king," Croy said.

"And right now, I speak for the king as regent."

Croy's teeth clicked together in anger. "No one has appointed you to that role! Only the king can name a regent, and he—"

"And he is fast asleep. I am the only man suited to the job. If he could wake long enough to be asked, he could name no one else."

"I . . . grant you that point," Croy said, the words coming from his mouth as if each was coated in poison. "But—"

"But? You have some better claim to put forth? Do you, Croy?"

"No," Croy grunted.

He could see that Easthull refused to be baited farther. "I have precedence here. That is not in question. So I *will* give the orders, and you *will* do my bidding." He sat down in a chair with his ankles crossed. The way a king would sit on a throne. "Kneel, Croy. Kneel on this floor, right now, and kiss my signet ring. Show me you have not forgotten who you are."

Croy took a step toward the Baron, breathing deeply through his mouth.

He had taken certain vows. The same vows every knight took.

He lowered himself onto his knees.

CHAPTER FIFTY-TWO

Money kept coming in, as it always had, and that was enough to keep the guild of thieves quiet. Not that there was much noise in the city anyway. The better share of the shops and workplaces in Ness had closed down, their windows boarded and their bustle silenced. As Malden and Cythera walked through the streets they'd always known, they kept remarking to each other how different it seemed.

One didn't notice the crowds, the clamor, the noisome smells and the piled filth until they were gone, really. "We should have a war every year," Malden japed, "if only to keep the streets clean."

Cythera laughed, but only softly, and not for very long. She was distracted that day. Something was on her mind. Yet when he asked her what it was she simply changed the subject.

"Look, Malden," she said, and pointed toward a little alcove by the entrance to a close. "When was the last time you saw one of those?" She indicated a small clay statue of the bloodgod, in the shape of a man with eight arms. Seven on one side, each holding a tiny clay knife or club. The eighth was alone on the other side, clutching the stem of a tiny flower.

"It's been a while," Malden admitted. Images of the bloodgod were technically forbidden by law, and most were kept behind closed doors. The Burgrave had never really bothered to tear them down—in fact, when Malden had broken into the palace earlier that year, he'd seen a quite large and beautifully gilded statue of Sadu inside. Still, such an ostentatious display was enough to comment on. The official religion of Skrae was the church of the Lady. Religious tolerance was unknown in Helstrow or Redweir—in those places anyone who publicly professed to worship Sadu could be arrested and fined. The bloodgod's followers had never quite died out, however—Sadu was too well loved by the common people—especially in Ness, where his worship was unofficially tolerated. Though the priesthood of the bloodgod had been outlawed and exterminated, his altars and his images ritually defiled or broken, the people continued his worship in their own small ways and the Burgrave had always been smart enough not to punish them too zealously for it.

Still, displaying his image was a risky act. "Devotion is on the rise," Malden said. "Religion is popular again in Ness. This was always such a sinful place. I hope people don't ruin it by becoming virtuous now."

"They're terrified," Cythera said. "The people, I mean. I suppose they have good reason."

"Even in Helstrow I saw men turning to Sadu for help," Malden told her. "He didn't seem to respond."

The tiny image was not the only sign of faith at large in the city. The Lady was widely venerated as well. Green and white streamers fluttered from every balcony, showing her colors. They'd been placed there by Pritchard Hood to remind the citizens that their lord was out on holy crusade and that they should remember him in their prayers. Hood made a daily speech to that effect in Market Square, though few stopped by to listen.

The new bailiff never missed an opportunity to appear in public and remind everyone he was in charge. Malden wished to know more about this man—especially how he could be bought. He and Cythera were walking toward a tavern where Malden expected to learn such things. When they arrived, he sent her in to get a bottle of wine and two cups, while he excused himself to use the alley. Velmont was waiting for him in the shadows back there.

The Helstrovian had much news, though none of it what Malden had wanted to hear. "This new bailiff's taken his master's word to heart, alright. Hood's employed thief-takers—just bravos, in troth, but sharpish men who'll get their catch, don't doubt it. It's just a question o' time afore he's got someone to hang."

Malden cursed. "Who is this bastard? Where did he come from? The old bailiff, Anselm Vry, was a corrupt and ambitious man. Pritchard Hood must be the same to have got the office so fast."

Velmont shrugged. "I asked a few fellas for his story, like you told me. They said Hood was an acolyte at the Ladychapel, but never took priestly orders. Found out he was better wi' the church books than at sayin' prayers. He worked fer Tarness as an exchequer until recent days."

"Any suggestion he was more creative with his numbers than the law would like?" Malden asked, hopefully.

"Not as I've heard. Your Burgrave took notice of him somehow and snatched him up last year. Put him in a place o' trust, and he's prospered every since. Now he's top dog in this city."

"We need to find out just how holy he really is," Malden said. "You've done good work getting this much. Go, now, and find out what you can about these thief-takers. Maybe we can grease them, and save ourselves some real trouble."

"Me hinges could do wi' a mickle oil themselves," Velmont suggested.

Malden nodded and spilled coins into the Helstrovian's hand. In an instant Velmont was gone. Malden headed into the tavern and found Cythera waiting for him with a smile.

There was one consolation to wartime, at least. He had

Cythera around as often as he liked. He resolved to spend the afternoon enjoying himself, and before he knew it, the sun was setting. For the first time in his life—a lifetime spent working mostly at night—he hated how soon the sun sank in autumn time. "Come," he told her, releasing her hands and draining his last cup. "I'll make sure you get home safe before night fully falls."

"That's very kind of you," she said, her eyes burning into his. They'd both had a bit too much to drink. Malden wondered if he would be invited to stay the night on the Isle of Horses. He could think of more romantic love-nests, but wherever Cythera was, he knew he could be happy.

He was laughing and holding her hand openly as they passed once more by the close where the image of Sadu had been put out. He wouldn't have given it a second look, had he not by accident trod on a piece of clay that shattered under his boot. He looked down and saw the arm of Sadu that held the flower. The idol had been dragged from its niche and smashed to pieces on the cobbles.

"Oh, that's not right," Cythera breathed, and bent to pick up the idol's broken head. "Someone knocked it down. Who would do such a thing?"

Malden glanced up at the alcove where it had stood. Green and white streamers had been tacked up in its place.

CHAPTER FIFTY-THREE

It didn't take long for the thief-takers to make their first catch. That very same night they discovered a thief in the Golden Slope. By dawn Pritchard Hood was ready to make an example.

Still, if he'd expected to draw a great crowd for the hanging, Malden imagined he would be disappointed with the result. A pall had settled over Ness since the Army of Free Men had decamped, a miasma of fear and worry that kept voices hushed and spirits low. Even as the thief was marched up to the gallows and the noose tightened around his neck, the jeers and shouts of the gathered crowd were subdued and almost mournful. Considering this was the best public entertainment the city had had all week, it was a sad showing. Malden barely had to push or elbow his way through the crowd to reach the base of the gallows.

The bailiff seemed unfazed by the dispirited crowd. His eyes were bright as he read out the charges. "Let it be known that one Janbart, a notorious rogue, is found convicted of stealing a pewter cup chased with bronze from the house of the guildmaster Harrit Fuller, said burgess of the city being absent from his home on night the last. Let it be further known that under the authority of Ommen Tarness, Burgrave, I have found this man Janbart guilty, and have imposed sentence of death by hanging on this day. Janbart! Have you anything to say, before the sentence is carried out?"

Janbart was a scrawny man of thirty, old before his time and none too steady of hand due to a fondness for drink. He looked even worse than usual up on the gallows platform—wasted and pale, as if he'd spent weeks in the gaol awaiting trial, though in fact Hood had pushed through the formalities with unheard of swiftness.

Malden was certain the man had been tortured after his arrest. The way he'd walked up the steps to the gallows suggested his leg had been clamped in an iron boot, and screws applied to his foot until he gave Hood what he was after.

He didn't have to wait long to learn just why Hood would do such a thing. The bailiff wanted more than a simple confession.

"Must I say it?" Janbart whispered. If Malden hadn't been in the front row of the audience, he would have heard nothing.

"You must," Hood told the convicted man.

Janbart bit his lips and looked out over the heads of the crowd. "I will say only this, let my death be a warning to them that would follow the crooked path. The—" Janbart paused, as if trying to remember words he'd been taught. "The Lady, verily, gave me every chance to be honest, and I rejected Her. Yet the blame is not entirely within me. If it were not for evil companions, namely one Malden, who is the master of thieves in this city, I would not be here today. I blame this Malden for my lowly end."

People all around Malden took a step back, as if afraid of being associated with him. Only Slag stayed close by his side.

"That's better," the dwarf said, when the two of them stood alone. "Now I can see."

A sack was placed over Janbart's head. Pritchard Hood bowed his head in a quick prayer and then nodded at the executioner, who placed both hands on the lever that would release the trap door under Janbart's feet.

"Janbart!" Malden shouted. "I'll see to your wife and children, have no worries!"

The convicted thief's head moved inside the sack as if he were trying to catch the sound of Malden's voice. Perhaps he might have said something more.

The executioner pulled his lever, and Janbart danced on the air. It was over quickly—the rope had been just the right length, so Janbart's neck snapped almost immediately.

Soon enough the crowd began to disperse. Hood left on foot, followed by a retinue of watchmen. He made no attempt to speak to Malden.

Feeling it was his duty, Malden stayed long enough to pay some boys to cut Janbart down and take his body away for burial. When that was done he and Slag were completely alone in the square.

"Well, lad," Slag said, softly, and not unsympathetically. "Now you're fucked."

Malden said nothing. He was anxious to get away from the scene. There were still things he could do. He would need to work quickly, giving reassurances and promises to those members of the guild of thieves who were already allying against him. He would need to consolidate those who would stand by him, and form his own alliances, inside the organization he supposedly governed. It was going to be a very long day.

Trailing at his heels, Slag muttered curses because Malden was walking too fast for someone with short legs to keep up. Malden did not slow down.

He did not know if he could do this, frankly. He felt reasonably secure for today, that no one would try to slide a dagger between his ribs when he wasn't looking. But tomorrow—

Malden had no doubt that tomorrow, at dawn, another thief would hang. And the day after, yet another.

CHAPTER FIFTY-FOUR

Slag followed Malden all the way across the Sawyer's Bridge into the Royal Ditch. Normally the narrow old bridge—named for the woodcutters who used it to carry firewood to the northern part of the city—creaked with the weight of all the pleasure-seekers heading across to the gaming houses and wineshops on the far side. Harlots had for ages walked back and forth along the bridge wearing red skirts and enticing day-time custom with their unshod feet and bare ankles, a living advertisement for the entertainments to be found on the far side. That day only a lone girl holding a house cat to her bosom was abroad. She waved cheerfully at Malden, but he had no more for her than an acknowledging nod.

On the far side of the bridge Slag dropped to the ground and begged Malden to stop a moment. "I can't run so fucking fast as I used to," he complained. "And this blasted sunlight makes me half-blind. I need to catch my breath. What's your hurry, anyway?"

Malden stared along Pokekirtle Lane, at the signs of the brothels there, all done in gaudy paint that stood out among the plain half-timbered houses. If it weren't for the porno-graphic pictograms on the signs this could be any other street in Ness. It was deserted enough not to show its tradi-tional commerce. "Something I need to work on. Something that might give me guidance and solve our problems."

"Ah. Cutbill's cipher."

Malden whirled around to face his friend. He'd mentioned the coded message to no one but Coruth and the three elders of the thieves' guild. "How did you know about that?" he demanded.

"Lockjaw's good at keeping quiet, aye," Slag said, sounding almost apologetic. "The other two never shut their fucking flaps."

Malden shook his head. If Slag knew about the message, then the entire guild must be aware of it by now. If they knew how it still mystified him, the thieves might start thinking he wasn't smart enough to lead them.

Maybe there was a way he could turn this to his advan-tage, though. "Listen," Malden said, "Will you do me a favor? Something that would help me greatly?"

"Depends what it is, lad. I've got my standards. I'm a dwarf, you know. We have a very exacting moral code we're expected to follow. Very strict."

Malden frowned. "I need you to tell a lie."

"Ah, well, that's fine, then."

"I need you to spread a rumor, actually. Let it be known that I've cracked the cipher. That I found Cutbill's advise-ment, and that it contains a secret that's going to save the guild."

Like all good lies, it was based on a kernel of optimism. Malden had made little progress with the cipher—it remained impenetrable. And yet he had come to believe, based on no evidence whatsoever, that the information the message contained in the cipher would be his salvation.

It was a thin thread of hope, but to a man trapped in a pit of confusion and despair, a rope as thin as a strand of hair could be a lifeline.

Malden gave Slag a moment to rest, then headed straight for the Lemon Garden—one of the less reputable houses of ease in Pokekirtle Lane. Malden had chosen it because he was known there, but also because it was one of the few businesses in the Royal Ditch that Cutbill hadn't owned any part of. The guildmaster of thieves hadn't wanted to absorb any of the Garden's debts. That meant it was less likely to house a spy for the rival factions that wanted to oust him from his position.

Normally during the day Malden had to announce himself repeatedly and hammer on the door to get in, but this day the Garden was open for business even in the early morning. Elody, the proprietress, welcomed him with a kiss on the cheek and explained. "Business is so bad I can't turn anyone away," she said, ushering Malden into the courtyard. A single scrawny lemon tree grew there, a few withered fruits still hanging from its boughs. Around its base were pallets of straw for the tupenny clientele. None of them were occupied at the time. "I've slashed my prices, offered delights to the public that I normally save for my most discriminating patrons—nothing seems to work," she went on, with a sigh.

Malden was saddened by this but unsurprised. The vast majority of Elody's customers had left town with the Burgrave. The very old men who remained were rarely in need of negotiable tenderness. Certainly Pritchard Hood and the handful of watchmen he retained didn't seem the type to dally in brothels. "I'll see if I can't send some custom your way," Malden promised. His thieves were one of the few groups of young men remaining in the city. Elody had been one of his mother's fastest friends, and had even sat by her bedside while she was dying of the sailor pox. He owed her something.

At that particular moment he owed her some silver, which he paid happily. "You've kept the room locked?" he asked her.

"Haven't needed it for anything else," Elody told him.

The silver coins disappeared into her sagging cleavage. "What about him?" she said, indicating Slag.

"He's alright. Slag, come with me—unless you see something here you like."

The dwarf squinted in the daylight but peered up at the gallery surrounding the courtyard. The women gathered there looked haggard to Malden, thin from hunger and tired from being up at all hours. They knew how to dress themselves, however, to show off their better features.

Slag shook his head, though. "Hairless as babies, all of them."

Malden raised an eyebrow. Like all the city's whores, the women of the Lemon Garden kept their hair very long and dressed with ribbons. It was one of their chief enticements, since most honest women in Ness kept their hair covered by hoods or wimples.

"I like a woman with some hair on her lip," Slag explained.

Malden laughed—for the first time in days—and brought Slag to the private room he'd hired from Elody. It was there he'd been working on the cipher. The room contained a large bed, of course, but this was now strewn with pieces of parchment, scratched on with a quill pen in abortive attempts to break the code. The original cipher was tacked to one wall, while fresh parchment, ink, and a book of grammar were waiting for Malden on a chair.

He set to work immediately, scanning the message over and over, looking for suspicious groupings of given characters. "Each symbol here must correspond to a letter of the alphabet," he explained to Slag—it was what Coruth had taught him.

"But how can you break it unless you know which character stands for which letter?" Slag asked. The dwarf looked intrigued—here was a bit of cleverness, a skillful science he had not mastered.

"The trick is knowing that some letters are more common than others," Malden explained. "For instance, the letter E is the most common in our language, so it stands to reason that the most common character in the cipher would correspond to E. Unless, of course, it actually represents A, which is also very common."

"It can't be that simple," Slag said.

Malden sighed and shook his head. "Sadly, no. I find combinations of common letters all the time here, but they never link up to form familiar words. I've been working on a theory that the message is not in the language of Skrae, but perhaps the written form of the script of the Old Empire, or even that of one of the northern kingdoms. The real problem, however, is that there are characters I can't account for. There are twenty-two letters in the alphabet I was taught. Yet there are far more different kinds of characters in the message. It's possible they stand for marks of punctuation, or numbers, or . . . anything, really. Musical notes? It's also possible there are two message interwoven here, each in a completely different cipher." He started to crumple a piece of parchment in his hand. Another wasted effort. He stopped himself in time, though—the stuff was far too expensive to waste.

"Cutbill meant for you to break the code," Slag said, laying a hand on Malden's elbow. "You'll find the answer, lad."

"I devoutly hope so, and that I find it soon."

He had things that needed to be done, far more pressing things. Luckily most of them could be done from the room at the Lemon Garden. He was able to send Slag out on various errands, even in the daylight when all sane dwarves were asleep in their beds. Runners came to him from the Ashes and from Castle Hill, where he had spies watching Pritchard Hood and his men. Elody eventually brought him a plate of herring and bread, and he realized he'd wasted half the day on the cipher. He didn't stop, however, and time sped by once more. When a knock came on the door and he rose to answer it he saw that night had fallen outside.

He'd spent a whole day working on the code, and was no nearer an answer.

Blinking away the cobwebs behind his eyes, he looked at who had come to him. He almost didn't recognize her at first. "Herwig?" he asked. "Where are your furs?"

The madam of the House of Sighs, the grandest and most

expensive brothel in the city, stood on his doorstep in a plain smock of wool. He had never before seen her when she wasn't dressed in ermine like a duchess.

"Sold, all of them, for this," she said, and she crossed his palm with gold. "It's what I owe you."

Cutbill had owned a sizeable interest in the House of Sighs. It had been one of his most profitable speculations. The gold must represent Malden's cut. "Feels a little light," he said by instinct.

"Business has been down," she said. "But it's all there."

"Very well," he said. "You have my thanks." He turned to go, but she put a hand on his arm.

"And now," she said, "I want what's mine."

CHAPTER FIFTY-FIVE

"Protection?" Malden repeated, when Herwig had told him what she meant.

"It was promised to me by your former master. I assume our arrangement still stands. My business has fallen away to nothing, but I'm paid up, now. So you need to meet your obligations."

"But—protection from what? Don't tell me some gang is trying to move in on you," Malden said. That was the last thing he needed—a rival organization working against the guild of thieves.

"In a fashion," Herwig said. "May I sit?"

Malden hurried to clear off the room's chair and bring it nearer the fire for her. Herwig had come up with his mother as well, though they'd never gotten along. Still, Malden honored all the women who'd survived on Pokekirtle

Lane long enough to grow old. It was a hard life with particular dangers most people never needed to face.

"I was visited last night by a group of men with knives in their hands. As bad as business is, I welcomed them. But they hadn't come for swiving. They slashed paintings in my vestibule, tore tapestries from the walls. Smashed several pieces of erotic sculpture I'd had shipped all the way from the Old Empire."

The art collection of the House of Sighs was one of Ness' more unconventional treasures. This was, in its way, a kind of desecration. Malden jumped to his feet. "I'll gather some bravos at once. We'll find them and make them pay you back for everything."

"You won't have to look hard," Herwig told him. She pressed her lips tightly together for a moment, as if holding back a curse. "They came from Castle Hill. Oh, they'd taken off their cloaks-of-eyes. But there are not so many watchmen in this city I didn't recognize one of them. I went to Pritchard Hood himself this morning and demanded recompense. Do you know what he told me?"

Malden shook his head.

"That images of lust were an offense before the sight of the Lady. I told him, of course, that I am not a worshipper of his new religion. He informed me, quite politely, that in times of war the Lady's favor was to be sought by all people. Believers and non-believers alike."

"He truly is a zealot," Malden said, and new hatred burned in his heart for Hood. The people of the Free City of Ness had always in the past been granted a certain measure of religious liberty. Clearly Hood intended to revoke that freedom.

Malden wondered, though, if this attack were purely motivated by faith. It was too well calculated to hurt him, as well. It was well known that Cutbill made more money from his investments in the Royal Ditch than he ever had from direct thieving. The gaming houses alone made Cutbill rich. Now that Malden had inherited all those accounts, perhaps Hood intended to beggar him by cutting off his sources of revenue.

Herwig exhaled noisily. "You need to do something,

Malden. You need to help me. You and I have never been close. But you are a friend to every working woman in this city—or so I've heard. Demonstrate that friendship now."

"I'd like to," Malden said, playing for time to think. "I have my own problems, you know."

It seemed Herwig would brook no excuses. She rose from the chair and headed for the door. Before she left she turned back to stare at him. "I've always found men to be useless when real needs arose. It's why I never married any of them, and instead found ways to make my own place in this world. For once—just for once—I hope I'm proved wrong."

She left before he could promise anything. Herwig was a shrewd woman, and he doubted she would have believed anything he said, anyway.

He was visited twice more that night by the madams of other houses, who told similar tales. It seemed Pritchard Hood had been very busy. The only house that hadn't been visited by the watch on some trumped-up pretext was the Lemon Garden, which gave credence to the theory Hood was trying to bankrupt Malden before he slaughtered him. In desolation, Malden did the only thing he could, and turned back to the cipher.

He made no progress at all. He worked well into the night, and nothing came to him. Slag returned, and kept him company, for which he was grateful. Yet Malden's frustration had grown to the point where he was afraid he would lash out at even his most faithful friend if he wasn't careful.

"It's gibberish!" he howled, tearing a sheet of parchment into ribbons and casting them into the air. They fell like the fluttering leaves of autumn. "There are just too many characters. Or too few. If it was two ciphers intermixed, there should be forty-four characters. But there are only thirty-seven."

Slag looked up from the plate of sops he'd been eating. "Thirty-seven?"

"Yes!" Malden, exasperated, grabbed up the grammar book he'd been using. "Which makes no sense at all. The alphabet of the Old Empire uses twenty-nine characters. Even in the northern kingdoms, where half their letters are draped in umlauts and circumflexes and diacritical marks no one can even remember how to pronounce, there are only thirty-one. There has never been a human alphabet in all our history that used thirty-seven marks, not even if you include full stops and question marks and the like."

"Not a human alphabet, no," Slag said, "but—"

"It's useless!" Malden shouted, and threw himself full length on the bed, crushing his wasted parchments and staining his tunic with ink. "Cutbill didn't want me to break this. I see it now. First he sent an assassin to slaughter me. When that didn't work, he gave me this job knowing I would foul things to the point my own thieves would turn on me. And he left a maze of meaningless characters for me to lose myself in, and waste so much time I would miss the killing stroke when it came."

"No, lad, I don't fucking believe it for a moment. He wanted you to solve this riddle. He knew what tools you would have on hand—Coruth, to teach you of ciphers, and, well, me."

Malden sat up suddenly. He said nothing, for fear of interrupting Slag.

"There are thirty-seven runes known to the dwarves. Exactly thirty-seven," Slag said, in a very, very quiet voice.

Malden got to his feet and walked over to where the dwarf sat in the chair, the plate of milky bread in his lap. He started to reach for the dwarf's shoulder.

He was stopped because there was a knock on the door. Before Malden could answer it, the door flew open and he saw Velmont standing there. The Helstrovian thief looked like he'd run all the way from the wall—he was gasping for breath and sweat slicked his face. "The thief-takers're at it again," he announced.

"Who did they get this time?" Malden asked.

Velmont wiped at his mouth. "Loophole," he said.

CHAPTER FIFTY-SIX

Croy knelt low in the brambles by the side of the road. He could see very little by the thin sliver of the moon, but every time a weed stirred in a night breeze or an owl swept down from the trees on some vicious errand, his whole body tensed and his hand tightened on Ghostcutter's hilt.

He had only a few troops at his disposal who he could count on not turning around and running at the first sign of danger. He was making a terrible mistake, and he knew it.

He had his orders.

From the trees well south of his position, he heard the cawing of a crow, and knew the time was coming soon. Crows flew by day, and slept at night, like reasonable creatures. That call was the signal that riders were approaching from the direction of Redweir.

There would be four of them, he knew. Four quick scouts, headed back to Helstrow with the news of Redweir's capture. They would not be Mörget's best warriors, nor would they be berserkers. He was relatively sure of that.

Before long he heard the sound of their hooves chewing up the half-frozen road. He did not see them until they were nearly at the trap. "Now," he whispered, and behind him there was a sudden, violent motion.

A stout rope leapt out of the road, trailing dust, and snapped taut at neck height. It ran all the way across the road and if you didn't know it was there it was almost impossible to see. It caught the first rider and yanked him backwards out of his stirrups to crash on the ground. His horse kept going. The second rider reacted in time not to be throttled, but did foul himself in the line. The barbarian grabbed for a knife to cut himself free.

Behind him, two more riders slowed their mounts to a stop.

That had gone far better than Croy had dared hope. Of course, it wasn't over yet.

What if the message they carried was in the saddlebags of the first horse? Croy wondered. He would never be able to catch the animal in the dark. If it was smart enough to run all the way back to Helstrow—

But there were more pressing concerns. "To arms!" he bellowed, and all around him torches flared to life. "Soldiers of Skrae, to arms!"

Croy's company swept out of the trees, pikestaffs and bill hooks jabbing at the mounted men. Croy unsheathed Ghostcutter and ran toward the man who had fallen. He could see well enough now to count the crosses on the man's neck, one for each time he'd gone reaving. How many villages had this barbarian put to the torch? How many women had he defiled, how many innocent throats had he cut? He was struggling to get up, to even roll onto his arms. His legs weren't moving at all—perhaps his back was broken.

Croy had his orders. Ghostcutter flashed down and cut through the man's throat, almost deep enough to behead him.

The snagged rider wheeled his horse and drew an axe with a long haft. Moonlight shone through quatrefoils piercing the blade. Ghostcutter rang as it parried the first stroke. The rider hauled backward on his weapon to recover and Croy moved in, stabbing upward. The rider fended off Croy's blow, but only by blocking it with his forearm. The sword bit deep into the man's flesh and blood spattered Croy's face.

The axe came around a second time, whistling in the air. Croy parried again—Ghostcutter was faster than any axe, no matter how well made. The rider tried to grab at the knight with his injured arm, but his fingers wouldn't close on Croy's tabard. Croy stepped in even closer, well within range of the horse's hooves. He had to finish this quickly. One good jab up into the barbarian's chest did it, and he rolled away before the half-mad horse could trample him. The rider swayed over in his saddle and was dragged as the animal broke for the fields at the side of the road.

His men had the other two riders pinned, but not wounded. The peasant soldiers had no idea how to use their weapons properly. Many of them were probably afraid to actually stab another human being. In another world, in a world the Lady ruled, Croy would have admired their gentility.

This was not that world. He grabbed at his own men and sent them sprawling in the dirt to make his way through their iron ring. The third rider smashed away bill blades with a boar spear and caught pike points on a buckler. He barely had time to notice Croy before Ghostcutter opened the long artery in his thigh. In a minute he would be dead from blood loss—Croy spun around and left him.

One more.

The fourth rider had managed to smash his way through a cordon of polearms. Two of Croy's men lay in the dust, one with his chest crushed in by a horse's kick, the other missing half his face from a sword cut. Croy could hear others behind him, wounded and moaning but alive, as the rider broke for the fields and escape.

"Don't let him get away!" Croy shouted, but he knew he was talking to himself. His men rushed backwards, away from the rider's swinging weapon. In a moment the rider had spurred his horse and dashed off into the fields.

Croy saw the horse of the third rider nearby. The rider was dead in his saddle but hadn't fallen off yet. Croy sprang up onto the horse's back, knocking the rider out of the way with his elbow. The horse bucked and reared but Croy grabbed up the reins in his free hand and viciously kicked the frightened animal in the ribs.

He had his orders. He had to give chase.

Away from the road and the torches the ground was a gray blur, the rider a smudge in the darkness. Croy could make out only his cloak fluttering behind him and the merest glint of light off his horsehoes as they flashed up again and again. Croy tried to stay hot on the heels of this last rider—as long as he stayed in the barbarian's trail, his horse wouldn't break a leg in some unseen mole hill or trip on a half-buried rock. He could hear the booming breath of both horses, hear his own heart beating, but that was all. Up ahead he saw an old barn, stars showing through a hole in its roof. The rider was headed straight for its open door. In the Lady's name, why? Croy couldn't guess.

He followed the rider right into the barn, however, and then jumped off the horse because he couldn't see a thing inside—all was darkness. Was this the rider's plan, to trap Croy in this shadowy place, and escape while the knight flailed in the dark?

Apparently not. Croy felt wind on his face and just had time to stagger backwards as a sword came rushing past him. Maybe the barbarian could see better in the dark, though Croy doubted it. Maybe he thought his only chance was this invisible combat, deadly for both of them—the rider must have watched Croy dispatching his fellows and wanted to even the odds.

Croy held his breath. Ghostcutter bobbed slightly in his hand, with the rhythm of his heart.

The barbarian's sword crashed into the armor covering his arm. A lucky blow—it cleaved through the leather joint between the steel plates of his rerebrace and his vambrace and sliced through the rough skin of Croy's elbow. Had the barbarian been able to see better, and judge the blow more shrewdly, he could have taken half of Croy's arm off with that strike. There was one thing the barbarian hadn't counted on, though.

It was Croy's left arm.

Pain seared through him, threatened to extinguish his senses but he simply clamped his eyes tight shut and held his breath as he listened for the sound of his enemy's feet moving on the floorboards. There.

Eyes closed, Croy visualized the barbarian's sword, saw the arm that held it, the chest, the heart of the barbarian—

Ghostcutter lanced out point first and impaled the barbarian, cleaving through the tight knot of muscle just to the left of the center of the chest.

The barbarian howled in agony, but not for very long.

Croy pulled Ghostcutter free of the death wound. He dropped the Ancient Blade on the straw-covered floor of the barn. Dropped to his knees and grasped his wounded elbow.

He did not open his eyes until his men came to find him with their torches, and he saw, for the first time, the face of the man he'd killed.

Or rather, the woman. Her face was painted to the favor of a skull. She had been one of Mörgain's female warriors. Croy had never killed a woman before—not even in self-defense.

But he had his orders.

CHAPTER FIFTY-SEVEN

I didn't want this job, Malden thought. *I never asked for it. Surely, this is Cutbill's punishment upon me. Yet what did I do to him, ever? I worked in his employ, helped to make him rich.*

Now I have to clean up the mess he left behind.

Loophole had been one of Cutbill's favorites, one of his oldest cronies. He was well loved in the guild of thieves. If he was to hang, the guild would tear itself apart—the thieves would blame Malden for the oldster's death, and they would remove him from office, in a rather pointed fashion.

Malden had no choice but to stop the hanging. He gestured for Velmont to follow him, then hurried out into the night.

The brazen doors of the Ladychapel stood open. Yellow light spilled out across its marble steps. Malden walked in to the smell of incense and the heat of braziers, and for a moment he was dizzy, his thoughts swirling in his head like a whirlpool.

At the altar, Pritchard Hood knelt with his hands clasped in prayer. A single priest dressed in green vestments stood

behind the altar, hands lifted in supplication. Behind him a
gilt cornucopia glared in the light of a hundred candles.

The air in the church was thick and still. Malden felt like
he was wading through molten glass. He was barely aware
of Velmont walking behind him.

Pritchard Hood did not stir as Malden approached. The
priest stared at the thief, perhaps expecting Malden to dese-
crate these holy precincts. As bewildered and frightened as
he was, Malden knew better than that. He did not know to
what extent Hood truly was a zealot, or if he merely had
taken up faith in the Lady as a shield, or a political gambit.
It didn't matter. If Malden did something rash now—like
spilling blood on the altar—he would have a thousand new
enemies to contend with.

"Pritchard Hood," he said.

The bailiff turned slowly, as if he were still lost in commu-
nion with his goddess.

Malden scowled. "You've taken an innocent old man."

"I would hardly call Loophole innocent," Hood said, with
a chuckle. "He's one of the most infamous thieves in Skrae."

"He's an old man. He hasn't stolen so much as a farthing
from you or anyone in this city." Malden crossed his arms
in front of him, careful not to let his hand fall to the hilt of
Acidtongue where it lay on his hip.

"He got his name by crawling through an arrowslit in
the barracks building on Castle Hill. He stole money from
the Burgrave's men."

"That was twenty years ago."

Hood smiled, showing all his teeth. "The Lady never
forgets evil done unto Her people. You would know that,
Malden, if you had any religious instruction. Those who
live good lives, by honest means, are rewarded by Her.
Those who do evil are punished by Her servants in this
world. Servants like me."

Malden shook his head. "The bloodgod's justice is more
to my liking. That comes to the poor man and the rich alike.
All are judged and tortured for their sins in the pit of souls.
Sadu needs no servants to wreak his vengeance for him."

The priest started to tremble as Malden spoke. "That

name is never spoken in this house," he insisted. "You violate the very stones of this church with your tongue!"

Malden ignored the priest. "Let Loophole go, Hood."

"Is that a threat, Malden? It means nothing to me. Your thief will hang at dawn tomorrow. And his last words will indict you. The Lady wills it, so let it be done."

Bile rose in Malden's throat, but he knew he was beaten here. He could not strike down Hood in the church. Even if he did, it wouldn't guarantee Loophole's freedom. But he had to do something. The entire guild of thieves would be watching him. There was no more time for delay, or appeasement, or begging for patience.

As he walked back out of the Ladychapel, he saw there was no more time for thinking, either. Half a dozen men stood on the steps, making a rather poor attempt at looking nonchalant. He knew them all—they were thieves, burglars and sharpers and robbers. They were the ones who had never had any confidence in Malden's leadership, and they were here to show him how low his reputation had sunk.

They were all armed.

"Velmont," Malden said, quietly, "can I trust you?"

"What color's your money?"

"It's gold, Velmont. Bright gold."

"You can trust me jus' fine."

Still—two against six.

"Gentlemen," Malden said, nodding at the six.

One of them stepped forward. His name was Tock, and Malden had recruited him into the guild personally. The guild's recruiting methods were not always gentle. Tock had reason to hate Malden long before Cutbill fled town. "You look tired, Malden. The strain of leadership getting to you?"

"They took Loophole tonight," Malden said, trying to appeal to camaraderie.

"So we heard. Now there's a man who deserved your protection. But where were you when he was taken? In a bawdy house, they say, holed up in a private room."

Malden didn't bother to explain himself. Cutbill never would have. Of course, Cutbill would have had armed bravos waiting in the shadows, ready to strike as soon as Tock made a move for his knife. "I'm going to get him released. You can help me with that, or you can try to stop me."

One of the six drew a long cleaver from his belt. Tock opened his hand, palm level with the street. This wasn't just a bunch of angry thieves, then. It was a crew—organized, if they'd bothered to work out signals. Able to fight as a unit.

Malden and Velmont had never fought back to back. He had no idea how the Helstrovian thief would do if it came to that.

"I'll say again, you can help me," Malden told Tock.

"You got a plan, Malden?" Tock asked.

"Always," Malden lied.

"You going up to Castle Hill, to the gaol? You going to sneak in and get Loophole, sneak out again with him over your shoulder?"

Some of the six laughed at the idea. Until that moment, Malden had been considering the very thing. Now he needed to rethink.

"No," he sighed. "That would be folly."

"Then what's your grand scheme?"

Malden closed his eyes. And heard singing. The priest inside the Ladychapel was leading the evening hymn service, and Pritchard Hood, his only constituent that night, was lending his voice.

"Ah," Malden said, because suddenly he had it. "I'm going to say a little prayer."

CHAPTER FIFTY-EIGHT

It wasn't easy getting the word out so late in the evening. The honest people of Ness (such as they were) tended to lock their doors after dark and go to sleep early—candles were expensive, and after a long day of work everyone just wanted to rest. The streets weren't safe after dark, no matter how deserted they might be. Malden had placed his hopes, though, on that segment of the population that made its living after the sun went down.

His thieves came first to Godstone Square, as they had before—alone, mostly. Some expressed quiet support for Malden's scheme, while others, Tock the foremost of them, had come because they expected it to fail and they wanted to see Malden destroyed. Lockjaw and 'Levenfingers came and stood quite close to the Godstone. Whether they believed in what Malden was about to do or not, they owed Loophole that much. Slag, like all dwarves, was at his most awake after dark, when the sun didn't burn his eyes. He showed up late, however, and grinned in apology to Malden—then held up ink-stained fingers to explain his tardiness.

Velmont moved pantherish through the crowd of thieves, looking for any sign of treachery. Malden had no doubt he found much, but for the nonce at least the knives stayed concealed.

The thieves were not alone for long. Coming in groups of six or ten for safety, the harlots of Ness arrived with some fanfare, the madams leading their girls in cheers of solidarity. Elody cheered the loudest, but Malden was pleased to find that Herwig had brought every working woman she could find. The House of Sighs must have closed its doors for the night, for the first time in living memory.

They were not the last to arrive. Malden's agents had gone deep into the Stink, even to the poorest neighborhoods where thieves weren't any safer than rich merchants. They had pounded on doors, and called out the news in ringing shouts. Malden had expected a few greybeards and old women to heed the call. He was surprised to see a goodly number of cripples, the sick, and even matronly women who should have known better arrive. Soon the square was so full the crowd spilled out into the surrounding streets, and window shutters flew open as the local residents looked to see what all the clamor was for.

Malden wasn't ready to start, however. Not until Pritchard Hood arrived.

For much of an hour, he waited, standing atop the Godstone just as when he'd addressed his guild, back when Ness had seemed a sane and safe place for a good-natured thief. He said nothing to the gathered folk, other than to welcome them and greet those he knew. He gave them no encouragement. What he was about to do was a solemn act, not the antics of a clown at a harvest season fair. Though never much of a believer himself, Malden was acquainted with the way the old priests of the bloodgod had acquitted themselves. They had taken their rites most seriously, and he intended to do the same.

When Pritchard Hood did finally arrive, along with six of his burliest watchmen, they shoved their way through the crowd until they stood directly beneath the Godstone. Malden was intrigued to see that the watchmen carried not their usual polearms but mallets and picks. Interesting. It seemed Hood had a demonstration of his own to make.

"I don't know what you think you're doing, Malden," Hood shouted up at him. "This place has been ritually defiled. There's nothing sacred about this piece of rock."

Malden smiled down at the man. "You think Sadu cared when the priests of your Lady washed this stone with vinegar and sang their little songs over it? Do you think He even noticed?"

"I think He trembled in His pit," Hood replied, looking around him. "I think He knew that His time was past, and that the age of the Lady had come."

"Ah, but your sort always think that gods can be cast aside when they're no longer wanted." Malden looked around the crowd. He saw the rapt faces, the strange calm in their eyes. "When it's politically convenient." He made his voice boom out over the crowd so all could hear. He only wished he could do this in the daylight, so people could see better. Loophole would hang at dawn, though, so he had very little time to spare.

"True believers know that gods do not die," he went on. "Sadu's children have not forgotten Him. Here, in Ness, we've always been guaranteed our right to worship whatever god we choose. Even if it's not in the Free City's charter, every Burgrave has upheld the freedom of each man to choose his own god. You seem to disagree with that liberty."

"There is only one goddess who can save Skrae now," Hood demanded. "What exactly do you expect Sadu to do for you tonight? What are you going to ask Him for? To crack open the earth so the walls of the gaol fall, and your old thief can run away? I'll just catch him again. Maybe you wish Sadu to send demons to aid you."

A murmur went through the crowd. Demonology was the province of sorcerers, and no one trusted them. If that was Malden's aim, he was about to lose any support he might have hoped for.

Luckily he had something else in mind. "I beseech the bloodgod for one thing only. The only thing he ever promised to us: justice, for every man and woman. And I offer him his chosen sacrifice in exchange."

He unsheathed his belt knife and, quick enough that he didn't even wince, slashed open the skin of his left palm. He showed the wound to the gathered people, then clenched his hand several times to make the blood flow.

"For you, Sadu!" he cried, and then bent low, so he could slap his bloody hand against the surface of the Godstone. Blood dripped down its face, dark in the moonlight so all could see.

For a moment not one person in all of Godstone Square breathed.

Pritchard Hood broke the silence by laughing. "Malden, you've undone yourself! You know blood sacrifice is illegal in Skrae, and has been for a hundred years. You know perfectly well that anyone making sacrifice to this stone is subject to penalty of death."

Malden glanced at the mallets and picks the watchmen held. "Come and catch me then, thief-taker," he said.

Had Pritchard Hood brought a ladder, and climbed up to bring Malden down, Malden would have been utterly lost. Had he sent an archer to the rooftops overlooking the square, Malden would have been slain on the spot.

Instead, Hood decided to catch two birds with one snare. "You've given me a wonderful excuse to do something no Burgrave or Bailiff has ever had the courage to do before. I thank you, Malden! You six—take it down."

One of the watchmen lifted his mallet, and brought it down hard on the face of the ancient stone. Cracks appeared on the surface of the Godstone, and fragments of its substance fell away. Time and weather had made it fragile, and it would not take long before the watchmen toppled it and broke it into rubble.

At least, if no one stopped them.

Pritchard Hood had made a grave miscalculation. The Lady, it was taught, put every man in his station by Her sacred decree. Those who prospered in this life owed Her their allegiance, for She was the giver of all wealth and bounty. The kings of Skrae and all their nobles, every rich merchant and guildmaster in the kingdom, every legally-sanctioned priest all worshipped the Lady and disdained the rites of the bloodgod. They had repressed—savagely—the worship of Sadu. They had fought wars against His faithful. But they had never quite wiped out the old faith.

The poor, the dispossessed, the outcasts of society never forgot Sadu's name. They would never let it be forgotten.

When word of the barbarian invasion reached Ness, all the rich citizenry had fled. All the merchants were gone, all the petty nobles and courtiers, all the hierarchs of the Lady's church had left the city to its fate.

The ones who had stayed behind had done so because they couldn't afford to leave. The same people who were Sadu's children. The true faithful, the ones who remembered the old ways, were the people who filled Godstone Square that night.

Before the watchman could swing again, and break the stone, the pure fury of the pit was unleashed.

CHAPTER FIFTY-NINE

An old fishwife with a face like a rotten parsnip threw herself in front of the Godstone and defied the watchman to strike through her bones. He hesitated a moment, just long enough for Pritchard Hood to grab her and pull her away. She clawed at his eyes and he could do nothing but hold her at arm's length.

The crowd shouted, then, voices blending together: "He's killing her!"

"He's manhandling that poor woman!"

"Let her go!"

"Disperse," Hood said, still struggling with the fishwife. "Damn you—let go of me. You—all of you. Disperse! Go back to your homes."

The crowd took a step inward, toward the stone.

"Back! All of you back!" Pritchard Hood howled. "You, men—keep them back."

A pick swung round and bit into the side of a thief who had come too close, one of the pickpockets who'd been in the guild longer than Malden. The man screamed. A mallet came around and cracked the skull of a blind beggar.

The crowd screamed with him. It screamed for blood.

It took another step inward.

"Break it! Break it now!" Hood shouted. A watchman lifted his mallet to smash the Godstone—

—and a thrown knife entered his throat, dropping him to choke on his own blood. The crowd roared like the ocean in storm and surged toward the stone, grabbing the watchmen and the bailiff even as picks crushed in heads and mallets bashed the sides of old men and lepers.

The crowd could not be stopped. It fell on Hood and his men like the vengeance of the bloodgod Himself.

"Hold them down!" Malden shouted, but he could barely hear his own voice over the tumult. "Don't let them fight back—don't let them kill you!"

The crowd needed no goading, and would heed no advice. Screaming, foaming at the mouth like an enraged bull, it seethed as one creature, unified in bloodlust. A watchman was torn limb from limb as Malden watched in horror, his blood slicking the cobbles underfoot so that many in the crowd slipped and were trampled by the feet of others, trying to get in closer, trying to tear and rend.

The watchmen fought desperately with their tools. The death count was horrible among the poor and the old—it was a massacre, plain and simple—but the watch couldn't hold out very long. Malden couldn't see Pritchard Hood under the piling crowd but he shouted anyway, "Seize Hood—we'll run him out of town on a hurdle!"

Hood might already have been dead before the words escaped Malden's lips. The bailiff was most certainly dead a moment later, when his broken body was hauled up on the shoulders of a group of whores and carried out of the square. No man could survive with his head barely attached to his body like that, or with his chest caved in at so many places. Blood slicked the bailiff's unmoving mouth and pooled in an empty eye socket. Malden had to turn away rather than see more.

The crowd wasn't satisfied, though. It screamed for more. More blood. More vengeance. All the tension of the last few weeks, as Ness waited to be sacked and pillaged by the barbarian horde, was being released in an orgy of rage.

Malden stayed atop the Godstone—trying to climb down would have been suicide—and shouted for order, for reason, for calm. He shouted for civility, for peace, for true justice. His words were completely lost in the din.

When the crowd swept out of the Square, headed in the direction of Castle Hill, tears ran down Malden's cheeks. What had he done? What had he set loose? He half expected the mob to burn the city in its rage. To slaughter every man and woman and child it could find, regardless of their guilt or innocence. When the square had cleared out enough to make it safe, he slipped down the side of the stone and landed hard on his ankle. His own blood was singing, though with fear rather than anger.

Bodies littered the square. Bodies of the poor, the crippled, of thieves. The crowd had taken the bodies of the watchmen with them, for what purpose Malden did not like to contemplate.

"Lad! Over fucking here!" Slag called. The dwarf had taken shelter in a doorway across the square. "Do you know how fucking dangerous it is to be this fucking short when the fucking world goes mad?" Slag demanded, his face wracked with terror.

"I—I didn't know they would—"

Slag shook his head. "Listen, Malden. There's nothing you can do now. Get somewhere safe—wait out this night." Slag peered around the edge of the doorway. "Fuck. Never mind."

Malden stared at the dwarf, deeply confused. Then he leaned out himself and took a look.

Coruth the witch was walking across the Square toward them, taking care as she stepped over all the bodies.

"Malden," the old woman said. "Come with me."

CHAPTER SIXTY

Coruth did not wait to hear if he would follow. She walked across the square and turned herself into a bird.

He'd seen that trick before, but it still made him uneasy. Coruth did not flap her arms, or say a spell, or even shrink in size that he could see. It was like she walked into a shadow and walked out of it with wings and a beak. Then she stretched her new wings and shot up onto the roofbeam of a house, and there waited for him to follow.

Malden climbed the house easily. The shingles of the roof were painted with moonlight and a tinge of red. He didn't know where that light came from. Coruth didn't say a word. She just fluttered across the street to the house across the way, and sat on a roof there, pecking at her side with her beak as if she were digging out a mite.

Malden shook his head. He had to follow her, of course. He'd learned enough about witchcraft to know it was unwise to disobey a witch. He ran across the roof, flat-footed to keep his balance, and leapt to the next house. Just in time to see Coruth take to the air and fly on.

He followed her like that halfway across the city. The roofs in this part of the Stink were steeply pitched but all of roughly the same height. It was nothing he had not done a thousand times before to move quickly and silently across that elevated sea of shingles and waterspouts. He swung along the gargoyles of a church. Leapt from a chimney pot to catch a balcony with his hands, and in one easy motion swung himself up to the second floor of a bakery. Eventually Coruth ran out of perches when they came to the Woolcarder's Bridge. Malden dropped to street level and crossed the bridge even before Coruth could leap into the air again. He knew now where she was leading him.

The Stink gave way to the Golden Slope, the district of mansions once held by the rich merchants of Ness. From the rooftops there was little to mark the change of neighborhood, except that the shingles in the Slope tended not to shift or crack when he landed on them with his full weight. Up ahead though lay the Spires, where all the buildings were made of stone, and many had lead-lined roofs to keep out the rain. Still Malden followed, clambering across the many-gabled dome of the counting house until he came to where he could look down on Market Square—and beyond, the wall of Castle Hill.

Now he saw the source of the reddish light. The square was full of firebrands, held aloft by a screaming mob. The crowd had lost none of its rage. The gate leading into Castle

Hill was sealed shut, but men who had never lifted a hand in anger before in their entire lives were rushing forward to pile firewood against the gate. Others cracked open casks of lamp oil and splashed it on the wood, on the gate, much of it on themselves.

Clearly the mob intended to burn down the gate and storm the palace.

Up on the wall, a handful of watchmen attempted to repel the invaders. They had bows and were firing recklessly into the crowd, perhaps too afraid to even pick proper targets. Every time an old woman or a one-legged beggar was pierced the crowd's howling grew in volume and intensity. The half-hearted defense served only to further incite the crowd.

Malden had never seen anything like it. Always in his experience the people of Ness backed down at the slightest show of force. There had never been a time when the people had truly loved the Burgrave, but always they had respected his authority—authority backed up with the point of a sword, or a line of halberdiers wearing cloaks-of-eyes. Malden had seen plenty of riots in Ness—plenty of moments when the people started picking up cobble stones to throw at their betters. Always before a man with a sword and a plume on his helmet had taken control of the situation and calmed everything down. Always before the unrest had been quelled before it could really get started.

This was different. This was outright rebellion.

"You see the power of belief," Coruth said. She sat atop the dome in her human form again, as if she had climbed down out of the sky in search of a comfortable seat. "Perhaps you made a mistake, Malden, when you took sides with a god."

"Pritchard Hood used religion against me—I thought only to fight back with the same weapon."

"It worked."

The crowd never faltered, even as the watchmen dropped stones over the wall to crush the attackers, as they called for more arrows, even as they tried to reason with the people. No matter what they tried the defenders failed to keep the mob from lighting their bonfire. The flames licked high at the wall, scorching the stones. The wooden gate held against the conflagration, but it couldn't stand up to that heat forever.

The archers stopped firing. The watchmen started hauling buckets of water up the wall to douse the flames, though this seemed to achieve nothing but to create great clouds of silvery steam. The watchmen were joined by palace servants and a few guards in green cloaks. The Burgrave had left precious few men behind when he rode out of the city, and now there were not enough for the task at hand.

"You need," Coruth said, "to start thinking what you'll do with this new power you possess."

"Power? Me? I have never felt more helpless in my life," Malden insisted.

Coruth laughed. "That's one of the first lessons I had to learn as a witch. The world is large, and the forces arrayed against us are numerous and vast. You do not gain power by opposing them. You gain it by becoming one with them. Every victory is a surrender to inevitability."

"Please, Coruth—no riddles, not now. I am sickened by this. I want no part in it. You speak of power! If I had any, I'd use it to stop this!"

The witch shrugged.

In the square, the gate began to shift on its hinges. Perhaps they were melting—or perhaps the wood of the gate was warping in the heat. Soon it would fall, and nothing would stand in the way of the mob.

Coruth turned to face him. "Tomorrow the people will own this city. There will be no civil authority left. I do not know if they will slaughter the Lady's priests. Their anger seems directed more toward the Burgrave who abandoned them. It matters little. Tomorrow they will look for someone else to lead them. To tell them what to do. Someone who has already demonstrated that their cause is his own. Someone who can take action, and speak pretty words, and convince them they were blameless for what happened tonight."

"Blameless! What they've done already sickens me."

"Best you don't tell them as much. They need someone to forgive them. They need someone to tell them what to do next."

"But that can't be me," Malden said. "I'm just a thief! No," he said, looking inward. "No, I won't do it. I can't."

"Be careful, Malden. If you will not take on that role, someone else surely will. Someone not of your choosing. You will do what you must do, Malden. No point in fighting it, not any more. When you need my help, come to me, and I will give it freely." She rose grumbling to her feet. He knew she was about to turn back into a bird and fly away, fly somewhere he couldn't follow.

Now there was power worth having.

"Wait," he called. He had to know something. "At least tell me how I should—" he began to ask, but Coruth was already gone.

He stayed atop the counting house all night, until the scene below him had played itself out. The gate fell. The defenders made a valiant stand. They were well-trained and well-armed. For every one of them, the mob could send fifty men and women against them. And the mob didn't care how many of its individual members died.

By dawn fire licked from the stone windows of the palace, and the roof of the barracks had been pulled down, and its stones broken.

Castle Hill was a ruin. Everything it stood for was gone.

CHAPTER SIXTY-ONE

In a muddy field just off the Helstrow road, Baron Easthull's plan was to be tested. In a few short hours, it would be seen whether the rabble of deserters and bandits could destroy a small force of barbarians.

Croy was not particularly hopeful for success.

Vapor twisted along the old furrows of the field, coiled around the stubble that was all that remained of the wheat stalks that had grown there all summer. Birds wheeled over the mud looking for any bit of grain dropped by the gleaners. At the edge of the field, where trees shadowed the soil, early frost made a crust on the water of an irrigation ditch.

The wound on Croy's arm was bandaged tight, and hidden by a broad shield he could just lift. The wound ached, but not as much as it would after a long day of fighting.

Perhaps he wouldn't live long enough for that to become a problem.

He looked out over a sea of expectant faces, and wondered what he should say to them. He did not believe many of them would survive the first wave of the attack. Scouts had reported that a force of barbarians on foot had left Helstrow before dawn. The scouts said they numbered more than one hundred, and were led by Mörgain herself.

Arrayed against her he had three hundred and sixty men. Every warm body he could find. They'd had minimal training, their weapons were of the poorer sort of steel, and they had never fought for their lives before. He'd seen them fight against a handful of scouts when they completely outnumbered their foes and still they'd make no headway. This time he expected most of them to turn and run when battle was truly joined. Which, ordinarily, might not have been so bad. Retreat was a valid stratagem on the battle-field—if you were outmatched, or unable to press a fight, it was always better to turn and run than to stand and be cut down. Against barbarians, though, retreat was suicide. The barbarians could run faster than the men of Skrae, and they didn't understand the concept of quarter.

Croy walked his horse back and forth across the line. Serjeants with green and yellow ribbons on their helmets struck at their men and bellowed curses at them to make them form up properly. Croy pretended not to hear the complaints and protests. He nodded at each man who met his eye. Then he rode back to the head of the column and stood up in his stirrups. The serjeants bellowed for silence.

Time to say something. Anything to give these men courage.

"You are men of Skrae," Croy told them, standing upright in his stirrups. "You fight under the Lady's watchful gaze. She will not desert you now, when you need Her the most."

He expected a cheer, but received none. Frowning, he watched their faces, looking for any sign of enthusiasm. If only Malden was here, he thought. Malden had always been good with words. He'd probably know a few sneaky tricks to even the odds. And having a second Ancient Blade would make a big difference.

Croy shook his head. "Alright. You know what to do. Hold your lines. Stand your ground. If you get any chance to hurt a barbarian—any chance—hurt him grievously."

That actually got a faint chuckle out of the men. Croy wasn't sure why—he hadn't been trying to be funny.

"Keep yourselves alive. Do not forget to parry and block their blows. I'm sure you'll all do fine."

He sat back down in his saddle. Some of the serjeants turned to stare at him, as if to ask if he was really finished. If that was it.

Croy raised a hand and dropped it. His one trumpeter blew an off-key fanfare, and then his handful of drummers started the march.

Once on the road they made good time, though Croy did not push the pace. No need to tire his men when the enemy was coming straight at them. He led them north, following the dusty ribbon of the road as it wound through a series of small bogs. Trees lined the road on either side, their dead leaves fluttering down in front of Croy like a grim echo of rose petals strewn before a conquering hero. He brushed them away from his eye slits as they flapped against his helmet.

The marching army made enough noise that he did not hear Mörgain and her company until they were nearly face to face. He lifted his sword hand, fingers spread, and the drummers ceased their beating. His little army took their time stopping behind him, men colliding with each other and grumbling about it. In time they formed up and brought their weapons round.

Mörgain sat her horse wearing no armor but a fur cloak. The paint on her face was freshly done and shockingly white. Behind her, scores of barbarians jogged on foot. According to the scouts they had been running all morning, and would already be tired, ready to take a rest. That was something, at least.

Mörgain spat out a word Croy couldn't make out. The barbarians stopped in mid-stride. They stopped as one, without a sound or wasted movement. Mörgain's eyes narrowed, making her face more skull-like than ever. She studied the army facing her but said nothing.

There was no need to state the terms of their meeting. Everyone knew why they were there, and that this would be a battle to destruction. No parley was necessary, for there was nothing to bargain for, or with.

Croy hesitated before he gave the order to charge, however. He had something he wanted to try, first.

"I understand," Croy shouted, "that among your people, there is a law of champions. That when two clans meet in battle, their leaders may agree to single combat. A duel, to the death, between the best warriors from either side."

Mörgain frowned and stroked the neck of her horse. "That is our way."

"Also, that when a champion loses such a contest, his clan must lay down their arms and surrender. They are bound by the terms of the duel."

"You know much of us."

Croy shrugged. "I knew your brother, once, in another time. I called him brother myself then, and listened when he spoke of your land and your people. I came to respect some of your traditions. Only some. But this one appeals to me. Dismount, and face me, one on one."

Mörgain shook her head. "Both parties must agree. You cannot force my hand, Sir Croy."

Croy's heart sank. It had been his best chance. "In my land, only a churl would call a woman a coward," he tried.

"In my land, no man would dare," Mörgain replied.

"You have much to gain, milady. There are three of us for every one of your men."

"I came ready for more."

Croy bit his lip. "Very well, then. If a lady wishes for

battle, a gentleman must oblige her. Let us waste no more time . . . *Princess* Mörgain."

Mörgain's teeth gnashed under her painted lips and she tore Fangbreaker from its scabbard. She was half out of her saddle—and Croy was getting ready to charge her—when her eyes went wide and she began to laugh.

"Very clever, Sir Croy!" she called. "But you cannot goad me to—"

Croy snapped his fingers.

He had spent enough time with Malden to have learned a little deceit.

From either side of the road, hidden by the trees, a dozen archers let fly. Behind Mörgain barbarians screamed and fell, their legs and arms and necks pierced by arrows. At that range, and with so many potential targets, even poorly trained archers couldn't miss.

"Charge them!" Croy shouted, and behind him his men started to run.

CHAPTER SIXTY-TWO

Mörgain's barbarians were distracted by the archers and turned outwards toward the trees to find and slaughter them. Croy rushed his own soldiers into the middle of the barbarians, racing his horse directly into Mörgain's teeth to keep her from countering the advance. His men struck fast and hard, as if they knew they would have only a moment's grace before the barbarians recovered enough to counter them.

Bill hooks tore through stinking furs and the unwashed flesh beneath. Pikes impaled reavers whose backs were momentarily turned. For a moment the battle seemed already

over, the men of Skrae making bloody inroads into the
barbarian mass, striking down the bigger, better-armed
barbarians left and right.

It could not last, of course. The barbarians knew how to
fight, and how to stay alive. They whirled about with axes
and crudely forged iron swords, hewing arms and heads
from civilized bodies, bellowing like bulls in their fury.

Croy's serjeants screamed for his men to press the attack,
to lose no momentum. Croy had no chance to see if they
heeded the call. He was far too busy with Mörgain.

He drove his horse shoulder to shoulder with her mount,
and launched into a frenzied attack, trying to catch her off
guard.

Mörgain just laughed.

She fought like no man he'd ever met. She was so fast
she made him dizzy. She had no shield but needed none—
Fangbreaker flashed even in the dull light, spinning around
to catch Ghostcutter every time Croy thought he saw an
opportunity for an attack. Her massive sword possessed a
fine balance no modern sword-maker could match, not even
a dwarf—heavy as it was, it seemed to float in her hand
like a wand.

Croy could barely lift his shield arm, but he had no choice
but to use it to block as she recovered from his parry and
took her own chances with sweeping strokes. Fangbreaker's
finely honed edge slashed deep cuts through his wooden
shield, which was held together only by its iron rim.

He could almost hear Bikker, his former instructor in the
arts of swordplay, speaking in his ear, pointing out all the
chances he missed, all the openings she left. Yet he could
not seem to take advantage of these lapses lest he leave
himself open. One good cut from Fangbreaker would shear
through even his steel armor and leave him bleeding.

Lift your shield arm, boy, Bikker shouted at him. *Catch
her point on your boss and swing—no, look out,
parry—parry—parry!*

He could not strike her without taking a cut himself. Her
speed made it impossible. And he was already wounded.
Yet if he didn't strike soon, or at least break contact with

Mörgain, he would be unable to command his men—unable to even look over and see how the battle fared.

Fangbreaker crashed against his shield with a mighty blow that made the boards flex inside their rim. One more blow like that would shatter it, he knew, and leave him defenseless.

No more time, boy. No more time for playing games.

With his wounded arm, Croy thrust forward with the ruined shield. Normally one blocked at an angle, so one's opponent's blade would slide off the shield and off to the left. This time Croy shoved the shield straight into Mörgain's attack.

The point of Fangbreaker sank through the wood, barely slowed as it sent a blast of splinters to tumble across Croy's breastplate. The sword kept coming straight at his heart, and clanged against his armor.

Croy slipped his feet from his stirrups and then twisted sideways, his wounded arm wracked with pain as he forced his shoulder down, between the two horses. The animals shied apart as he fell toward the road surface, swinging his leg up and over his saddle.

Mörgain's sword was trapped by the twisted iron rim of his shield. She had to either follow him down or let go of her blade. He prayed for the latter.

She chose the former.

Croy looked between the legs of the horses on his way down, and saw something that revived much of his flagging strength. The men of Skrae were prevailing.

The barbarians must never have recovered from their initial surprise. They had moved fiercely to attack, but as individuals—each man choosing a foe from among the attackers and concentrating all his strength on a single enemy. The men of Skrae, on the other hand, seemed to actually remember the little training he'd given them, and fought together as units, flanking and mobbing the barbarians. There were three of them for every one of Mörgain's soldiers and though any given barbarian might cut down two opponents, the third could still strike in return. The road was a heap of bleeding bodies, and most of them were dressed in fur.

He started to call for his serjeants to press the attack,

but the breath was knocked out of him as Mörgain fell full on him, her death's head face so close to his he could smell the paint she wore.

"Ha!" she gasped. "Is this what you wanted all along? To bed me? You should have just asked!"

He could not frame a proper reply. So instead he reared up and smashed his armored forehead into her nose. Bikker had taught him that move, too.

Mörgain rolled off of him and sat in the dust, wiping blood away from her upper lip. She looked stunned. Croy changed his grip on Ghostcutter's hilt and readied himself for a swing.

Before his arm could lift, her eyes focused once more and with her free hand Mörgain punched him on the side of his head. His helmet rang like a bell and his head bounced around inside it. He felt like he'd been struck with a battering ram. His face flew sideways and for a moment he could see nothing but bursting light.

Bikker shouted in Croy's head. *Get up, damn you. A man lying down is a dead man.* The words sounded like they were being shouted through a pipe, but Croy forced himself to get one foot down on the ground, to lever himself up onto one knee using Ghostcutter as a crutch.

When he could see again, Mörgain had Fangbreaker free of his ruined shield and was lifting it high over her head for a killing stroke. Croy wasn't sure that he had the strength to block that cut—not against a sword so heavy.

He never got to find out. As Mörgain howled for his blood, an arrow pierced the bicep of her sword arm. The thin shaft seemed to appear out of nothingness, but it hit with enough force to knock her sideways. Her blow came down and cut deep into the road surface, missing Croy by a good foot.

She hadn't expected the swing to carry so far. She was off balance. Croy kicked her legs out from underneath her and scrambled to his own feet.

"Serjeants! Form your men—let no barbarian live!" he shouted.

The battle was nearly won. Only a few knots of reavers

remained, fighting back to back now and holding the men of Skrae off as best they could. They could not hope to prevail for long against massed pikes. They may have been better fighters in every possible way, but they lacked the better weapons and better tactics of Skrae.

Had Easthull been right, Croy wondered? Maybe this was exactly what the baron had planned. A humiliating victory over one of Mörg's chief lieutenants, the very daughter of the Great Chieftain. If they carried this day perhaps the clans would have no choice but to sue for peace—

"You will die!" Mörgain shouted, jumping up behind him. "Even if my men perish here, you will not live to see it, Sir Croy!"

Croy whirled around in a flawless arc, Ghostcutter's point whistling through the air. Bikker would have been proud of his form, of his speed.

It didn't hurt that Mörgain was bleeding copiously, or that the muscles of her sword arm had been injured. When Ghostcutter's flat smacked against Fangbreaker with a resounding ring, Mörgain's sword jumped from her hand and spun in the air. She tried to dive for it, to catch it before it hit the ground.

Croy could not allow that. He danced in through the follow-through of his strike and shoved Ghostcutter's point into the hollow of Mörgain's throat. Just short of piercing her skin.

"Ask for quarter now," he told her, "and observe my mercy. You may have your life, if you surrender."

Mörgain's lips split in a defiant grin. Then she shoved two fingers in her mouth and let out a piercing whistle so loud it made Croy wince backwards and shut his eyes.

When he could open them again, she had grabbed Fangbreaker and scuttled away from him. "You think I fear death?" she mocked. "Death is my mother!"

Croy's ears were still numbed from her whistle. Yet he could distinctly hear something, a rumbling noise like an earthquake beginning. Soon he could make out individual voices in that roar—gibbering and wailing, and the chattering of teeth.

Out of the trees, a horde of berserkers came for him.

CHAPTER SIXTY-THREE

Spittle flecked their red-painted lips. They came running with blood in their eyes, flourishing axes high over their heads and biting their shields. Croy had seen them before, at the gate of Helstrow, but then he'd had a wall at his back and a gate to retreat behind. Now they surrounded him on all sides.

The few of Mörgain's barbarians left on the road broke off from the combat and moved out of the road, making room for their reinforcements. The men of Skrae, perhaps heartened by their near victory, fell back into ragged formations, making tight squares bristling with pikestaffs. Not even a cavalry charge could break a properly formed pike square.

The berserkers were beyond awareness of the danger. They threw themselves on the points of the pikes, impaling themselves even as they slashed at the long hafts with their axes. Pikes exploded in bursts of splinters and the squares began to fall apart. The berserkers, jabbed in a dozen places, their wounds running bright red, did not even slow down. When a pike square broke the berserkers leapt into the gap, hewing left and right with no concern for their own safety.

"Break and run!" Croy shouted. There was no cowardice in fleeing this madness. "Serjeants, disperse your men!"

It made no difference. Croy's men could not hear him over the roaring of the berserkers.

He turned to see Mörgain leaping onto the back of her horse.

"They'll slaughter friend and foe alike. Their fury can't be quenched but by blood," Mörgain told him. "If you're wise, you'll do as I do."

Croy frowned at her. "You expect me to leave my men here to die?"

"I hope you will," she told him. A strange wistful look

came into her eyes. "I'd like to see you again. At the point of my sword or—otherwise." Then she laughed and kicked her horse into a gallop. In a moment she was gone around a bend of the road.

Croy cursed in frustration and ran toward the fray. Ghostcutter tore through the spine of the first berserker he found, cutting the man's back to ribbons. The berserker fell but his legs kept kicking at the dust as he tried to get up.

Another man with a red-painted face howled at Croy and swung at him with his axe. The blow could have chopped down a tree, but it was ill-timed. Croy ducked underneath it and ran the easterner through the heart.

The berserkers died like anyone else. They just took longer to realize what had happened. Croy laid low two more before he'd reached the first pike square. "You, men, get out of here," he screamed at his own soldiers. "You only have one chance!"

As the serjeant smote and bellowed at his men to obey their orders, one by one the men of Skrae broke for the trees. Many of them were caught by berserkers but a few escaped. Unfortunately that left Croy alone with a pair of berserkers who had no other target for their wrath.

They moved fast, though not nearly with the speed of Mörgain. Croy turned their headlong recklessness against them, tripping one as he stepped inside the reach of another. Ghostcutter rose and fell as he slew them. They made no attempt to parry. Croy paused only a moment to make sure they were dead, and would not come biting at his ankles.

Suddenly another berserker was right next to him. A wicked axe blade came down on the side of Croy's helmet. It bounced off but it left his head ringing and his helmet slid to the side so he could no longer see out of the eyeslits. Blind and deaf, Croy jabbed straight out with Ghostcutter and tore the helmet off with his free hand.

Two more berserkers faced him. They were still ten yards away. More than enough time to think of how to dispatch them. Or just enough time to try to break up another doomed pike square. Croy sought the nearest group of his own soldiers—

—and found none.

Maybe they'd been smart enough to break and run without waiting for his command. He saw mounds of bodies, though, and this time, he recognized most of the dead faces. Nowhere on the road could he see men of Skrae still standing. What he did see was red-painted faces and rolling, bloodshot eyes.

He was alone, with at least thirty berserkers.

Croy no longer had a duty to dispatch. Without men, he had no orders to carry out. He raced for his horse, as fast as his legs could carry him. Jumping up onto its back, he gave it a sharp jab with his spurs and grabbed up the reins as he tried desperately not to fall off.

As fast as his horse could run, though, the berserkers gave chase. They ran after him, whooping and brandishing their weapons, covered in blood. Croy felt like he was in some terrible dream where no matter how fast he rode he would never get away.

Little by little, though, he gained ground. His horse panted for breath as its hooves flashed on the dusty road. He leaned forward into the charge, to avoid the naked tree branches that flashed by overhead. He was going to make it. He was—

A berserker leapt from the side of the road and grabbed onto his saddle. The man's legs dragged behind him on the ground but his hands clutched with white knuckles at Croy's tack.

Croy stared down into eyes gone wholly to madness. He saw anger there, only anger—anger at the world, at the gods, at anything that could bleed. The berserker grabbed at the reins with his teeth and started chewing through them.

Croy didn't have time to cry out in surprise. He lifted Ghostcutter high and brought its pommel down hard enough to smash in the berserker's skull. The madman's hands finally released the saddle, and the body fell away.

Easthull, Croy thought. He must go at once to the manor. The baron, the king, the princess were there. He needed to move them somewhere else, perhaps far to the west. Perhaps as far as Ness.

There was no time to waste.

PART 3

A CHANGE OF STATION

INTERLUDE

"Halt, here," Mörgain said, and the paltry remnants of her band formed up behind her steed. Wincing a little—Sir Croy had given her many new bruises to remember him by—she dropped from her horse to the surface of the road. Behind her a dozen reavers stood glancing at each other as if they wondered what she was up to. Let them wonder in silence, she thought. If they started questioning her decisions she would act then.

She had seen something lying in the dust and she wanted to know what it was. Some half-formed thought was wriggling at the back of her mind and she wanted to let it hatch from its chrysalis and try its wings.

Stooping, she picked up an apple and studied it carefully. Then she looked up at the trees that overhung the road, trying to see where it might have fallen from. Most likely it meant nothing. Still . . .

It was Halvir, one of her strongest warriors, who chose to speak for the rest. "Chieftess, we need to return to Helstrow as quickly as possible. The Great Chieftain needs to know about the Skraeling resistance we met."

"We broke Sir Croy's force," she said, turning the apple back and forth in her hand. Not looking up. "He'll be no trouble for us now, even if he survived the berserkers." Those trance-crazed warriors were still out in the trees, either attacking every living thing they saw or having already collapsed into the deep slumber that always followed their mania. She would round them up tomorrow and reward them for carrying the day. In the meantime she had only this handful of reavers, the only survivors of Croy's well-orchestrated attack, to work with. It might be enough.

If she returned to Helstrow now, she would gain glory

and tribute from her father. She had, after all, broken a surprise attack from a superior force. Yet it would not be enough for Mörgain. Mörget was returning as the conqueror of a city. His achievement would eclipse hers and he would never let her forget it.

No. Mörgain would bring something else back, when she returned to the Great Chieftain. She would be able to say she'd met the last army of Skrae—and crushed them, utterly annihilated them. And that meant finding their hiding hole and burning them out.

Mörget would not be able to match that.

Since her birth, Mörgain's glory had been sullied, overshadowed by the greatness of her father and brother. Scolds sang songs about their journeys and their duels, about how Mörg had seen every land in the world, and how Mörget had bested every man who ever stood against him. The songs they sang about Mörgain made men laugh. The girl who would play with knives, they'd called her. Then the girl who would be chieftess. Of late they'd stopped singing the songs—she'd killed enough men that her exploits didn't seem so funny anymore. Yet still she was considered weaker than her brother. Until she could prove herself Mörget's better, she would never be satisfied.

"We have some time to play with. Time to strike another blow. Perhaps a fatal one," she said.

Halvir had been made bold by her near defeat on the road. "We're wounded and tired, and long to return to the fortress, Chieftess. Why this delay?"

She stared at him in surprise. Her brother, she knew, would strike the man down just for defying him. He would never allow his men to speak to him in such a way. Yet perhaps Mörgain had inherited some of her father's wisdom. Mörg, she knew, always wanted to hear what his subordinates thought. He understood they might have seen something he missed, or have come up with some creative solution to a problem that vexed him.

She decided to take a middle course, and pretend his defiance was beneath her notice. The buzzing of a pesky fly. "Is there not a manor house near here?" she asked. "There was one on the map I saw in Helstrow."

The reaver frowned. "Aye, a place called Easthull, not so much as a quarter mile away. Yet we had reports from Mörget's men that it was abandoned. There was no smoke from its chimneys and its gates were locked up tight. No lights showed at night. He assumed it was untenanted. That all the Skraelings fled from this part of the road."

"Apparently not all of them," Mörgain said. She held the apple up where Halvir could see it.

Someone had taken a bite out of it. Recently. Its pale flesh was brown around the edges, but not yet rotten.

Halvir scowled. He didn't seem to understand.

"Look up," she said. Above them an apple tree bent its branches over the road. Here and there a red fruit sagged on a limb, though not so many as one might expect. And there were no rotten apples lying on the side of the road, nor any others trampled in the dust. Only the one she'd found. "Someone has been collecting these. Perhaps storing them away for the winter. Someone who lives close by, but who is clever enough not to show himself when we ride past."

Halvir's nostrils flared. Did he see it now? Or was he only angered that she'd showed him up? For many men that was the only possible reaction when a woman demonstrated she had a brain in her head—or an arm capable of swinging a sword. She wondered idly if she would have to kill Halvir before the day was out. As an example to the others, and to stop his wagging tongue.

"You saw the men Sir Croy led against us," she told him. "A rabble, poorly trained. Barely clothed. But they had one great advantage—they were organized. Better so than we were, and that cost us many men. Croy gathered every man he could find to fight us and he trained them himself. He must have had some place to bring them, a staging ground from which to plan his attack."

"So you would raid Easthull, and find that place," Halvir said. He turned his head away, but he nodded. "Perhaps find Sir Croy as well. His head would be a good prize to bring the Great Chieftain. Yet if we find the manor deserted and empty—"

"At the very least we'll have a place to sleep tonight," Mörgain pointed out.

Halvir seemed not wholly convinced. Yet he knew better than to challenge her further. Mörgain mounted her horse and led the way. The manor was very close indeed, and easy enough to find if you were looking for it. As promised the gates were locked and the house shut up, but Mörgain's nerves keened as she approached anyway. This was the greatest glory she knew, the finest pleasure. To approach a place with sword in hand and no idea what one would find.

The thrill of discovery, she thought. The thrill of finding new enemies to destroy. Who knew what was inside that house? Dust and shadows? Sir Croy, nursing some wound that left him helpless to fend her off?

The body of the long sought-for king of Skrae? Now *there* would be a prize.

They tied ropes to the gate and used her horse's strength to pull it down. It fell into the road with a great thud. Surely anyone inside the house would have heard that sound, but no door opened, there was no flash of color at a window as someone peered out to see what was happening. Mörgain drew Fangbreaker and moved in, crouching low as if she were braving an enemy revetment and expected to be peppered with arrows.

Behind her the dozen reavers came on, not nearly so cautious.

"Look at the door," Halvir said, loud enough to be heard inside the house.

Mörgain did not turn to chastise him, but instead did as he'd suggested. Fallen leaves had piled against the bottom of the manor house's door. No one had gone in or out that way in weeks, it looked like. Mörgain began to wonder if she'd made a mistake after all.

"I weary of this," Halvir said, and strode forward, past Mörgain.

So when a western peasant jumped out of a tree above their heads, he landed on Halvir, not Mörgain. The little man knocked the reaver to the ground and started pounding on his head with a rock. Blood flowed and Halvir shouted in pain.

It seemed Mörgain would be spared the task of killing the reaver herself.

Mörgain lunged forward with Fangbreaker and skewered the peasant. The civilized man screamed and died, even as two dozen of his fellows erupted from side doors of the house or came running out of the stables, crying for blood and swinging weapons.

The reavers behind Mörgain had all fought in raids before. They formed up in a tight knot at her back, swords and axes ready. They were outnumbered. Yet Mörgain only took one look at the weapons the peasants carried—sticks and farm tools—and a wicked smile bloomed on her face.

She'd found what she was looking for, surely.

CHAPTER SIXTY-FOUR

Malden grabbed onto a window ledge and hauled himself upward. One foot on the casement, he thrust his arms up to grasp the sharp edge of a roof, then swung himself up with a grunt and scrabbled up the shingles toward the roof ridge. Dancing around a chimney pot, he dashed to the edge of the roof and leaped into empty space, barely catching the head of a marble statue in the square beyond. Before he'd lost his momentum, he kicked off the statue's shoulders and somersaulted onto a second floor balcony across the way.

Through the windows of the house he'd landed on, he saw a family of four sitting at table, taking their midday meal. The father looked up and for a moment made perfect eye contact with Malden—a thief, climbing around on the outside of his house.

The man gave him a cheery wave and rushed to the window to fling it open. "Lord Mayor! Lord Mayor!" he called, but Malden was already up on his roof and running up the slope of shingles as fast as he could.

There had been no time to acknowledge the change that had come over Malden's life. No time to reflect and even think about what he was doing. He'd been so busy since the people had carried him through the streets and put a garland of dried roses on his head. Too busy to think or even stop and reflect on the burden he now bore. The only peace and quiet Malden ever got anymore was on top of someone's roof, running as if every man in the watch was after him.

Except there was no more city watch, and the people chasing him all wanted to shake his hand and express their gratitude.

In the week since the death of Pritchard Hood, things had changed in Ness. The people owned their own city now. It had always been a Free City, and the people of Ness had always enjoyed certain liberties. Freedom from royal taxes. Freedom from conscription. Freedom to own property, and to keep their own money. All those things had been guaranteed in their charter, a piece of paper Juring Tarness had signed eight hundred years ago. They had a saying in Ness: *City air makes you free.* Of course, there had been limits on that freedom. All other rights not specifically listed in that document were still the province of the king.

Now there was no more king. There was no more Burgrave. Only, now, a Lord Mayor. There had been much debate about what to call the new leader of Ness. The title they'd eventually chosen was not a Skraeling honorific at all—it was the name given to the men of the Northern Kingdoms who were elected to serve as the leaders of their mercantile cities. It was technically incorrect, since Malden was no lord by birth or right, but the people did love calling him by his new title.

A title Malden hated, because it made him the enemy of freedom.

Freedom was one of the few things Malden truly loved

or believed in. Freedom was what he'd sought all his life, even as all the lords and knights and kings tried to take it away from him. Freedom was wonderful—at least, it was until your neighbor decided to be free with your property, or your spouse, or your life. Then someone had to step in and take away his freedom to preserve yours.

Malden, who had spent his entire life hating watchmen and judges and especially rulers, was now the one who sent people to the gaol. The one who sat in judgment at their trials and decided who was worthy of freedom and who must be constrained for the good of Ness. The one who would have to punish miscreants, as soon as he figured out a way to do so that didn't make his stomach cramp and tie itself in knots. There had been no hangings in Ness since the night Castle Hill was razed. There had been a dozen murders, though. Just that morning he'd had to send Velmont and a crew of thieves into a bad part of the Stink. Because there were no watchmen left, it was up to the thieves to maintain order—something they found hilariously funny, though Malden had not been laughing when he asked this of them. There had been a man, a citizen, deranged in his faculties, who had killed his own daughter. He'd claimed he was going to take her blood to the Godstone, and there make proper sacrifice. The madman thought that reinstituting human sacrifice was the only way to drive off the barbarians.

Malden had him put in chains. After talking briefly with the man he had been convinced that should the murderer's freedom be returned to him he would only find somebody else to kill. The murderer had six more daughters, and two infant sons.

"Enough," Malden said out loud, up on the rooftops, because all this thinking nearly made him miss a step. Twenty-five feet above ground, on a roof of crumbling shingles, a misstep would be fatal.

And if he died here who would keep Ness from descending into anarchy?

He ran the rest of the way to the Lemon Garden feeling like a black wind was howling through him. When he dropped down into the courtyard beside the withered lemon tree—all its fruit was gone now, he saw—he felt almost human.

Unfortunately, the courtyard wasn't empty. The whole city knew that Malden had taken the private room upstairs as his office. Men and women from every corner of Ness came now, and paid the tuppenny fee Elody demanded (the price of her quickest and least sanitary engagements) just to get in the door.

"Lord Mayor! There's no one working the grist mill in Chapeldown Lane—I can't get the flour I need to make bread!"

"Lord Mayor! My wagon threw a wheel this morning, but the wheelwright says he can't find any bodgers to make new spokes!"

"Lord Mayor! I put an image of the Lady in my window last night, you know, just in case—and a gang of boys broke my window with rocks!

"Lord Mayor, please, a moment!"

"Lord Mayor!"

"Lord Mayor!"

Their breath filled the courtyard, cutting through the chill in the air but making Malden's head spin. They pressed close and grabbed at his clothing, all trying to get his attention, just for a moment.

Malden felt faint. He felt a desperate need to escape. He scuttled up the swaying trunk of the lemon tree and jumped to the gallery above. More supplicants awaited him there, but he was able to duck inside his private room and bar the door before they could do more than shout his name. They knocked and begged through the portal but for a moment, at least, he was alone.

Or rather—alone with the one person in all of Ness he wanted to see. On the bed, Cythera turned over and opened one bleary eye to look at him. Then she smiled.

There were some small compensations for being called Lord Mayor.

CHAPTER SIXTY-FIVE

Malden leaned down and kissed Cythera gently. She wrapped her arms around his neck and pulled him into the bed. They lay there together for a while, just holding one another. Lovers in a busy time, stealing precious seconds.

In a moment, Malden knew, he would have to get up and go back to work. He could ignore the people knocking on his door, ignore their constant pleas, for a little while, but it turned out that having power mostly meant having to listen to every person with a complaint and finding some way to reassure or help them—lest one lose that power again.

He would have given it up for a bent farthing. He didn't dare give it up for all the treasure in the world's coffers.

"You seem to like men of position," Malden said, with a smile, as Cythera ran one finger up and down his arm.

"Some positions more than others," she laughed.

He brushed hair away from her forehead. He had so many questions he wanted to ask her. So far he hadn't dared. The night after the sacking of Castle Hill, she had come to him. It had not been their first night together, but it had felt different. It had felt like something real had grown between them. Something fragile but invaluable. Something that could be lost as quickly as it was found.

This was Cythera. He knew—knew it with all his heart—that she was not merely attracted to his new powers or the money that came with them. Yet he didn't understand why she had chosen this moment to show it.

"I could buy us a house, now, on the Golden Slope," he told her. "We could live there as man and wife."

Her shoulders tensed. She couldn't seem to meet his eye. "Why would I want that?" she asked, her smile gone. "I've spent the last seven nights in a whore's bed, and there have never been seven sweeter."

Malden ran a hand across the coverlet. He hadn't considered that he had brought her to a bawdy house, or how she would see that. The place just felt like home to him.

"I had Elody change the sheets," Cythera jested.

"Marry me," Malden said, suddenly urgent.

He had asked her as much a thousand times. He'd made a game of it, because every time she said no, but in such a way as to suggest she might one day change her mind. That she longed to be his wife, as much as he longed to be her husband.

"No," she said, again.

This time there were no promises hidden in her eyes.

Malden sighed and laid back, his head on a pillow. He wanted to ask why not. He wanted to force the issue. When would it ever be the right time, if not now? Yet he was terrified of finding out why she would be his leman, but not his lady. He was terrified of what she might say.

Especially because he had begun to suspect he might know the truth.

"Seven nights of bliss," he said, wandering around the subject, "but eight nights ago, I spoke with your mother. Together she and I watched Castle Hill burn. She told me I would have to take up this mantle, or someone else would, someone not of my choosing."

"She sees much. Perhaps more than she should," Cythera told him. She reached over and grasped his hand tight, as if afraid a great wind would come and blow away everything they had.

"Even before that I think she knew this would happen. When I tried to give my sword to Ommen Tarness, I could not lift it. Witchcraft held it down."

Cythera closed her eyes.

"I think I know why she would not let me be rid of Acidtongue. A blade I never wanted, nor ever learned to use and can't even sell. She made this happen. She made me defy the Burgrave, so I would become Lord Mayor."

"Coruth didn't do anything of the sort."

"What?"

"It wasn't Coruth who cast that spell."

Malden sat up in the bed, perhaps too fast. If it hadn't been Coruth, then . . . He could feel Cythera moving away from him, flinching as if she'd been struck. That had not been his intention. "Cythera—"

"I hear the fear in your voice, Malden. And I know why it's there," Cythera whispered. "Be not afraid. Ask me the question in your mind, and I'll answer it."

"You?" he said, almost a whisper. "You did it?"

She turned away from him. "Croy gave you the sword for a reason. He believed you were its rightful wielder, not the Burgrave. That's all." Which didn't answer his question at all, but only forced another.

"Croy," Malden said. "Who was once your betrothed."

"Croy," Cythera repeated. "Who is very far away, now."

She reached for him, and he took her hand. Drew closer to her, so that their faces were nearly touching. He was still Malden. She was still Cythera. Even if she was something else now, too. "You're a witch," he said, his lips moving against her forehead.

"Not yet," Cythera told him. "But I'm learning."

"But—why? Why would you want that, when you could have . . . something else?" he asked. When she could be his wife, he thought.

"When I was a child I begged Coruth to teach me more. So many times I begged." She sat up in the bed. "Malden, women in this world don't have it easy."

"I know it too well," Malden said. His own mother's life had been a litany of sorrows. Poverty, hunger, disease. An early, painful death. Yet she had always said how lucky she was to have never married. Men in Ness regularly beat their wives as much as the law would allow. Getting pregnant was always half a death sentence—a woman would watch her belly swell with love and pride, yet always wonder if she would live to see her child's first breath, for one of every two women died in their birth pains.

"No, you don't. You don't understand what we suffer, and you never can. I grew up believing I was the equal of any man. Smarter than most. Mother's magic kept me healthy and my father's teaching made me strong of will. Yet when Croy fell in love with me, and asked for my hand in marriage, I understood. It didn't matter who I was, or what I wanted to become. My life's course was already set. I was never going to be a person of importance. I was going to be a person of importance's wife."

Despite himself Malden felt the need to protest. "Croy never wanted anything for you but happiness," he said.

"Oh, I know it. He was the sweetest trap I've ever sprung. He was gallant, and so very kind. And he would take away every freedom I owned. Not because he wanted to harm me, or even to own me like livestock. Yet that was all he could ever offer me. A room in his castle, where I could do embroidery and read silly love poems until eventually I died trying to give him an heir. If I was very lucky, I might live long enough to hear that he had been killed on some foreign battlefield, and spend the rest of my days alone, aching for companionship. Even on the night he proposed I think I knew I could never marry him. I wanted to run away. I wanted an antidote for love, and an excuse that would let me say no to him."

She sighed deeply, and stared into Malden's eyes. "I knew only one thing that would make it so. I went to my mother, and I begged her to make me a witch. To train me in her art. A witch can't be owned by any man—not even a handsome knight."

"But that was some time ago," Malden pointed out. "She must not have—"

"She refused me, then. She said she'd seen enough of my future, and that she had reason not to give me power. She would not explain further. I hated her that day." Cythera shook her head. "I didn't understand. I didn't know—she wanted me to see the world. She wanted me to know love. She wanted me to meet you."

"She saw us together?"

Cythera shrugged. "She saw I could have some kind of life. The very thing I wanted. Even if it could only last a little while."

Malden held her close. "It can last the rest of our lives, if you choose."

"No, Malden. It can't. When we first returned to the city she had a surprise waiting for me. She told me she'd changed her mind. That it was time for me to begin my training."

"Your training as a witch," Malden breathed.

"Please don't look at me like that," Cythera told him. She grabbed his hands, pulled him up so he was sitting facing her. Leaning forward very carefully, she placed her lips against his.

"You'll be a witch. Like Coruth."

"She feels the times coming upon us will be hard. Very grim. She feels I'll need every bit of power I can muster." He could see in her eyes there was more to it, but he didn't press. "She feels the same way about you. It's why she—and I—guided you toward taking this job."

"A witch," Malden said, because he couldn't stop thinking it. A witch like Coruth. There were worse allies a Lord Mayor could ask for than a pair of resident witches. Though for some reason the thought of Cythera wearing shapeless robes and staring into other places with wild eyes made him feel weak and alone.

A witch could not be owned by a man, she had said. And what man would want such a dangerous creature for his own? Malden might have answered that question. And yet he sensed there was more at stake here than Cythera simply becoming a woman with her own power.

Where witchcraft was involved, there were always rules. Rules only a doomed man would fail to follow. Rules no man could ever know.

"I don't understand," he said, his body going limp with a sudden weakness.

She wouldn't let him go. She pulled him towards her, and he lacked the strength to resist. "Don't shy away from me now," she said. "I haven't even had my initiation yet. Let's make it seven nights and a day." She reached up and started unlacing her bodice.

CHAPTER SIXTY-SIX

Loophole would never walk easy again. When the mob seized Castle Hill, someone had been smart enough to free him from the Burgrave's dungeon before they set the place to the torch, but one night in the torture chamber had been too much for the old thief. He had spent too long in the iron contraption known as the boot.

Malden had found him a crutch in an abandoned apothecary's shop. It was well-made, with a comfortable pad to fit under his arm, and its shaft was inlaid with mother-of-pearl. Loophole was just able to hobble around on it, though clearly it pained him to do so. Moving at all pained the oldster now that every bone in his left leg had been shattered.

"Don't mind me, lad," the elder said as he winced around Cutbill's headquarters. "Just glad to be alive."

"Tell me everything you require," Malden said, one hand over his mouth so Loophole wouldn't see his fallen face. "It shall be yours. Food, wine, female companionship— you'll be honored, old man, as only those thieves who escape the gallows are. Gold. Fine clothes—"

"It's not the first time I got out of a noose," Loophole laughed. "Of course, last time I was eighteen years old. I knew a trick, y'see, that you can use when they tie your hands. You tense up the muscles in your forearms much as possible, that makes 'em bigger. Here, like this." He showed Malden how it was done. "Then later, you relax your hands again, and your bonds are loose. So when they put the rope around my neck, I waited until they started reading the charges, then slipped my hands free. I grabbed the rope over my head, like this—" Loophole reached above his head. The crutch slipped out of his armpit and he twisted around on his good foot. Malden barely caught him before he fell.

Carefully he led the old man over to the comfortable chair behind Cutbill's desk. Loophole gasped for breath for a while, his mouth puckering and blowing like he was a fish that had jumped up onto a dock by mistake. Blood flushed his face and his eyes couldn't seem to focus properly. Malden began to worry the oldster was succumbing to apoplexy, but after a minute, Loophole calmed down again. "Mayhap I'll tell you the rest of that story some other time," he said.

"Of course," Malden said. "I'd like that." He went to the door and called for Tyburn. The man who came at his call had been Cutbill's personal bodyguard, once. Malden had made him the castellan of the underground lair. "Let Loophole stay here as long as he wants. See to his needs."

"Yes, milord," Tyburn said. "Velmont's been asking for you. Says it's urgent. And 'Levenfingers came by this morn, said some of the thieves are getting restless."

"What now?" Malden asked.

"They say they've looted just about the whole of the Golden Slope. All those abandoned houses, and no watchmen—well, the work went fast. They're running out of things to steal."

Malden had been afraid of that. Thieves would be thieves, and needed prodigious quantities of coin to pay for all the ale they quaffed while they weren't actively working on a job. Meanwhile a delegation of honest citizens—the same honest citizens who had torn Pritchard Hood limb from limb—had petitioned him to offer them protection from robbers and cutpurses. He would have laughed them off if he didn't already know that pickpocketing and footpaddery were running rampant in the city, right when the non-thief population was having trouble making ends meet. If this kept up, there wouldn't be any coin left in Ness that hadn't been stolen out of one pocket to be spent from another. He was probably the first guildmaster of thieves in history to actually have to find a way to reduce crime. It galled him, but he couldn't just ignore it.

The Golden Slope had provided one outlet for the thieves. The houses there were boarded up and abandoned—but not empty. The rich folk of Ness had left plenty behind when they'd fled the city, and so Malden had turned his men loose

on the unguarded treasure. At first he'd thought they would
resent this work as it was just too easy. He'd underestimated
the base laziness in the heart of every thief. The whole point
of being a thief was to get at the easy money. They had
cheered him and offered to pay him a tenth of everything
they stole, even before he thought to ask for it.

"When the Slope is wrung dry, when there are no more
abandoned places to rob, talk to me of this again," Malden
said.

Tyburn nodded. He didn't look happy but since Malden
had become Lord Mayor, he'd learned that politics was not
the art of making everyone happy, it was of making sure no
one became so miserable they were willing to stab you in
the back. "And Velmont? Will you hear what *he* has to say?"

"Yes. Let me just grab my cloak."

Velmont had become Malden's eyes and ears in the city,
proving himself more valuable every day. The Helstrovian had
no friends in Ness, but he brought a pair of fresh eyes that
could see problems Malden might miss. To Malden, Ness had
always been on the verge of collapse—he knew too well how
shoddy and unstable the institutions of his home city could
be. In the midst of the general chaos no individual problem
stood out in high relief. When Velmont saw a problem,
however, Malden knew it had to be fixed immediately. This
was one summons Malden had no choice but to accept.

CHAPTER SIXTY-SEVEN

He already knew what his Helstrovian second-in-command
wanted, but still he let Velmont explain it in the most
dramatic terms. That, at least, meant spending some time

on the rooftops. The two of them raced each other across the Stink and up into the no longer aptly named Smoke, that zone of manufactories and work yards that girdled the city and which now lay mostly quiet, cold, and unproductive. Even the terrible smell of the place had dissipated. "There, brother, what do you see?" Velmont asked, pointing down into the courtyard of the city's biggest grain mill.

"I see wheels that aren't turning, and wheat rotting in sacks," Malden said. The giant mills needed oxen to turn them, and the rich merchants had taken all the best livestock when they fled the city, long before Malden's return. Now the mill wheels stood silent and unmoving. Some needed replacement, too, but none of the workers remaining in the Smoke—a bare handful of what there had been, before the Burgrave enlisted all their fellows—knew how to lever a mill wheel off its axle.

"Slag says he has a solution," Malden told Velmont. The dwarf had been working even longer hours than Malden on one project or another. "A way to use the current of the river Skrait to turn the wheels."

"Won't the grain get wet if you put 'em in yon river?" Velmont asked, looking confused.

"Don't second-guess a dwarf when he says he's invented something new," Malden told the Helstrovian.

"Won't matter, anyroad," Velmont said, his shoulders slumping. "Come, keep up if you can, and follow me uphill. There's more to see, and worse."

The two of them hurried across the roofs of the Smoke and up the Golden Slope toward Castle Hill. It was not a place Malden truly wanted to see ever again. The burnt-out stones of the palace and the fallen public buildings there were a mute accusation of guilt he would never be able to atone for. Yet when Velmont led him along the fire-besmirched wall to a place near the back of the courtyard, Malden saw why they'd come, and his stomach fell.

Six square towers stood along the back wall of the Hill, each of them windowless and very tall with a single thick door at the bottom. Each had once possessed a steep conical lead-lined roof to keep snow and rain off, but the roofs had all melted in the fire.

"Not the granaries," Malden moaned.

"Aye, yer lordship. Ever last one of 'em." Velmont squatted on the battlements and then leapt over to the top of the nearest tower. Malden followed him down through the ruined top of the granary and they clambered down through scorched support beams to the level of the grain inside.

An entire harvest's worth of wheat had gone into these towers before the barbarians came to Skrae. A winter's worth of flour, once it was ground and sifted. Winter was always a lean time in Ness, a time of hunger when many of the poor died for lack of bread. The Burgrave kept these granaries full so that when the coldest months came, he would have something to distribute to his people, if only to keep them from rioting while he dined on succulent venison and rare sweetmeats in his palace.

This year, there would be nothing to hand out. Malden knelt in the grain and picked up handfuls of it to study in the dim light. That which wasn't burnt outright was soaked through by exposure to the elements.

He dropped his hands and let the roasted grain fall from his fingers. It smelled wonderful, frankly. Its smell made his mouth water. In one way the fire had probably done them a favor. Malden had spoken with enough bakers and millers since his ascension that he'd learned more than he ever cared to know about the proper storage and processing of wheat products. For instance, he knew that roasted grain was harder to mill into flour, but it didn't spoil as quickly.

Which was one small saving grace on top of a very serious problem. Roasted grain might be better preserved, but only if it was kept dry. It had rained several times since the fire melted those leaden roofs, and Malden could feel the damp rising off the stored food. Mold was probably already spreading through the towers, and rats wouldn't be far behind. Malden could repair the lead roofs of the granaries, but the damage was already done.

Malden had lived through enough famines in his brief life to understand that what he saw here, what Velmont had shown to him, could easily be the end of his career in politics.

He tried to think of what they could do. "We'll need a

small army up here to move the grain to better bins," Malden said. "We'll salvage what we can."

"Won't be near enough," Velmont pointed out.

"You have a better idea?"

The Helstrovian shrugged. "Maybe. Maybe you and me don't go home tonight. Maybe we light out for greener hills. Surely there's a need for high-toned thieves like us in the Northern Kingdoms, or maybe the Old Empire. Bein' Lord Mayor's a plum job, certes, but—"

"But once people start starving, it won't be mine for long." Malden nodded unhappily. "How I wish I could do what you say. But no—the people of Ness are depending on me. I have to find an answer."

CHAPTER SIXTY-EIGHT

Dead bodies littered the forecourt of Easthull manor. Not a single one of them had been a soldier. These had been the baron's servants and those few peasants he'd kept to work the last of his fields. Croy saw no weapons in their cold hands, no sign they'd put up a struggle at all.

The roof of the manor had fallen in, and the entire south wing was rubble.

He'd come too late.

He'd ridden his horse until it died, and then he had walked. Through mud and fens up to his chest, he'd walked. He'd shed his armor as it became too heavy. Thrown away everything but Ghostcutter. He had not slept, nor eaten, since the berserkers took away his army.

He could barely stand. Yet he walked into the forecourt, sword in hand, just in case Mörgain had left behind anyone to watch the place. Anyone to pick off stragglers foolish enough to return.

Inside the house, birds lifted from a sodden floor and dashed past his face. He waved them away. Found the hearth cold. All the food gone.

He would not have eaten, even if he could. Not until he knew for sure.

In the apartments of the baron he found blood everywhere. The wooden door to the receiving chamber was scarred by axe blows and the lock had been hacked out of its mounting. He pushed open the door, which squeaked noisily on its hinges. Inside something moved furtively.

Croy crouched low, Ghostcutter held before him. He stepped inside, into shadows. He saw the baron's desk. The maps were gone, as were all the reports Easthull had gathered. Whatever the baron had known about the defense of Skrae was old news now to the barbarians.

A beam of yellow light came through a stained glass window at the back of the room. It fell on a scrap of cloth stained dark with blood. Croy stepped closer and picked it up. Linen. It was wrapped around a severed finger. Croy guessed the signet ring had been hacked off the baron's hand.

Behind him something stirred. He swung around instantly, ready for a fight.

One of the baron's hounds came limping toward him. The animal was unkempt and mad with fear. It bared yellow teeth and snarled.

There was fresh blood on its muzzle.

Croy pushed past the dog. It whimpered and snapped at him, but he ignored it and headed back out toward the kennels at the rear of the house. He found the baron there. Easthull had been butchered and fed to his own pack. The dogs had not finished with the head yet, or Croy would not have been able to identify the nobleman.

He could only imagine what the barbarians had done to the king. Or Bethane, the king's daughter. Mörgain had no love for princesses. Thinking about what Bethane might have gone through before she died, Croy began to weep.

Sharp iron touched the back of his neck.

Croy wheeled about, and Ghostcutter sliced through the wooden haft of a bill hook. The blade clattered to the ground. Croy started into a second stroke, one that would cut his attacker in half.

He barely managed to stop when he saw it was no barbarian who had accosted him, but an old woman in a russet tunic. A peasant. How had she even possessed the strength to lift the polearm?

Croy supposed that if the need was great enough, the strength could be found.

"Are you the one they call Croy?" the woman asked. She did not seem frightened, even though he had disarmed her and almost killed her. "Answer me, lad, or it'll go hard for ye."

Croy almost laughed. But then he bowed his head. Sheathed his sword. "I am he."

The old woman nodded and turned away from him. She started walking and he followed, because this felt like a dream—or an enchantment—and there were rules about such things. When a guide presented itself, you had to follow. All the stories agreed.

Stories. Malden used to laugh at the old stories of gallant knights and noble crusades. The stories that had nourished Croy in his infancy, as surely as his nurse's milk. Croy had always believed the stories held a deeper truth, a layer of reality beyond the gray banalities of the mundane world. He had always thought a man with a pure heart and a good cause really could prevail, no matter the odds.

Yet here he was. Doubly masterless, a knight errant without so much as an old story to lead him onward, any longer.

Perhaps . . . perhaps the Lady would let him see Cythera again, now. Perhaps he would see his beloved again before he died at the end of a barbarian's blade.

The old woman led him into a copse of trees not quite deep enough to be called a forest. A wood lot, really, a place for the baron's men to collect firewood. Deep in the shadows of the naked branches lay a cottage, a sawyer's hut. Croy had never seen such a crude dwelling. Its roof was moldering thatch, its walls made of wooden withes smeared with horse hair and dung to keep the wind out. It had no windows and its door was a simple plank that the old woman lifted free of its frame. She couldn't even afford hinges.

Inside was a room that smelled of old fires and rotten vegetables. There was a fireplace Croy could not call a hearth. Most of the room was so thick with shadows he could see nothing. The old woman stepped inside and replaced the door, leaving him in darkness broken only by the dull light of the coals in the grate, and those illuminated nothing.

"You saw his face?" the old woman asked, in the blackness. She wasn't speaking to him. "It's the one you wanted?"

Had he been led here by assassins? Brigands who would take his sword and trade it for a jug of wine? Croy wondered if he had the strength left to fight such.

"I saw it. Make a light, goodwife," a new voice said. A voice Croy recognized.

Still—he could credit it not, until the old woman lit a stinking rushlight, and he saw. There was no furniture in the tiny house, but a pile of straw had been shoved into one corner to make a pallet. Ulfram V lay upon it, sleeping.

And standing next to him was his daughter, Bethane, who would be queen hereafter.

Croy dropped to his knees. He had only the strength left to utter, "How?"

"When they came we had very little warning," Bethane explained. "A man came running down the road, screaming. It was enough. I dragged father back here. Baron Easthull sacrificed himself by staying behind. He knew Mörgain would not rest until she'd found a noble who'd dared to stand up to her. He died swearing he was alone in the house, and I suppose she believed him."

There was no passion in Bethane's voice. Her words were as flat and uninflected as those of a parish priest reading a very dry passage of the Lady's word.

"I saw much of what happened, though I dared not go so close as to help. I saw them die," Bethane went on. She did not weep. "I saw my country dying. Before it was over I came back here, and knelt by my father's side, and prayed the Lady would take him into her bosom before ever he awoke. I do not want him to know what has become of his kingdom."

Croy lowered his head in grief.

"It was not good for him, to be dragged through mud so far, nor is the air in here fit for royal lungs. Come, Sir Croy, and listen. Tell me what this sound means, though I know it too well already."

Croy moved to kneel over his king. Ulfram lived still, but the breath that came in and out of his lungs rattled and choked. A sound that could have been mistaken for snoring, if Croy had never heard it before.

"It is his death rattle," he agreed.

"Sit vigil with me tonight," Bethane said, and he obeyed. They knelt together, deep in prayer and meditation. Time went away.

In the morning the old woman rose from the pile of blankets she had instead of a bed, and she stirred the fire. "I need to get some water on, if we're having pottage," she said. Neither Bethane nor Croy responded. The old woman went out, letting light into the room when she moved the door.

The sunlight fell across Ulfram V's face, and showed it pale, and the eyes empty, open, staring upwards.

Croy broke his reverie long enough to place one hand against the king's neck. There was no pulse, and the skin was cold as ice.

"The king is dead," he whispered. "Long live the queen." It was only then Bethane allowed herself to cry.

CHAPTER SIXTY-NINE

"The king is dead," Coruth said, plucking at long blades of yellow grass on the shore of the Isle of Horses. She said it off-handed, as she might comment on an unusual formation of clouds overhead. "Skrae is in tatters."

Cythera shivered and pulled her cloak around her shoulders. Then she went and gathered some more driftwood, and piled it on the fire.

Coruth had set up a small kettle on a tripod well clear of the house, and it was Cythera's job to keep it hot, tending the fire beneath it as necessary. From time to time Coruth came over and threw a handful of herbs in, then replaced the thick iron cover.

"You care about Skrae," Cythera pointed out, when her mother was silent for too long. All day Coruth had been distracted, staring endlessly out across the waters of Eastpool. Cythera knew perfectly well that her mother was not looking at the clutter of shacks and houses on the far shore. She was sending her mind out—not all of it, not as she did when she flew on the wings of birds and saw the whole of the world. Just feelers, tendrils of her consciousness, testing and probing at the flow of events. "I would have thought witches were above petty politics."

Coruth snickered. "Do you mean, am I heartbroken that we've lost Ulfram V? Hardly. The man was better than his father, but not overmuch. He had a habit of speaking to everyone as equals rather than subjects. I liked that."

Cythera remembered meeting the king, back before the barbarians came. Back when she had thought she knew what the future would hold. That seemed a long time ago. "He seemed a straightforward man."

"But a fool. Too concerned with small matters, the daily accounts and business of running a kingdom. He could not see the larger picture. No, there will come better kings. If there will be any kings at all." Coruth rose to her feet and came over to tend to the kettle. When the lid came off it let loose a stink that made Cythera's head reel, a must of old graves. The liquid in the pot had thickened to a gelid consistency with a crust of foulness at its top. It had the color a fish's eyes get after it's sat too long in a vendor's cart. With another few hours of heat it would congeal even further until it became as stiff as wax.

Cythera thought she knew exactly what this substance

was for. And it made her so cold she couldn't bear to look at it.

"You'll be interested to know," Coruth said, "that Croy is still alive."

"I—" Cythera said, but the thought she'd had, the immediate emotional reaction, died inside her as soon as it was born. "Croy," she said. "Is he in danger?"

"Always," Coruth cackled. "He's an Ancient Blade. He lives to fight. How could a man like that ever be safe? But for now he's still on two feet. If that still matters to you."

"It does," Cythera said, looking down at her feet. It always would, she knew. No matter how her love for Malden grew, there would always be a little room in her heart where Croy would live. A room with a door that could not be locked.

Coruth came and stood next to her, looking down into the kettle of ointment. "Almost ready," she said. She had changed, become more present—more fully integrated with her own body. "You know what this is, don't you?"

Cythera went to get some more wood for the fire before she answered. "It's witch's unguent. It opens up the inner eye. Brings on the second sight."

"Yes," Coruth said. "When it's ready—when all the preparations are ready—we'll begin your initiation."

Cythera closed her eyes and tried not to weep.

CHAPTER SEVENTY

A thousand barbarians marched north, pulling wagons full of books from Redweir. They grumbled at the load, wondering what the Great Chieftain could possibly want with words. Mörget ignored their complaints and ordered a doubling of the pace. He was anxious to see his father again. He had something to say to the old man.

"Slow down, you bastard. We've been walking so long I've got blisters all the way up my legs. For fuck's sake, I've got blisters so far up my arse I can taste them."

Mörget hauled in Balint's chain. The dwarf staggered toward him, her eyes wide with terror. He was in a good mood for once, so he didn't hurt her. Just grinned down into her hairy face and laughed his dark and booming laugh.

Mörget in a good mood was still a frightening thing.

Ahead he could see the walls of Helstrow. He'd been walking for days to return to the fortress, leaving his horses behind. There were so few of them left that every mount was needed for the dwindling number of scouts Mörget could command. The scattered men of Skrae had been busy killing his outriders. No matter—if that was the best they could do, then victory was assured.

There was a nagging doubt in the back of Mörget's mind, a curiosity about what he would do once he had conquered the west. What would satisfy his bloodlust then, when every man on the continent was his thrall? The barbarian put such pointless wonderings behind him. There was always the Old Empire, across the sea to the south. There were always more lands to crush.

At the gate of Helstrow, Mörgain received him with honors. She placed a wreath of dry roses upon his head in mockery of western pomp. She'd even pruned off all the thorns—which he thought might be a subtle jab at his toughness. He was used to her disdain, however. He thrived on it.

"I hear you laid low a baron," he told her. "A silly little man in linen and fur."

She bowed like a western courtier. "Milord, you are too kind to remember my paltry accomplishments. Though I see you've forgotten I also defeated Sir Croy."

"I forgot nothing. He still lives."

Mörgain laughed. "I left him in a welter of berserkers. We've heard nothing of him since. Though, if he is alive—I want him. He's beautiful, in a decadent way. I want him stripped and staked in my tent. I want to see what soft western skin feels like under my lips. I want to know the secrets of courtly love."

"Him you may not have. I must slay him myself."

"You give me orders now, chieftain?" Mörgain's eyes flashed dangerously. The two of them had never fought a true blood duel. Never had their Ancient Blades met when the intention was to draw heart's blood. Mörget wondered briefly how long it would take to kill his sister. Whether she would be a satisfactory opponent, the foe he'd been looking for so long.

She was still useful to him, though. He grabbed her by the throat—she did not try to stop him. Her eyes danced and she smiled as he squeezed.

"What do you really want, Mörgain? I need your aid today. Tell me your price and I'll pay it."

"I want," she said, picking her words carefully, "to serve my clans. To obey and enforce the decisions they make. I want nothing for myself. I am their chieftess, and what they want is all that matters."

It was a variation on the oath every chieftain took when he won his clan. She would deny him the true secret of her heart's desire by parroting words he'd spoken himself so many times. Words their father had composed.

He let go of her. For a moment he expected her to draw Fangbreaker and try to cut him down, but she merely laughed.

"Ah, this tender scene explains quite a bit," Balint said. She had sat down on the grass outside the gate to capture this stray moment's rest. "I was wondering how you lot got so pig stupid. If all brothers and sisters in the east act like this, it's no more a fucking mystery. You know what they say about the get of incest."

Mörgain slapped the dwarf hard across the face. "We kill sibling-fuckers! And we kill anyone who makes false accusations, as well, tiny bitch."

Mörget considered letting his sister kill Balint. It might be briefly entertaining. Yet he still needed the dwarf. He knew what to say to save her life. "A scold can speak thus with impunity," he told Mörgain.

Mörgain screamed in defiance. "She's no scold! Scolds are warriors, who have earned the right to speak truth to their betters. Who has she killed?"

"Hundreds—at the Vincularium, and at Redweir," Mörget pointed out.

Mörgain wouldn't have it. "She's never held a blade in her life."

"She may not have the training of a scold either, or know the kennings and the couplets, but she can speak oaths and curses better than Hurlind." He hauled Balint to her feet by the chain. "And every chieftain may appoint his own scold, as he chooses."

He had Mörgain there, and she could not gainsay him.

"Come, scold. Mörgain, you come with me as well. I take it your thralls can see to my men?"

"It will be done." Mörgain fumed darkly and stalked inside the gate ahead of him. Mörget followed behind her.

"Listen," Balint said, "my feet—"

Mörget picked the dwarf up and tucked her under his massive arm. He thought that would be enough to silence Balint, but it was not.

"So I'm your scold now, as well as your engineer? I want no more responsibilities from you, you daft giant prick. I don't even know what a scold is supposed to do!"

"Oh, you know it all too well. But I did not give you this honor without reason. What you said to my sister—it was unforgivable. She was well within her rights to cut off your head, then and there."

"Because I said she was inbred?"

"That's our way. Slander is not permitted. Except when spoken by a scold. Scolds are expected to mock one and all, and no man may seek revenge for their jeering. Scolds alone are allowed to speak the truth—and by so doing, keep the chieftains from believing their own boasts. By making you my scold I have saved your life. Now you must find a way to repay me."

"Lovely," Balint said. "Where are we going now?"

"I go to see the Great Chieftain. You will wait for me, until I choose to return for you." He tied her chain around a post standing before the gate to Helstrow's inner bailey. The rotting head of a Skraeling knight still sat atop the post, dripping black fluids. Mörget laughed to see Balint strain against her spiked collar, trying to avoid getting any of the putrescence on her clothes.

When he felt he'd been amused enough—that, after all, was another responsibility of a chieftain's scold, to keep him entertained—he headed into the inner bailey with Mörgain at his side.

Mörg waited for his children on the steps of the palace of justice. He received them there with wine for his daughter and milk for his son, and they all listened with varying degrees of impatience as Hurlind the scold recounted their great victories with a minimum of chiding. Sometimes a scold's duty was to tell when a man was worthy of honor.

While they stood and listened to Hurlind's accolades, the dog that followed Mörg everywhere came trotting out of the hall and curled around the Great Chieftain's feet. All that animal ever did was sleep. Mörget hated it so—no barbarian would ever be allowed such lethargy or uselessness, yet Mörg loved it more than he had loved Mörget's mother. He imagined all the different ways he could kill the dog while he waited for Hurlind to finish.

"The eastern half of Skrae is ours. Redweir has fallen," Mörg said, at last, and put a hand on Mörget's shoulder. Normally the son would have shrugged off the father's touch, but this time he tolerated it while he grinned nastily at Mörgain. As usual, Mörget thought, he'd shown her which of them was the stronger. As usual he swelled with the satisfaction of showing her up.

Yet Mörg took his hand away all too soon. "More importantly, the remaining soldiers of Skrae are vanquished, and all resistance conquered," he said. "Mörgain, you have given me half a kingdom by slaughtering that baron who was the last to stand against us. You of all my chieftains have achieved the most."

Mörget's jaw dropped. He could not believe this outrage. He had brought low an entire city! What had Mörgain done, but crush a defiant rabble? This could not stand. This was not acceptable, that he should be slighted this way!

And yet—what could he do? Mörg had already honored him. To demand greater laudation now would be the petulant whining of a child who is not given enough of his mother's milk to suck. He seethed and glowered at Mörgain, but she did not even meet his eye. Why should she? She was the hero of the day.

Mörg lifted his hands high and smiled at his children. "We have won this war, thanks to my get and my ain. You shall both have coffers overflowing with gold, and thralls by the hundred to do your bidding."

"I'll trade my gold for you calling me by my proper name," Mörget growled. It had been a long time since he'd let anyone refer to him as Mörg's Get. He would be damned if he was to be called by that shameful name now.

"As you wish it, Mountainslayer. Hmm. I've never saved that much money by giving a man proper respect before. I must do it more often," Mörg said. He was very drunk, and in a merry mood.

"I'll keep my gold," Mörgain said, looking deeply satisfied. She had always seemed bizarrely proud to be known as Mörg's Ain, that is, "one of Mörg's". The names had not been meant to bring honor to the children, but rather shame them—they had no true names for themselves, not until they earned them. Yet Mörgain acted as if her name was a badge of distinction. Perhaps she thought, like the decadent Skraelings, that glory could be passed on to one's descendants the way you would pass down a sword or a shield. "Gold's worth more than words, any day," she said. "Though it would please me to be called Baronkiller, I confess."

"Sorry, the price is non-negotiable." Mörg laughed and stepped forward to place a hand each on their shoulders. "I will give you each one thing for free, and that is my pride. You've both done very well."

"We've done nothing yet," Mörget insisted, thrusting away his father's hand. Perhaps there was a way he could turn this around—to downplay Mörgain's accomplishment and gain another chance to reap glory for himself. "The western half of Skrae is unconquered. My spies tell me of a new army massing against us, this Army of Free Men. They say it is led personally by the Burgrave of Ness. As long as he opposes us we have only temporary claim to this land."

"You desire to march out of here again so soon?" Mörg asked.

Mörget began to answer. Then he bit his tongue. He'd been about to demand it for himself, but he remembered what Mörgain had said outside the gate. Perhaps she had something to teach him, after all. "I want nothing for myself. I am a chieftain, and it is what my clans want that matters."

Mörg nodded respectfully, as a man will who appreciates a move his opponent makes in a game of counters. That meant far more to Mörget than his father's *pride*.

"Winter is coming," the Great Chieftain said. "This morning the water in my basin was frozen. I had to break it up to wash my face. It will be a hard thing, campaigning in a strange land in wintertime. I myself was going to suggest we spend the season here, and renew the fight only when the grass grows green once more."

"My clans long to complete this war," Mörget insisted. "To crush Skrae while its leadership is in disarray. If we press the fight now we face scattered troops hiding under their beds. Resistance in the eastern half of Skrae may be broken," he said, waving one hand in the air as if to suggest this was no great thing. "Yet there are plenty of men to oppose us in the west, still. Right now they are an untrained rabble, the kind Mörgain has proved so effective in dispersing." Her eyes narrowed and Mörget wondered how far he could push her before she drew her sword and attacked him. Part of him would relish the chance to match his Ancient Blade against hers. "If we wait until spring there may be a real army prepared to stand against us."

Mörg shook his head from side to side. "Meeting even a scattered army on the battlefield means many casualties. Is it not better to let them come to us, where we have strong walls to aid us?"

"You assume they will attack if we do nothing. If it were wise for us to sit and wait, why would it be folly for them?

They will not wish to fight in winter, either. Let us use that to force them into a decisive battle."

Mörg looked up at the sky, as if trying to gauge when the first snow would fall. "You. Chieftess. You speak for one half of all my clans. What do you say?"

Mörgain could not speak for a long while, as her skull-painted face contorted in rage. Clearly Mörget's gambit was working and he had robbed her of her glory. "My clans desire to hear the word of their Great Chieftain before they make a decision." Mörgain turned and stared into Mörget's eyes. "For myself, I desire many things. But of course, what I want does not matter."

Mörg nodded. "Very good. You've heard my decision. Take it to your chieftains, argue it all night over mead and contests of strength. Tell me tomorrow what you decide, and that will be our answer."

There. It was out in the open. Mörgain did want something. His own heart's blood, probably. It did not matter, though.

If she refused to march west now she would look the weakling. She would be begging the scolds to call her Mörget's cowardly sister. He knew Mörgain could never live that down. She would offer her clans to accompany his because she had no choice. All the clans would agree that the war must be taken to the west, as far as Ness and the mountains beyond, all the way to the far sea, until all of Skrae was under their heel. As for Mörg, he would never gainsay the clans when they were unanimous in their choosing.

And even if he tried to do just that—well, he could be replaced. And with Mörgain on the defensive, able only to react to Mörget's moves, there could be only one warrior ready and capable of being Mörg's replacement.

He walked away from the palace of justice with a vast smile deforming his face, despite how he'd been slighted by the Great Chieftain. No one dared asked him what he found so pleasant. He returned to the wall between the inner and outer baileys and collected Balint once more. As he headed toward his tent he told her all that had been said between father, brother, and sister. He wanted to know if she thought his plan to invade the west was brilliant or headstrong.

"Does it truly matter? It means more blood, and that's what you're really after," the dwarf asked, her jeering tone gone for once. She sounded afraid. "It means you get to kill more men of Skrae."

As usual, when she wasn't trying to be funny, she made Mörget laugh the hardest.

"Oh yes," he agreed, "that's certainly a benefit." He boomed out with laughter that shook the windows in the houses all around him.

CHAPTER SEVENTY-ONE

"The Godstone is cracked. The cracks need to be repaired. Only blood will do. Blood is what He wants! How can you not see this?" The madman, the child-killer, was chained to the bars of his cell in the gaol. He looked badly used. Bruises covered his chest and one eye had swollen shut. Clearly his keepers had been beating him.

Malden wondered if they had done so in self-defense, or because they hated his crime. He supposed he couldn't blame them for being angry. Still, he sighed. "I want him made as comfortable as possible. He's beyond rationality—beyond knowing right from wrong. There's no reason he should suffer because he's lost his wits."

"You could end his sufferin' right now," Velmont said. The Helstrovian thief didn't look angry. He looked like he pitied the man. Yet it seemed he could imagine no better way to express that pity than slitting the madman's throat.

The laws of Skrae—and the customs of Ness—agreed.

If anyone but Malden had been in charge of his fate, the man would already be dead. But there had to be a better way—didn't there? Mercy had to mean something.

"No," Malden insisted. "There will be no executions while I'm Lord Mayor. The Burgrave hanged beggars for stealing a loaf of bread. Things are going to be different, now."

"There's only six cells in this gaol," Velmont pointed out. "There'll be more like him, an' soon enow."

"Then we'll build more cells," Malden said, and headed up the stairs toward the ruins of Castle Hill. Velmont was right, of course. The gaol wasn't going to serve his purposes for long. It was meant only for holding criminals until they could be brought to trial. It had not been designed for keeping anyone more than week at a time. The sanitary facilities were rudimentary. There was no air or light down there. Prisoners would sicken and perish if they were locked away in that hole for long.

Yet he knew he was right. Killing a man for a simple crime didn't redress the original offense. It wouldn't bring back the madman's child. There had to be a better way, and it was up to him to find it.

Maybe, he though for the first time, he'd been given this unwanted responsibility for a reason. Maybe he could use his power, instead of being used by it. Maybe he could change things for the better.

If he was only to be given a chance.

Up in the air again, he turned to Velmont and asked, "How much grain did we save from the stores?"

Velmont shrugged. "Enow fer a month, if we're lucky."

"We may have to ration it to last longer," Malden said. He knew that would not be popular. In the two weeks he'd been Lord Mayor, the complaints he daily received of people being unable to get flour to make bread had tripled. It was bound to get worse. Hungry people would want to know why he wasn't feeding them. Starving people would start to think maybe they'd be better off with someone else. Every time he tried to explain the situation, he was met with blank stares.

The worst part was he couldn't blame the people of Ness. He couldn't get angry with them when they didn't understand. Back when he'd just been Malden the Thief, he would have had the same reaction. Living in a city, so far from farms and fields, people forgot that food had to be grown and harvested and brought to Ness and stored. When you could just go down to the market and buy a loaf of bread you never had to think about its provenance.

"Perhaps we should form details of men to go outside the walls and search the closer farms. There may be stores of grain left behind when the farmers fled. Though I imagine the Burgrave probably raided them. He'll need to feed his army, and—"

Malden stopped because he'd heard a noise coming from beyond the wall of Castle Hill. A great jeering roar, full of boos and hisses.

"That can't be good," he said. They rushed to the broken gates and hurried out into Market Square. A crowd had gathered before the Cornmarket Bridge, a rough mob of women and old men who were throwing garbage at a train of wagons. Malden's first thought was relief that the subject of the crowd's ire was not himself.

His second thought was that it was his job to find out what was going on—and to stop it.

"We need to get through there, and see what's happening," Malden said.

"On't," Velmont said, and started grabbing people from the crowd and thrusting them out of the way. Cursing and kicking, he forced a path through the gathering and Malden swept through until he stood at the end of the bridge, where rotten vegetables and bits of refuse coated the cobblestones, the remains of garbage thrown by the crowd.

A dozen men and women huddled there, sheltering themselves from the stinking missiles. They were dressed in heavy mantles and scarves as if they intended to travel a great distance. Behind them mules pulled three wagons overloaded with bundles and crates.

"What's going on here?" Malden asked.

The leader of the group lifted his arm away from his face. It was the priest of the Lady who'd ministered to Pritchard Hood the night the bailiff died. The others, Malden realized, must be those few people left in Ness who still worshipped the Lady. The last few weeks had been difficult for them, Malden knew.

The priest stared pure hatred into Malden's eyes. "I'm taking my flock to a better place."

"Beyond the walls of Ness? It's dangerous out there."

"Less so than staying," the priest insisted. "We are attacked by ruffians in the street. Our images are smashed. Our churches defiled by thieves and whores! You've driven the Lady's face away from this city, Lord Mayor, and you will suffer the consequences."

Malden grunted in frustration. He'd heard tales of violence against the Lady's adherents, but had been able to do little about it. His staunchest supporters were those most devoutly attached to the bloodgod, who seemed to think that the Lady's priests were fair game.

"Don't go," Malden beseeched. "I'll protect you. I'll make it illegal to persecute anyone for their belief." It had been one of the things he wanted to do, anyway. He'd assumed he had some time before he had to start convincing people that they should accept all religions. Apparently it was now or never.

"We'll take our chances with the barbarians, thank you very much. If you really want to help us, move this throng out of our path."

Malden shook his head. "Where will you go?"

"The northern kingdoms do not worship the bloodgod. Their interpretation of the Lady's word is different from ours, but we share some articles of faith. Perhaps they will listen to our preaching there. If not, well, the Old Empire knows many faiths. The emperor tolerates all religion as long as no one preaches against his rule. We can live there without fear of being murdered in our beds, simply because we believe in the true faith," the priest said. He looked tired already. Malden wondered how far he would get before bandits killed him and his people for the contents of their wagons. Ten miles? Twenty? The Northern Kingdoms were two hundred miles away, and crossing the sea to the Old Empire would take months—assuming the pilgrims weren't slaughtered by pirates or wrecked by storms.

"I won't stop you," Malden said, when he'd considered doing just that for a minute. He turned around and faced the jeering crowd. "All of you get back and let them through. And stopping throwing that filth! They're leaving. Isn't that what you want?"

Grudgingly the crowd moved back to make an opening. They kept jeering and shouting insults, but they kept their garbage to themselves. Malden bowed to the priest and gestured for him to go through.

Velmont, however, had thought of something Malden had missed. "Boss," he said. "What've they got in yon wains?"

For the first time Malden paid close attention to the priest's wagons. They were filled to bursting with bundles of clothing, tents and tools. More importantly, they were full of bags of flour, casks of lard, whole sides of salted beef and pork, and barrels of small beer.

Food. Enough food to get them to their destination. Alternatively, food that could feed a hundred people in Ness for a week.

Malden wrestled with himself. He could not, in good conscience, do what good politics demanded of him.

But he needed that food.

"Hold," he said. The priest glared at him. Malden took a purse from his belt. It was full of silver coins and a few gold royals. "I'll give you fair recompense for the food you're carrying," he said.

"We'll need it on the road," the priest said. But there was a new look in his eye. A look of fear.

Malden tried to push the purse into the priest's hand. The old man wouldn't take it. "You can buy food on your way. It'll make your load lighter."

"Let me pass," the priest insisted. His voice was weak. He knew that without Malden's approval, he would never make it as far as the city gates.

"You can stay here, and keep everything. Or you can leave the food behind on your way out of Ness," Malden said, through gritted teeth. His heart shriveled in his chest, just speaking the words. "Take the coins, damn you."

"Every demon of the pit will take turns gnawing on your soul," the priest said.

But he took the coins.

CHAPTER SEVENTY-TWO

"Be of good cheer, lad," Slag said, as he led Malden down toward the Meadlock Stair. "Think of the fucking bright side, already." Ahead of them the river Skrait was at its narrowest, and it ran cold and fast, swollen with melted snow from the north. That morning white flakes had settled for a moment on the courtyard of the Lemon Garden, melting before Malden could be sure they were real. Winter was almost upon them.

Malden could barely imagine a bright side, much less see one. He strained for optimism, and came up with only the barest rationalization. "The pilgrims will die on the road, long before they would have had need of those foodstuffs," Malden said, mostly for his own benefit. "In this weather— they'll freeze before they starve."

"That's not precisely what I meant. Here, let me show you something I think will please you," Slag said. He headed down the steps toward the river, where his latest creation was spinning freely on a massive steel axle. It looked like the bloodgod's own wagon wheel, twenty feet across and made of massive beams of wood. All along its circumference paddles stuck out like the oars of a war galley. The paddles dipped into the water where the current pushed against them and sent them speeding upward again, water spilling from them in a constant torrent. "The force of the river, you see, is transmitted to the axle as angular moment, and from there to a reducing gear which—"

"I don't speak dwarven, and you know it," Malden said. He followed Slag up a rickety scaffolding to look down on what had once been a yard for the storage of tar barrels. Now it had been turned into a grain mill. The steel axle of the waterwheel was connected by some ingenious bit of clockwork to a wooden shaft as big as a tree trunk. This rotated constantly, turning as it did so a millstone that busily churned out crushed wheat. The human millers down there looked afraid to touch the mechanism, but they worked spryly enough at gathering up the grain and scooping it into sacks.

"This rod turns that rod, which turns the arsing stone," Slag explained, a bit testily. "It works, that's the important thing."

Yes. Yes, it was. As little grain as Ness still possessed, it was worthless if it couldn't be ground into flour. Now, at least, that part of the problem was solved. Malden felt hope blossom in his chest for the first time in days. "Slag," Malden said, "you've done it again. Is there no end to your invention?"

"Now, I can't rightly claim to have thought this one up," Slag admitted. "There's wheels like this in Redweir, turned by the Strow. Or at least, there used to be. Who can say what's come of that town?"

Malden nodded solemnly. News from the eastern half of Skrae was rare as hen's teeth, but all of it bad. Those few travelers who actually came as far as Ness now reported a countryside ravaged by barbarians, full of bandits and starving peasants too terrified to leave their homes in search of food.

"For the nonce, at least, we'll have flour," Malden said, because that was what Slag wanted to hear. "You've done a wonderful job here. The city will give you a medal, or some commendation. I'll see to it."

"Lad, bollocks on that. You know I don't care for honors. I'm trying to help you, that's all. And maybe I can offer you something else today, if you'll step into my office." The dwarf's eyes burned with excitement as he led Malden into a shack at one corner of the millyard. It was cold inside, and cramped—the ceiling was far too low for Malden's comfort—but once he saw what the dwarf had in mind, he could not look away.

A piece of parchment lay weighted on a table. On it was a message written in dwarven runes, with beneath each rune a character from the alphabet of Skrae. This second set of characters was grouped into individual words.

"You've deciphered it?" Malden asked, breathless. Cutbill's message had become a touchstone for him, a hope he could cling to no matter how dark things got. He had convinced himself, with no evidence whatsoever, that if he could only read it all his problems would be solved. In his more lucid moments he knew that was folly, but with so many people believing in him, he needed something *he* could believe in. "But no," he said, glancing at the alphabetical marks. "No, it's still gibberish."

"Trust a guildmaster of thieves to be paranoid," Slag said. "He used not one cipher, but three. First the symbols on the original ledger page, which were then revealed to be substitutes for dwarven runes. I had to convert the runes to your tongue, by comparing the sounds they stand for. That wasn't simple! And even then the wrong man wouldn't be able to read it, because he ciphered the runes as well." Slag shook his head. "Crafty bastard."

"One step closer," Malden said. He had not expected it to be easy.

"More than that. Look here. This last word in the message—ASRZGJJ. Does it look familiar at all?"

"Not in the slightest."

Slag groaned. "Think, lad! Use the damned skills Coruth gave you. It's a substitution cipher. A rotation cipher, I warrant, or blind me with a stick. Seven letters. The last two the same. Think!"

Malden wished the dwarf would just tell him the answer. He hadn't slept more than an hour or two in days. Every time he closed his eyes he saw only the fear in the priest's eye as his food was taken away. He could use something easy, for once. *But—alright*, he thought. *Work it through. Seven letters. Two the same, at the tail. Think of words that end with a double letter, most of them end in TT, SS or—ah—LL . . .*

"It's a signature," Malden exhaled. "It's—"

"Cutbill's name, ciphered!" Slag agreed. "And more than

that, it's a partial key to the whole fucking thing! Now I know every time the letter J appears in the message, it's actually an L. Every A stands in place of a C. Fill in the rest, and we have it."

"We . . . have it," Malden said.

"Together we can solve this in an hour," Slag said, nodding happily.

A strange fear gripped Malden. So close. He desperately wanted to read the message. And yet—if he did—his one hope would be gone. There couldn't possibly be anything in the message to solve his problems. It just wasn't long enough.

Yet he had to know. He must know what Cutbill had deemed so important it had to be kept so carefully secret.

"I'm supposed to go address a meeting of the wool carders' guild right now," Malden said. "After that I'm supposed to sit in judgment at the hall of justice. Velmont has my whole day sewn up with meetings and audiences," Malden said.

"So—you don't want to work on this right now?"

"Blast you, no, that's not what I meant at all. I meant bar the door, so when Velmont comes looking for me, he can't get in. And hand me that quill!"

CHAPTER SEVENTY-THREE

Croy kept his horse to a walk as they crept slowly through the fens north of Easthull. This was Greenmarsh, once the most politically influential district of Skrae. Now it was firmly entrenched with barbarian pickets. He had to maintain constant attention on the hunched trees around him that could hide anything and also the soft ground, lest he become trapped in the mire.

Bethane's presence behind him did not help. They had been unable to find another mount for her—the barbarians had scoured this land for every bit of horseflesh they could find. Having to share wasn't the problem, though. The girl was light enough not to over-burden Croy's horse, and she never complained about her uncomfortable position sitting on his cantle. She kept her arms wrapped around his waist, but not so tight that he couldn't breathe.

No, the problem was that she kept talking. He had convinced her to keep her voice to a low whisper, but she was his queen, and he could not command her to be silent. He never responded to what she said, but that didn't seem to dissuade her.

"When I am reinstated at Helstrow," she said, excitement plain in her voice, "I will command a great tournament to honor the sacrifice of all our brave men. Knights will come from every land to prove their mettle and their honor. There will be bright pavilions all around the fortress, a great sea of them in every color. Of course, preference will go to the green tents, and the white."

Croy had been following a deer trail through the swamp, a narrow track barely visible even by brightest daylight. His horse could find it better than he could himself, shying on its hooves whenever it stepped off the trail and into the thicker vegetation to either side. Now that the sun was setting, the horse seemed less sure of itself, and Croy wondered how he would find his way in the dark. But they could not stop now.

"There will be jongleurs, and fools, and the dwarves will demonstrate their marvelous creations. I will have a great fountain built, that will spray water ever so high in the air, so that men will delight to watch it go up, and wonder at how long it takes to come down again. There will be falcons, and much sport from their flights, and their handlers will be gallant men with steely eyes who never speak except to command their fierce birds."

Up ahead something blocked the trail. Not a roadblock—the barbarians would never waste time closing off a path so far away from civilization. No, it looked perhaps like a massive deadfall, as if a cyclopean chestnut tree had fallen, and its roots were sticking up in the air, thick with moist earth. Croy searched the ground around this obstacle with his eyes, looking for a way to circumvent it.

"The ladies of my court will be all in linen and velvet, and they will embroider teasing mottoes inside the sleeves of their gowns, so that any man who ventures to peek inside will find himself made a figure of fun. And there will be great competitions of skill. Archery contests that will go on all day. And men will try to climb greased poles, or capture chickens set loose in a paddock. Oh, it will be humorous to watch their antics."

As they came closer Croy finally made out the truth of the obstacle. It was no fallen tree. Instead, it was a pile of corpses clotted with gore, their bones picked at by birds. Even from a distance he could see the wounds that had slain these men. Axe cuts had lopped off arms and ears and faces. The bodies were still dressed in the colors of Skrae. Were these some men from his rabble, the one he'd lost on the road to Mörgain's berserkers? Or were they simple deserters, thinking to save themselves from certain death, only to find it again here, in this forgotten place? Whomever had slaughtered them had deemed them unworthy of even a simple burial. They had been left to rot where they lay. Croy's shoulders stiffened at the sacrilege, and he felt Bethane lift her head.

"Is something wrong, Sir Croy?" she asked.

"No, your highness." Croy tried to think of what to say. How would Malden handle this? The thief had always been a great flatterer, and very good at smoothing over unpleasantness. "I was only . . . struck by the grandeur of your vision. Please, close your eyes, the better to see such beauties, and the better to relate them."

Bethane sighed and leaned against his back. "You're right. I can see it better like this. Oh, Sir Croy! The place you will hold on that day. You'll be by my side, of course. You will be my champion, when I am properly crowned and established in my station."

Croy urged the horse forward, moving as carefully as he might around the pile of dead men. The animal snorted and balked at the smell of death, but Croy rubbed its neck and it settled down.

"You will be heaped with honors, of course," Bethane went on. "Your colors will hang from the highest tower, next to mine, and every knight on the field that day will bow in recognition that whatever victory they may win, they shall never match your achievements."

Croy had fought in tourneys, once. He had jousted with lance and spear, fought in mock melees with wooden swords. Like a child playing at war. He had won great honors and tributes from lords and ladies. He had held himself up as an example of honor and virtue, and thought everyone would gain from just seeing him, that he would inspire them to make the world a finer place.

Now he was a man on a horse, with a girl clutching to his back. The horse was near death and the two of them were dirty and saddle-sore and so very hungry. The world she spoke of had never existed, not really. There had only ever been this muddy place where death waited around every turn in the road. The sun had been a little brighter in summertime, that was all, and it had fooled him into thinking the green grass and the blue sky would last forever.

To the north, he thought. He must take Bethane far to the north, as far as the Northern Kingdoms, where she would be safe. She would reign in exile while the barbarians despoiled her own country. But she would live. And perhaps someday, some descendant of hers would travel south again, with a proper army, and take Skrae back. Or what was left of it.

"I see the groaning boards, Sir Croy! Laden with every kind of roasted meat, and every succulent dainty my cooks can make. I see the boats on the river Strow, their flags snapping in the breeze . . ."

CHAPTER SEVENTY-FOUR

Malden reached up and grasped the snout of a gargoyle. It started to pull free but the iron staple that held it to the wall was still strong, even after so many years of neglect, and it took his weight. He clambered up onto its stone back and rested for a moment.

He'd had steadier climbs. He'd gone places in Ness he felt more easy. The Chapterhouse did not have a good reputation.

An octagonal building with a high spire, it was an anomaly in the Stink—one place in all that stew of humanity that no one ever went, a massive stone pile in a sea of wood and thatch, forlorn and shunned. It was supposed to be the most haunted building in the Free City, with a far more dire reputation than even the Isle of Horses, because its evil had continued to take victims long after the tragedy that cursed it.

In the early days of Ness—in the early history of Skrae—the Learned Brothers of the Lady had been a strong institution, a beacon of reason and erudition in a benighted land. They had tended to the sick and fed the poor in a time when the priests of the bloodgod could do nothing but demand larger and more savage sacrifices. The Brotherhood had brought thousands of converts to the then new religion of the Lady. They had also been rumored to possess secrets even the dwarves had never plumbed. At Redweir they had built the Sacred Library, the greatest concentration of books and manuscripts outside of the Old Empire. In Ness they had built the Chapterhouse, a meeting place for all seekers of knowledge and enlightenment. It had originally stood outside the city's precincts and been protected by its own high wall. When the Free City grew it had swallowed the Chapterhouse but the building had remained cloistered and aloof. Inside its towering edifice the Learned Brothers had kept the rules of their order, and no Burgrave had ever dared intrude upon their laws or customs. Rich merchants had sent their more bookish sons to the Chapterhouse to be tutored, and it had become tradition that these scholars would become the distinguished Professors of Ness' burgeoning university.

Any organization of celibate men, however, will eventually fall under suspicion from more cosmopolitan minds, and the Chapterhouse was no exception. Tales were told of initiation rites that went beyond harmless hazing, of license and formalized pederasty. The once-honored title "Chapterhouse Pupil" came to be slang for a catamite. The Learned Brotherhood gained a bad reputation. How much of it the monks had actually earned was unknown, but two hundred years before Malden was born, one Jarald of Omburg came to be High Scholiast of the place, and within a year it was empty and abandoned, its doors chained shut and its fires of learning quenched.

The Burgraves had never revealed the true account of Jarald's crimes, but Malden had grown up hearing tales of hundreds of monks being driven from the city in chains, of watchmen fainting dead away at the discovery of dismembered boys inside, their wounds violated in horrible fashion. His mother had used the Chapterhouse as a bogey, warning him that if he did not behave he'd be sent there to become a student of Jarald's ghost. It had not been a toothless threat. Those few thieves or vagabonds who had been desperate enough to try to break into the Chapterhouse had vanished without trace, and even vandals who besmirched its outer wall with graffiti were said to have been punished by spectral forces.

It took a lot to keep thieves away from any building in Ness. The city was famous for its thrice-locked doors and the dwarven traps that protected the houses of wealthy men. The Chapterhouse needed no such protections—thieves shunned it the way they shunned the gallows.

And now Malden must enter its deadly confines, and plumb its darkest corners. He had been taken aback when he finally read the message Cutbill had left for him. He'd seriously considered tearing up the letter and forgetting its contents. Yet it promised so much he could not resist. Properly deciphered, the message read thus:

FOR MALDEN SHOULD HE RETURN

YOU HAVE MANY QUESTIONS I HAVE BUT ONE ANSWER
COME LET US TRADE IF YOU LIKE THE TERMS I SET
CLIMB TO THE ONE HEIGHT YOU NEVER YET SCALED
IN ALL THE FREE CITY AND YOU WILL FIND MY TRAIL
FOLLOW IT WITH CARE FOR I AM NOT UNPROTECTED
FOLLOW IT AND FIND ME I WILL AWAIT YOU THERE

CUTBILL

On his gargoyle perch, Malden studied the transcribed parchment one last time. It confused him more than ever, even more than when it had been a meaningless clutter of symbols. Just like Cutbill to be so cryptic—and so forbidding. Just like Cutbill to put such obstacles in his way, knowing full well he would have no choice but overcome them. And yet how unlike Cutbill to put himself at such risk. Malden had assumed that the guildmaster of thieves had fled the city like every sane man wealthy enough to do so. He had assumed Cutbill was willing to donate his entire enterprise to a young and untried thief, rather than stick around and take his chances with fate and the barbarians.

The message suggested otherwise. It suggested that Cutbill had gone into hiding—right in the middle of his own city. That he'd been in Ness the whole time just waiting for Malden to track him down.

Cutbill was playing a deeper game than mere survival. That, Malden should have expected.

He climbed higher. The steeple of the Chapterhouse was one of the highest places in Ness, even though it was well down slope from Castle Hill. The building must be twelve stories high not including its superstructures. All of its windows and doors had been sealed off quite firmly but Malden was certain once he reached the top he would find a way in.

Nor was he disappointed. The peak of the spire had been

blasted by lightning and never repaired. One whole side of its apex had fallen away. Malden slipped inside the remaining three walls and found himself in a narrow space full of the droppings of bats, the walls wooly with cobwebs. No furniture or appurtenances remained in the room, but there was a simple trap door set in its floorboards. He tried lifting this portal and found that its hinges had completely rusted away. The square door fell through its jamb and clattered down through rafters and support beams below, into total darkness. Echoing up through that open space, Malden heard the clattering sound of gears and clockwork lurch sluggishly to life.

He had expected the Chapterhouse to be dead inside— empty, its furnishings long since rotted away, even its ghosts having eventually given up in boredom. The last thing he'd expected was the sound of well-oiled machinery turning and cranking away. What in the bloodgod's sacred name had Cutbill found inside? Or what had he built there himself, to confound his disciple?

Malden knew better than to expect Cutbill to come climbing up through the trapdoor and welcome him with a hearty smile. But what *was* down there? What game was the guildmaster of thieves playing, this time?

Only one way to find out.

CHAPTER SEVENTY-FIVE

Malden lowered himself through the trap door by his hands. He swung his feet back and forth until they came in contact with a solid surface that felt like it would hold his weight, then jumped to crouch atop it. He pulled a candle from his tunic and lit it with steel and flint. When the wick caught, he placed the candle in a tin reflector that Slag had made for him. It gave him a good beam of yellow light he could direct wherever he liked.

Aiming the beam downward, he saw that the inside of the steeple and much of the spire was open space, some of the floors below having fallen away over the years so that he was inside a high shaft leading down into darkness. He crouched atop one of the few remaining support beams that hadn't rotted or burned away over time.

He could hear gears churning below, and a rhythmic whirring sound as of something very large spinning very quickly.

The interior walls of the spire provided ample foot- and hand-holds to make an easy descent, at least for the first fifteen feet down. Where the floors had fallen away, little more remained than narrow ledges now fringed with broken bits of floorboard. As rudimentary as they looked they would give him plenty of purchase. Beyond that the space opened out and became far more regular. He could see little more than that by candlelight. He climbed quickly down to a place where a corner of ruined floor remained, still braced by rotting beams. Looking down further, he finally saw the source of the whirring noise.

Where the spire ended and the main building began, a wide circular opening separated the two. Filling that opening was a massive iron blade that spun around and around, forbidding all access to the lower floors. It moved so quickly he could not see how many vanes this obstruction possessed. Not that it mattered. He knew if he tried to jump through it he would end up shredded.

Yet there had to be a way to pass it.

He found a place where the plaster had come away from the wall. Underneath, the laths that had once held the plaster were exposed. He was able to tear one free, a good strip of wood an inch wide and six feet long. Creeping down as far as he could get, he thrust the lath into the whirling blade.

He was not surprised when it was torn out of his hand and then cut into splinters. It had not been thick enough to jam the mechanism. Malden wondered if this blade explained the vanishing of every thief who'd tried to enter the

Chapterhouse before him. Then he rejected the idea. He'd spent enough time around Slag to know that such complicated devices couldn't remain in working order for two hundred years, not without someone to periodically clean and repair them. Cutbill had put this blade in motion, not the long-passed monks who'd built the Chapterhouse.

Malden needed a way to stop the blade. He had Acidtongue at his belt and he supposed it would be strong enough, but he didn't want to risk the blade on such a risky enterprise—especially since he thought he might need it later. There must be something else, though, something he could use. He sought around him for something better than a lath, and quickly found it.

A series of stone columns ribbed the interior of the spire, some of which had cracked and broken. One had fallen away entirely, and lay in pieces on a corner of broken flooring. It almost looked like it had been left there intentionally for him to find.

That wouldn't surprise him. When Cutbill created a puzzle, he always managed to leave the solution somewhere in plain sight. This was not simply a way to keep trespassers out of the Chapterhouse. It was a test.

The broken section of pillar was too heavy for Malden to lift. It was three feet long and as thick as his arm, and made of very solid stone. He considered rolling it over the edge to crash down on the blade, but knew he would only get one chance at this—if the stone fell through the gaps between the vanes of the blade he would be out of luck. He needed a way to lower the pillar into the blade, a way he could control.

He had brought along a length of rope—he never went climbing in new places without a line. Now it was kept coiled around his waist like a sash. It was strong enough to hold his own weight, but he wasn't sure if it could support the pillar. There was, as usual, only one way to find out. Malden lashed one end of the rope around the fluted end of the pillar, then carefully rolled the stone over the edge of the broken floor. The rope creaked and complained and started to fray almost at once. In a few moments, Malden knew, it would snap.

Perhaps not before he made use of it, however. He paid

out the rope as quickly as he dared, careful not to let the pillar jerk too much at its end. Foot by foot, second by second as the rope twisted and frayed, he sent the pillar down toward the deadly blade.

It made contact just as the rope broke. The pillar bounced off one vane of the blade and then fell away into the darkness below. Malden cursed in rage for a moment—then stopped himself as he saw what happened next.

With a horrible clanging whine, the blade slowed and then ground to a shuddering stop. The pillar had bent the blade out of true and it no longer fit inside its prescribed mechanism. Still it tried to turn, but could only grind slowly around its arc as it dragged against its own rim.

Malden scurried down through a gap between two of the blade's six vanes before it could start again. Underneath the blade was a small square room almost entirely filled with huge iron gears and an enormous coiled mainspring that drove the blade. A lever stuck up out of the floor, clearly a controller for the deadly engine. Had Cutbill stood here only minutes before, and pulled that lever to start the whirling blade?

Thinking it best to stop the blade for good and all—he might have to climb back out this way—Malden grasped the lever and pulled it toward him.

He had only himself to blame when the entire floor of the small room fell away on a hinge, dropping him into darkness.

CHAPTER SEVENTY-SIX

Malden's candle fell from his hand and flickered out instantly. He could just see the last orange ember of its wick tumbling away from him. In the last guttering flare of the light he'd seen chains hanging around him, but beyond that nothing.

He was falling, weightless, a condition he knew could only end in a sudden stop—and very soon.

Desperately he lashed around him with his arms. His fingertips brushed the rough surface of a chain and sent it flailing away from him. Malden's left leg hit another chain and he grabbed at it with his feet, trying to tangle himself in its length. It slipped free of his grasp—but not before he twisted around and got one hand on it.

He stopped falling with a wrenching jerk that nearly pulled his arm out of its socket. His fingers started to tremble but he managed to get his other arm wrapped around the chain so it would hold him up. Powdered rust sifted down across his face but he held on, just held on, until he could breathe again.

He couldn't see a thing. There was no light at all inside the Chapterhouse. He couldn't hear anything, either. Not so much as wind whispering through abandoned eaves.

He could smell something, though. A sharp odor of stale oil. Perhaps it was just the smell of grease on the chains, gone rancid over the years. He didn't like it, though.

Slowly, once his hand had stopped shaking, he began to climb down the chain. It swayed and shook as he moved— clearly it wasn't attached to anything at the bottom. He had no idea what awaited for him at the bottom of the chain. Perhaps common sense indicated he should climb upward instead. Head back up through the whirling blades, get out of the Chapterhouse altogether.

But he had to know. He had to find Cutbill, and get his answer. The mystery was like a demon at the back of his brain, goading him forward. So he climbed down.

Eventually he reached the end of the chain, and had no idea what to do next. Stretching himself downward from its farthest extent, he still couldn't find a floor beneath him. If he just jumped he could fall for dozens or hundreds of feet, and break a leg or his neck when he finally reached bottom. Or the floor could be just inches out of reach. He had no way of knowing without a light to see by.

He soon had more light than he wanted.

Above him, the broken pillar he'd used to stop the whirling blade had lodged in the clockworks. As the blade stuttered forward, it dislodged the pillar. It fell right past Malden, clipping his ear with a searing pain. It kept going, and eventually struck the floor below.

Malden heard a sound like pieces of metal grinding against each other, followed by a heavy splash. He heard the sound of air rushing into a vacuum. And then he was blinded by brilliant light.

He clamped his eyes shut. He felt heat rising up toward him, and smelled smoke. When he could see again, a little, he squinted downward and saw the cunning trap he'd been saved from only by his hesitation.

Upon the floor below him was an enormous tub filled near to the brim with lamp oil. Atop the tub had been lain a grid of interwoven strips of material. Half the strips were made of a dull gray material like stone. The other half were shiny metal, discolored here and there by rust.

The strips must be made of flint and steel. Any pressure upon them at all caused them to rub together and create a spark that ignited the oil. Had Malden dropped the ten feet to the floor, his impact would have been enough to set off the trap and he would have been roasted alive. Instead the broken pillar had ignited the oil while he was still up on the chain, still uncooked.

For the moment, anyway. The heat was intense and the fumes made his head spin. It was arguable whether he would swoon first from asphyxiation, or if the sweat already beading on his hands would loosen his grip and he would fall into the flames.

As fast as he could, Malden started swinging back and forth on the chain, hoping desperately he wouldn't be overcome before he could get down. There was a clear space of wooden floor visible on one side of the tub of oil. If he could just swing himself over there before he let go—

He landed badly, one ankle twisting beneath him. The bones didn't break but he would be limping for a while. Down on the floor the heat of the tub was beyond intense. He could feel the hairs on the back of his neck curling as they were singed off just by being near that conflagration. He looked around for any shelter from the heat. The tub was mounted on a wooden scaffolding, a few feet above the actual floor of the room. Looking between the struts of the scaffolding he saw a spiral staircase leading downward, directly beneath the tub. He ducked under the tub, careful not to touch its underside lest he be burnt, and hobbled down the stairs.

Below lay a corridor leading forward into darkness. He had no more candles. There could be as something as basic as an open pit trap ahead of him, or something as insidious as a pressure plate he had to avoid to keep from being studded with poisoned darts. He had no reason to think he'd reached the end of the traps.

There were ways of dealing with such difficulties, but they involved spending enormous spans of time moving in the most careful way possible. Malden was not going to be given that much time, he presumed.

His suspicion was borne out a moment later, when the trap came following him down the stairs.

He heard a dripping sound, and the smell of oil billowed from the staircase behind him. A steady stream of oil was leaking down the steps. The fire must have melted right through the tub.

"No, no, no," Malden groaned, as the trickle turned into a steady stream—and the stream caught fire. A river of burning oil started inching toward him across the floor.

He ran forward, into the dark. He could just see the walls of the corridor on either side and, by the light of the fire, a little of the floor and ceiling. He tried not to look behind him to check how quickly the burning oil was catching up with him, but he did take one quick glance backward—

And had to stop stock still, as his left foot came down on nothing at all.

He shot his arms out to the side, desperately trying to keep his balance as his weight shifted back and forth, supported entirely on his weak ankle.

A pit lay ahead of him. The simplest, most ancient trap of all. It stretched six feet down the corridor, and it was not disguised in any way. At its bottom he saw broken wood and masonry. Plenty of exposed nails and sharp edges.

He looked up and saw nothing on the ceiling. The walls on either side were perfectly smooth, and showed no signs of tampering.

Behind him the river of burning oil had become a flood. He jumped for it, kicking off the floor with his injured foot, and sailed unhindered across the pit to the other side. The ceiling didn't crash down on him in mid-leap. The floor on the far side wasn't rigged to fall away from him as he landed. Behind him the oil poured into the pit, and couldn't follow him across the gap.

Fair enough, he thought. He'd take it.

Slowly, cautiously, he rose to his feet and headed farther down the corridor. It only ran another twenty feet before it came to a door. A nice, normal, wooden door with no lock. He hesitated quite a while before touching its latch.

Behind him the pit was filling up with burning oil. He did not know how long it would take to overflow.

He pressed down on the latch, and the door swung open ahead of him. Beyond was a pleasantly appointed room lit by many candles, with a fire burning in a hearth. He stepped inside, wondering what deadly ploy Cutbill would unleash on him next.

CHAPTER SEVENTY-SEVEN

Malden closed the door behind him and bent low to look at the gap between the door and its jamb. He didn't want the burning oil to come seeping in after him. Fortunately it seemed the pit was deep and wide enough to contain the oil—it never came over the edge of the pit. The volume of oil in the tub must have been less than the capacity of the pit, something Malden was sure had been taken into account when the traps were installed.

He heard someone moving in the hidden apartment and he stood up straight to see what was coming. He was not entirely surprised when Cutbill emerged from another room, a cup of wine in one hand. The guildmaster of thieves evidenced no shock whatsoever to find Malden in his hiding place.

Cutbill held up one finger for a moment's silence. Then he finished his wine and placed the cup on a small, elegantly carved table. Smiling—Cutbill almost never smiled, and when he did it put Malden's teeth on edge—he walked toward Malden and then knelt on the rush-strewn floor before him. Without saying a word, Cutbill lowered his head to expose the back of his neck.

Cutbill was not an imposing man, physically. He was slight and small of stature, and his features betrayed a clerkish sensitivity that didn't quite jibe with his station. Malden thought about the ogrish one-legged boss of the thieves in Helstrow—the one Velmont had butchered when they came to a disagreement. He could not imagine two more different men, even though they were opposite numbers.

Of the two, Malden knew Cutbill was the far more dangerous.

Cutbill had hired an assassin to end Malden's life. Malden had the proof inside his tunic—a warrant for his own murder signed with Cutbill's symbol, a heart transfixed by a key. Malden expected Cutbill to make another attempt. He expected another cunning trap, one even he would not be able to avoid. A hidden blade, a dozen killers hidden in a nearby closet just waiting to spring out and attack. Perhaps a tripwire at ankle height that would bring down the whole Chapterhouse on his head.

He had the sneaking suspicion that he was facing something even more devious. Cutbill did not move or speak. He simply knelt there, waiting for Malden to make the next move.

"What are you doing?" Malden demanded.

"Presenting myself for execution," Cutbill told him. His

voice was calm and level, quite matter-of-fact. As it always had been. "You've brought your sword. I assume you've come to exact your revenge."

Malden's blood burned inside of him. "Damn you," he said, biting off the words. "You could at least have the decency to cower." He pulled Acidtongue from its scabbard. Drops of vitriol hissed on the rushes.

"You're well within your rights to lop my head off this very moment," Cutbill said. Was it an apology? Malden couldn't make any sense of this.

"So you don't deny it? It was you who sent Prestwicke the assassin to slaughter me?"

"Oh, yes," Cutbill said.

Malden brought the sword up high, as he'd seen Croy do when he wanted to make a devastating cutting stroke. He gripped its hilt with both hands, ready to bring it down fast. The blade could slice through anything, if it was driven with enough force. Cutbill's flesh and bones wouldn't stop it for a moment.

One cut—and Malden would be avenged. He would have satisfaction for the great injustice this man had done to him. Perhaps more importantly, he would be safe. Cutbill would never be able to turn on him again.

So why did it seem the exact wrong thing to do?

"I never harmed you!" Malden gasped. "I lined your pockets with gold. I strengthened your organization."

"You were my best thief," Cutbill agreed. "Perhaps the best I ever saw." He glanced up at Malden for a moment. "You'll want to move your left foot back an inch or two. It will give you a better swing. And please, aim for the thinnest part of my neck, here, just below my jaw line."

"I never plotted against you, if that's what you think. I would never have betrayed you! So why in the name of Sadu's eight elbows would you turn against me like that? I trusted you. I—I honored you. And you repaid me with treachery!"

"Is that what I did?" Cutbill asked.

"Yes! Unless—" Malden's face was sweating. What wasn't he seeing?

"Unless?"

The traps in the rooms above had been deadly, Malden thought, but not quite deadly enough. He'd believed that Cutbill's summons was merely a lure to lead him into a place where he was certain to die. Where the job could be completed, the task that Prestwicke—Cutbill's hired assassin—had been unable to finish. The coded message was itself the first trap, an irresistible lure to bring Malden to a place that would be his death. Yet—Cutbill must have known that Malden could overcome the blade, the tub of oil, certainly the pit in the hallway. In his career as a thief Malden had gotten past far more sinister snares.

But no one else could. Anyone without Malden's experience would have been slaughtered. Anyone less quick than he. Anyone less lucky.

"Unless it was all a test," Malden said. "Unless you meant me to come to this room. At this moment."

"In truth, I'd hoped you would come sooner. I didn't think it would take you so long to figure out my cipher."

"Don't anger me!" Malden shrieked. "Your life is forfeit!"

Cutbill laughed. "I think not. Not anymore. A moment ago, you might have done it. But not now. You have to know. You have to know the *why*. Which might be explanation enough in itself why I chose to do this to you. Because you are wise enough, Malden, to never react to a misfortune until you know why it had to happen."

Malden relaxed his grip on the sword. He could still do it. He could still bring the sword down. Take the bastard's head.

But no. No, he would not. If he killed Cutbill now, he would never learn the truth.

He put the sword in its sheath.

"Get up," Malden commanded. "Get up, and start talking."

Cutbill raised his head. "Nothing would give me more pleasure."

CHAPTER SEVENTY-EIGHT

"Malden, no one loves me," Cutbill said. He poured two cups of wine from a pewter jug. He held them both out to Malden to choose which he would drink from. Malden took the one on the left. Cutbill quickly took a drink from the one on the right, to prove he hadn't poisoned them both. It was all done without much attention, a formalized ritual they both instinctually understood.

"That isn't . . . completely true," Malden said. "The thieves of your guild—"

"They fear me," Cutbill said. "Perhaps some of the more intelligent among them, who understand a portion of the things I do, even respect me. Please don't misapprehend me. I have no desire to be loved. I never have. When I was first putting the guild together, I had to make of myself a completely unlovable villain. Do you know anything of how I became who I am?"

"Is this another test?" Malden asked.

"If you like."

Malden sat down in a comfortable chair, laying Acidtongue in its scabbard across his knees. He thought back on what he'd heard—rumors and hearsay, mostly, but over time he'd established a few real facts. "There's some mystery about where you came from originally. Whether you were born in Ness or some other place. What I'm sure of is that you took a crew of common thugs and criminals and turned them into the most lethal gang in the city. This was, when— twenty years ago?"

"Twenty-five," Cutbill corrected.

Malden frowned. Cutbill must be older than he'd thought—or he must have started his career in crime much younger than would seem probable. "By murdering the leaders of other gangs, you consolidated your power. Many of your rivals tried to draw you into open warfare in the streets, but you favored the knife in the dark, the carefully-staged accident, and on occasion," he finished, looking down into his cup, "poisoning."

"The city watch cared little if one thief or another turned up dead in an alley come morning—but they would never have tolerated gangs of villains attacking one another in broad daylight." Cutbill shrugged. "Further, had I butchered thieves indiscriminately I would have been left with a weakened force of my own. When I killed one man, I could absorb all his crews, and my organization grew."

Malden nodded. "In other words, you rose to power because you were nastier than any other criminal in Ness."

"Instead, say I was more efficient. More practical. I had to make many difficult decisions back in those days. Respond to threats in the same hour they arose. I did not sleep like a normal man, not for many years. Even today the slightest sound or even an odd smell will waken me. It is not a life I recommend."

"And yet when you absconded from your post, you gave that life to me."

Cutbill laughed, a short, unpleasant sound that did nothing for Malden's nerves.

"Why?" Malden demanded. "I originally thought you were afraid of the barbarians, like all the rich men. That you had escaped to some safer place. Yet here you are—hiding in the very place you supposedly fled. Why disappear at all?"

"Because it was your turn."

Malden just stared at Cutbill.

"You are capable of the one thing I could never achieve. Because of the things I've done, the people of Ness think me a shadowy villain. A bogey to scare children with, like Jarald of Omburg." Cutbill looked up at the ceiling, at the Chapterhouse above them. "You, Malden, are quickly becoming a folk hero. The son of a whore, penniless and despised, who became the most daring—the most dashing—thief in Ness. And now, so much more. They'll write ballads about you some day."

"You flatter me."

"Never," Cutbill said, quite serious.

Malden shook his head, trying to make sense of this. "But even so, what of it? The guild was doing a brisk business. The money was coming in faster than anyone could spend it. Despite the fact the city's deserted, we're actually turning a nice profit by looting abandoned homes. Why wouldn't you want to be in charge of that?"

Cutbill said nothing for a while. He went to the hearth and poked at the fire. Drained his wine and refilled their cups. Malden wondered if he was trying to think of the proper words. He'd never imagined Cutbill could be at a loss in that regard.

"Because," he said, at last, "I saw what was coming."

"The barbarians," Malden guessed.

"Not the specifics. But I knew that things were about to change. There are signs, if you know how to look for them. I knew I'd taken the guild as far as my abilities allowed. Already there were forces in place that threatened to destroy all I'd made. The relationship I enjoyed with the Burgrave had become increasingly strained. Once he and I shared an understanding. He believed that the guild of thieves served a needful purpose by keeping crime in the city to a certain acceptable level. In recent years, however, my power continued to grow. It was only a matter of time before he decided I was too influential to be allowed to continue. I knew the jig was up when Pritchard Hood became the new bailiff, a man who would have slit my throat with his own hand if he could."

"He certainly tried to slit mine," Malden agreed.

"If my organization was going to survive, I needed to prune away the one thing that would hold it back, keep it from growing. From developing into something new. And that one thing was me. I needed to vanish so people would forget how much they feared the guild—it had to shed its evil reputation. But that meant I would need a successor. You were the obvious choice."

"Because people love me?"

"Because of that, yes, and because you have a brain in

your head. You don't always use it, but when you do you can think your way out of most scrapes. You see beyond the immediate circumstance, and grasp the why and the wherefore."

"So you tried to kill me, knowing I would survive," Malden guessed.

"No. I tried to kill you, knowing if you didn't survive, then I'd made a mistake that could have cost me everything. There was no guarantee for you, Malden. There couldn't be. I chose Prestwicke very carefully, as well."

Malden frowned. "Prestwicke." He considered something, something he didn't like very much. Which made him think immediately that it must be true. "If he had killed me—if he had met the terms of his contract—"

"Then," Cutbill confirmed, "he would be sitting in that chair, holding that same sword. Drinking my wine, even now."

Malden swallowed thickly.

"You both made promising candidates. I needed to know which was the better choice. That's why I tried to have you killed."

Malden jumped to his feet, wrapping his hand around Acidtongue's hilt. "Prestwicke was a sadist. A madman!"

"And a devout servant of the bloodgod," Cutbill pointed out. "The people wouldn't have called him Lord Mayor. They would have called him High Priest. But the result would have been the same." Cutbill placed one hand on Malden's shoulder. Malden fought the urge to shrug it off. "For many reasons, I'm glad it was you. But he would have served. Now, will you sit down and hear what is to come?"

CHAPTER SEVENTY-NINE

"The barbarians will arrive within the week," Cutbill told Malden.

"That soon? I thought they were bogged down in Redweir," Malden replied, feeling his heart race. He had hoped—in vain, it now seemed—that the barbarian horde would be stuck in the east for the winter, unable to push west against bad weather and a lack of food. Of course, he'd met Mörget before and should have known better. The barbarians thrived on death and destruction. They would probably laugh in the teeth of winter storms and eat frozen grass rather than slow their advance. "We aren't ready," Malden said. "I'm not sure how we could ever be ready, but now—"

"How many archers have you trained?"

"Sorry? Archers? Ah," Malden said. Why hadn't he thought of that? He'd seen the archers practicing at Helstrow, under edict of the king. He should have implemented the same program for his own people. "Well—"

Cutbill shook his head wearily. "I'm sure you've had other things to worry about. Have you at least reinforced the gates? The only real advantage you'll have against the barbarians is the city wall. It will keep them out for a while, but those gates are weak points that must be shored up if you hope to have a chance."

Malden could only shrug. Those gates were massive portals of wood reinforced with iron. It had never occurred to him that they *could* be reinforced further.

"Get Slag on it at once. Give him everything he needs— he'll definitely prove your best ally in what's to come. You are about to be besieged. You need to know how these things are done, Malden." Cutbill rose and went to a shelf behind

Malden's chair. It was stuffed with books and old manuscripts. "The Learned Brotherhood left some things behind when they were driven out of the Chapterhouse. I saved what I could. Here," he said, handing a book to Malden. "This is Rus Galenius' *Manual of Fortifications*. It's the best volume on the subject that I've found."

Malden opened the book and flipped through its pages. There were copious illustrations. One showed men standing on battlements, turning a crank mounted on the side of a giant kettle. Below them other men threw their arms over their heads as a rain of hot oil or perhaps molten lead came down toward them. Many of the illustrations were cunning diagrams, showing the proper employment of fascines and mottes, or exploded views of siege towers and mantlets. The text was in a language Malden didn't know, however. "I can't read this," he admitted.

Cutbill stared down at him along his nose. "It's the high tongue of the Old Empire. Until very recently, every book written in the world was in that language. You don't even know the basic grammar?"

Malden frowned. "I learned how to read so I could keep the books of a brothel. I was lucky to get that much of an education. I never had a chance to study foreign languages."

Cutbill nodded sagely and considered this. He reached for another book, then shook his head. "There's no time for you to learn it now. Slag can at least make sense of the drawings and charts, but you'll need a translator for the text. The priests of the Lady are all fluent in the high tongue."

"Perhaps, but they've all fled," Malden said. *Which*, he thought, *you should know already—your spies should have told you as much*. Even locked up in the Chapterhouse, Cutbill would have eyes and ears everywhere in the city, and some way of keeping abreast on developments. For Cutbill to claim ignorance now meant he was hiding something. Malden wondered what was really going on here.

Cutbill sat down and steepled his fingers below his nose. "Of course, I can read it. Yes, that's what we'll do. You'll have to come back here every so often for lessons."

And advice, Malden thought. *Whether I want it or not.*

He saw the game here. When one dealt with Cutbill, one always needed to be looking for the hidden stratagem. Missing it was fatal. He looked back over the recent events of his life, seeing how Cutbill had shaped them, step by step. When the Burgrave had wanted to kill Malden, Cutbill had forced the lord of the city to spare Malden's life. When Malden had refused to go to the Vincularium, Cutbill had made sure he had a very good reason to want to leave the city. When Malden returned to Ness, the leadership of the guild of thieves was waiting for him. Cutbill had made sure all the pieces fit together. If Malden hadn't opposed Pritchard Hood in quick order, he wondered how Cutbill would have forced that confrontation. He was certain Cutbill would have had a plan.

Cutbill was a master manipulator because he followed one simple rule. He made sure, always, that when he wished to convince someone to do his bidding, no other course of action was even thinkable. He never told anyone what to do directly. He merely spelled out the dire consequences of doing anything else.

"I'll advise you on every element of the city's defense. I'll give you lists of things you need to get done, and the sooner the better," Cutbill said. "Together we'll make a stand, and save Ness."

"What if I refuse?" Malden said.

Cutbill blinked. "I beg your pardon?"

"What if I decide I won't do your bidding? You've groomed me for this role. You've given me no choice so far. But a free man always has a choice."

"I'm offering you help at a time when you desperately need it," Cutbill pointed out. "What fool would turn that down?"

"The kind of fool who knows that everything has a price. You said earlier you wanted a man with a brain in his head for this job. But that was a lie, wasn't it? You only want a puppet. A figurehead, capable of being loved by the crowd. But entirely beholden to you, and bound by iron chains to your counsel."

Cutbill stared at Malden for a very long time without

speaking. Finally, he looked away. "I think you should consider carefully before you make a grave error," he said.

Malden rose to his feet and put a hand on Acidtongue's hilt. "You didn't prepare for this, did you? You don't have a gambit ready in case I do balk."

Cutbill glanced down at the blade. "Are you sure of that?"

Malden drew the sword an inch out of its scabbard. Acid dripped on the rushes and sizzled.

Cutbill didn't flinch. "You could kill me now, of course," he said. "We've already established that. Think of what you'd lose, though."

"A job I never wanted? A master who treats me like a raw apprentice?"

"Malden," Cutbill said, very slowly. "I've heard how well you fared against Sir Hew at Helstrow. How you showed that a man with a sword is no match whatsoever for a man with a sword who also knows how to use it."

"I don't see you holding a sword," Malden said.

"When I was half your age, I led a gang of beggar children. We fought on the streets every day for a few rotten peelings of a turnip or enough coin to let us sleep in a stable on a cold night," Cutbill said, very softly. "I haven't forgotten what I learned back then. I know more dirty tricks than you do."

Malden stood his ground.

"Alright," Cutbill said, with a sigh. "You've threatened me. I'll even do you the honor of believing this is no bluff. But fighting you now would help no one, and hurt a great number of plans I've been working on for years. Put that sword away. I'll buy my life from you."

"I don't need gold. I have plenty of my own," Malden said.

"I wasn't going to pay you in coin. I possess something far more dear than money. Through that door," he said, pointing across the room, "is a store of foodstuffs. I knew this would be a bad winter, so I laid in provisions for a very long wait."

"You're going to buy your life with a cask or two of salt pork?"

"I have a hundred barrels of flour back there. I bought them at the peak of harvest time, when the price was quite low. They're yours, Malden."

A hundred barrels of flour would feed the entire city for a week. Malden needed that flour. He considered killing Cutbill and taking the flour anyway.

But in the end, he shoved the sword home and lifted his hands in a gesture of peace. "I'll take what you offer. The flour, and the advice. But I want you to know one thing—I don't work for you anymore," he said. "You work for me. As a counselor. I will make my own decisions, and if they align well with your advice, that's well to the good. If they deviate from your plans, I will not apologize."

Cutbill smiled. "I wouldn't have it any other way," he said.

Malden wondered then whether he had won a small victory—or if the confrontation had played out exactly as Cutbill had hoped from the start.

CHAPTER EIGHTY

Mörget tramped up the frost-crackling hill, naked axe in hand, and flourished it in the air. An arrow arced through the wind, tumbling as it came, and landed on its side on the hard ground next to him. He ignored it. "Come closer, you cowards! Come and fight me!" he shouted, his voice booming down to the frozen fields below.

An army stood there, watching him. The Army of Free Men, they called themselves, though they took their orders directly from a man on a horse wearing a crown. Mörget pointed his axe at the front ranks of the army and it fell back, some of its individual members tripping over those behind.

"Fear belies you! Fear makes you her slaves. Free men, ha! Fight me!" Mörget howled.

Another arrow came toward him. At this range he had time to bat it out of the air before it reached him. Mörget turned around and looked back down the hill, toward where Balint hid in the shelter of a lightning-blasted tree. The few leaves still clinging to its branches were clotted with ice.

"You're good with taunts," Mörget told the dwarf. "Tell me what to say to them. Tell me how to make them angry!"

Balint looked around as if afraid the men of Skrae were sneaking up on her, as if he had given away her position. Hardly likely, Mörget knew. The barbarians had caught a few pickets of this Army of Free Men. They had tortured them to learn what they could, then given them proper deaths. Now even the most daring scouts of the Burgrave's army wouldn't come within arrow flight of Mörget or his clans. Every time the two armies got close and Mörget thought they would at last come to blows, the cowards of Skrae would disengage and withdraw with all possible speed.

Even now, with Mörget well in range, they were pulling away. The man with the crown signaled to his serjeants, whirling a flanged mace over his head and repeatedly pointing north. The serjeants got the men moving. They couldn't seem to keep proper formations, but they were glad enough to move away, and it didn't take long before the entire army was marching away in retreat.

"Tell me how to insult them. I'm no scold. What will offend them most?" Mörget demanded.

Balint shivered, but she found her voice. "Drop your breeks. Show them your arse and spread your buttocks so they can see your little ring. That'll give them a bullseye to target," she said.

Mörget shook his head and came stamping back down the hill toward her. He grabbed her up under his arm and carried her back to the road, two low hills away, where the barbarian horde was marching west. The clans were tired and foot-sore, and on short rations, but they gave Mörget a hearty cheer when he appeared above them.

Mörget hurried toward the van where his father and sister rode before their standards. He jogged alongside Mörg's horse and called up to him, "They're retreating again. They're demoralized. If we gave chase, we could take them easily."

"Aye," Mörg said, as if he was seriously considering it. "We could break their main force in an afternoon. But only if we spend two weeks chasing them down. They want us to follow. They want to lead us as far from Ness as they can." He shook his head. "No, Mountainslayer. If there's no fight in them, why bother?"

Mörget was stunned. The clans had spoken for war. They had already questioned Mörg's judgment once, when they forced him to march west from Helstrow. Now he would defy them by refusing to let them fight?

It was Mörg's right to make decisions for the entire horde, of course. That was his function as Great Chieftain. Yet to so openly deny his people what they wanted most . . .

Wheels began to turn inside Mörget's mind. "Father," he said, intentionally addressing Mörg in the most familiar, and therefore least respectful way possible, "a warrior does not show mercy to his enemies when he meets them on the field."

If Mörg understood the subtext of what his son said—that the name Mörg the Merciful was not an honorific—he chose to ignore the challenge. "I have every intention of destroying that army. Just not yet. When we take Ness, they'll have to come to us—and we'll be in a far better position to crush them. We'll be well-fed, well-rested, and behind strong walls. The key to Skrae is to hold the three cities, Helstrow, Redweir, and Ness. Once we're properly invested they'll never loosen our grip. You wanted to conquer this land. Let's do it properly."

Mörget fumed but he resisted the urge to call his father a coward. That could only end one way, with one of them dead. Instead he tried to think strategically. It was not his forte. "We'll be leaving an army behind us. Astraddle our supply lines," he countered.

Mörg turned and looked at him with something akin to pride. Mörg could not remember the last time that had happened. "Good thinking. But we'll also leave them with no base to operate from. Strand them out here in these empty fields all winter—they'll freeze so solid when we emerge in the spring, we'll have to chip them out of the ice just to make them thralls."

Mörget fell back and fetched his own horse. He rode among the chieftains of his clans—dark men, grim as he was. There was much muttering, some of which he joined. When they stopped to camp for the night, one of the chieftains took him aside behind a tent. "Your father's making a mistake," the man said. "He's made a lot of mistakes already."

Mörget eyed the man critically. His name was Thürbalt, and his beard was shot with white, but his arms were near as thick as Mörget's own and he'd never lost a wrestling match. He commanded two hundred men and thralls, most of whom he was related to either by marriage or bastardry, and he had a right to speak his mind. Mörget couldn't remember the last time he'd done so, however.

Now—he had chosen to break his silence now. With a dire accusation, indeed. Chieftains who made mistakes did not remain chieftains for long.

Not when they could so easily be replaced.

"Who do you speak for?" Mörget asked.

"Myself alone," Thürbalt said, which was cautious, but proper.

"When you speak for all, you tell me." Mörget had to be cautious himself. Questioning Mörg's decisions wasn't sedition, not among the clans. But gathering men of like opinion, muttering in darkness, spreading mistrust—these things had a way of quickly moving from speech to action. "I obey the will of my clans," Mörget finished. It was an old formulation, a figure of speech. It could also be a promise.

In the morning, the file marched through a plain of frost-hard fields that extended to the horizon in every direction, where birds circled endlessly looking for one last forgotten seed or bit of fallen grain. Mörget, lost in his thoughts, saw little of it, and was only brought up from his reverie when a messenger came back from the van to tell him Mörg wanted him.

Jogging forward, Mörget wondered idly if Mörg had heard the whispers in the night. This might be a chastisement—or a challenge to his honor. Perhaps things would come to a head far sooner than he'd expected.

Yet when he reached the van, he saw Mörgain dancing with arms raised high, giving thanks to Mother Death. Some of the berserkers had joined her. Mörg stood high up in the crotch of a dead tree, one hand shading his eyes.

"I thought you'd like to see this, Mountainslayer. Come up, to me."

Mörget clambered up the creaking branches to perch next to his father. "What is it?" he demanded. "I haven't broken my fast yet."

"No time for surly words, my boy," Mörg said. He could not hide the excitement in his voice. "There! Look! Surely your young eyes see it better than mine."

Mörg looked. And there it was. Across the plain, no more than four hours' march away, stood a strangely regular shape, a form of straight lines and shining brick that circled a cloven hill. A wall. A city wall.

The wall of Ness.

PART 4

THE SIEGE OF ness

INTERLUDE

In theory there were no officers in the Army of Free Men. There were serjeants, of course, because no army can function without men to scream at the soldiers and give them their orders. But there were no lieutenants, no captains, and no generals.

There was of course Ommen Tarness, the Burgrave of the Free City of Ness. The man who had organized the Army in the first place and its de facto leader. Yet he went to great pains to remind the men that he was a common soldier like any of them, and that if they accepted his commands and followed his decrees, it was simply because they recognized he had the best ideas and the most meaningful contributions to their effort.

Together with a cadre of the Army's finest scouts, he went in person to spy on the barbarian horde when it arrived at Ness. Like a common scout he lay in the mud on a hill a half mile away so he could see what the Army would face in battle.

Of course one had to be practical about such things, so he had a bear hide to lie in, while his fellow soldiers had to suffice with moldering blankets. His wineskin was full of fine malmsey as well, and he had dried venison to chew on while his men sufficed with weak ale and pemmican. And of course he wore—as always—his golden coronet, which marked him out in any group of men.

"There," one of the scouts whispered, and pointed down the hill. "That'll be the first of them." The scouts had been lying in their perch since before dawn. The sun had been up for three hours with no sign of the enemy—they were certainly in no hurry.

Before the van of their force the barbarians sent vedettes ahead—mounted sentries who watched every side of the road as if they expected some sudden ambush. One rider wheeled his horse around right below the wall of Ness, well within bowshot. When no one tried to shoot him he let out a piercing whistle that the scouts could hear quite plainly, even from so far away. The rest of the vedettes moved to take up positions on the sides of the road. They stayed watchful, even though no trace of resistance had been offered them.

Perhaps they were as surprised as Tarness. What he could see of the city beyond its defensive wall looked much as it always had. Smoke rose from a hundred chimneys. Shutters were open to catch the morning air and dispel the night's closeness. Tarness could even see people moving about the streets, going about their everyday tasks.

It was as if no one inside was even aware that they were about to be besieged. "I expected slightly more of Pritchard Hood," Tarness said. There were certain things one did when facing a siege, things that should have been done long since. The wall showed no trace of hoardings, nor were any ballistas or onagers set up on its wide battlements. The gates were closed up tight, but so were the sally ports—small doors set into the more massive gates, through which defenders could emerge to harass the incoming horde. There was no sign at all of such a force, however. There was not so much as a delegation of parley to speak with the barbarians when they arrived.

Down in the road Mörg and his children came now on horseback, and behind them an honor guard of berserkers. The red-painted faces of the manic warriors were slack with exhaustion, but they jogged to keep up with the ambling horses. They had their weapons over their shoulders in good order and they looked ready for anything the city might throw at them.

"Strange. There should be flags flying on Castle Hill," one of the scouts said.

Tarness frowned. The man was right. Not so much as a pennon flew at the top of the city. In fact, the more Tarness looked at his old palace and the barracks where his guard resided, the more he got the feeling something was missing. He couldn't make out much detail from so far away, but he got the impression that the walled enclosure from which he'd previously ruled the city was deserted.

The main force of the horde came down the road on foot, thousands of reavers and berserkers and thralls in no particular formation. They carried packs on their backs or drove wagons loaded with supplies. Tarness saw bundles of long stakes and countless acres of deer hide for tents, a round score of anvils, casks and barrels by the hundred to hold mead and beer, flour, dried meat, turnips and pickled fish.

Tarness had been a general for a very long time, far longer than any of his men suspected. He was struck by how orderly the wagons were loaded, and how well supplied the horde was. Most armies lived by foraging—the Army of Free Men lived on the produce of the land, for instance, on whatever game its soldiers could catch and whatever supplies of grain they could requisition from local farms.

When you intended to lay siege to a city, though, you couldn't just send out all your men each day to hunt and gather for themselves. The land around the besieged city would be picked clean in the first few days and you would be forced to send your foragers out ever farther in search of food, stretching your lines until you could no longer effectively storm the city should the opportunity arise. The barbarians had a reputation as reckless fighters, but apparently this Mörg the Wise had more foresight than some civilized generals Tarness had fought against.

While the scouts watched, the barbarians set up their camp a quarter mile away from the city walls. Far enough away to avoid any missile fire from the walls, but close enough no one could escape the city without being caught. The camp went up with remarkable speed, as if the barbarians had done this a thousand times before. Small knots of men set about erecting a thousand tents, while others dug neat latrine pits well clear of the main camp. Others set up makeshift forges for the blacksmiths who would keep their weapons in good repair, or built stone ovens to bake bread to feed the camp. The work was done well before nightfall, when most of the horde turned in to sleep. Others stayed at watch around blazing campfires or stood picket duty at the edge of the camp.

It was all done with such efficiency and trim as Tarness had never seen before in any civilized army. It would have taken the king's own troops weeks to achieve all that. By full dark the barbarians were settled in fully to their new home.

One woman, her face painted like a skull, broke open a series of barrels and let the men fill horns and leather cups with thick mead, which made them laugh so brightly Tarness could hear it on his ridge. Mörg himself stood on a crude platform and gave a speech, and received a great cheer.

Mörg's son, whose face was painted like a berserker, broke off from the rest and went to stand outside the Hunter's Gate of Ness. He simply stood there while darkness fell and lights came on inside the city. Stood and stared at the wall, as if he could bring it down by sheer effort of concentration. Perhaps he was waiting for someone up on the wall to call down to him, to make some effort at communication. He waited in vain, if that was the case.

He was still there when Tarness indicated that the scouts should withdraw. He'd seen enough. Rising stiffly from their perches, the men headed back down the side of the ridge to where they'd left their horses.

Tarness had a lot to think about. What he'd seen had been instructive enough—but what he hadn't seen was far more troubling. Hood should have offered some resistance, surely. He should have at least shown the colors of Ness in defiance of the siege. "Something, anything, to show he was unwilling to give up," Tarness muttered. Unless Hood had betrayed him and struck a deal with Mörg, to open the gates and let the barbarians move inside. But no, that was impossible. Tarness had picked Hood for his zeal and his utter hatred of anyone who didn't worship the Lady. And furthermore Mörg had set up camp exactly as if expected a protracted siege.

What in the sacred name of the Lady was going on?

"We'll ride back to headquarters at once," one of the scouts said, in that deferential way the Free Men had. They'd learned not to ask Tarness directly for an order, but instead to state what they expected him to say as if they'd come up with it themselves. Then he would approve or disapprove as if he was offering counsel only, and not an actual command. Tarness nodded and the scouts mounted up.

Another of the men leapt up onto his horse and drew his sword. "In two days we can be back here with the Free Men, every one of them ready to die to relieve the Free City. We'll show them what they get for picking a fight with Ness!"

The others looked to Tarness. They seemed ready to cheer the idea but they needed his approval first.

Sadly he couldn't give it. He sighed and climbed up into his own saddle. "Yesterday," he said, "I watched our men drilling at pike squares."

The scouts looked at each other as if wondering what he was getting at.

"Most of them," Tarness said, "have figured out how to march in a straight line. They can even turn when they're ordered to. Though some of them still have to put down their weapons to look at their hands and remember which direction is left and which is right. Half of them are stricken with camp fever, and the other half with the sailor pox from all those camp followers I told you to drive off. Their armor is rusty, their weapons are falling apart. Not a single one of them has ever fought in an actual battle."

One of the scouts shook his head. "They've got heart, though—they love their city and will be fierce in its defense."

Tarness smiled at the man. In his experience that did count for something—but not as much as soldiers who knew how to shoulder arms or brace for a cavalry charge. "You know that my ancestor, Juring Tarness, was a great general. He had a saying which has been passed down through the generations. 'If one wants to be renowned for one's great victories, the best thing to do is not fight any battles where one might lose.'"

Tarness glanced back in the direction of Ness, though it was hidden now by the side of the ridge. He didn't need to see it to remember what it looked like. "No, I advise we hold off for now. Keep drilling the men, make them as ready as we can. But it would be suicide right now to take on an army that well organized and blooded. Ness will have to hold out on its own a while longer."

"How much longer?" a scout asked, his eyes wide in the

moonlight. He looked almost angry at what Tarness had suggested.

Tarness smiled. "Until some miracle occurs, and we actually have a chance. But don't worry." He flicked his reins and got his horse moving. "The Lady is on our side."

CHAPTER EIGHTY-ONE

North of Helstrow, Croy took to the road.

It was risky, but it meant they covered far more ground every day. The barbarians seemed wholly uninterested in the land beyond the royal fortress. He had not seen any sign of patrols or even pickets for days. For that matter, he hadn't seen any sign of life at all. The farmland that passed by on either side of the road was frozen solid, and if there were peasants still living in that cold region, they wisely stayed indoors. He was a bit worried by the fact that he hadn't seen a smoking chimney for some time, but he assumed the locals were just being careful.

He should have followed their example.

Bethane had fallen asleep against his back, and he was paying more attention to making sure she didn't fall off the horse than he did to the road. He was vaguely aware they were about to enter a copse of trees that narrowed the road on either side, but gave it little thought—until he heard someone cough.

He pulled up sharply on the reins. His horse bridled but dragged to a stop, just as Croy heard a taut rope being cut with a twang. A heavy log shot down from the tree tops, swinging on the end of a line so it arced directly across the road at the height of Croy's chest. Had he not stopped in time, it would have knocked him clear off the horse and left him sprawling and broken in the road.

Instead it collided with the rearing horse's neck. Croy heard bones shatter and the horse screamed, its hot breath lancing upward in the air. Beneath him he felt the animal falter and begin to collapse.

Ghostcutter jumped into his hand as he leapt to the ground, dancing backward to avoid the falling horse. Bethane, wakened by the horse's pitiful cry, slid down and was nearly crushed by the dying animal. Croy had no time to get her clear as three monstrous shapes came rushing toward him out of the trees.

They were bundled so heavily in furs he could not get a sense of how big they really were, or if they were even men. They wielded hatchets and hay forks with wickedly sharpened tines. One jabbed at him before he was fully ready and he felt metal pierce his flesh.

Perhaps thinking they had him, the other two men moved in for the kill. Croy swung wildly with Ghostcutter and sheared through the haft of a fork. A hatchet came swinging down toward his face but he kicked out and caught its owner in the chest, knocking him backward and off his feet.

The bloody fork swung low for another attack and Croy smashed it aside with the flat of his blade. His side sang with agony as he twisted at the waist to block another blow, but he ignored the pain and swung hard for the opponent who had wounded him. Ghostcutter bit deep through layers of fur until it found flesh and laid open the veins of the man's neck.

The man let out a gurgling scream and dropped to his knees. Perhaps realizing that Croy was not such easy prey as they'd believed, the other two turned and ran for the trees.

Croy was breathing heavily as he stepped back toward the horse, intent on making sure Bethane was alright. His heart raced when he saw she was not there.

Casting about wildly he saw a fourth man running away across an open field. Bethane was over the man's shoulder, kicking and punching at him. He probably couldn't even feel the blows through all that padding.

Croy gave chase but the kidnapper had a long lead on

him, and the wound in Croy's side slowed him so that he couldn't sprint. He followed as best he could, desperately trying to keep his quarry in sight.

He nearly lost them—but then he heard Bethane scream his name, and he raced toward the sound. The kidnapper had hurried toward a leafless orchard a quarter of a mile away. Croy pressed one hand against his side and ran into the trees. It could easily have been another trap, but he didn't care. He would fight his way through whatever they sent him, or die in the attempt. He could not let them have the queen.

In the middle of the orchard stood a humble croft, a low house with a thatched roof that descended to within a foot of the ground. The entrance was more hatch than door. Croy found it locked, but he bashed in the latch with Ghostcutter's pommel and threw open its panels and stumbled inside.

He nearly tripped and broke his leg. The house was mostly dug out of the ground and was accessed by way of a ladder leading down to a muddy floor. Croy had not expected that—he had assumed that the floor inside would be level with the ground outside, so he fell into the dugout room, the floor rushing up to meet his face. He managed to twist to the side—he felt his wound open wide as he did so—and crash down into a bin of moldering apples.

There were four people in the room. One was Bethane. Two others were holding her down while she struggled. The fourth held a rusty knife.

Croy rolled out of the bin and drove Ghostcutter straight into the heart of the knife-wielder. Before the others could react he cut them down, groaning in pain as the wound in his side oozed blood. When they were all dead, he slumped down on the floor and could do nothing but listen to Bethane scream for a long time.

Eventually she stopped. Eventually she came over and lifted his cloak away. His side was clotted with blood. She cleaned his wound and bandaged it. He thanked her as best he could. He could not stand up.

Bethane went over to one of her kidnappers and started pulling furs away from the dead man's face. Perhaps she wished to know if her attackers had been barbarians or men of Skrae. Croy didn't have the strength to stop her.

"By the blessed hem of the Lady's green robe," the queen said. Croy looked over and saw the face of the thing he'd killed. It belonged to a boy. A child, not much older than Bethane herself. He'd slaughtered a child.

Perhaps it was his wound that kept him from feeling the guilt that honor demanded. He closed his eyes and tried to just breathe. His wound was deep, and he feared it might have touched his vitals.

"But what could they have wanted from us?" Bethane asked. "They didn't ask us for money. I would gladly have given them coin for safe passage."

Croy didn't answer. He was afraid he knew, but he couldn't say it aloud.

It was only when Bethane approached a soup pot on the hearth that he found his voice again. He knew she was hungry—they'd eaten little but mushrooms and tree bark tea for days. The soup smelled divine, hearty and rich and well-spiced. It smelled of good, fresh meat.

"Don't," he managed to say. "Don't even look in that pot."

Did she understand? He couldn't tell. If he'd had the strength, he'd have made up some story about witch's cauldrons and the foolish people who tasted their contents. Or about northern peasants being accustomed to a diet that would be too crude for a royal stomach to digest.

"Don't look," he said, which was all he could muster.

She stepped back from the pot, and came to curl up by his side.

CHAPTER EIGHTY-TWO

"Nock! Draw! Fire!" Herwig the madam shouted, beating time against her leg with a fan. A row of women loosed their bows and their long arrows flashed through the air. Most of them at least hit the archery butts at the far side of the square—they'd been practicing nonstop since Malden first recruited them as archers, and Herwig had proved a merciless drill instructor. "Nock!" she called, and the women, all of them harlots from the House of Sighs, lifted arrows to their bows, rested them against their thumbs as they'd been taught. "Draw!" Herwig shouted, and her charges did as they were told, though one very young woman at the end of the row managed to drop her arrow before she'd managed to draw fully. The others laughed at her. Herwig came storming down the row, cold fury in her eyes.

"Is there a problem, Guennie?" she demanded.

"It's just—I bumped my breast on the draw and it—startled me," the young whore said, looking down at her feet.

"In the Old Empire they tell stories still of the female warriors of Thune," Herwig said, raising her nose in the air. "They were fiercer than the men by far. When they encountered this very same problem, they thrust torches to their bosoms to burn off their own left breasts. That," Herwig said, "made it much easier to draw. Perhaps you'd like to do the same?"

"No, milady," Guennie said, her eyes very wide.

"Then prove to me you don't need to," Herwig said. "Pick up that crooked little thing you call an arrow and draw!"

Slag laughed as the whore archer bent to do as she was told and Herwig rapped her across the neck with her fan. Malden just shook his head.

"Cutbill was right. We should have been doing this weeks

ago." He'd seen real improvement in the last few days, but the female archers were hardly ready—Herwig's company of archers were the best of the lot. Elody's women were barely able to string a bow yet. The thieves of the guild more often than not failed to show up for practice at all, though Velmont threatened them with dire punishment.

The thieves and the whores were all Malden had, though. Of the honest population of Ness, by far the great majority of the men were old and infirm or too young to even lift a bow. The honest women were needed elsewhere.

"Will they be ready, when we need them?" Malden asked, mostly to himself.

The dwarf laughed again. "They'll not be sharpshooters, that's for fucking sure. But with all those barbarians out there, they're like to hit one or two if only by mistake," he pointed out. "Anyone can hit a target as big as an army."

"Come on," Malden said. "We're not helping here—we're probably just making them nervous so they don't shoot as straight. Let's go see how the other work is progressing."

Malden and Slag hurried north to see to the reinforcement of the Reeve's Gate. Under Slag's instructions, the women of Ness used cranes and winches to stack pompions—wicker baskets full of rocks—against the gate, while others hammered a scaffolding of wooden beams together to hold the stacks in place. There was not enough iron available to properly bolster the scaffolding, but a one-legged blacksmith oversaw the construction of a massive bracket that would help a little.

"It won't be as strong as the wall around it," Slag said, inspecting the work, "but I'd like to see the battering ram that could get through that." He seemed very pleased with himself.

A lot of people did, that day. For all their fear of Herwig, the archers had been rosy-cheeked and ready at the crack of dawn to get to work. The crews at the gates joked amongst themselves and sang songs while they toiled.

Everywhere the people of Ness were, for once, happy and productive. Maybe just having something to do was better than huddling in their houses waiting for death to come. Maybe it just helped they couldn't see over the city wall.

"You'd think the barbarians weren't out there," Malden said. He had seen over the wall. He'd seen plenty, and now he couldn't seem to forget it. Every time he closed his eyes he remembered what he'd seen from the top of Castle Hill. The barbarians had encircled the city and their tents stretched out across the fields as far as the eye could see. Berserkers danced endlessly on the banks of the Skrait, while Mörgain and her skull-faced crew rode circles around and around the circumference of Ness, daring each other to come closer and closer to the wall.

So far not a shot had been fired from either side. The barbarians had made no attempt to attack, nor even communicate with the defenders inside the city. Malden knew that would not last. There were very dark days to come.

Yet for the moment Ness was ruled by good cheer. Even the ceaseless flood of petitions and demands on his time as Lord Mayor had slowed to a trickle. The guildmasters of the mercers and the cordwainers had both sent him messages of support and confidence. The beggars of the city had declared a holiday and thrown him an impromptu, if slightly odorous, parade.

"Don't they understand that we're all probably going to die, or at the least be enslaved, within the week?"

"Ah, lad, you're overestimating the faculties of human fucking reason," Slag told him. "That's still seven days away. Right now, they're safe and reasonably well fed. And they're learning something dwarves have always known—if you don't have time to sit around doing nothing, you don't have time to fucking complain."

It was true. There was so much to be done that Malden had found employment for every idle hand. Wooden hoardings had to be built at strategic locations atop the wall, then covered in hides and wetted down so the barbarians couldn't set them on fire. An enormous arsenal of weapons had to be cleaned, sharpened, and rubbed with animal fat to keep off rust. Arrows by the barrel full had to be carved, straightened, fletched and headed. Everyone who could stand on two legs and fight with at least one arm had to be trained and made ready.

There had been a time, Malden thought, when even the prospect of hard work or—bloodgod forbid—sacrifice was enough to start a riot in Ness. Now the entire city was energized with the effort of the counter-siege.

"They're united for the cause," Slag said, finally. "They're working towards their own buggering salvation, and they know it. Show a little civic spirit yourself, you dumb bastard!" Slag slapped Malden on the forearm and laughed uproariously.

It seemed the dwarf shared the peoples' spirit of camaraderie against the common enemy.

"I just wish any of it felt like enough," Malden admitted. "Most of this will make no difference. The barbarians know how to fight against archers on a city wall. They didn't batter down the gates of Redweir—we still don't know how they breached the wall there, but they didn't go in through a gate. At Helstrow simple trickery and momentum saw them through. If only I had some secret weapon, some power uncheckable to draw on . . ." He thought of Coruth, and how she was training Cythera to be a witch. Magic would come in very useful right about then, but he knew better than to count upon their arcane assistance. History books were stuffed full of examples of lords who'd relied upon witches and sorcerers, and paid for it when magic proved more fickle than iron.

"Lad," Slag said.

"Hmm?" Malden had been lost in his thought.

"Lad, come over here," the dwarf whispered. He led Malden around a corner into the shadow of a mews. "Lad—maybe I can give you just that."

The thief felt like he'd been doused in cold water. "Give me . . . what?" he asked, carefully.

"A power fucking uncheckable." The dwarf's eyes blazed in the darkness. "It won't be easy. Or cheap."

"You have my full attention," Malden promised.

"You remember that book I found in the Vincularium?"

"Not really," Malden confessed.

Slag shook his head. "Alright, alright. You remember how Balint managed to bring the place down?"

"Vividly."

Slag nodded. "I'm going to need a workshop, somewhere in the Smoke will do, some place private. This is not something we can let anybody talk about. No-fucking-body talks. And I won't make you any promises it'll work."

"What do you need?" Malden asked.

"Well, now, let me see . . . charcoal, for a start, as much as you can get. As much stale urine, too."

Malden grimaced.

"Don't look at me like that. Fullers use piss all the time. It's part of how they make felt. There'll be barrels of it in every woolery shop in town. And we can start collecting it from the citizenry, too, though we'll need a good cover story for that. Then there's the last ingredient I need, and it'll be hard to come by—brimstone."

"Don't tell me you've taken up sorcery and need to conjure demons. Though if you do tell me that, I'll ask you how many demons you had in mind and when we can expect their aid."

"Maybe something better than that, lad. Just—trust me. I'll also need workers. Alchemists, apothecaries. I'll take fucking tanners if they don't stink too much. Bakers and millers would be good. Anybody who can grind and mix ingredients. I'll need all manner of equipment. Best I make a list and you have Velmont fill it. Mostly, though, I need time. This is untested stuff. Purely experimental."

"Time is the one thing I'm short on," Malden said, "but you'll have as much as I can spare you, I promise."

"It's going to be dangerous, too. I'm likely to burn myself to a cinder working with this stuff. If that happens—promise me one thing."

"Of course," Malden said.

"You'll give me the biggest damned funeral this city ever saw. No expense spared. But you'll keep the coffin closed. If this goes up in my face, what's left of me won't be pretty."

"That's a hopeful thought."

Slag laughed again. Malden had never heard a dwarf laugh so often. "Optimistic to a fucking fault, that's me. All part of that damned civic spirit, eh?"

CHAPTER EIGHTY-THREE

"Halloo! Halloo! Ness! People of Ness! Is someone in charge up there? There must be someone in charge. The people of Skrae can't clean their bottoms without someone telling them how to do it. Halloo! Oh, cowards! We'd like to speak with you, cowards!"

Hurlind the scold had been shouting up at the walls outside King's Gate all day. He was growing hoarse, and still no one would come out and address him. There had been a few attempts early in the day to throw garbage down on the scold, but that had just encouraged the clown.

Mörget itched with the desire to slap Hurlind down into the mud—just to get some quiet. He didn't dare, however. Hurlind was operating under Mörg's direct order. The Great Chieftain wanted to talk to the leaders of Ness. Convince them, through reason, that it was in their best interest to surrender.

"That's unlikely to work," Balint pointed out. The two of them sat in Mörg's tent, brooding. Outside a thin freezing rain was falling. It didn't seem to bother Hurlind.

"You think them unreasonable people?" Mörget asked.

"Hardly. They're smarter than you lot. Of course, a bucket full of spotty turnips is, too. No. They'll have heard what happened at Helstrow. Of the way dead king Ulfram tried to make parley with Mörg, and got skewered up the shitpipe for it. No, they won't come out and play nice."

"Let us then, you and I, discuss better ways," Mörget said. "We took Redweir quick enough."

"By sapping? Sure, we can try sapping," Balint said, with a shrug. She seemed to have accepted the collar around her neck, finally. She rarely ever complained about her thralldom anymore. "The walls here are better built than at Redweir, though. Thicker, better reinforced, and they go down deeper, in proper casements. Turns out a Burgrave can afford better engineers than a bunch of impotent monks."

"So it can't be done?"

"I didn't say that," Balint admonished. "But it'll take longer, and we'll need to dig multiple tunnels. It'll take a week or so."

"What could you do in the meantime? What other ideas have you?"

"We could build siege engines," she said. "I don't have the tools or the skilled laborers here for proper mangonels or siege towers but I could probably build some simple trebuchets. Won't bring down the wall, but we can make the people inside wish they could crawl up their own arseholes."

Mörget nodded in interest. "Could they be rigged to throw balls of flaming pitch? We could burn those wooden hoardings off the walls."

"Now there you're thinking, old son. Why, I know some recipes for—"

At the flap of the tent, someone cleared his throat. Mörget jumped up at once and grabbed his axe. It was the Great Chieftain, Mörg himself, eavesdropping on them.

"All good ideas," Mörg said. "It might come to that. But for now, I want you two to stop this talk."

"You don't want us even thinking out loud?" Balint asked. "We weren't planning anything for real, yet."

"For now I want to try a more gentle option," Mörg told the dwarf.

Mörget's eyes narrowed. "Great Chieftain. There are murmurings in the tents. They have been calling you Mörg the Merciful again. It is my duty as your man to give you warning."

"And so you have. I give little credence to men who

whisper. Those are men afraid to act. When they talk openly of revolt, tell me again," Mörg said. "Now, come with me, Mountainslayer. Ness has finally agreed to talk."

Father and son tramped through the mud of the barbarian camp. This had all been fields, once, fertile fields full of waving grain. Now it was a great brown soup that sucked at their boots and threatened to swallow the camp entire.

There was little of the romantic in the investment of a siege. Everywhere barbarians were bending their hands to construction work—building enormous bread ovens, constructing crude mantlets, fencing in paddocks for livestock. The vast majority of the horde languished in their sodden tents, however, getting drunk. They knew they might be here all winter and wanted to get started on warming themselves now.

"Father," Mörget tried again, as they wended their way through the randomly-placed tents, "they say you've lost your fire. That you won't fight—and if you won't fight, they want someone else for Great Chieftain. Someone who will crush this place."

"If it comes to that, I say good luck to them. You've besieged how many cities, Mountainslayer? One? And it fell within a week. I'm very proud of that, my boy. But until you've sat outside a curtain wall for six months, getting fat and lazy but always wondering if today is the day, the day you have to try your iron against that of some desperate man who just wants to defend his children . . . well. Don't try to teach your grandmother how to skin a deer."

They came to the end of the camp. A broad open space two hundred yards across separated the camp from the city wall—enough distance to make archers think twice before wasting arrows on pot-shots. Mörgain and her riders were the only ones daring enough to enter that disputed zone. Now Mörg led Mörget into the yellowed grass and together they looked up at the wall.

"That right there," Mörg said, "is what separates us from the westerners. They can build things like this wall. That's where their strength lies."

"There's none in their arms, we've proved that," Mörget

laughed. "Great Chieftain, we have no need of walls! Tents are enough for your warriors." Walls had always been the emblem of the great injustice that had locked the clans away on the dry and harsh eastern steppes. The people of Skrae had pushed them first from their walled cities, then back beyond the Whitewall Mountains, where they'd been all but imprisoned until the day Cloudblade fell. In the stories the scolds told, walls were objects of hatred and derision. "Walls! I'd tear this one down with my own hands, if I had the time."

Mörg sighed. "Look at it. Really look at it. Right now it looks like cowardice and frustration. But imagine, if you can, what it would be like to own that. To be able to stand behind it and never worry about enemies raiding your camp again."

It was impressive, Mörget had to admit. Twenty-five feet of closely-fitted stone, mortared together and then dressed to give protection to the mortar. No amount of strength-of-arms could penetrate that defense. They would have to find a way in through stealth, or engineering, or, as Mörg seemed to want to try, promises. "They called down a few minutes ago," Mörg told his son. "They're going to send someone to talk to us. Finally."

"Talk. They wish to talk," Mörget muttered.

"Yes. If one wishes to offer terms of surrender, one must be able to speak," Mörg pointed out. "Oh, don't get too excited. I doubt they'll give in so easily. They'll want concessions, and we'll need to prove we bargain in good faith. But if we could take this city without losing a single berserker, I'd not balk at the price."

"There's more glory in breaking our way in by force," Mörget pointed out.

"Glory. Yes. Tell me, Mountainslayer—if we bring down that wall, what do we gain?" Mörg asked.

Mörget hated it when his father asked him leading questions. It meant there was a lesson to be imparted. His face burned even as it was flecked with cold winter rain. "We could storm inside, slaughter the inhabitants, and take the city for our own."

"And hold it for how long? The Army of Free Men is sticking close. Right now they're afraid to engage us, but what if we stole their city? Do you think they would hold back, then?"

"I would relish the chance to destroy them!"

"Ah," Mörg said, "but would you get that chance? Once we were inside, we would become the besieged. We would be the defenders. And if the wall is damaged at the time the Burgrave arrives—if there is a massive hole in one side of our only protection—how will we defend ourselves? I want this place intact, Mountainslayer. I want it in the same condition I found it. Otherwise we gain nothing by taking it. I'll remind you, it was your plan to come out here in the first place."

Mörget seethed, but said nothing. The whispering in the tents was growing louder every day. When it became open muttering, he would move.

But not until then. Mörget trusted his own arm. He trusted the steel of his axe. But he was wise enough to know that without the support of the clans, his own strength would not be enough to get him what he wanted.

"Halloo!" Hurlind shouted again. "You in there! Come show us some sign you haven't forgotten us. You'll break our hearts! Halloo! Show yourselves or we'll write songs about how craven you were. Do you want your children to hear songs like that? Do you want history to remember you as cowards?"

Mörg pointed upwards. There was definitely movement atop the wall now. A man was coming forward. He wore a coat of plate that covered him head to toe in steel, and a great helm with a gilt cornucopia welded to its top. He seemed to have trouble walking as if he was not accustomed to wearing so much metal.

The man bent forward at the waist, so that he could look down over the side of the wall. Then he fussed with his helmet, as if trying to get a better view through its eyeslits. Mörget heard him cursing, his voice hollow and echoing inside the helmet. Then the man of Ness shrugged off the great helm with a sigh of disgust, and for the first time Mörget saw his face.

"Malden?" he shouted upwards.

The little thief stared back down at him. "Mörget? Fancy meeting you like this."

"Imagine my surprise, at being hailed by a thief," Mörget shouted back.

"It's Lord Mayor Malden now."

"They put you in charge?" Mörget boomed out a violent laugh. "Malden! I must admit, it's very good to see you up there! I was worried this place would be defended by an actual soldier!"

"Is that some kind of jibe at my expense? I never could figure out your wit, Mörget. But then, I never went looking for it with a magnifying glass. Look, what do you want? You—the other one—you're Mörg, right? The barbarian king?"

"We don't have kings," Mörg said, with the air of a man repeating words he had spoken a thousand times before. "The clans rule themselves. They call me their Great Chieftain."

"Mörg the Wise! Mörg the conqueror of North Tyndale, Mörg the Master of Helstrow, Mörg, friend of dogs! Mörg whose sword is not magical, but who needeth not such toys to—"

Mörg shut Hurlind up with a pointed glance.

"So you're the famous Malden?" the Great Chieftain asked, when he had quiet again. "Well met, friend. Mörget's spoken often of you. He said you were instrumental in helping to bring down Cloudblade. Without you he might have stepped into a trap under the mountain and hurt his foot."

"Oh, now you're just insulting me," Malden said. "I'm ever so deeply offended."

Mörg grinned. He looked like he found Malden entertaining. Mörget had always found the little man annoying, himself. Such a weakling. He'd never understood why Croy had chosen this rodent to carry an Ancient Blade.

Mörg bowed low to the thief. "Forgive my transgression. I've come to make you an offer."

"Please don't be surprised when I tell you to go fuck yourself," Malden called down. "But I'll do you the honor of hearing the offer before I reject it."

Mörg nodded happily. "Alright, then! We all know each

other. Perhaps we can talk like rational beings. Malden, you're in trouble. I think you know that. If we have to take this city by force, my clans aren't going to be polite about it. They'll rape your women, cut ears off your men, and eat every animal they find inside your walls. That's just their way."

"So I've heard," Malden said. "That's why I didn't invite you in to break fast with me this morning."

Mörg shrugged. "I won't be able to stop them if it comes to that. I can't tell them what to do, not in the heat of victory. What I can do is give you another option. You can open your gates now. You can march out with whatever you can carry on your backs. I'll give my word that no citizen of Ness will come to any harm."

"I've heard about your word, as well. Ulfram V trusted your word. Every man in Skrae knows your secret, Mörg: you cheat. That's the only way you can win."

"I won't make this offer again," Mörg pointed out.

"Good," Malden said. "Then I won't have to tell you to dine on my shit again. I've never enjoyed profanity." With that, the thief disappeared from the battlements.

Mörg looked almost saddened that his offer had been rejected. Had he seriously believed the westerners would even consider it? No warrior could have borne the shame of just walking away from a battlefield. Of course, Malden was no warrior—Mörget knew that from personal experience.

The Great Chieftain turned and headed back into the camp, with Mörget trailing after him. They headed directly for Mörget's tent, where Balint waited for them. Outside the tent Mörg sighed deeply. He stared down at the frost-withered grass and seemed to be convincing himself of something. Mörget left him to his thoughts, knowing he'd already pushed his father enough that day.

After a while Mörg nodded to himself and pushed his way into the tent. Mörget followed close behind.

"Nice chat with the locals?" Balint asked. "Did you achieve much?"

The Great Chieftain sat down on a stool and bowed his head. "I must take this city, and soon," Mörg told the dwarf. She nodded, her eyes suddenly bright with excitement. "I want to keep the wall intact. I don't want to set the place on fire with balls of burning pitch, either." He sighed deeply. "Other than that, I'm open to suggestions."

CHAPTER EIGHTY-FOUR

"Get me out of this ridiculous stuff," Malden growled, trying to yank the gauntlet off his left hand. It felt like some of his fingers would come off with it if he pulled too hard. Slag hurried forward with a screwdriver to help Malden out of the armor, but Cythera just stood back and laughed at him.

Velmont couldn't stop peeking over the wall. It was as if the Helstrovian thief had never seen a horde of barbarians before.

Well, of course, he hadn't. Malden had given strict instructions that no one was allowed up on the walls without his permission. He'd said it was so no one would become a target for some sharp-eyed barbarian bowman, but really he just hadn't wanted anyone to see what they were up against and lose heart.

A piece of steel dug hard into his side. It felt like it drew blood. "Quicker, if you please," Malden snarled.

"You want it done fucking right, or you want me to take half your skin off?" Slag asked. When Malden had decided to actually hear what the barbarians had to say—it was that or listen to their scold shout himself mute—it had been decided that he had to look like an actual knight. The problem had been that the Burgrave, when outfitting his Army of Free Men, had already taken every complete set of steel armor in Ness. The few pieces Slag had been able to scrounge had been of different sizes and some showed the signs of repeated and ill use. The Burgrave had left these pieces behind for good reason. Getting Malden into the armor had been torture—getting it off was going to be worse.

"You told him for certes," Velmont said, in the voice of a man who has just seen a ghost. "You told him good. Did you e'en hear him, though, what he offered?"

"To let us all walk out of here? It was an empty promise," Malden said. Slag started disassembling the complicated pattern of rivets holding his breastplate together. Ignoring the constant pinching of his skin, Malden tried to focus on the Helstrovian. Velmont didn't just look scared. He looked like he was about to soil himself. "Mörg might have kept his word and let us walk out of the gate. He said nothing about what would happen to us afterward. Most likely he would have enthralled us all. Even if he meant to let us free, then what? We don't have any food left to carry with us. We could starve out there in the fields, with no place to go. Alternatively we can stay here and starve where it's warm."

"You could've asked for time to ponder," Velmont said. "Bought us some breathin' room, at the very least—" He shook his head and seemed to recover himself. "Sorry, boss. There's just so many of 'em. I don't like our chances, is all."

Malden could hardly disagree with that.

Velmont came over to help Slag with the greaves and soon Malden was naked on the battlements, freezing in the wind. Cythera draped a cloak around him and led him down to the level of the streets. As they made their way back toward the Lemon Garden, Velmont and Slag gave him reports on where they stood. The food shortage was the main topic of conversation. Even with strict rationing the people of Ness would be without so much as a crumb in two weeks. Malden had already recruited a legion of oyster rakers and fisherman to try to drag food up out of the Skrait, but eight hundred years of cultivation had left the river a poor pantry. Short of food dropping from the heavens (or, slightly more likely given the city's religious bent, flowing up from a crack in the earth, stinking of the pit) people were going to starve.

"Galenius tells us that starvation is the most effective weapon in siegecraft, far more powerful than any catapult or ram," Malden said, thinking out loud. He had learned this in one of his frequent sessions with Cutbill. The former guild-master of thieves was reading to him from the *Manual of Fortifications* like a mother telling stories to her toddler to help him sleep. The contents of the book, however, had left Malden with more than one sleepless night. "The siege of Hollymede, four hundred years ago, lasted two and a half years. There were a hundred thousand men and women inside the city walls when the siege began, and only six thousand still alive when the gates were opened—and the invaders never fired an arrow or bloodied a sword. Of course, many of the deaths were the result of disease and thirst. We have plenty of small beer on hand and if we have to we can drink water, but we'll need to watch for outbreaks of plague. Velmont, make a note of that—I want a committee of the public health set up. Any sign of disease must be taken seriously. Report to me if anyone gets so much as a running nose."

"Mother and I can help with that, a little," Cythera said. "Much of learning how to be a witch is the study of health and sickness."

Malden nodded appreciatively. "Slag—how many archers can I muster, right now? If the barbarians decide to scale the wall in the night, will we be able to repel them?"

"Depends how serious they are, lad," the dwarf admitted. "If they all came at once? Not a fucking chance. If it's just a few we might be alright."

He turned to Cythera next. "Has Coruth been keeping an eye on the Burgrave and his free men? Galenius makes it sound like the only way to break a siege is with help from outside. We need them to move, and now."

Cythera sighed. "I wish I could tell you otherwise, but the truth is Tarness is building a winter camp, thirty miles north of here. He's staying close, but he shows no sign of moving to rescue us."

"The bastard!" Malden swore. "He's getting revenge for what we did to Pritchard Hood, most like."

"Or," Slag said, carefully, "he simply knows he hasn't got an arsehole's chance of beating Mörg, and he doesn't want to lose everything just to make a demonstration."

Malden sighed. "Alright. We've done what we can. Galenius is also quite clear on the fact that the most important skill a besieged general needs to learn is when to sleep. We might be here quite a while, and we all need to keep ourselves as rested and sharp as possible. I'll see you two in the morning."

Velmont and Slag glanced at each other and shared a discrete smile.

Malden shrugged it off. He didn't care who knew that he and Cythera spent every night together now. He loved her—he'd always wanted the world to know that. He'd only kept it secret so long because he knew Croy would kill him if he ever found out.

That seemed the least of his problems now.

Cythera turned down the sheets of their bed upstairs at the Lemon Garden and warmed it with coals in a covered pan. Malden watched her in this simple domestic task and found his heart nearly broke. He'd never expected her to be a real wife to him. Not the way most men seemed to think of their spouses—as free labor they could exploit mercilessly, and beat if they ever complained. That was something he'd never wanted, and especially not from Cythera. He'd never thought she would cook for him, either.

He'd never thought she would mend his hose. Or share a roof with him. Or hold him in her arms when he woke screaming in the middle of the night, terrified the barbarians were already inside the walls.

He'd never thought she would truly so much as love him.

Yet here she was, warming his bed. Literally. In a moment she would do it again, figuratively. "I love you," he said, because it was the only thing he could feel at that moment.

"I love you, too," she said, with a smile.

It couldn't last much longer. Already Coruth was preparing for Cythera's initiation. And witches didn't marry. No one would give Malden a proper explanation for why they couldn't, but everyone knew it. Witches lived alone, growing old and twisted as their powers expanded. There were scores of old stories about famous witches, and not one of them included a man about the house.

In a few days Cythera would be a witch, and this domestic bliss would be over.

A few more nights would have to be enough. That night Malden was too tired for much lovemaking, but he took what he could get. Eventually, they fell asleep in each others' arms. Malden thought he could sleep the whole day through like that.

Alas, it was not to be. Just after dawn, a crashing noise tore through the city, a report loud enough to make their bed jump on its four feet. Malden leapt out from beneath the covers and threw open the window that faced Castle Hill.

Just in time to see the spire of the Ladychapel fall into Market Square, with a noise far louder than the one that woke him.

CHAPTER EIGHTY-FIVE

Malden hurried through the streets, headed for the bridge to Castle Hill. He doubted anyone had been inside the Ladychapel when it fell—the place had been abandoned since the priest and his followers left—but there might have been plenty of townsfolk in Market Square, setting up what few market stalls still had anything to sell.

He hadn't covered three blocks when the barbarians struck again.

He saw it coming—saw the impossibly big stone hurtling through the air. Its shadow fell across his path and he danced backwards as if it was going to fall right on him. Then it was gone, past the rooftops on the far side of the street.

Malden grabbed a timber on the front of a house and pulled himself upward, reached and grabbed for the edge of a balcony, hauled himself up to the shingled roof. He ran to its ridgeline and looked out over the city, trying to see where the stone had gone. Then it struck home with rumbling boom and he nearly fell from his perch as the whole city shook underneath him. He struggled to get upright again, to get his feet underneath him so he could see what had happened.

As he watched, a house in the Stink collapsed in on itself. Timbers and plaster shredded with a series of horrible shrieks, stones rattled and bounced. A plume of dust swirled up into the air. And then he heard a woman screaming, and knew that this time there had definitely been casualties.

He was trying to determine where he should go first— Market Square or the Stink, both of them about equal distances away—when he heard someone calling him.

"Lord Mayor! Get down from there! It's not safe!"

Malden ran back to the edge of the roof and looked down. A one-armed beggar was in the street, waving at him. The man ducked his head as a third stone came flying over the city.

Maybe the beggar had a point. Malden hurried down the side of the house and grabbed the man's shoulders. "Go home," he said. "Get to a cellar—anywhere but out in the open." The beggar hurried away, moments before Malden realized that the last place anyone wanted to be when a flying rock hit their house was underground.

There was nothing for it. He couldn't chase after an unhurt man while citizens might lie dying in the rubble. He hurried toward Market Square, thinking he might be able to help there. Do something. Anything.

When he arrived he found he wasn't the only one who'd had the same idea. Say what you wanted about the people of Ness—that they were corrupt, lazy, and mostly stupid. True enough. But they did come together in a crisis.

The falling spire had deposited itself as a line of rubble and debris all the way to the gate of Castle Hill, cutting the square in half. Teams of citizens were hauling away rocks and broken wood, piling it on the cobbles as if they wanted to sort through it later.

"There's a girl in there!" someone shouted at him.

Malden rushed up and grabbed half of a broken gargoyle. He passed it to a man who appeared behind him. He thought of nothing else as he worked, his back aching and his arms weak with fatigue. It didn't matter. Little by little he cleared the rubble. He only stopped when he heard joyous shouting and he looked over to see a group of women digging furiously at one spot in the mess.

Hurrying over, he used his status to make a way through the crowd of onlookers. He found that the women had already unearthed the girl by the time he arrived. Her face was white with dust except where saliva had etched a clean track down one side of her mouth. Her eyes saw nothing. When the women picked her up, her head and limbs hung as limply as a doll's.

"Is she breathing?" Malden asked. One of the women shrugged, but another thought to check.

The girl was breathing. She was alive. It looked like half the bones in her body were shattered. Malden didn't know if she would live long enough for them to set, but he didn't care, either. The girl was alive.

"Take her to the Isle of Horses—Coruth the witch will help her, if anyone can," Malden commanded. A cart was brought up. There were no horses to pull it, but a band of old men offered to stand in the traces. They were turning the cart around, making ready to go, when a fourth stone flashed across the sky.

It came down inside the defensive wall of Castle Hill and bounced around the ruins there for a while. At least no one was in there to be hurt, Malden thought—and then he remembered his prisoners inside the gaol were inside that wall. He called for help and rushed to the gate to help them, if he could.

The stone had stopped bouncing when he got inside. It had settled in the great courtyard before the palace, where once the Burgrave's personal guard had marched in parade order. The stone was four feet across and some effort had been made to carve it in a regular shape. It didn't look nearly as big, or as dangerous, as it had when it had been flying through the air.

Malden ignored it and ran down the steps to the gaol.

The men inside were screaming to be let out, or to be put to death instead of suffering so, or just to learn what was going on. Dust filled the air and a wide crack ran across one wall. The gaoler was nowhere in sight—most likely he'd gone to help the people in the square. Malden found the keys to the three occupied cells and opened them one by one. He had no idea what he was going to do with the men inside. One was a rapist, one a bravo who had killed for money. The third was Malden's first charge, the madman who'd killed his own daughter for the bloodgod's favor. The lunatic was raving as Malden hauled him out of the cell and dragged him toward the stairs. "You two," he said to the rapist and the bravo, "go up top and help the people there. There could be more people in that mess."

"What's going on?" the bravo demanded.

"The barbarians are attacking with some kind of catapult," Malden told him. "They knocked down the spire of the Ladychapel. Now go help!"

The madman couldn't find his own way out of the gaol. Malden had to lead him every step of the way. When they reached sunlight, a crowd was waiting for him.

"There! There, do you see!" the madman shrieked. He pointed at the ruined stump that was all that remained of the Lady's church in Ness. "Sadu has spoken! He made it fall. He made it fall!"

Malden tried to push his way through the crowd but the madman kept grabbing at onlookers, snagging his fingers in their tunics or their hair.

"He must have His blood. He must have His blood. He must have His blood," the madman blathered. Malden wondered if he could find a safe place to put the man in the Ashes, where his raving wouldn't bother anyone. Then he considered the folly of that. A safe place? What place could possibly be safe when stones fell from the sky?

"He must have His blood, or we are all doomed. Give Him His blood!"

"Be quiet! I'm trying to think," Malden demanded, but the madman shouted over him.

"His blood! Give Him His blood! His blood!"

There was something wrong with the sound of the madman's voice. Had Malden been deafened by the noise of the falling stones? It was like a strange echo accompanied the madman's chanting.

"His blood! His blood His blood His blood His blood!"

Then he understood.

"His blood!"

"His blood!"

"Give Him His blood!"

"He must have His blood!"

It wasn't just the madman. Half the crowd was chanting for blood as well. They'd taken up the raving cry.

Did they think Sadu could make the barbarians stop? Did they think the bloodgod could grab the stones out of midair and save them?"

"His blood! His blood! His blood! His blood! His blood! His blood!"

CHAPTER EIGHTY-SIX

"Fascinating. In the space of one night they built three trebuchets? I would have thought the technique far beyond them." Cutbill mused silently for a moment. "Unless they had help. Perhaps an engineer seized at Helstrow. Or a dwarf."

"For all I know Mörgain has a degree in divinity from the university at Redweir. For all I care she may have two," Malden insisted. "You're missing the point. They're throwing stones even now!"

"What does Slag say? I assume he's had a look at the engines. Was he impressed or disdainful of their construction?"

Malden ground his teeth together. "Disdainful, on the whole," he admitted. "They're using traction engines, apparently. That means that instead of using counterweights, they actually have teams of men pulling on ropes to launch the stones. He seemed to find that grossly inefficient. I understood very little of his reasons why. I was too busy looking at the great heaps of missiles they had ready to fire at us. Those heaps were as big as houses!"

"They'll run out eventually. There are no proper boulders out in the farmland where they camp," Cutbill pointed out. "Most likely they've already taken to demolishing stone buildings for ammunition."

"You're not seeing this," Malden insisted. "My people are dying."

Cutbill leaned back in his chair and turned his eyes to face the ceiling. He sighed deeply for a moment, then said, simply, "Malden. You must think, not feel."

The thief—the Lord Mayor—jumped to his feet. "What? What say you now? Is your blood so cold you can't even mourn your fellow citizens? A little girl—just a little girl, crushed—broken as if she'd been worked over by torturers for a month. An entire family in the Stink, dead, save their piteous wretch of a mother, spared by uncaring fate just so she could watch her babies die—"

"Malden," Cutbill said again, perfectly calm.

"What, damn you?"

"Malden, this is a war. I thought you understood that."

"I've thought of nothing else in days!"

Cutbill sighed again. Malden had grown to hate that sound. "In war, people die."

"Volunteer soldiers, perhaps. Foreign mercenaries. The enemy. But—"

"You've had your first real taste of war, and it galled. That's perfectly understandable. Only a bronze statue of a man would not have this reaction. Yet you must not let this horror consume you. If you don't steel yourself now, you'll be mad in a week," Cutbill pointed out. "Many people will die. You may lose half your constituents before this is over. And if you don't win this battle, the other half will be enslaved. Or worse."

Malden's heart seized in his chest. He cried out, an inarticulate noise of rage and fear and utter sorrow. "I never wanted this! I never even wanted to be Lord Mayor. I didn't want to take over your guild! I never asked for any of this responsibility, and I don't want it now. I've done all this only because no one else would, or could—because if I didn't the people of Ness would be without a protector. And now I've failed them!"

"It is to the good, in some part, that you feel so much for them," Cutbill said. "That will help you when you must inspire them to fight on in the face of despair. Your sincerity will be a far greater weapon than your magic sword."

"I cannot bear this," Malden moaned.

"You can, and you must. Every prince in history has felt this way, I imagine. They learned to cope. The good ones anyway. And so shall you. They learned that pawns on a game board cannot be treated as individuals. That one must think strategically, even when one's heart is breaking."

Malden fell back in his chair and stared at the man.

Could anyone truly be so callous?

But yes. Yes, they could. He'd seen it with his own eyes. Every time the Burgrave had ordered some man hanged as an example, just to improve the public order. Every time some bastard reeve in the field had beaten a peasant because he wasn't working hard enough, because the crops had to be harvested or everyone would starve. He'd seen it a million times in his life, this ability to armor one's heart against cries of mercy and compassion, and do the hard thing.

He'd fought all his life against the men who ran the world. He'd learned to sneak around their rules and controls, and find some space of breath, some freedom, for himself. Always he had hated them for their cruelty.

And now he was one of them.

"If you are going to prevail," Cutbill said, "you must find a way to take the battle to the barbarian. You cannot simply hide your head now. Let us discuss methods for repaying this injustice, shall we? I think we'll begin with a reading from Galenius. We were discussing, on your last visit, the proper use of fascines and ramps. Make yourself comfortable, and we'll begin."

Malden got up and started walking toward the door. "Not now," he insisted.

"Malden, if you have an ounce of sense you'll come back here and—"

"I said not now," Malden grated, and pushed his way out into the sunlight. Somewhere in the distance he could hear screaming.

CHAPTER EIGHTY-SEVEN

Bethane slumped down to sit on a rock and rub at her feet. If she had as many blisters as Croy, every step must be torture to her. He wished he could carry her on his shoulders, but even his strength had flagged over the last few miles. The wound in his side was festering and he could barely lift his left arm. So instead he knelt before her and carefully unwrapped the rags he had wound around and around her feet. The rags stank and were blotchy with blood and pus. He used some of their precious water to wash her feet, then wrapped them up again in the same dirty rags because he had no fresh cloth. Eventually she managed to stand again, and start shuffling forward, again.

Neither of them said a word the whole time. It was not the first time he'd washed and wrapped her feet. It would not be the last.

North of the orchard where Croy had been wounded, the Whitewall mountains curled to the west and shrank to rough hills, their tops cluttered with wind-slumped trees. It was bad country, dry and cold, and in many places snow gathered in ravines and defiles deep enough to swallow a man whole. That snow was their only source of water, but to get it he had to make a fire, and every fire they lit was a beacon to their enemies. There was no food to be had there at all.

The hills were going to kill them, Croy believed. He would gladly have turned south, turned away from that desperate country. But the hills also represented his only hope. They formed a natural border between Skrae and Skilfing, the closest of the Northern Kingdoms. If he could cross that treacherous land he would have fulfilled his duty and delivered Bethane to some kind of safety.

Then, he thought, perhaps he could lie down and die. If not for Cythera.

His betrothed was in his thoughts at all times, though such fancies tortured him as much as they spurred him onward. Cythera. The Lady had brought her into his life, surely. No one else could have done him such an honor. His mind kept casting backwards toward the day in Ness when she had almost signed the banns of their marriage. When, but for a bottle of spilled ink, she would have been his. Instead they had postponed things and raced off to the Vincularium for one last adventure before they entered a new life together.

Croy had laughed so much, back then. He'd had a fair hand to kiss, and a lady's kerchief to tie around the end of his lance. It had made so much sense.

Now Cythera was hundreds of miles away, if she wasn't already dead. He had no way of knowing whether the barbarians had taken Ness yet. He was certain that if they had, Malden would never have allowed them to take Cythera alive—the thief was a good friend, and would know what Croy would want done if things came to that pass. That was the true reason why he'd given Acidtongue to Malden.

He'd told himself—convinced himself—that he thought Malden could someday be an Ancient Blade. That the thief had the potential to be something more. No one had taken the idea seriously—not even Malden himself. Croy had persisted in this folly, because he knew on some level Malden cared for Cythera almost as much as he did himself. Croy had treated Malden like a knight, because he wanted the little man to act like one. He'd wanted someone to take care of Cythera when he couldn't.

He hoped he'd made the right choice.

Ahead of him on the path Bethane tripped over something and fell forward on her face, barely catching herself with her hands. Croy rushed to her side and helped her sit up. The palms of her hands were scratched and filthy. She made no sound of pain or discomfort, though. Both of them were well past feeling small scrapes. Croy brushed as much dirt off her hands as he could and helped her stand.

He looked back idly, trying to see what had snared Bethane. An exposed tree root, probably, or maybe just a rough patch of ground. He did not expect to see the haft of a poleaxe lying astride the trail.

Bethane didn't even look. She started hobbling forward again, one small step at a time. Croy didn't tell her to stop—every foot of ground they covered was precious.

Bending as low as he could without groaning, Croy studied the forlorn weapon lying on the ground. The wooden haft had once been polished to the point of smoothness, but this was no parade weapon straight from a cobwebbed arsenal. The polish had been worn down by long use until the wood was dull. He ran his eyes along the length of the weapon to the massive blade, a wicked-looking axe head with a recurved tip. Quatrefoil holes had been drilled through the blade to lighten it. It was not a barbarian weapon—it was too well made, perhaps even dwarven in manufacture. The thing that worried him the most was that the blade shone with luster. There was not a spot of rust on it. Someone had maintained the weapon with care. And recently. This was no long-lost souvenir of some ancient battle.

Croy closed his eyes and tried not to panic. Then he stood up, opened his eyes again, and hurried as much as he could to catch up with Bethane. She had walked twenty feet in the time it took him to inspect the poleaxe.

Together they walked another half mile before the sun set. They made camp in the shelter of some trees, with a rock wall behind them to lean against. He balanced caution against the threat of freezing to death and made them a small fire, and they sat back to back quite close to it, greedy for its warmth.

Bethane picked at the rags on her feet, perhaps for lack of anything better to do. Croy sharpened Ghostcutter, rhythmically drawing his whetstone along the iron half of the blade, letting it slide free at the point, bringing it back down toward the hilt.

Between the sound of his whetstone and the crackling of the fire, he expected to hear nothing else. Yet when a twig snapped somewhere out in the darkness, every muscle in his body jumped.

Bethane noticed his alarm, but she had learned over many days of travel not to react or ask questions. He held his left hand low, palm toward the ground, to tell her to hide herself and be still. She did as she was ordered, whether or not she was his queen.

Rising stiffly, Croy stepped away from the fire until his eyes adjusted to the darkness beyond. He could see little of the rocks around him—there was no moon and clouds hid the stars. A little light, just a dim glow, outlined the tops of the hills, so he looked up there—and saw it.

A man sitting a horse. Very far away. Too far away to be the source of the noise he'd heard. So there were more than one of them out there.

He hurried back to the camp and kicked out the fire. Bethane had taken shelter under an overhanging rock. The rock hung so close to the ground she'd had to cram herself inside. Croy shoved himself in after her, his greater bulk making it difficult. He ignored the way the rock scraped at his back and shoulders and squeezed himself inside.

In the last embers of the fire he saw Bethane's eyes, and the fear there. It seemed she was still capable of feeling something, then, if only terror. He placed a finger to his lips, and she nodded in response.

He heard no more sounds that night. Whoever had come looking for them in the dark didn't find them—or didn't think the game worth dragging them out of the rock. Croy spent every moment of the night watching anyway, watching and listening, his ears straining to pick up the slightest noise.

Eventually gray light streamed along the world outside their hiding place, and dawn lightened the sky.

Though they had slept not at all and Croy's body had become as solid as the stone around him, he managed to haul himself out of the crevice and then pull Bethane out after him. They had nothing with which to break their fast, so they just started walking again.

Less than an hour later Croy saw the rider once more. This time he made no attempt to conceal himself—standing at the top of a hill he was hard to miss. The other pursuers, however, were harder to find, though he could hear them moving through the trees.

They could be hillmen, the notorious savages of these untamed rocks. They could be bandits or deserters or high-waymen from Skrae. They could be barbarians. Croy had no way to tell.

Bethane looked at him with eyes she kept barely under control.

He nodded, and pointed at the trail ahead of them. She kept walking.

He drew Ghostcutter from its sheath and held it close to his leg. His one comfort just then was that he knew exactly what to do. If the rider's men attacked, he would try to fight them off. If there were too many of them, though . . .

For one of royal blood like Bethane, there were fates worse than death. He could not let her be captured. If it came to that, if honor left him no other choice—

He thought he could do it.

Cythera, he prayed, for he could think of no words the Lady would like to hear. *Cythera, forgive all my sins. Remember me fondly. I did my best.*

CHAPTER EIGHTY-EIGHT

The whispers became murmurs. The murmurs became disgusted looks in the midst of the camp. Mörget said nothing, but made certain every man of the horde knew he was willing to listen.

And still, no word came from inside the walls of Ness.

A warrior came to him from one of the lesser clans, a weakling of a man who should have been weeded out long ago. His name was Horfnüng, and he was known far and wide for being a thrall to his wife. Still he had the courage to speak to Mörget, man to man. Mörget led him inside his tent and together they sat on stools and shared the warmth of Mörget's charcoal stove. "The snow lies on the ground today, and does not melt," Horfnüng said.

"I saw it," Mörget told him. He wanted to smack the man with the backside of his hand for wasting his time, but instead he nodded sagely, as if this were some grand observation.

"This morning I went to make water, and by the time I was done, my piss had frozen on the ground," Horfnüng went on.

If the man did not get to his point soon, Mörget would gut him.

"Every day we throw rocks over this wall, like bad neighbors throwing garbage over a fence," the little man said. "Inside the city, they sleep in warm beds, and enjoy their women. I want a bed." Horfnüng smiled, as men do who are about to make a joke they think hilarious. "I want to enjoy their women."

"Mörg, my father—ah, and chieftain of us all," Mörget said, very slowly, "has decreed the city must not be harmed. So we can enjoy it more when it is ours."

"Every day he tells us this. And nothing changes.

Meanwhile, an army camps not thirty miles away. An army we could walk over with bare feet. Mörg, your father, leaves them in peace."

"Such is his decision. Some, in the past," Mörget said, "have called him Mörg the Wise."

"Some now call him Mörg the Merciful," Horfnüng said, spitting out the insult.

Mörget nodded sagely again. "Who do you speak for?" he asked.

"Only myself," Horfnüng admitted.

"Ah. Very good. I am glad to offer you the hospitality of my tent," he said, and stood up. Horfnüng was smart enough, at least, to rise as well, and take his leave.

At the flap of the tent, however, Horfnüng stopped a moment. "There are many others who would say the same things."

"Let them come to me and speak, for there is no harm in it. Now—get out of my tent. You're letting in the cold," Mörget said, and took a step toward the flap.

Horfnüng all but ran away.

"Spittle of a man," Mörget cursed, when he was gone.

Balint raised her head from where she lay on a pile of furs in the corner. "That almost sounded like a real insult," she said. "You must be learning from me."

Mörget snarled. "I would wipe my arse with his kind, if—"

"—if you didn't need their support," the dwarf said. "Aye, barbarian, you can't do this thing alone. If you're still committed to doing it at all. You need to make up your mind, you know. A man sitting on a fence too long gets a post up his backside."

But Mörget had already decided. Horfnüng had spoken true when he'd said many others thought the same as he. Mörget had heard similar veiled threats from a hundred men already, and knew there would be no question when he made his move. Mörg's plan for taking the city wasn't working fast enough. The barbarians were not famous for their patience. "I'll go and make the challenge now, if you like, little one." He reached for his axe.

"Don't you dare. If you get cut down, they'll make me one of their thralls. I'll have to carry rocks and sharpen weapons for the rest of my life," Balint said. "I could probably fuck my way out of thralldom in a month, of course, but it would be a very smelly, very sore month. No—you need to do this the classical way. In the middle of the night when no one's looking."

Mörget scowled. He would have preferred to kill his father in broad daylight. But he supposed she had a point. Mörg cheated—he was famous for it. Perhaps it was time to see how he felt when someone broke the rules on *him*.

CHAPTER EIGHTY-NINE

The rocks kept coming, though not as frequently as when the bombardment began. Most of the missiles struck Castle Hill—sticking up above the level of the wall, it made an excellent target—and did little harm. The constant fear of attack might actually have helped Malden a little, since it kept people off the streets.

On top of everything else—starvation, greedy thieves, a horde of barbarians—now he had to worry that the city would be overrun from within, by a mob of zealots.

The cry for blood sacrifice had been taken up all over the city. His thieves and whores seemed mostly immune, but the honest folk of Ness had given themselves over to religious mania. Every day more people claimed that if the proper sacrifices were made at the Godstone, the barbarians would have no choice but to pack up and leave. Conversely, a rumor started making the rounds that failure to appease the bloodgod would cause the city wall to collapse.

That was not based entirely on conjecture, either. Malden had heard a rumor when he as a child—grisly stories being a favorite topic of conversation for street urchins—that when Juring Tarness built the wall eight hundred years ago, he had sacrificed his three chief architects to Sadu and mixed their blood with the mortar that held the bricks together. He had thereby made the wall impenetrable to mortal weapons. In eight centuries that theory had never really been tested. Now it seemed an article of faith that the shield of blood must be replenished in time of need.

On his daily patrol of the city, Malden started finding the carcasses of animals lying before the Godstone. He knew better than to forbid it—even though the city desperately needed the meat. The common people of Ness, it seemed, would rather starve than risk the eternal punishment of their god. The looming altar had been ritually desecrated back when the Burgraves had decided to outlaw the priesthood of Sadu, but it seemed the stone had been rededicated to the bloodgod. For the first time in centuries it was being used for its original purpose.

The old religion had never died. It had slept for a while, but now it was waking up again, and bringing with it all the old madness. Sadu called out for blood, and the people were afraid enough to answer that demand.

He went to Cutbill to ask for advice. "This morning," he said, when he was seated comfortably by the ex-guildmaster's fire, "a deputation came to me. Five men who said they wished to be ordained as priests of the bloodgod."

"Interesting. They think you have the power to bless them, now?"

Malden raised his hands in bafflement. "They treated me like a prophet, with much deference. And it's not as if anyone else has that right. There hasn't been a true priest of Sadu in how long? A century?"

"Longer than that," Cutbill told him. "Royal decree outlawed that priesthood three hundred years ago, and the Burgrave of Ness reinforced the ban a few dozen years later. And for good reason."

Malden nodded. The priests of Sadu had performed human

sacrifices to appease their god, once. Some of them had not
been above kidnapping and murder to make sure of a steady
flow of blood—since volunteers had always been hard to
come by. It had not been unheard of for one of Sadu's priests
to work as an assassin, taking money from clients and blood
from victims. That had been the priesthood that Prestwicke
had tried to revive. The men who had come to Malden wanted
a slightly more orthodox office to be set up, but still, they
wanted the right to sacrifice animals and even humans at the
Godstone. "I made them swear they wouldn't kill anyone.
But that wasn't what they were really after. They said they
would need some kind of official position in order to convince
the people they really were agents of the bloodgod."

"Official position? So they wanted more than just your
blessing. They wanted to be part of your government."

"They wanted me to put them in charge of distributing
foodstuffs."

"Ah. So they wanted to be the ones to eat first."

"Everyone's hungry. I told them as much—that I couldn't
afford preferential treatment for any of my citizens. They
seemed offended. I told them I thought the whole point of
Sadu—the only reason the poor still worship Him—was
that every man was equal in his sight. That we all had to
die and be judged, and that no social station made a man
less blameworthy than his neighbor. That made them leave
in a huff. But they warned me as they went. With or without
my sanction, the priesthood will be renewed. And the sacrifices will start again."

"You can hardly complain about their faith now," Cutbill
told him, without sympathy. "Since it was that belief that
raised you to the heights of fame in the first place."

The former guildmaster had a point, of course. Yet it was
enough to make Malden wish he'd forced the priest of the
Lady to stay in Ness. The Book of the Lady forbade blood
sacrifice in no uncertain terms. The laws of Skrae had been
founded on that book and they had eliminated the practice
everywhere in the kingdom. Yet now those laws were
ignored—statutes decreed by a dead king, issued from a
fortress far away, impossible now to enforce. Malden knew

that in the absence of such laws, it was just a matter of time before he found one of his citizens at the base of the Godstone, throat slit in just the right manner. The priest of the Lady might at least have preached to the people about why human sacrifice was wrong. Now it felt as if no one remained who held that particular view—no one except Malden.

If he was going to fight religion, he decided, he would need help from the occult. As soon as his duties allowed it, he headed down to the Isle of Horses. Coruth had promised him all kinds of assistance, but since the siege began the witch hadn't so much as showed herself in the city. He borrowed a boat at the Ditchside Stair in Eastpool (the Lord Mayor didn't have to pay a security deposit) and rowed himself over to the forbidding island just as the sun hit the top of the wall.

Climbing up onto the withered grass on the Isle's shore, he braced himself for another attack by phantom horses. It didn't come. There was a light burning in Coruth's shack but no one approached him or welcomed him. He started walking slowly toward the door, expecting some nasty surprise, when he heard a shriek from within.

It sounded like Cythera. He broke into a run.

Coruth met him at the door. She shoved it open with one skeletal hand and beckoned him to follow her. "You're late," she said, as if they'd had an appointment.

Malden had no time to wonder what she really meant. He was too busy being horrified. Cythera lay on a pallet in the front room, naked save for a sheet that covered only one leg. It looked like she'd thrown it off her in the convulsions of some terrifying dream. Her skin was pale and clammy and slick with some foul-smelling unguent. Her eyes were wide open but when she blinked he saw that arcane symbols had been painted on her eyelids.

"The Guardian of the Gate!" she screamed. "He sees right through me! He judges me!"

Malden started to demand to know what was going on. Then he stopped himself. He knew. This was Cythera's initiation. The ceremony that would transform her into a witch. He knew there were rules about such things—ironclad laws that no man dared break. If Malden spoke at the wrong time, the consequences could be dire.

Coruth stared at him with one bloodshot eye. The old witch looked like she hadn't slept in weeks. Normally she stood tall and erect but now she was as stooped and grotesque as—well, as a witch in an old woodblock illustration. Had she sprouted a wart on her nose and been clutching a broom, she might have been a caricature of her profession.

"Here," Coruth said, and shoved a dagger at him. He took it, for the same reason he'd kept silent so far. The weapon was a thin-bladed knife wholly without ornament, and seemed unfit for ceremonial purposes. Its point looked very sharp.

"What do I do with it?" Malden asked.

"Put the point here," Coruth said, tapping a point just left of Cythera's sternum. "If I give you the signal, drive it straight into her heart."

"I can't do that," Malden said. "Not—not to her."

"Worried about losing your swiving-partner?" Coruth said, and her mouth curled into a wicked smile. "All good things should come to an end, boy. Only true evil is eternal. It's got no bottom."

Malden didn't know what to make of that. "My love for her is true."

"Every boy in the history of fucking has said as much. And they were all honest, at least at the moment they said it. You think I don't understand love? You think I never had a leman? I had to give all that up to become a witch, and I did it, because Skrae needed me. Cythera will make the same sacrifice, because the times require it."

"Surely there's another way—she could renounce magic and—"

"Stop your blathering, boy. Time is tight. Put the point where I showed you."

"I can't kill her!"

"Unless she's a bigger fool than I think, you won't have to," Coruth told him. "Now do as you're told! Much more than you know depends on it."

Malden bit his lips for a moment, but in the end he did

as he was asked. He made sure to touch the point so lightly to Cythera's skin that she would barely feel it.

Not that she was likely to feel much. Her eyes were unfocused, and her pupils changed size rapidly as he watched. Cythera was looking at things invisible, perhaps things very, very far away.

Occasionally she struggled, as if trying to break the grasp of some unseen monster. Occasionally she cried out. Sweat ran in thick rivulets into her hair though she shivered with cold.

"I see the old man with the lantern," Cythera reported, at one point. "His light shines on a forest. He is so very lonely—he wants a kiss."

Malden glanced up at Coruth. The old witch shook her head.

"No, I understand now," Cythera said. Malden had a feeling she wasn't talking to anyone in the room. "His vigil can't be interrupted. I'll go down to those woods, in case he tries to follow me—oh. Oh! The trees are—the trees are alive. They're so . . . alive."

"Where is she?" Malden whispered.

"It's not so much a place," Coruth told him. "It's a path between two places. It only exists in a relational sense."

"Ah," Malden said, as if that explained everything.

"There are two paths through the forest, but which is the right one?" Cythera asked. "The path on the left is so straight. It goes right to the end of the forest. It's paved with gold, with . . . with power and . . . fame."

Coruth leaned close to Cythera's ear and shouted, "What of the other path?"

"What? Someone . . . someone is whispering . . . I—oh, the path on the right looks so hard. It bends and curls back on itself, and there are so many thorns. I don't think it even goes where I want to go!"

Malden would have told her to take the easier path, to get out of those woods as quickly as possible, but Coruth silenced him with a glare.

"Choose wisely," Coruth shouted. Then she nodded at Malden.

This was the moment. The moment when she would tell him to stab his lover through the heart. He couldn't—there was no power in the world, not god or man or witch, that would make him do that.

But then he understood exactly what was at stake. It was like he gained the second sight himself, if only for a moment. Cythera could choose the path of sorcery, the path of demonology and pure will, which way lay madness and deformity and evil, but also great power. Or she could choose the path of the witches—magic that she herself could not control but only influence, magic that came from the world around her. Magic with rules.

If she chose sorcery, he would be asked to kill her on the spot.

And still he knew—he would not do it. Even if she was to become like her father Hazoth, wicked and cruel and utterly without sympathy, he would still rather have her alive.

Coruth disagreed.

Luckily for them all, she chose the path on the right.

Her suffering was terrible. "The thorns tear my skin! My feet are bleeding," she moaned, as she writhed on the pallet. "Where am I headed? I can't see anything—I'm blind! I'm dying!"

There was more—much more, and none of it Malden could understand. There were trials for Cythera to face, gates for her to pass. She met every trial with fear and pain but passed them all because she'd been trained how.

Eventually her voice trailed away into raving syllables that failed to form words at all. Malden worried that some deadly test had been failed . . . but Coruth sank back in a chair and closed her eyes. Soon she began to snore.

Malden threw the dagger on a table and knelt by the pallet, clutching at Cythera's hands. Her fingers were limp in his and he doubted she could even tell he was there, but still he clung to her. For hours he waited by her side. He understood now that Coruth hadn't just wanted someone to hold the dagger. She had brought him here—though he thought he'd come of his own will—she had brought him to comfort Cythera. To comfort himself.

The day wore on. Once Malden heard a great stone crash into the city, but for the first time he didn't care where it landed. He had no thought but for his love.

Who was his no more.

Eventually Cythera's eyes fluttered closed, and she slept. She stopped shivering and her body relaxed. Malden pulled the sheet up over her form. It was cold inside Coruth's shack. It was winter time.

When she woke her eyes were bleary, and she lacked the strength to even sit up. But she smiled at him and placed one warm hand against his cheek. They began to whisper to each other, saying nothing at all, really. He didn't ask what had changed, because he already knew. She made no promises, nor did she need to.

They let Coruth sleep.

In time, when Cythera rose from the pallet, she wrapped her arms around herself, hiding her nakedness. Malden rushed to find one of her velvet gowns so she could be clothed, but she shook her head. Instead she took a shapeless robe from a chest in Coruth's bedchamber. The robe of a witch. She pulled it over her head and lifted the hood over her sweat-greased hair.

When she kissed him, it felt wrong. Like being kissed by a statue, perhaps.

"Marry me," he begged. Desperation overcame him and it felt just like fatigue. "It can't be too late. Give this up and marry me."

She placed a hand on his cheek. She neither smiled nor frowned. "It's forbidden of a witch," she told him.

"By whom, damn it? Is there some council of covens I can appeal to? Is there a witch queen somewhere who makes these decrees and tells you all what to do?"

She shook her head. "Hardly. There are so few of us in the world . . . no, Malden. We have no laws, only vows that each of must take. A witch can't marry because she must remain above worldly concerns, that is all. She has to make decisions on the behalf of other people. She must not be attached to one person—not when so many others depend on her."

Malden cast about for any way to save what they'd had.

To keep the love he'd found, even though he knew it was already gone. "Your mother and Hazoth were lovers," he pleaded. "There is no rule of celibacy that binds you now, is there?"

"Their union was all about power, not love," Cythera said. "Nor did my mother consent to it." Her smile was so sad. "I can't belong to you, Malden. I can't belong to anyone, anymore."

"You never did," he told her, his voice very small.

CHAPTER NINETY

The rider had come very close, now. He could descend upon Croy and Bethane in the space of a moment and run them through with his lance. A quick death might be the best they could hope for.

"Your majesty," Croy said, "when I tell you to run—run fast, and do not look back." He drew Ghostcutter from its sheath. He could hear Bethane gasping for breath already. She must be terrified.

If he could, he would spare her what was to come—but not yet. Not when they still had some slim chance. Croy had been in this position before, on foot and facing a man on horseback. He knew how it was done.

He only wished he could see the others.

He knew he was being guided by the horseman, driven toward some ambush up ahead. There would be footmen there waiting for him, ready to encircle him, to stop his flight. He did not know how many there would be or how well armed they would prove. He would have to improvise and use his best judgment.

Croy could barely walk. His feet were numb, his legs just blocks of wood that he could still command but not rely on. His left arm was useless, and the wound in his side had stopped throbbing—always a bad sign.

But he was an Ancient Blade. He could still fight.

"*Var!*" the horseman called. Croy didn't recognize the word. "*Var uit!*"

Was he calling to his prey, or to his fellow predators? It didn't matter. The rider had driven them along a high ridge, a rocky escarpment with only one clear way down. Up ahead on the path the rocks fell away from a narrow cut, perhaps the remnant of some long dry creek bed. Walls of stone rose on either side. It was the perfect place for a trap. Croy looked to his left, away from where the horseman ambled toward him. That way lay a treacherously steep slope of broken rock. He could break to the side and run that way but it meant hurtling down a hillside of loose scree. The grade was too sharp for him to climb down that way—at best, he could manage a controlled fall down the slope. A few withered trees stood up from the slope, little more than skeletal bushes. Even if he could get Bethane safely to the bottom of the hill, there was precious little cover there.

He looked again at the cut, at the place where the footmen would surely be waiting. There was no longer any choice.

"Run," he shouted, and pointed with Ghostcutter's blade. Bethane hobbled forward and at once started skidding down the loose stony soil of the hill. She screamed as her feet flew out from underneath her and she kept sliding. Croy threw himself after her, his feet barely touching the ground as he danced down the hill. He reached out with his left hand and tried to grab at one of the tree trunks, but he lacked the strength to get a proper hold on it. The rough bark tore at the skin of his palm and only slowed him a little.

"Sir Croy!" Bethane screamed, as she slid on her back, small stones bouncing around her face.

He bent his knees and jumped, arcing through the air to hit the ground again just next to her, rolling and bouncing as he tried desperately to slow his descent, to regain any kind of control on the steep slope. Her hands grabbed at his tunic and she pulled herself toward him just as he saw a tree coming straight at him.

For once he was glad for the numbness in his legs. He slammed into the tree with his left foot, hard enough to make his bones rattle. Somehow he got his knees around the trunk so he could hold on. Bethane whipped past him, her momentum pulling one of her hands free of his tunic. His left hand couldn't grab her, not in time, and it certainly couldn't hold her. The sword in his right hand had to go.

It felt so wrong—but he let go of Ghostcutter and watched it slide down the hill away from him as his right hand grabbed for the collar of Bethane's dress. The sword was his soul—but she was his queen.

He managed to snag her garment with two fingers. His knuckles turned white as he took her weight. "I have you," he called. "I have you, stop struggling!"

He glanced down at the bottom of the slope, looking for Ghostcutter. Without it he was defenseless. His fingers ached abominably but he cast this way and that with his eyes, seeking the blade.

Instead he saw the footmen. They were down there already, at the bottom of the slope. Waiting for him. Two dozen men carrying polearms. Their faces were hidden by the steel helmets they wore.

"Croy," Bethane said, "please—please hold on—I can feel you letting go!"

Croy glanced at his right hand and saw she was right. His fingers were shaking. Little by little they uncurled, loosening their grasp. He was too weak to hold her weight.

"Croy, you are my champion," Bethane said. "You are my protector, my—"

His fingers lost their grip, and she slid away from him. Right toward the footmen.

He shouted her name and pulled his legs away from the tree trunk. Let himself fall as well. He would be by her side down there, at least. He would fight those footmen with his bare hands, if he must. He gritted his teeth as he rolled end over end down the slope. He would fight to his last breath, to his last ounce of strength—

A rock slapped him across the temple and his vision went blurry. For a moment he was blind and his ears rang. He fought to regain his senses, fought to clear his head but he was rolling, rolling out of control and he couldn't think, couldn't concentrate, couldn't—

At the bottom of the hill he smashed into a boulder, right next to Bethane. His bones jumped inside his flesh and new agony erupted down his injured side, but he managed not to cry out. He was too busy looking at Bethane. She was unconscious but seemed not to have sustained any mortal injuries.

A clatter of steel made Croy's heart leap. Suddenly the footmen stood in a circle around the two of them, polearms ready to skewer them. Croy tried to jump to his feet and found he could barely move his head.

He heard hoofbeats and then the rider came galloping around the side of the hill. The horseman slid out of his saddle and came running over. The footmen made room for him—was it to be his right, his honor, to kill a queen and a knight?

The rider came and stood over Croy, peering down into his face. His eyes were wide as if he were surprised at what Croy had just done. "*Var aus,*" he said, as if Croy should know what he meant. "*Var aus gevuirten, ha?*"

"Give me one chance to stand up, and fight me like a man," Croy howled. He tried to spit in the rider's face but he couldn't work up the saliva.

The rider shook his head and pointed at his ear, then his mouth. He shook his head again. He was trying to convey a message—that he couldn't understand what Croy had said. Then he pointed at Croy's chest. "You Skraeling," he said, and nodded as if Croy had agreed with him. Then he placed his hand on his armored chest. "Me, Skilfinger." Then he reached down as if he would take Croy's hand. As if he would help Croy sit up. "Skrae *ut* Skilfing," the rider said. "Skrae *ut* Skilfing friends."

CHAPTER NINETY-ONE

The Skilfinger knight wore a byrnie of chain mail that fell in long triangular tappets around his knees. Strips of steel hung from the chain links across his chest and jangled merrily as he rode. "You. Come," he said, for the hundredth time, gesturing westward with his lance.

Croy grunted but kept walking after the horse. On either side of him, the knight's retainers—rail-thin men in boiled leather armor, carrying poleaxes like the one he'd found on the trail—jogged effortlessly along. They didn't seem to mind the slow going, but the knight seemed impatient with their progress. He had to keep his horse to a deliberate walk so that Croy and Bethane could hope to keep up with him. Croy had asked a thousand times that the knight let Bethane ride behind him, but apparently that was forbidden. The knight practiced a severe religion that would not allow a man and a woman to touch each other unless they were married.

Of course, by right of precedence, the knight should have dismounted and given Bethane the horse. In the days since their capture, Croy had attempted to tell the knight who Bethane was in several different ways. Yet among the score of Skraeling words the knight possessed, and the half-dozen or so of the Skilfinger language Croy understood, "queen" was not among them.

"It's alright," Bethane kept saying. "At least we're safe." She gave him one of her small treasury of smiles and he nodded back.

They had recovered Ghostcutter from the scree of the hillside, and let him put it back in its sheath. That was something. Other than that, however, Croy wasn't sure what the Skilfingers intended. He knew he had no choice but do as they said.

His strength was at its very ebb. The wound in his side was getting worse. Every time he lifted the bandage there the smell nearly made him swoon. The old wound in his left elbow made it impossible to even close that fist. His feet felt like raw stumps.

Had the Skilfingers intended to slay him or Bethane, he would not have been able to resist.

Yet it seemed that was not the plan. Instead, the knight herded them westward, along the border rather than across it. The knight seemed uninterested in telling Croy where he was taking them. If they kept along this course they would soon reach the shores of Lake Marl. The fishermen who lived around the lake traded with Skrae, and surely someone there would speak his language. He would be able to find someone to translate and he would be able to tell the Skilfinger knight just how important it was that Bethane be taken to safety.

Yet he had a sinking feeling they would not be going that far.

And he was right.

That night they camped in a box canyon with the wind whistling by high overhead. The knight gave them food and comfortable bedrolls but made sure they were watched at all times by at least two of his retainers. Croy was allowed to keep his sword, but he knew if he tried to draw it they would just take it away from him. So little strength remained to him that he doubted he could fight off even one of the well-trained soldiers.

Croy and Bethane had slept curled up together for warmth when they were alone in the hills. Now the custom of Skilfing demanded they sleep at least six feet apart. Croy found he missed the human contact more than he'd expected.

In the morning, he woke with a fever. His vision swam and he could barely swallow the thin wine they poured down his throat. In a daze he watched Bethane argue with the retainers and then with the knight until some kind of agreement was reached. Bethane knew even less of their language than Croy did but somehow she got her way. He supposed that was part of her inheritance as a daughter of a long line of kings.

Croy was lifted by the retainers and then tied to the back of the horse. There was no law against two men riding together, it seemed.

All that day he drifted in and out of consciousness. His wounds pained him grievously when he was awake and when he slept he was plagued by horrible meaningless dreams. He saw the hills flashing by, now as if the horse were galloping, now as if they moved more slowly than a cloud across a summer sky—trees, rocks, everywhere lichens sprouting, he could almost see them grow as he watched—

—and then they rode up a long promontory of rock, a kind of natural highway flanked on either side by high walls of stone. They came out on the side of a hill overlooking a valley swaying with dead yellow grass. It hurt Croy's head to watch it bend and shift in the wind, so he focused instead on the shapes that didn't move.

Tents, he saw. Hundreds upon hundreds of tents. Not the crude animal-skin tents of the barbarians, either. These were neat pavilions, organized in militarily exact rows and columns, and each had a standard in front of its flap. Every standard flew the black and yellow colors of Skilfing, except for one. One especially large tent near the mouth of the valley flew green and gold.

The colors of Ulfram V, and now, the colors of Bethane I.

The queen came running up to grab at Croy's dangling chin and cheeks. "Croy!" she said, with excitement so long buried it cracked the wind-chapped skin around her mouth. "Croy, do you see it?"

He could not answer. The Skilfinger knight took him down the hill, the horse picking its way with excruciating care. They rode up to the large tent flying the royal colors and then, finally, they stopped. The knight's retainers lined up in perfect order. The knight dismounted, then untied Croy and lowered him carefully to the cold ground.

Croy tried to sit up. Found it impossible. Bethane helped him, tucking a bedroll under his head so at least he could look around him. He saw someone come out of the tent—saw their greaves of steel, at least, from that vantage. The greaves were of Skraeling manufacture and design.

He struggled to turn his head enough to look up, to see the face of his fellow countryman.

When he did he could only believe he had lost consciousness again, and was being harried by a ghost from one of his fever dreams.

It was the smiling, worried, oh so very long missed face of Sir Hew, Captain of the King's Guards. But of course Sir Hew had died at Helstrow, with the rest of the Ancient Blades. Sir Orne and Sir Rory and Sir Hew, all dead in the first hours of the barbarian invasion, only Croy remaining of their brotherhood—

"How?" Croy managed to ask.

Sir Hew seemed to understand what he meant. "Sir Rory and I attempted to reach the keep, to organize a final defense, but we were too late. Mörget and his men cut us off before we could reach the inner bailey."

"Sir Rory," Croy said.

Hew shook his head. "He died at Mörget's hand, seconds after you left us. The barbarian cut him in half. Even worse— he broke Crowsbill with the same blow. An Ancient Blade, shattered in one blow by a barbarian!"

Croy thought of Bloodquaffer, which had suffered the same fate. It seemed even magical swords of ancient provenance were no guarantee against Mörget's strength. His heart sagged in his chest, and not just to hear that his friend Rory was dead.

"Mörget tried to come for me, then, but I was busy. Killing every man I could get my hands on. I thought only to sacrifice myself in delaying the barbarian advance, to give you more time." He shook his head. "I achieved nothing in that regard. A berserker knocked me over the head with an axe while I stood trying to defend the bridge over the Strow. I fell in the river and started to drown. Wearing that much armor, I should have. But the Lady had other uses for me. She washed me up on a bank two miles south of the fortress. I found a horse and came straight here."

"Sk-skif—"

"Enough. I'll answer every question later. For now, be at peace. You've done a man's service," Sir Hew said, "bringing us the girl. I take it that Ulfram is dead."

Croy nodded. It took some effort.

"Long live the queen," Hew said. "Now, hero—sleep." Hew's face swam away from Croy's vision, as he followed the direct order of his superior.

CHAPTER NINETY-TWO

Mörg was no fool.

He would have heard some of the murmurs in the camp. Of late it had become open talk—how could he have not heard it? Though still the chieftains turned their faces away and fell silent when he came near, he must understand it would not always be that way. A challenge was coming.

Mörget watched his father's tent all day, endeavoring to be no fool, himself. He watched as those most loyal to the Great Chieftain found excuses to always be near the tent. Mörgain went into the tent early in the day, coming quickly as if she'd been summoned. She left again a few moments later, fury twisting her face, striking out at every man who got in her way. She did not return, but always there were berserkers and loyal chieftains standing around, warming themselves by the fire Mörg kept, drinking his mead. Even those with specific duties elsewhere—those tasked with finding more stones for the trebuchets, those who were stationed to watch the walls of the besieged city, looking for signs of new defenses—found time to come around and joke with Hurlind, or feed morsels to Mörg's filthy hound.

And always—always—there was Torki, the Great Chieftain's champion, standing like an oak tree before the flap of the tent. Torki with his burnt face and his massive double-bladed battle axe. Torki did not move. He did not smile when Hurlind made jest of him. He did not drink when the mead horn was passed around.

He only stood, and waited.

"If you don't strike soon," Balint told Mörget, "you'll lose your chance. Mörg's smarter than a crow sitting on a gallows tree. He'll find some way to convince the chieftains his way is the right way."

"They've grown tired of this waiting game," Mörget insisted. "They are ready for action."

"They're bored, and looking for some passing diversion," Balint said. "If you don't provide it, someone else will. They'll back your throw only if it promises them some reward. Mörg can make promises, too."

Mörget roared and grabbed her up off the pile of furs. "Shouldn't you be building another trebuchet right now?"

"Why?" she asked, as he dangled her in the air. She was no coward, he had to admit. "There aren't enough stones for the three we have."

He dropped the dwarf and went to sharpen his axe again, even though it was already keen enough to cut through steel.

Night came quickly, and with it snow. Huge soft flakes filled the air and collected everywhere, danced in the guttering flames of the camp's many fires, collected in beards and on hair. The temperature dropped to the point where even barbarians wanted to be inside and away from the wind. Suddenly the berserkers and loyal chieftains weren't crowding around Mörg's tent so thickly, anymore. Hurlind went to fetch his master's dinner.

"This is the moment!" Balint urged. "If you keep anything in those breeches at all, you'll do it now."

"I don't need your advice," Mörget insisted, and kicked at her. She managed to roll away before he broke her in half.

Torki was still there, his face that of a frost giant, his battle axe white with rime.

It didn't matter. Mörget had bested the man before. He threw his own axe down, unbuckled his sword belt and dropped it as well. Then he stepped out into the storm.

Torki didn't move until Mörget was within striking range.

Then he only shifted on his feet, and opened his mouth to speak. "The Great Chieftain is busy," he said.

"I have a right to speak with him at any time," Mörget insisted.

"Not even chieftains may bother their leader when he takes his meals," Torki said.

"But sons may," Mörget said. "Look at me. I am unarmed." He threw open his furs to show that he carried nothing more deadly then a belt knife. Then he grabbed for the flap of Mörg's tent and tried to step inside.

The flat of Torki's axe caught him in the ribs and sent him sprawling. "For my next blow, I use the edge," the champion said. And then he went back to standing still as a stone, waiting for Mörget to try again.

"A son has rights to his father's house!" Mörget shrieked. And then he threw himself at the champion.

Torki had not attained his post for being slow, or for flinching from combat. The battle axe came up faster than Mörget had expected and swung for his neck. Mörget dodged to the side even as Torki started to recover and brace himself for another blow.

An axe that big, that heavy, could cut a man in half—even a man as thick and sinewy as Mörget. It was a slow weapon, though, and its momentum was not easily checked. Mörget let Torki start his second stroke—then moved slightly to his left and punched Torki in the nose as hard as he was able.

Blood spurted down the champion's face. Torki barely flinched. Barely, but enough. Mörget ducked low and got his shoulder into the champion's armpit. He brought his fists together and hammered downward with them on Torki's hand where it held the axe. The bones there cracked audibly and the axe fell into the snow. Still Torki didn't cry out.

After that it became a wrestling match, and Mörget had been winning those since he was six years old. Torki tried to grab Mörget's belt, perhaps intending to throw him to the ground, but Mörget spun around him and threw an arm around the champion's neck.

A crowd had begun to gather—made of equal parts of Mörg's reavers and Mörget's own loyal chieftains. None of them rushed to Torki's defense. They only stood there in the blowing snow, watching with wide eyes. Mörget studied the crowd, looking for Mörgain, but didn't find her.

Good. She could ruin everything with a word or a single blow. He hoped she was far, far away.

Torki fought valiantly as Mörget squeezed down on his windpipe. The champion bashed and scratched at Mörget's flesh but Mörget could take a little pain and blood. Little by little he felt Torki's life draining away as the champion struggled for air that wouldn't come.

Torki fought for long minutes, his face purple, the veins on his neck and shoulders standing out and then popping one by one. Mörget squeezed ever harder, until he heard vertebrae crack inside the champion's neck. Only then did he let go.

Panting a little, sweating under his fur cloak, he made eye contact with as many men in the crowd as he dared. He challenged them all to step forward, but none did. Then he picked up the fallen battle axe and stormed inside the tent.

Inside Mörg sat naked on his furs, feeding morsels to the pathetic dog. When the Great Chieftain looked up and saw Mörget standing there, he patted the dog's back and told it to run off. Looking confused, the animal darted between Mörget's legs and out into the snow.

"Look me in the eye," Mörget said.

Mörg yawned and stretched his arms over his head. Had he been sleeping all day? He looked utterly unconcerned, for a man who was about to die.

"The clans have spoken," Mörget told him.

Mörg simply nodded. He poured himself a horn of mead, and drank deep.

How many times had Mörget dreamed of this moment? As a child, growing up in this man's shadow, he'd envisioned it a million times. As he grew into manhood he'd realized how difficult it could be—how wily an opponent Mörg was. As a chieftain he had given it true and serious thought. He had planned it out thoroughly. Seen it from all angles. He had never doubted for a second that this appointment would come. That he would be the one to take his father's life.

In those daydreams, Mörg had always pleaded for mercy.

He had begged to be exiled, which was the worst fate a warrior of the clans could imagine. Or sometimes he had looked on his son with approval, knowing this was just. Rarely, in his imaginings, Mörg would pause to impart some secret wisdom. An answer to a question Mörget could only ask himself in dreams:

Where does my rage end? What is its purpose?

Mörget hesitated. The axe grew heavy in his hands. He could feel events conspiring around him, could feel the gathered clans outside drawing a collective breath. He stalled for time.

"Mörgain came in here earlier. She did not like what you told her."

Mörg spoke for the first time. "I told her I loved her."

Mörget's blood hissed in his veins. *Love?* Love was not something a Great Chieftain expressed to his chieftains—or to his children. It was what he spoke of to his thrall concubines. Perhaps to his horse.

"I told her I was proud of her, and that I loved her." Mörg sighed. "It's something I've always wanted to say, though I knew she would take it hard. And she did. But now, when it's come to this—I can think only of myself. Enough! Who else is there that I should think of now? And soon, I will cease thinking even of my own petty sufferings. Death will take away all my concerns. It will leave me at peace, something I've always wished for. It's odd, I never considered that before. So many years searching for a calm place in the storm of life. And here, now, I find it."

"What—of me?" Mörget asked. He could not frame the words properly.

"Make sense, boy."

Mörget scowled and grunted and thumped himself hard on the chest. "You had words for her. Do you have any for me?"

Mörg looked up at him, then, with eyes as deep as oceans. There was nothing there but wisdom, not anymore. Mörg the Wise, they called him. For the first time in his life, Mörget thought he understood what that meant. The torment of it. What horrors had Mörg seen in his time? Bad enough to watch a thousand men die. But understanding it—understanding everything. What greater curse could there be?

"You have a *wyrd* on you, boy."

The word could mean many things. It could mean 'destiny,' or it could mean 'doom'. In the language of the barbarians there was very little distance between those concepts. It meant a driving fate, a power that possessed a man and made him do things others would go white to even imagine. Things that would destroy him—and make his name glorious.

"You think I don't know that?" Mörget asked.

"You want wisdom, now? From me? Why do I owe you that? Don't answer. I know the answer. You'll say that you are my son." Mörg nodded to himself. "And you'll be right. Very well."

Mörget took a step closer. He did not put the axe down.

"Here: take this message, as you please, and use it as you see fit. Mörget Mountainslayer, you will not be able to stop yourself. You are too weak to defeat your own strength. Someone else must stop you, and you should hope they do it soon."

Mörget screamed in rage. "You give me riddles, like a scold!"

"Some truths," Mörg said, "cannot be made clear. They must be lived to make sense. Now."

"What?" Mörget demanded.

"Do it now. Before you lose the stomach for it. Now, while you hate me! I could not bear you to love me when you do this thing!"

Red light burst behind Mörget's eyes as the axe came down. And down again. And again. He did not swing it like a blade, but dropped it like a hammer, over and over, sometimes the edge catching on flesh, sometimes the flat smashing against bone.

When it was done the red ruin on Mörg's furs was not a man at all, but raw meat.

Mörget plunged his hands into the gore, and used his father's blood to paint his face. Berserkers painted half their face red, because they were mad only half the time. Mörget covered his shaved scalp, the back of his neck, plugged his ears with blood. It still was not enough.

Outside the tent the cold air could not touch him. The snow turned to steam when it tried to land on his face or hands.

He was aware of people all around him, of gasping mouths and staring eyes, but they seemed unconnected to him. They did not seem to matter. He thought of something. "The dog," he said. His father had loved that dog. The dog had loved Mörg back. Was that what Mörg wanted from his children? He would not let Mörg have that, not even in death. "Find the dog. Bring me its skin, so I may wear it around my neck, and every man know what I've done!"

If anyone responded he did not hear them.

He went back to his own tent, blind to the whole world, knowing nothing but fury.

He threw himself upon his furs and waited for his rage to cool. When he could finally talk again without shouting, he turned to look at Balint.

"At dawn, you will do your worst. If even my father's blood cannot cool my brow, I will have this city for consolation. Whatever devious scheme your black heart can concoct, I will make it happen."

"I've been waiting for you to say that," she told him, her voice low and husky. "You just made me happier than a nine-month's pregnant girl on her wedding day."

CHAPTER NINETY-THREE

The workshop stank of brimstone and urine, enough to make Malden's eyes water. It was hot inside, despite the snow that lay six inches thick on every surface outside the windows. Slag had his workers skimming orange crystals off the top of reeking vats or burning wood for charcoal, night and day. Other workers sat at narrow benches, grinding together the three necessary substances, or mixing it together with their fingers until it formed grains the size of corn.

"Finer! Grind it finer than this, you fucker" Slag said, sifting black pebbles through his fingers. The apothecary's apprentice he had admonished ducked his head and bent over his mortar and pestle again. "Malden, it must be ground finer. I need some kind of mill, maybe an upright wheel to crush the substance. And some kind of multiple-sieve refining sleeve to break it up smaller. I'm also going to need some kind of carriage for the device. I need iron, or better yet—bronze. As much as you can get me."

Malden shrugged. "There's a bronze statue of Juring Tarness in the Golden Slope. I doubt he'll mind much if we melt it down." He had no idea what Slag was after, really. The dwarf had tried to explain the nature of his secret project many times—apparently it was some kind of huge siege engine, far more powerful than a ballista, but operating on completely different principles. There was fire involved, and some kind of projectile, but beyond that it made very little sense to Malden. He assumed the dwarf knew what he was doing.

He had other things on his mind. He doubted that Slag cared much about what happened outside of his workshop— dwarves were notorious for their obsessions when they had a project to work on. Still, Malden needed to talk to someone about this, and Cythera was . . . no longer available. "Six cows, slaughtered and left to rot before the Godstone. Someone must have been hiding them when I did my last census of foodstocks. Do you know how much soup we could have made of those animals?" he asked. "Now they're frozen to the cobbles so solidly no one can shift them, not even with pry bars."

Slag shrugged. "Humans and religion. Never figured that one out, myself, lad. Seems like you lot need somebody to tell you what to do. If there isn't an overlord looming over your shoulder all the time, you invent one."

"The barbarians only sent one stone over the wall today, so far," Malden said. "The people seem to think these sacrifices are having an actual effect."

Slag gave him a dubious look. "You ought to nip that in the damned bud," he said. "They'll start thinking soon that a human sacrifice will stop the attacks altogether. Or maybe they'll try something far worse."

"Worse than slaying each other for their blood?" Malden asked.

"Aye. Maybe they'll think dwarf blood will work even better, since it's a much rarer commodity. You! Don't just dip your ladle in that piss! Skim the surface, skim, like this!" He made gentle sweeping motions with his hands. "All we want is the crusty bits from the top."

Malden put a hand on the dwarf's shoulder and squeezed. Slag winced out from under his grasp. "You—mind that brimstone! The stuff burns if you get it too close to the fire, you clumsy fucker!"

Malden took his leave without a farewell. Outside the cold air felt good on his face. It smelled better than the air inside the workshop, as well. Malden, who had grown up in a city without any kind of public sanitation, where the only known method for dealing with waste was dumping it in the river, had never imagined that Ness could smell good, before.

Ness. His city. Imperiled and fraught with confusion it might be, yet he still loved the place more than he hated it. He truly wanted to save it from destruction. If he could only figure out how. So far he'd just found ways to delay the inevitable. He strained his mind for answers, for solutions. His thoughts grew less focused as he walked. Perhaps he was just tired, having slept very little in weeks. Perhaps he was just—

His reverie came to an abrupt halt when he heard a cry from the top of the wall. "Archers! Archers to your posts!"

That couldn't be good. He scampered up the side of a tavern that abutted the nearest stretch of wall and jumped over the battlements. Men and women were running everywhere, gathering up quivers and bows. No one stopped to tell him what was happening. A hoarding stood nearby, a wooden gallery built over the edge of the wall from which archers could fire without being exposed themselves. Malden ducked inside and peered out through the firing slit.

Down below, the barbarian camp was a sea of movement and hurry. A wave of fur-clad warriors was headed right for the wall, and they were carrying ladders. Clearly they intended to scale the wall and fight their way inside. *This is it*, Malden thought. This was the moment he'd been dreading, because he knew that in a direct confrontation with the barbarians he could not win.

That didn't mean he was allowed to give up. Croy had taught him that.

"Forks!" he called. He grabbed the man nearest to him—a thief who was so nervous he couldn't seem to string his bow. "Get every able-bodied man up here you can, and have them bring forks."

The thief looked confused. "What kind of forks?"

"It doesn't matter! Pitchforks, turning forks, any bit of wood with a hook on the end, anything. Go! And send word I need Velmont."

Rus Galenius, in his *Manual of Fortifications*, described scaling ladders in exquisite detail—the best wood for their construction, the proper time and manner of their use, the number of men who should be on one at any given time. The counter-strategy for dealing with ladders was so ancient and so simple the author seemed to disdain its mention, giving it a single sentence. Malden had actually been paying attention the day that Cutbill read him that passage, however.

The first ladder touched the wall not a hundred feet from where Malden stood, and berserkers started scrambling up the rungs. "You," Malden said, pointing at a group of female archers in the next hoarding over. "Don't let them reach the top!"

Bows flexed and arrows shot downward at flat angles. The berserkers were easy targets, unable to move out of the way as the archers poured shafts into them. Soon the men near the top of the ladder looked like pincushions for all the arrows sticking out of their arms and backs. Unable to feel pain, they kept climbing until they died and fell away.

At the base of the ladder a hundred more men waited their turn.

An old man carrying a pitchfork came up to Malden and saluted. It took Malden a second to remember how to salute back. "Thank the bloodgod you're here," Malden said. "Do you see that ladder, where its end sticks up over the wall?"

The oldster nodded and gave Malden a wicked grin. He hefted his fork and made toward the ladder.

"Wait," Malden said. "Not quite yet." He waited until the topmost berserker on the ladder had nearly crested the wall. Below him the ladder bowed with the weight of half a dozen more. "Now," Malden said.

The old man caught the top rung of the ladder with the tines of his fork and heaved. The ladder weighed too much for him, so Malden grabbed the end of the fork and lent the strength of his own back to the effort.

The ladder twisted and bent and then fell backwards. Some of the men clinging to it jumped free. Some lacked the presence of mind to do so. Bodies made horrible crunching noises when they struck the frozen ground below. The ladder shattered as it spun away from the wall.

"Good," Malden said. "Like that! Every time. Wait until they're nearly at the top, so you get as many of them as possible. But don't wait so long that even one of them gets over the side." He turned to look around him. "Where is Velmont?" he demanded.

His Helstrovian lieutenant appeared a moment later. "I came as fast as I could," he pleaded.

Malden grabbed his forearms and dragged him out of the hoarding, making room for more archers to crowd inside. "Something's changed," he said. "I don't know what, but it's not good. Last night they were still intent on waiting us out— letting us starve in here, until we begged them to come in and feed us. Now they've lost their patience. I don't know why. But this is what we've been dreading. A real attack! Get every single archer you can up here. Get me watchers at every tower along the wall, get me reports—I need to know if the attack is just in this one place, or if they're everywhere. Go! Quickly!"

Velmont dashed off to do Malden's bidding. Malden

needed that information. And yet, in the pit of his heart, he already knew what Velmont would report.

This was the moment Ness would be lost. All the planning he'd done, all the hard work, had been designed around one simple principle: that the besiegers would wait him out. Clearly that belief had been founded on the wrong principles. There would not be enough archers, nor enough old men with pitchforks, if the barbarians were serious about scaling the wall. And in his experience, he'd never known Mörget's people to be less than serious about anything.

CHAPTER NINETY-FOUR

"They're scaling Ditchwall now, and there's no one to stop them!" Cythera sent her consciousness winging over Ness, trying to watch in every direction at once. "There are two more ladders at Wheatwall. One just fell, but—no! Malden!"

"He's not your lover anymore," Coruth growled. "This is why you had to renounce him. Do not tarry with him—tell me where else the barbarians are attacking."

Cythera watched as Malden hurried toward Ditchwall, shouting for forks and archers. If the barbarians reached the top of the wall and surrounded him, even Acidtongue wouldn't save him from—

"Tell me what you see, girl!"

Coruth's voice was tinny and small, as if she were very far away. Even though she sat directly next to Cythera in the main room of their house on the Isle of Horses. It was so hard to stay aware of her body, to keep talking even while her eyes saw things in a hundred places at once. How could anyone do this? How could any witch bear seeing so much, and not slip free of her body altogether?

"You may be one of the initiated, but you're still learning," Coruth told her, and suddenly the older witch's voice was much louder. Cythera felt like her being was yanked sideways, pulled away from Ditchwall, as if she were a kite whose string had been tugged. "Look, daughter. Look everywhere—we must know what they're doing."

"But why?" Cythera demanded. She couldn't see Malden anymore—was he overrun? Was he already dead? "What's the point? Just knowing where the barbarians are doesn't help anyone. We can't tell them where to concentrate their forces. We can't fight them ourselves."

"Do as you're told!"

Cythera tried not to think of Malden, to spread her consciousness wider. It was so hard—she'd just learned how this was done a few hours before. "Mother, the city will fall in the next hour—there are so many of them!" At Ryewall a barbarian climbed up on the battlements, only to be struck down by three arrows fired from different directions. At Westwall a fork pushed away another ladder, even as the barbarians raised two more. "We have to stop this. We have to do something, not just watch!"

"And what would you do?" Coruth demanded.

"Cast a spell. Set the ladders aflame, or—or call down a storm, they can't climb if the ladders are too slick with rain to hold onto."

"You think those things are in my power?"

Cythera couldn't bear it. Ness was about to be overrun—the siege broken. The barbarians were about to take the city and there was nothing she could do. "They'll kill everyone, mother. They'll kill every single person in this city."

"So now you've seen the future?"

"I've seen enough to know how much blood they'll shed, once they're inside the walls," Cythera insisted.

"So the time has come," Coruth said.

"What time? Mother, we have to help!" Cythera said. She felt as light as a scrap of silk floating on the wind. Her head reeled and her senses were on fire.

A slender thread snapped somewhere, and twanged like a broken bowstring. Cythera felt as if she were being pulled through the air faster than a trebuchet ball, and then she was falling, falling so fast.

With a start she lurched forward and found herself sitting in her chair, back on the Isle of Horses. Her consciousness was firmly back inside her body. She tried to extend her vision again, to see farther, but she could not. It was like she'd never been trained to be a witch at all.

Beside her Coruth sat, her eyes rolled up in the back of her head. "You're done for the day," she said.

"What? But the attack—the barbarians—"

"There's supper to get ready," Coruth said, as if it were just an ordinary day. "And you need to sweep out the grate. There's a week's worth of ashes piled in there. I expect it all done by the time I return."

Cythera couldn't believe it. The siege was about to be broken and her mother could only talk of chores? "Wait— when you return from where?"

"I had hoped there would be more time to train you before things came to this dark pass," Coruth said. "I can only hope you've learned enough." And then her body erupted in a welter of black birds that winged around the room, smashing against the walls and ceiling as they desperately tried to find their way through the open window.

The chair where Coruth had sat was empty.

CHAPTER NINETY-FIVE

There seemed to be no end to the berserkers willing to scale the wall, even when every ladder was knocked away, even when Malden's archers kept cutting them down. Messengers kept running in to tell him of new ladders reaching for other sections of the wall—the barbarians were too smart to let him mass his archers anywhere, and instead were sending up ladders on every side of the city. They must have constructed hundreds of them overnight. The ladders were easily destroyed, pushed back by forks, and every time one fell a half dozen barbarians fell with it.

Yet they kept coming.

"Two at Swampwall!" a messenger shouted. Malden dispatched archers that were already too thinly spread where he stood on Ditchwall. He raced around the circumference of the city, calling for more forks, more people to push the attackers away. He had no lack of volunteers—women and men were pouring out of the Stink, looking for any way to help. They found things they could use for forks, things Malden would never have thought of—threshing flails on six foot long poles, the long brass candle snuffers from the ruins of the Ladychapel—and he put them to work as soon as they presented themselves. Still more ladders came.

A team of old women pushed a ladder away from the wall not a hundred yards from Malden—but not before one crazed berserker was able to grab on to the hoarding there. He swung by a hand for one moment as archers peppered him with shafts, but he did not lose his grip. Like a demon out of the pit he laughed and struggled to pull himself up onto the wall. No one could stop him. The moment his feet hit the top of the wall, the fur-clad attacker came at the old women with axe in hand, clearly not caring who he killed, only wanting blood. Malden had to dash in with every ounce of his speed to beat him to his kill. The barbarian was foaming at the mouth and his bloodshot eyes never blinked as Malden drew Acidtongue and sliced his head off. The head went bouncing down inside the city to smash off the chimney pot of a house far below. Malden kicked the body the other way, to crash down on the frozen soil outside the wall.

It was the first time he'd ever killed a human being with his magic sword. His entire body shook, and he thought he might throw up. But now he understood. This was why he wasn't allowed to give it to the Burgrave. This was why Croy had demanded he take it. Why fate had decreed he should hold it.

He hated the world in that moment. The world where such things were necessary.

"Lord Mayor," someone said. It sounded like they were very far away. Then he looked up and saw one of Elody's girls staring into his eyes. She couldn't be more than sixteen. She held a bow in one hand and an arrow in the other and she looked like a little girl playing with toys. She was terrified, and she needed someone to make everything okay. "Lord Mayor, please—they're still coming."

Malden looked down at the sword in his hand, at the blood on its blade, and suddenly he could think again. He looked down, over the parapet, and saw another ladder reaching upward toward him, more barbarians scrambling up its rungs.

"Archers! Bring me more archers!" he screamed, though he knew there were no more to be had. There was so much wall to cover that if the archers spread out evenly all around Ness, they would have to stand a hundred feet away from each other. There was no way they could cover every part of the wall, and no way they could kill every barbarian that tried to climb up. It took half a dozen shots to bring down even one berserker—Malden wondered if he'd even had enough arrows made, or if they would exhaust their supply before long.

"Pick your shots with care," he instructed, and Elody's girl nodded grimly. "Only shoot the ones at the tops of the ladders—they're the ones most likely to get in. Aim for their eyes—no—aim for their hands. Leave them unable to climb, and they'll stall the ones below!"

He ran everywhere, trying to see every side of the city at once. But Ness was too big. His archers were too spread out. He saw barbarians clambering up over an unprotected section of wall. He ran toward them, knowing he had gotten lucky with the berserker he'd beheaded, that if it came to a real fight he would be unable to hold them back. "Get me anyone who can fight," he shouted. "And archers! More archers!"

He waded into the midst of the barbarians coming over

the wall, Acidtongue whirling around him, cutting open arms and stomachs and faces. Some of the barbarians screamed and fell away from the wall, but others— berserkers—didn't seem to notice they were faced by a madman with a magic sword. One gnashed his teeth at the blade as if he would take a bite out of it. His axe swung at Malden's head, and Malden knew he couldn't block it in time. He winced backwards, expecting to die.

A dozen arrows appeared in the barbarian's neck and side and back, knocking him backwards. Blood spurted from the wounds. The barbarian tried to bring his arm down, tried to follow through with his axe stroke—and five more arrows cut through the muscles of his shoulder. He fell away in tatters, stumbling over the parapet to fall into the streets below.

Malden whirled around to see who had saved him—and saw a dozen archers standing there. He thought they must have come from all over the city and left huge stretches of wall unguarded, only so they could save him. Except there was something wrong with these men—they stood in a perfect line, each of them with their feet spread exactly the same distance apart, each of them holding their bows at the same angle. They even seemed to be dressed identically. He studied their faces and found the features of Tyburn, one of his thieves. They all had Tyburn's face.

Malden turned slowly around, and saw another dozen archers behind him. Every single one of them looked exactly like Guennie, one of Herwig's girls. As he watched, flummoxed, the Guennies lifted their bows and easily picked a barbarian off a ladder. Their arrows flew in perfect synchrony and hit the same man, the points hitting his flesh no more than an inch apart from one another. More barbarians came scurrying up the ladder, but six identical one-armed men heaved at a fork they'd made by lashing their crutches together, and the ladder spun away to fall and collapse.

The archers, the one-armed men, they didn't look like ghosts. They looked as real to Malden as he was. Yet it was impossible, utterly impossible.

"Witchcraft," Malden gasped.

Over Castle Hill, a flock of dark birds were circling,

faster and faster. Watching them made him dizzy. Malden turned to look at the next section of wall over, the length called Ditchwall. It was crowded with archers and fork-bearers. They stood side by side, so close their elbows touched. No—not just touched. As they moved to pick new targets or rush to push back a ladder, they passed right through each other, no matter how solid they seemed. They were illusions, products of some spell Coruth was casting.

And yet their arrows were wickedly real. The forks they wielded pushed with real force against the ladders. How could it be? In Malden's experience, such phantasms could never touch the living, and certainly could offer them no harm. He thought of the ghostly horses on Coruth's island, or the illusions he had bested inside Hazoth's villa the summer before. Those had been diabolically clever and had led him toward destruction, but they'd been unable to hurt him on their own.

Coruth's doubles were killing barbarians as fast as they could come at the wall. The energy she was expending must be enormous. He looked at the circling flock again, and saw one of the birds falter and drop like a stone. For a second Parkwall was bare of archers again, but then they flickered back into existence.

Coruth could not have kept the spell going much longer. Fortunately, she didn't have to. When they saw what they were facing atop the walls, someone in the barbarian camp was smart enough to call a retreat.

As quickly as it had begun, the attack broke off. Ladders fell, abandoned, against the wall. Bodies were left to lie where they'd broken. The phantom archers kept up a withering fire that followed the barbarians all the way back to their camp, and more than one berserker, too far gone into rage to properly retreat, was cut down while trying to rush the walls with his bare fists.

In the space of minutes, however, all was at peace again—the barbarians safely out of range, the archers lowering their bows. They flickered out of existence one by one as they were no longer needed. Only the original men and women from whom they'd been copied remained.

Over Castle Hill, only a few birds still flew, circling

madly. Eventually even they slowed and flapped wearily toward the nearest roost, utterly drained.

Malden waited another hour, to make sure the barbarian retreat was not just a ruse. Eventually he sat down on the battlements and rested his face against the cold stones of a merlon.

It was there that Slag found him.

"Lad," the dwarf said, "there's something you need to see."

CHAPTER NINETY-SIX

M alden followed the dwarf down a flight of stairs to the level of the streets. The bodies of dead barbarians lay here and there on the cobbles, having achieved a glory few of their fellows could boast—they had actually made it over the wall.

"I'm feeling rather pleased at the moment," Malden said. He felt giddy, actually. Like he'd drunk too much wine and was about to pass out. "We've accomplished something here. Bloodied their noses, at least. Why do I have the feeling you're going to ruin this all-too-rare mood?"

Slag frowned and shook his head. "I don't want to piss in your puncheon, lad, but—"

Malden closed his eyes and sighed. "Alright. Just tell me what is wrong now."

The dwarf led Malden down a street that ran alongside the Ryewall. The street was only six feet wide in places, flanked on one side by the wall itself, on the other by a row of tall houses that formed a close. It was here that Slag had set up a strange tableau. Only a little snow had fallen into that artificial canyon, but even so Slag had swept patches of the cobbles perfectly clean. Then he had laid out a series of shallow bowls, each ten feet from its neighbor.

He had a cask of wine under his arm and he proceeded to extract its bung. Malden grabbed the cask from him and held it over his head so the wine fell into his mouth. "My thanks. I needed a drink."

The dwarf grabbed the cask back with a growl. "That's not for you, lad. Normally I'd use water for this purpose, but it's so arsing cold out here the water would freeze. Wine will serve just as well." Moving from bowl to bowl, he filled each with an inch of wine. Then he knelt next to one of them and stared into its surface.

"Scrying?" Malden asked. "I thought dwarves never used magic. Although these are desperate times."

Slag stood up and glared at him. "Take me for serious, lad, for what I'm about to tell you is no joke. I believe the attack on the wall was just a feint."

Malden had been worried that was the point of all this. All the jests he could think of wouldn't put off the truth. "What makes you think that?" he asked.

"If I'm right, all that noise and blunder was just to distract our watchers while they started coming at us from a different direction. Look, and be still, now. Watch the surface of the wine."

Malden knelt down next to Slag and tried not to so much as breathe on the bowl. At first he saw nothing—but then the barest shimmer passed across the surface of the wine. A moment later it came again. It could have been the breeze, but—no. There was a rhythm to the movement of the wine. Again. Again.

"This is an old trick we use in our mines, up north," Slag whispered. "If you think somebody else is digging too close to your claim, you set out bowls of water to track 'em. The vibrations from their tools run through the earth and make the water dance. If you set out enough bowls, you can triangulate and work out how far away they are and what direction they're coming from."

The wine shook again. Again. Again.

Slag jumped up and moved to the next bowl. He waited a moment over it, then ran to a third. "Here. It's strongest here," he said. Malden came and stood beside him. The wine there shook more visibly, distinct ripples forming in the surface.

"What does it mean?" Malden asked, softly.

Slag's shoulders tensed. "Sappers. Fucking sappers. They're digging a tunnel under the wall. Propping up its roof with loose timbers. When the tunnel's gone far enough, they pull out the timbers, and—crash!—the wall won't be able to support its own weight. It'll collapse into the empty space."

Malden thought of something. "We heard a rumor that Mörget managed to bring down the wall of Redweir in just three days. I assumed that meant he used picks and drills, but—"

"Aye, lad," Slag said. "He must have had sappers there, too." Slag shook his head. "Between this and those trebuchets he built, when nobody ever heard tell of a barbarian with a siege engine before, well. I think we ought assume Mörg has a fucking dwarf on his side. Somebody who knows about this manner of skullduggery."

A dwarf, working for the barbarians. It was hard to imagine—and it did Malden's composure no good at all. Combine the technical skill of a dwarf with the remorseless bloodthirst of a barbarian and you were up against an unstoppable enemy.

"How long, do you think, before this tunnel is complete?"

Slag shrugged. "These walls are sound, and sunk deep. It'll take time. Maybe a week. Assuming we don't stop them first."

"We can stop them?" Malden asked, hope springing anew in his bosom.

"Perhaps, lad. In theory it's simple enough. We just have to dig our own tunnel that intersects theirs. Then we kill every fucking one of them."

"But then there will be a direct tunnel from their camp to the inside of the city. What's to stop the barbarians from sending through a whole army?"

"They can try," Slag said, with a half-grin, "if they don't mind us collapsing our tunnel on top of 'em once they're in so deep they can't turn back."

"Remind me never to cross you," Malden said. "I don't think I'd enjoy your revenge overmuch. This is excellent work, Slag. The city will thank you, somehow. Is there some reward I can offer you?"

"Put about ten more hours in each fucking day," Slag said. "Between digging a counter-tunnel and working on my secret project, I'm going to need 'em." He shrugged. "I'm in this with you, lad. It's my head, too, if we lose now."

Malden grabbed the dwarf's shoulder. This time Slag didn't flinch.

CHAPTER NINETY-SEVEN

Croy could stand, and if he used Ghostcutter as a cane, he could even walk. He pushed aside the hands of the Skilfinger nurse who had tended to him and stepped out of his tent. His head swam and black spots appeared in his peripheral vision, but he was determined not to stop now.

The Skilfinger camp was busy, always, with soldiers running here and there on errands, working on digging ditches and building palisades or simply practicing their drills. They were incredibly well disciplined and organized. Had Croy possessed a company of them when he met Mörgain in Greenmarsh he would have carried the day.

Unfortunately they were some two hundred miles from where they needed to be. Croy hobbled across a parade ground and up to the tent where Sir Hew and Bethane were in constant council. When he lifted the tent flap, eighteen inches of steel blade leapt out at his throat. He was just able to wobble backwards and avoid being beheaded.

Hew said something in the tongue of Skilfing, and the

guard withdrew his weapon without apology. Croy demanded none—the guard was only obeying his duty.

"You're up and about," Hew said, nodding in Croy's direction. "Good. You can tell us the situation at Helstrow. Her Highness has been kind enough to tell us what she could, but of course she is untutored in military strategy. I mean no offense, my queen."

Bethane was seated in a carved wooden chair at the back of the tent, wrapped in heavy quilts. "None taken," she said. Then she jumped up and ran to throw her arms around Croy. "I thought you would perish, my champion."

Croy did his best not to be knocked over by her embrace. "Your highness. There are matters of decorum and—"

"I don't care. Without you, I would be dead right now," Bethane told him. "And surely, I have a royal prerogative to touch any of my subjects I choose. Especially those wounded in my service. They tell me that my touch can cure scrofula now, did you know that?"

"I've . . . heard as much," Croy said. Personally he'd never actually seen it happen. But it was one of the legends of the kings and queens of Skrae that they could cure a variety of diseases simply by personal contact. He shook his head, remembering the direct manner and plain speech of Ulfram V. Clearly the father had passed this trait on to his daughter. "Sir Hew, I need to speak with you at once."

"Of course. We're planning our next move. As an Ancient Blade, it is proper your voice should be heard," Hew said, ushering Croy inside the tent. It was open and airy inside, and everything was washed with the colors of the painted canvas. A dozen Skilfinger knights stood with Hew around a table bearing a map of all Skrae. All of them were armored in shining steel, as if they expected an attack on the instant.

"I thought we might speak alone. These men are—mercenaries, is that correct?"

"It is. Ulfram V, Lady remember his name, was wise enough to send for them even before the barbarians arrived. The contracts are signed and the retainers paid. You can trust them. Anyway, none of them speak our language."

Croy met the gaze of one of the knights. It was the same

man who'd found him in the hills and brought him to Hew. "Very well. I have come to ask your help in the rescue of the Free City of Ness."

Hew shook his head and bent over his map. "You have my regrets, but no. Ness is a lost cause. Eight thousand of the barbarians have surrounded the city and my latest reports tell me Ness will fall in a matter of days. No, we'll be marching on Helstrow, and we leave tomorrow."

Croy limped over and leaned on the table. "I must ask you to reconsider. If the horde takes Ness, they'll control half the kingdom, and—"

"And if we take back Helstrow, and then Redweir, we'll have the other half. The eastern half. We'll be between them and any reinforcements they might call up from beyond the Whitewall." Hew drew one finger down the length of the map. "If we control the river Strow, we'll be well on our way to taking our land back." He pounded on the table and looked up, into Croy's eyes. "I know your sentiment is with Ness. It's where you've lived so much of your life. But you must think like a general now."

Croy closed his eyes for a moment. Hew was right. He could see that much from the map. He *knew* that much if he trusted his military instincts. Helstrow would be poorly defended, and Redweir would be garrisoned by only a skeleton crew of barbarians. Two easy victories that could turn the war around—turn certain defeat into sudden and almost bloodless success.

It didn't matter. "If you allow the barbarians to have Ness, the suffering of the people there will be unthinkable," Croy said. *Cythera's suffering will be . . . unbearable*, he thought. It was possible she was already dead. No, he would not accept that. The Lady had spared his life so many times. Surely she would have just let him die, if he was not meant to do this. To save Cythera.

If he followed Hew's lead, and rode with him on Helstrow, they might win the eastern half of the kingdom before winter choked the land. But then it would be many months before they could even think of moving on Ness. Cythera would be alone, and defenseless, that whole time.

That was not acceptable.

"This is war, Croy. People suffer in time of war. Even people we love."

Croy nodded. "I understand that. I've seen it with my own eyes. I was there when Baron Easthull made the last stand against the barbarians, in Greenmarsh. I was on that field."

It was an ungallant blow, to point out that while Sir Hew had been running for his life, Croy had been fighting for Skrae. But it could not be unsaid.

Hew pulled back the chain mail hood of his hauberk and the padded cloth gambeson underneath. He chafed at his ears as if they were burning. "I've given you a place on my council, Croy. Don't mistake the bounds of that authority. Don't forget your station."

"I'm an Ancient Blade, same as you," Croy said.

Another few words, another challenge to Hew's supremacy here, and it could come to a duel. An Ancient Blade's honor was his most valued possession, and if Croy took this any further he would be trampling all over Hew's honor. Croy had been forced to kill Bikker, his teacher and the former bearer of Acidtongue, because of poorly chosen words. He had no desire to face Hew and Chillbrand just because he couldn't accept the place he'd been given.

Yet he couldn't back down. He'd fulfilled one sacred compact by getting Bethane to safety. Now he must continue with another. He thought of begging a horse and riding for Ness on his own, if he had to. Yet what would that accomplish? He would be slaughtered by the first band of barbarians he ran into. Dying that way would do Cythera's memory honor, but it wouldn't save her.

No. If he was going to rescue her, he needed the Skilfinger mercenaries. He needed an army.

"You, my friend, are a knight errant. And I," Sir Hew said, obviously choosing his words with great care, "am the Captain of the King's Guard."

An insult—and a piece of logic. Hew was giving Croy one last chance. He could choose to take umbrage with being called a knight errant, and challenge Hew to a duel then and there. Or he could accept the fact that Hew outranked him, and be relegated to the status of a lieutenant. And lieutenants didn't lay orders of battle.

Croy's hand was already on Ghostcutter's hilt. If he drew the sword even an inch from its scabbard, the choice would be made. He tightened his grip.

"What of the Queen's Guard?" Bethane asked, softly.

Hew and Croy turned as one to look at her. The Skilfingers, who could not know what was happening, looked at each other and shrugged. They filed out of the tent, clearly intending to let the knights of Skrae settle their own differences.

"Your Highness," Hew said, his brow furrowing. "It was your father's intention that I continue to serve in that post, as guardian of your self and your crown."

"My father is dead," Bethane pointed out. "I can choose my own protector. And if I base that choice on who has more experience guarding my life, my choice is clear."

Hew's face darkened with anger, or perhaps fear. "My queen, I may be forced to remind you that you have not yet come of age."

"That is true," Bethane said. She didn't look concerned.

"Until your eighteenth summer, when you attain your majority," Hew said, very carefully, "you do not, in any official capacity, rule Skrae."

"I know the law," Bethane said. Her face did not change.

"And thus, I am truly sorry to tell you, you cannot abnegate my rank or my posting," Hew finished, as if reciting the final element in a mathematical proof.

Bethane nodded agreeably. "All correct, Sir Hew. All quite correct. I cannot command you yet. However, is it not also true that in such a case, when the reigning monarch has not yet reached her majority, that the law requires the appointment of a regent? One of proper age and attainment who may rule in her name, and at her pleasure? I believe the law to be unclear as to who selects the regent. Traditionally it is the royal family, meeting in conference, who appoints to that role."

Sir Hew said nothing. He could only swallow meekly and stare at the girl. At his queen. Perhaps he was thinking the same thing as Croy. That he had never seen better evidence for the royal blood in Bethane's veins. She spoke not as a fourteen year old girl, but as a monarch. As a ruler.

"Seeing that I am the last surviving member of the royal family, at least as far as anyone knows—I find that I must appoint my own regent. So, Sir Hew, you remain Captain of the Queen's Guard. And you, Sir Croy, may approach me and kneel."

Croy did as he was told, though he nearly fell trying to get down on his knees.

"Be my voice, and my will, and in the Lady's name, serve always Skrae," Bethane said. "Do you swear to uphold the law and protect the people?"

"In the Lady's name, I do," Croy said.

"Then it is done. I give you all the powers of my crown, and all rights, ranks, privileges and titles thereby appended, for the remainder of my minority. Lord Croy, please stand, and be Regent of Skrae."

Croy rose stiffly. He turned and faced Hew, careful not to let a mocking smile cross his lips. That would be ungallant to a fault. "Please advise your mercenary knights," he said, keeping his tone formal, "that tomorrow we march for Ness, and the relief of the people there."

Such a difference one pronouncement could make. For the next four years, Croy would rule Skrae, with every power of a king. As far as the law was concerned, he *was* now the king of Skrae.

He allowed Hew a moment to wrap his mind around that. Then he raised one eyebrow, because the knight had failed to respond. He stared Hew down until his old friend bowed stiffly from the waist, and rose again.

"As you command," Sir Hew said, his face a wooden mask. "My liege."

CHAPTER NINETY-EIGHT

A single trebuchet stone arced over the city that day. It landed on Castle Hill in the ruins of a building already smashed to pieces and did no harm except to scare a few people. The day before no stone had come. Since the attack on the walls was repulsed, the barbarians seemed to place far less trust in their siege engines.

It was enough to create an illusion of peace and safety. Malden was glad for it, even if he knew how false it really was. The barbarians hadn't given up, not at all—they had simply moved their attention elsewhere. Slag had started work on his counter-tunnel, but had also reported that the sappers moving under the wall were craftier than he'd expected. They had dug a sort of maze down there, full of dead-end passages and parallel tunnels that they then filled up with refuse and tailings just to foil his attempt to find them. "Which means I know they're there, and they know I know they're there, and they know I know they know they're fucking down there. They'll put traps in the fake tunnels, just in case I think to break through on them in mid-dig. They'll have armed guards in the real tunnel to make me sorry I found it." The dwarf shook his head in dismay. "I haven't given up yet, lad. But you better have a good back-up plan, in case they beat me to the punch."

"What about your secret project?" Malden asked.

"If it's ready in time, aye, and if it actually works—mind, I make no promises—it'll be good for one big fucking surprise. One. It won't end anything, just buy us a little more time." He looked down at his hands. "I'm sorry. I know you were counting on me—"

"You've already been of better service than I could ask," Malden told him. "We'll survive this. I'm going to see

Cutbill. He's forgotten more dirty tricks than you or I will ever learn."

"He is a sneaky bastard. I wonder, though, if you can trust him much more than you can trust those giant pillocks outside."

"At this point every friend I have is precious," Malden said. He left the dwarf's reeking workshop and headed across the city toward the Chapterhouse. For once he took the streets, like an honest man. He wanted to make a point of showing himself to his people. If they saw him walking past their homes, safe and cheerful, it might help their morale.

He should have known better, though, because before he reached his destination, his own spirits were flagging. Everywhere he went he saw signs of religious mania. Every house now was decked with red ribbons, emblems of the blood sacrifice that Sadu demanded. Images of the eight-armed bloodgod were being erected in every square and inside every close—most of them crude idols made of bits of wood nailed together and hung with weapons and animal teeth. More than once he passed by an old woman or a crippled man with nasty scars on their arms or hands, worn proudly to show they'd made their own private contribution to the war effort—by shedding their own blood.

When he reached Cutbill's hidden office, he could only shake his head in grief. "The barbarians just have to hold out long enough for us to bleed ourselves dry," he said.

Cutbill let him in without a word. He had a folded piece of parchment in his hand and he kept looking at it as he poured Malden a cup of wine. Then the ex-guildmaster of thieves sank down into one of his chairs and placed a hand on his forehead.

He seemed uninterested in talking about what bothered him. Malden had never seen Cutbill so agitated, and that unnerved him more than he liked to admit. He tried to shake Cutbill out of his melancholy by sharing some news.

"There's been a change outside the walls—I can't say what it is, but they've completely altered their strategy. Where before they seemed happy to starve us out, or crush us all with rocks, now they plan on bringing down the wall."

"A change. Yes," Cutbill said. He glanced down at his paper again.

"Something bad, there?" Malden asked.

"A report from one of my spies," Cutbill admitted. "Mörg is dead."

"Mörg? The Great Chieftain? Why, that's the best thing I've heard today!"

"Hardly." Cutbill got up from his chair and started pacing. Eventually he threw the parchment on the fire and watched it burn.

"Hold a moment," Malden said, because something had occurred to him. "You have spies among the barbarians? And you never told me?"

"Not spies. Call them contacts. I had one. Now I have none."

Malden couldn't believe it. "Mörg worked for you?"

Cutbill shook his head. "No, Malden. He was a friend. A . . . colleague. He never betrayed his people or gave me anything you should have known. Nor did I give anything away in my messages to him. We were simply two men who respected each other's intellect. That's all."

Cutbill was the smartest man Malden had ever met. He found it hard to believe that a barbarian could be his equal in a match of brains. "You need to tell me everything, now. In plain detail. I don't like this."

The ex-guildmaster sighed deeply, but then he nodded. "I've spoken of how I built up my organization, before. But not of the time since then. When I had Ness under my control—half the public officials on my payroll, the other half terrified I would have them assassinated if they displeased me—I started wondering how to expand my horizons. I reached out to others like myself in other cities. Other criminals, first. The pirate queen of the Maw Archipelago, the Beggar Prophet of Ranmark, their like. At first they distrusted me, thinking I meant to supplant them. Eventually I convinced them we could aid each other from afar without competing. I sent my tendrils farther, as well, looking for thinkers sympathetic to my own philosophies, even honest folk. I found many among the dwarves, for instance, and among the Learned Brotherhood, and the College of Deans at the great university of Vijn. Eventually I found Mörg. A more perfect mind I have rarely encountered. And so desperate to achieve something with his legacy! Something more than conquest and bloodshed. He wanted to make his people stronger, Malden."

"Any stronger and they'll be able to punch through the wall with their bare fists."

Cutbill hissed in frustration. "He understood that the strength of a people is not in their arms or their steel. It's in their ability to work together, and of each man to make the right choices for himself without a sword at his neck telling him what to do. In many ways the nation he built out of the clans is more sophisticated, more equable, than ours will ever be."

Malden held his peace. He could tell Cutbill was grieving. A dozen jests rose to his tongue, but he kept them inside the cage of his teeth.

"Now that's lost. The nation he wanted to create couldn't survive his death—that was his great fear. That his children would not learn the lessons he wanted to teach. You've seen Mörget and Mörgain."

"I . . . have," Malden said.

"One of them will become the new Great Chieftain, it's almost certain. The strange peace you've felt, recently? This change in the bombardment? It will only last until they decide between themselves which it will be."

Malden swallowed painfully. He was pretty sure he knew already who would win that contest. Mörgain was a formidable woman, but Mörget had the heart of a wounded lion. "And when it is decided?" he asked.

"Then they will come at you like a hammer toward an anvil. Both of them are smart enough to know they must demonstrate their power if they want to keep it. They will crush Ness no matter what the cost. I believe you have at most two more days of this quiet, Malden. You had better be ready when it ends."

Malden forgot what he'd come to talk to Cutbill about, after that. He made an excuse—he was tired, he claimed, and needed to sleep—and took his leave. Once outside the hidden door of Cutbill's lair he leaned up against the cool stones of the Chapterhouse and tried to calm his raging thoughts. Eventually he could breathe again and his pulse stopped pounding in his temples. It was not the threat of a renewed attack that distressed him so, however, but one simple fact—

Cutbill had possessed a spy in the barbarian camp! And now that priceless resource was lost—without providing any useful information. Damn Cutbill! Damn him that he hadn't told Malden this earlier. How much could they have learned? Now he would never even know the name of this lost informant.

He turned to go. It was only then he noticed the mangy dog who had curled up next to the door, as if waiting for his master to come home. Malden frowned at the animal, wondering what it was doing there—Cutbill had never showed any interest in dogs, not as far as Malden knew.

He stooped to pet the creature, mindful of fleas, before he left. The dog arched his back and panted happily at the touch. It felt good to be kind to someone—even a beast—who wouldn't repay him with harsh words or dire imprecations.

CHAPTER NINETY-NINE

Malden wrapped a loaf of bread in a silken cloth—the loaf was the more precious commodity now than the silk—and headed down to the Isle of Horses, intending to thank Coruth. She had saved the city, or at least given it one more day of freedom, and he meant to honor what she'd done.

When he arrived at Eastpool, however, it was to find the water frozen over and all the boats hung upside down and covered in sailcloth for the winter. The only person he could find at the Stairs was an old woman who sat by a hole cut through the ice, a fishing pole in her hand.

"No way to get across now, Lord Mayor," she said, cackling. "Unless you choose to walk."

Malden stared out across the expanse of ice separating him from Coruth's island home. It thrummed and sang in the sunlight, while dark water bubbled up from underneath. It looked like it might crack open at any moment.

Malden steeled himself. "I'm quite light on my feet," he said.

When he took his first step onto the slick ice, though, he wondered if even he was nimble enough to get across. With each step the frozen pool shifted underneath him and icy water surged up around his leather shoes. He took it slowly, spreading his legs as much as possible so as to distribute his weight, but before long he heard the ice start to crack. Ahead of him a dark spot appeared as water flooded up from beneath to splash against the thinnest layer of rime, and then that thin ice collapsed into greasy shards.

"Blast," he said, and turned around to head back. He would have to wait for a colder day. He took a step back toward shore.

And under his foot, the ice cracked open, a jagged fissure opening up that spread across the surface of the ice with a noise like paper being torn.

Malden danced sideways, onto what appeared to be firmer ice—and felt it tilt beneath him, the near end submerging into cold water, the far end lifting up to glint in the sun. He started to slide down into the freezing pool and just managed to jump away before he fell, landing on a more solid floe.

It was a temporary reprieve at best. The islet of ice he'd found refuge on was surrounded by black water on every side. The sun burned down from a pitilessly clear sky and made new jagged cracks appear all around him.

The floe he stood on was not broad enough to hold his weight. A fraction of an inch at a time, it started to sink.

Malden knew how to swim, had in fact learned how in this very water. But he was certain that if he fell in now he would freeze long before he could swim to shore. The water would soak through his heavy cloak and the thick tunic underneath and bog him down. The cold would eat into his bones, make his muscles lock up—

Had he survived so many perils, lived through a barbarian invasion and a deadly siege, only to perish from sheer folly like this? He started cursing his fate.

He stopped, however, when he saw Cythera come out of Coruth's shack and walk through the snow down to the rocky shore of the Isle of Horses. She waved at him—no, she was simply raising her hands in the air. Her head tilted back and her eyes fluttered closed.

All around him the ice crackled and popped. Malden felt the floe he stood on tilt wildly as new ice pushed up all around it. The surface of Eastpool brightened as long crystals of ice snaked over its ripples, then joined together to form a path of solid ice from where Malden stood directly to the island. Malden did not waste time wondering at the miracle. Instead he dashed along the path, feet sliding crazily beneath him, until he could leap up onto the rocks near where Cythera stood.

Cythera opened her eyes. Instantly the ice behind Malden fell to pieces. She gasped, and looked like she might swoon. Malden got an arm around her waist to hold her up, and she sagged against his chest. She was burning up as if with fever, though he knew it was only the etheric energies she'd conjured, still flowing through her blood and bone. He helped her stagger back toward the shack.

Inside he handed her the wrapped loaf he'd brought. She stared at it numbly as if she couldn't imagine ever eating again. "This is too much," she said. "People are starving all over Ness, and you bring us a full loaf?" She stared at him. "This must be worth its weight in gold, right now. When was the last time you ate anything?"

"I had a handful of oats this morning," Malden said. "I'm fine. Anyway, your mother deserves a far greater reward than this."

"Mother . . ." Cythera pressed a hand against her cheek as if she felt faint. "Malden—you should come see her. Tell her that yourself."

"Gladly," Malden said, though there was something in

her tone that worried him. She led him into a room at the back of the shack, a room thick with heady smoke from braziers full of burning herbs. The medicinal smells covered up something more sickly, something foul that Malden didn't want to identify.

A massive canopy bed filled most of the room. Lying on its mattress was Coruth. Or what was left of her.

She looked tiny in the middle of all those blankets. It was strange. Malden had always thought of Coruth as enormous, a towering, looming figure who was always bigger than anyone she spoke to. Thinking back, though, he realized he had always been considerably taller than the witch and much broader through the shoulders. When he tried to understand why he'd always thought her so big, he could only think of his own mother. She'd been a slender woman, and not overly tall, but when he was an infant she had seemed a giant. Coruth must have had a similar effect on him.

Now sickness had wasted her body until she was a bare scrap of a thing. Her iron-colored hair was strewn across a pillow and her haughty face was slack with sleep. As he watched, horrified, he saw her turn over on her side and bring one hand up from beneath the sheets. The fingers of that hand had turned to twigs—actual wooden twigs, one of which sprouted a tiny shriveled leaf. Her arm looked more like the branch of a tree than like human flesh.

"Is she—?" Malden asked, unwilling to say the word 'dying' in her presence.

"Perhaps," Cythera told him. "It's also possible she'll just transform for a while. When my father imprisoned her, she turned herself into a rowan tree, do you remember?"

Malden nodded. It was how Coruth had appeared when he first met her.

"There is something about that form that allows her to heal." Cythera shook her head. "I'm starting to grasp the concept, but the details are still lost to me. The process of transformation is a simple matter of altering the weave of one's constituent atomies," she said, "but how that allows the body to accelerate its natural processes, well . . ."

Malden bit his lip. Cythera was a witch, now, just like her

mother. Such mysteries were open to her, if she went looking for the answers. To him they would always be obscure.

"This," Malden said, gesturing at the woman in the bed, "this is because she over-extended herself, am I right?"

Cythera nodded.

"She made an illusion, made it appear we had far more archers than we actually did," he said, thinking back to what he'd seen the previous night, up on the wall. "That wouldn't have consumed her so. But then she made the illusory arrows real. Real enough to kill."

Cythera looked away from him quickly. Malden frowned, wondering why she wouldn't meet his gaze. He had only been stating a matter of fact. "Did you . . . aid her in casting that spell?" he asked.

"It was a powerful operation," Cythera confirmed. "A conjuration even a sorcerer would find daunting. It would have destroyed me to even assist her. No—she had to do it herself. She nearly perished."

"She saved us all," Malden said. He sat down on the edge of the bed and placed a hand on Coruth's forehead. Her skin felt waxy and stiff. "The city thanks you. I thank you."

He nearly jumped off the bed when one of Coruth's eyes fluttered open. It stared right into him and he felt transfixed, as if her very gaze could pierce him like steel. She tried to whisper something, but he couldn't make out the words. Leaning close, his ear almost touching her mouth, he heard only a little.

". . . never too late. Through the heart. Her father . . ."

There were no more words. Coruth's eye closed again. When Malden sat up, he was shocked to see a tiny brown leaf attached to one greasy lock of iron-colored hair. The effort of speaking must have cost the old witch dearly. Clearly she had been desperate to get some message across.

Sadly, he could make no sense of it at all. Yet another mystery, one he had no time to decipher. He got up to leave. No point in disturbing her rest, now "Can you help me get back to shore?" he asked of Cythera.

The new witch nodded and led him back to the door of the shack. "Malden," she said, when they arrived at the ice.

"She knew this would happen. She knew it would take more than she had to aid you. She understood the necessity. I hope you do, as well."

Malden bowed his head. She was explaining why she couldn't be with him any longer. "I understand that fate plays dice with us all, and rarely do any of us get a natural throw." He shook his head. "I understand what your mother did, and what it cost her. Her sacrifice moves me in ways I cannot find words to express," he told her.

"That was her way," Cythera told him. "The witch's way. We go places other people do not dare, and take risks others cannot countenance, for the good of all. It's a noble calling, and one I'm proud to have accepted. She saw this would happen, and she made sure I was initiated before she exhausted herself—so that you would still have a witch on your side afterwards. I see that now."

Malden reached for her hand, but she thrust it under her shapeless cloak.

"You need to understand, though," she went on. "My witchcraft is still slight. I can effect some minor workings. I can harness a few natural energies better than others, but—I couldn't even begin to do what she did last night. I couldn't even have created the illusion. Don't count on me, Malden. Don't make plans that require powerful magics for success. I'll help you when and where I can, but it may not be enough."

"I'd rather have your love than all the sorcery in the books of Redweir. Maybe it's not too late," he said. "Maybe . . . maybe you can still give it up. Give up your witchcraft, and come be just a woman with me."

"Oh, if it were so simple," she said, very quietly. "But could you just be a man, with me?"

"When I'm with you," Malden said, "That's all I ever am. Your man."

She made no reply.

He opened his mouth to speak again, but she had already lifted her hands and tilted her head back. The ice began to firm up just off shore. Malden knew she couldn't hold it very long. Hardening his heart, he raced for the far side, for the Ditchside Stair and solid ground.

CHAPTER ONE HUNDRED

The Lemon Garden could no longer hold all the supplicants who wanted a piece of Malden's precious time—and some of the more devout citizens had begun to object to having to enter a whorehouse just to make their points heard. Malden took offense at that, but he knew better than to alienate his people by venting his personal feelings on them. So he took over the Moothall, a massive stone building in the Spires just off Market Square. Once the masters of every guild in the city had come there to discuss public policy. Now that the guildmasters were all gone, fled long before the barbarians arrived, it stood empty and its hearths cold.

Velmont built a fire in the enormous fireplace of the main meeting hall, while Malden walked around and around the long oak table, studying the coats of arms hung up by the rafters. The guilds those heraldic symbols belonged to had built Ness, and made it free, even more than had Juring Tarness—it had been the money they accumulated that had given Ness its power. Many, many times in its history the kings of Skrae had tried to tax the city, or to enslave its population despite its charter. Always they'd been bought off with tributes and fat bribes. Ness had bought its safety and its freedom, with money earned by hard work and shrewd dealings.

That was the official story, anyway. It ignored the fact that since the beginning of the guild system the actual workers—the laborers, the unskilled and the eternally apprenticed—had been exploited and ruthlessly kept down, all so the merchants who sat in this hall could squeeze out another farthing from their misery.

"I was downstairs in the cellar, earlier," Velmont said, when his fire was blazing cheerfully away and the room began to warm up. "They got some flash regalia down there. Guild symbols all in gold, and enow ermine and sable to make a menagerie."

Malden nodded. "They had a grand procession every year. They would trot out the symbols of their mysteries— ornamental tools, ceremonial robes and hats and the like. Basically a way to celebrate their own importance."

"I was just wonderin'," Velmont said, a sly look in his eye.

Malden sighed. He knew what Velmont was asking for. For the first time a stab of conscience struck him. The regalia down there was steeped in mystery and tradition—it was part of Ness' folk heritage, and now Velmont wanted to plunder it? How dare he?

Malden, once called Malden the Thief, could only laugh at himself. How far he had come. There had been a time when he would have tricked Velmont just so he could get first dibs at the stuff.

Now he could only think of how to use the regalia to firm his grasp on his people. "Get a team of thieves down here. Pick the ones who are the best archers, and the most loyal. Cart it all away, but be quiet about it." The thieves had begun to grumble again, now there was very little left in the city worth stealing. They were happy to serve Malden as Lord Mayor, they said, but if he was also going to be the guild-master of thieves, he needed to line their pockets. He could not afford to lose their favor, not when they still represented the best pool of able-bodied men under his command.

The whores, conversely, had never complained once. It seemed that they got what they truly wanted—recognition as full citizens, a little respect—just by being associated with him. He could count on Elody and Herwig and the other madams, at least.

Of the honest folk, who made up ninety percent of his constituents, he could be neither sure nor comfortable he knew how to appease them, and that worried him. If Cutbill was right and the siege was about to come to a head—and he had no reason to doubt it—then now was the time he had to solidify his power. Now was when he had to make common cause with his people, so when he asked them to fight—and die—for him, they would not hesitate.

For nearly a week he had refused to meet with any civic group, because he'd had more important things to worry about than their petty concerns. If they were starving, or terrified by the bombardment, or just desperate for recognition, he'd had no time for their feelings. Now that was starting to feel like a mistake. Perhaps they would not have turned so maniacally toward the bloodgod and supernatural aid if they had thought they had their Lord Mayor's ear.

He was in a mood to give them anything they wanted, that day. As long as it didn't mean losing the city in the process.

Velmont ran out just as the first supplicants of the day started filing in. Malden recognized them at once, though they'd changed their clothes. They were dressed in scarlet and crimson now, with even their leather dyed burgundy.

The self-ordained priests of the bloodgod. Perhaps the worst of his enemies, he thought. At least he knew where he stood with the barbarians.

There were three of them. Thin, wild-eyed men with shaggy hair and beards. He could barely tell them apart. Only one of them spoke, which meant Malden didn't need to remember three names.

"Hargrove, is it?" Malden asked, falling down into a chair at the head of the table. He threw one leg over the arm of the chair and studied his nails. "I'll ask you to be plain and not waste much of my time. I have a war to fight, you know."

Hargrove scowled and made a complicated gesture before his face. Most likely some exhortation to Sadu. "Milord, we have not come here to condemn you, nor to censure you. You are His chosen instrument in this world," he said. "That much has been made plain to us. Yet questions do remain."

Malden rolled his eyes. "Of what sort?"

"Lord Mayor, you've never shown any sign of true piety. At least not since you re-sanctified the Godstone. You don't come to our services. You've made no sacrifice since then. The people wish to know you believe as they do."

"The people would be better occupied helping me break this siege," Malden said.

"But that is exactly the point! The barbarians cannot be repelled by strength of arms. Not any such strength as we possess. Our only chance of turning them away is through divine assistance."

"Mmm. My mother was a good woman," Malden said.

Hargrove's face crawled all over itself. It was known everywhere, of course, that Malden's mother had been a whore. "May I inquire what that has to do with—"

"It was she who taught me about religion. About Sadu."

All three priests lowered their heads at the mention of the bloodgod's name. They clasped their hands together and said something quick and formulaic.

"At that time the bloodgod had no priests, nor any church in the city. Yet people still worshipped Him in their hearts. They kept that flame alive, no matter what the Burgraves did to try to snuff it out. My mother taught me that was all that was necessary. That we thank Him every day for the justice he brings to this world—the only kind of justice the impoverished will ever see."

"Things have changed," Hargrove said. "Now we have a better way to approach Him. A more effective method of beseeching His aid."

Malden nodded. He knew what this was really about. "A more visible, more—pragmatic way. A way to show our faith in public, and to share it with each other."

Hargrove actually smiled. "Exactly! A living church, for the first time in centuries. But that church cannot exist on private faith alone. If you were to make an appearance at one of our services, or—"

"Or if I were to grant you some kind of official commission?" Malden asked.

"Well, ah, that would be most useful in bringing the fire of belief to those not as—as firm in their faith, here in Ness."

"Very good. Let's see. The first time you came to me, you asked to be allowed to distribute the city's food supply."

"It was always the province of the church to do so, in olden days. Grain was gathered by the church in autumn, and portioned out over the winter by the priests. It was the only way to make sure the poor received enough to eat.

This tradition of charity kept Ness alive through many a hard winter."

"None so hard as this one," Malden said. "Well, far be it from me to stand in the way of charity and compassion." Or graft, he thought, or hoarding, or making sure the priests get to eat first, before all those less righteous people who come demanding a bit of bread to keep their families alive. "I'm of a mind to give you exactly what you want. In exchange, I wish only your blessing—and that you not question my piety any more."

"I can assure you," Hargrove said, bowing low, "such questions have fled altogether from our minds."

Malden saw the priests out of the moothall. He found Velmont standing by the door, having already rounded up enough thieves to clear out the cellars.

Malden waved the others on, toward the regalia in the cellars, but he grabbed Velmont's sleeve as the others filed cheerfully in. "How much of my audience did you hear?" he asked the Helstrovian thief. "Did you hear what the priests asked for?"

"I heard you givin' 'em what they hankered for this whole time, e'en after you turned 'em down before." Velmont looked confused.

"Ah, but back then there was an actual stock of food to be considered. How much is left now?"

"A mite," Velmont confessed. "A few days, if everyone sticks to one meal a day, and a paltry one at that. What kind o' fool gives up his last crust o' bread to folk that'd spit on his shadow?"

"The kind who doesn't want to be in charge of foodstuffs tomorrow. Tomorrow, when there is no more. When the bread runs out the starving people will have to ask the priests for food, not me. I'll be able to say I gave over responsibility for that to the most trustworthy men in Ness. Furthermore, there may be a few head of livestock still tucked away somewhere. How likely are the priests to waste those animals in sacrifices, if they know they'll have no other source of meat?"

Velmont laughed, long and loud. "Ye're getting' good at this, boss."

"I've had a good teacher," Malden told him. "Alright, send in the next beggar who wants something I can't afford to give away. I'm ready." He went back to perching himself on a carved wooden chair, one leg over its arm in a pose of carefully studied insouciance. The image he presented was half his power. Cutbill had taught him that, too.

CHAPTER ONE HUNDRED AND ONE

The wailing of Mörgain's female warriors set Mörget's teeth on edge. For six hours they had sat outside the dead Great Chieftain's tent, tearing their hair and howling at the sky. They followed an ancient custom that hadn't been practiced in a hundred years, making that horrible noise to drive away the hungry ghosts that might come and snatch Mörg's soul before Death could claim it. Some of them beat on tabrets, while others clashed swords together to add to the din.

Alone among them Mörgain was silent. She sat in the snow outside the blood-splashed tent, Fangbreaker naked across her knees. She kept her eyes closed—everyone knew you couldn't see the ghosts when they came, you had to hear them dragging their bloody feet along the ground—and the paint on her face had never looked more like a real skull.

"She thinks to sway the chieftains by this show of loyalty to a dead man," Mörget said, brooding in his tent. He got up frequently to peek through an opening in the flap and see if his sister had moved at all. She had not.

"She's trying to make you look bad," Balint agreed. "Stop letting the cold in, will you? I could cut my meat with these nipples already."

"You think she does this to shame me? I did nothing wrong. I acted on the will of the clans," Mörget insisted.

"You told me this ritual is never used for warriors who die in battle."

"No, of course not. Everyone knows Death comes directly for such. After all, she's already on the battlefield, walking with her children."

Balint sighed. "You easterners are so transparent, yet you always think your motives are so well hidden. What she's doing is as plain as your mother's face. Your sister's claiming you cheated Mörg out of a proper death, by slaughtering him when he wasn't ready for you. She's trying to ruin your chances of being chosen as the next Great Chieftain by insinuation." The dwarf shook her head. "You just don't understand women at all, do you?" She got up and put another knot of wood on the stove. It was one of the last pieces on the pile— fuel was getting scarce. If Mörget didn't take the city soon, frostbite would start mutilating the clans camped outside.

Mörget stared at his dwarven scold for a while. "Shouldn't you be digging a tunnel, right now?"

"I have a team of twenty of your best men doing it for me. They had nothing else to do."

Mörget's blood surged in his veins. He jumped up and grabbed Dawnbringer and his axe. "Damn you. And damn her. If she thinks she'll be chosen instead of me—"

"She has a chance at it," Balint interrupted. "Half the clans are loyal to her, and she'll have all the chieftains who remained loyal to Mörg."

Mörget narrowed his eyes. "Not if she's dead. They can't choose her if she's dead."

He did not like the look on Balint's face, then. It was far too smug. Was he really that predictable? He thought of what Mörg had said, right before he'd died. That Mörget was under the influence of a *wyrd*. Such a fate could drive a man headlong, like a horse wearing blinders, until his bloodlust took him right over a cliff.

It could also drive him to everlasting glory. Often at the same time. He stormed out of the tent and across the camp toward where his sister sat vigil. "Get up," he told her.

"Brother," she said, without opening her eyes. "I heard your feet dragging in the snow. Have you come to sit in my place, and protect our father's soul?"

"You know damned well I have not," Mörget told her. "It can wander the world forever, for all I care. Let him haunt me if he feels I acted wrongly. No real man would agree with him. I said, get up."

"I am quite comfortable. This snow is soft as any pillow in a westerner's bedchamber. And my grief keeps me warm."

Mörget growled. "You and I need to talk. Alone. If it comes to an election between us, the clans will never be properly united again, no matter who wins. We need to choose for ourselves."

"You mean, we two must choose you." She opened her eyes and stared up at him. Her pupils were two different sizes. He realized she must have been drinking black mead until she could feel nothing at all. Yet her voice had none of the manic pitch associated with the delirium-inducing drink. "I am not done yet with my vigil. Nor is this the place to talk. Do you know the place a mile from here, where a gallows stands at the crossing of two roads?"

"We tore the gallows down for firewood a week ago," Mörget told her.

She watched him without blinking.

"Yes, I know the place," he told her.

"I will meet you there in three hours," she said.

Mörget looked for the sun. It was already low in the sky, a bright patch behind roiling clouds. The time she'd chosen would be well after dark. Perfect.

He turned and left without another word. Then he went to the blacksmith's tent, and had a new edge put on his sword.

When the time Mörgain chose for the meeting came, he was at the place she'd named, ready for anything. Perhaps she thought to ambush him with her cadre of woman warriors. Perhaps she wanted only to talk, as she'd suggested. Regardless, he intended to bury her there, and say she had run off because she knew she could not bear losing to him.

Yet when she came, he did not see her arrive. Nor did

she reveal herself so he could strike her down. He only heard her voice, carried along by the wind.

"Brother," she called. "I would know—what did he say to you, before you slew him? Or did you strike fast, so as not to give him a chance to defend himself?"

Mörget turned around slowly, looking for her. If she wanted to kill him, she'd picked the right place. He could see no further than the blade in his hand by the little moonlight that cut its way through the clouds. The wind made it impossible to tell what direction her voice came from. There was even a good hiding place, a cluster of rocks at the exact intersection of the crossroads.

He faced the rocks and lied to her. "He said I should be the next Great Chieftain. And that I should think of some great reward for you, as compensation."

Mörgain laughed, a noise like funeral bells chiming.

"I know what he said to you," Mörget announced. He took a slow step toward the rocks. Was that hiding place too obvious? "He said he loved you." He put as much scorn in his voice as he could muster. "What did you make of that?"

"I thought to slay him myself for the affront. And to steal your glory."

"You didn't, though," Mörget said. Another step closer.

"In the end I decided to do him honor, in a way he would understand. So I swallowed my bile and told him I loved him, too. It was what he wanted to hear."

Mörget grinned wickedly. "It is good for a woman to think of what a man wants, and give it to him."

Mörgain laughed again. "Let us speak of what you'll give me, in exchange for my chieftains. A great reward, you said."

"Yes," Mörget replied. "What will you have? You asked me for dwarven steel, once. And gold."

"I can have those things now for the effort of stooping to pick them up," she told him. "You'll have to do better."

Where was she? He was close enough to see the rocks as more than shadows, now, and to realize they weren't rocks at all. They were tombstones. None of them bore names or dates, but they had the round-topped shape of western grave markers. He recalled that in Skrae suicides and traitors were buried at the crossroads so their ghosts could not find their way back to haunt the living. Another subtle message, Mörget thought, that Balint would make much of.

"I have another gift I can give you. I can give you all of the east. The land where we were born. Be great chieftess there, while I rule Skrae."

That was enough to shut Mörgain's mouth. Mörget cursed silently. He had hoped to shock her into showing herself.

"That land is not yours to give. It belongs to the chieftains."

"You think they will gainsay me?"

"No," she said. "They would never dare. They are afraid of you. But I *know* you, brother. You would never give up so much power."

"Unless I know I cannot hold it. When this war is won, when Ness is taken and Skrae belongs to us, the clans will be spread too thin. No one man—or woman—could rule it all. I'll share it with you—if you bow to me now."

That made her laugh.

Was she hiding behind the tombstones? Mörget knew if he stepped in between them, she would have him at a disadvantage. He would be too aware of the danger of tripping over one of the stones to be sure of his footing. Interesting.

"So you do not want power. Then tell me yourself! What do you want? In exchange for not opposing my candidacy as Great Chieftain, what will you take?"

He struck Dawnbringer across the top of a gravestone, a ringing blow with the flat. The blade lit up as if it were white hot, light searing through the darkness for a moment. It was enough to show him that Mörgain was nowhere among the stones.

Then she answered him, her voice coming from close by. Even before she'd finished talking he felt her presence. She'd been behind him the whole time, throwing her voice on the wind.

"Vengeance for the only man I ever loved," she said. He had time to see she'd darkened her furs and face with soot to make herself nearly invisible in the dark. Then Fangbreaker came up and glinted in the paltry light, distracting him.

By Mother Death she was fast with that blade.

Before Mörget could even raise Dawnbringer, she slashed a line across his throat. Blood spewed from the wound, dark venous blood, and he knew she'd cut his jugular.

It was a hasty stroke and the sword failed to bite very deep—yet it was placed perfectly, and any other man would have fallen on the spot. Mörget was not just any man, however. Surprised, hurt, even with Mother Death's hand on his shoulder he still had the strength to bring his axe down with one of the mightiest blows he'd ever struck.

The weight of the axe drove down hard, and bit through old iron. Mörget's bones rattled but he did not flinch.

For the third time, he cut right through one of the Ancient Blades, and sent half of Fangbreaker's forte spinning into the snow.

He turned, intending to stab Mörgain through the heart with Dawnbringer.

But she was already gone. As fleet of foot as a deer, was Mörgain.

"Coward!" he called after her, his voice full of bubbles.

Once that word would have burned her heart and forced her to turn back and finish the fight. But he knew she had no need to prove herself to him now. Not when he was going to die in a few seconds. He found the broken piece of Fangbreaker lying at his feet. In its polished surface he could see the wound across the front of his neck and the blood that was pouring down his cloak. He was bleeding to death.

He dropped to his knees in the snow.

You will not be able to stop yourself, Mörg had told him. *You are too weak to defeat your own strength. Someone else must stop you, and you should hope they do it soon.*

His own strength—strength Mörgain shared. So this was what the old man meant, he thought. This is my ending. I found the foe I could not beat, and she was there all along. His *wyrd* was complete.

So why did he still seethe for more death, for another chance to prove himself?

"You're a mess, boy," Balint said, hurrying out of the darkness. She had a piece of cloth in her hands, and a needle, and some thread. He had not known she'd followed him. Now he stared at her as if she were a ghost come for his soul.

"Don't try to thank me," she told him. "If you do, your head will probably fall off, and while even that probably wouldn't kill someone as stubborn as you, I don't carry enough thread to go all the way round." Then she started mopping at his wound and digging her needle into his flesh. "Don't ask me why I'm doing this, either, because it's pure folly. I'd be leagues better off without you."

But Mörget thought he knew. The dwarf had her own *wyrd*, didn't she? She needed to make mischief in this world, wherever she could. It was what she lived for. And he would give her every chance to do it.

He started to laugh, and didn't care that it made dark blood jet outward from his veins.

CHAPTER ONE HUNDRED AND TWO

"Come forth! Step up, and receive Sadu's bounty! Food for all, a feast from your God. See the miracle He has wrought!" The red-dyed priest handing out loaves of bread in Godstone Square was not one that Malden recognized. The bloodgod's ministers had been ordaining more of their kind every day. They'd been busy in other ways, too. They had established formal churches in many districts of Ness, and clearly they'd been baking night and day to prepare for this. After Malden had turned over the last paltry stores of grain, the priests had announced a city-wide prayer fast. He'd thought they wanted to hoard the remaining food for themselves. He had put up with the complaints, and with the pangs of his own belly, because he thought he had given the priests just enough rope to tie their own nooses.

Now, however, he could not be sure.

The priest stood on a wooden platform, as high as a gibbet. Behind him, stacked neatly in enormous wicker baskets, were hundreds of loaves of bread, enormous crocks of pottage, and dozens of meat pies. Meat! Where had they gotten meat?

There could only be one answer, of course. The priests must have been hiding an entire herd of animals somewhere, a herd of livestock they must have been saving for their sacrifices. Now it seemed they thought food more important than the ritual shedding of blood.

He knew them too well to think they would just stop making sacrifices. They must have some other source of blood hidden, as well. Or maybe they were just preparing for their first human sacrifice.

"Come forth! Food for all! Sadu heard your prayers, He knew your hunger, and He has provided. A loaf for every man, pottage for every family!" The starving people of Ness jostled and pushed each other trying to get closer to the bounty. Acolytes in tunics stained pink handed out the loaves, each time saying a little prayer over the bread before they let it go. "Enough for all! None of us are forgotten in His mercy!"

Malden turned to speak to Velmont, but the Helstrovian thief had slipped away. Malden scanned the crowd and found Velmont bowing his head over a pie, while an acolyte whispered in his ear. If he was praying, it was an especially long and fervent prayer he shared with Velmont.

The Helstrovian thief finished with a nod and a sly gesture, then came running back to Malden's side. He already had the inedible crust off the top of the pie and was picking out morsels from inside with his fingers. The look on his face was one of sheer ecstasy. How long had it been since Velmont tasted meat? Malden wondered when the last time he'd had any flesh himself had been. He'd made a point of taking no larger a ration of food than he allotted to any of his citizens.

He found himself licking his lips as Velmont sucked and

chewed at each dainty in turn. "Blind me, it's fresh piglet," the Helstrovian said, tears in his eyes.

Malden fought off the urge to run up to the platform himself. "What did that acolyte say to you? Did you learn anything?"

Velmont blushed, but he didn't stop eating. "Nothin' you'll want to hear, boss. I asked him if this was a one-off, you know, did they have more where this bunch came from. He just told me his god would provide, like, which is what priests always say, ain't it?" Velmont looked away.

"That's all he said?" It looked like they'd shared far more words than that.

"That," Velmont said, shrugging, "and a lotta holy babble I ne'er really heard. When the stink of this meat hit me nostrils, I was a trace distracted."

Malden nodded. He had an uneasy feeling about this. He was almost completely sure that there was no supernatural element at work here. The priests had simply used up every last bit of food in the city for one big banquet, and when these pies and loaves were gone, there would be nothing left. They had bought themselves a day's grace, but in the end it would hurt them, still.

Funny how he wanted them to fail. He was willing to let people starve, if it meant the priests suffered in consequence. A pang of guilt stabbed through him, driving away his own hunger. Had he come to that point where he started thinking of people as tokens on a game board, as Cutbill said he must?

He'd never wanted that.

He'd never wanted any of this. Not the title, not the responsibilities. Certainly not the duty. Duty was Croy's province.

"Come on," he said. "We need to go check in on Slag. You can eat while you climb." He led Velmont up the side of a house and then across the rooftops, jumping nimbly across the narrow streets, climbing cold chimney pots to scout out his next leap. He still had the rooftops. He could still travel across his city, near as free as a bird. They hadn't taken that from him.

"What's the mood of the city?" he asked, as he paused

atop a steeple in the Spires. His vantage point was near the top of the arsenal. Ahead of him lay the university cloister. Slag had set up a new workshop in its courtyard, claiming he needed thick stone walls around him for some reason. The cloister was abandoned—the university's students, young, strong, and idealistic, had been among the first to join the Burgrave's Army of Free Men.

"The fear's been ebbin' away, since the bastards stopped throwin' stones," Velmont told him. "And the priests've been makin' merry, spreadin' cheer. There's been some grumblin', mostly about food. That'll be quieted today."

Malden grunted assent. Tomorrow would be a different story, when the food ran out—but for today at least his position was secure. He'd been given a little room to breathe in. If Cutbill was right, it wouldn't last. As soon as Mörget and Mörgain settled their differences and elected a new Great Chieftain, the siege would turn bloody. And still the sappers progressed inch by inch under the city's walls, and still Slag could not find a way to stop them.

If he had been given a moment to think, he needed to use it. He needed to plan, and prepare, and make ready. He needed to—

Down in the University Cloister, the bloodgod's pit opened up, and a ball of hellfire burst through into the mundane world.

Orange flames shot through with purple sparks leapt toward the sky and a wave of smoke and force blasted past Malden, knocking him off his feet. He just managed to grab onto a gargoyle with one hand. Velmont went skidding past him, and in a frozen moment Malden watched the Helstrovian's face open in a gaping parody of surprise, as the remains of his pie floated around his hands and chest.

It was a fifty foot drop to the street. If Velmont fell he would be shattered like a porcelain doll. Malden grabbed at the man with his free hand and missed. Then he felt a heavy weight jerk him downwards, and his grip loosened on the gargoyle. For one sickening moment he was falling, and death rushed toward him.

Somehow he managed to catch a carved balcony railing

on the way down. With both hands he clung on for life. Smoke boiled around him, and debris pattered down on his head and back, some of it big enough and falling hard enough to knock the breath out of him. He nearly fell again.

When he could see—if not breathe—he looked down and saw Velmont clutching fast to the glass-lined scabbard of Acidtongue. The Helstrovian was pulling him down, and Malden considered kicking Velmont away, kicking him to his death.

No. He was better than that. Using every ounce of strength he possessed, he got one elbow over the balcony, then pulled his chest over the stone. That freed up his hands enough that he could reach down and help Velmont clamber up beside him.

Neither of them could talk. They could do nothing but cough and wheeze. Malden broke through the stained glass window that opened on the balcony, and threw himself inside, away from the falling detritus.

He found himself inside the arsenal, on a gallery over-looking racks of old polearms and crossbows whose strings had rotted away. Down on the ground level a dozen workers had been busily polishing and scraping rust off old iron blades. They stared up at him now as if he was a demon come to claim their souls.

There was no time to reassure them. Once he had a good clean breath in his lungs, he grabbed Velmont's arm and hurried him down a flight of stairs to the level of the street. Outside the cobbles were thick with dust and ash. He raced toward the university, just as a second blast rocked the entire city on its foundation.

One whole wall of the cloister had come down. Inside, in the courtyard, he saw nothing but fire and destruction. "Slag!" he called. "Anyone alive in there! Call out if you hear me!"

The smoke was so thick it made him gag on his own words. It stank of rotten eggs and brimstone—the breath of Sadu Himself.

"Lad," he heard someone call. The voice was weak and distant, and he realized he could barely hear anything other than his own heartbeat. The noise of the explosion must have partially deafened him.

He raced toward the voice and found Slag buried under broken stone, only part of the dwarf's face and one arm visible. He grabbed Velmont's arm and pointed and together they began clearing the rubble away. When Slag was mostly clear, Malden pulled at his body to get him out of the wreckage.

The dwarf's left arm came off at the shoulder as he came free. It had been hanging on only by a shred of skin and then it was gone. The rest of Slag wasn't in much better shape. Malden cradled the small, skinny body in his arms, certain the dwarf would die at any moment. Slag's face was scorched and his beard was burnt away. His eyes were yellow and red and gelatinous tears clung to what remained of his eyelashes. Blood slicked down the entire left side of his body.

"Lad," the dwarf croaked, "I finally got the ratios right. Fucking . . . right. It works! It works! It will fucking serve!"

And then the dwarf started laughing, laughing for joy.

CHAPTER ONE HUNDRED AND THREE

Croy rode at the head of an army of two thousand men, of which only one in a hundred could understand his orders. It did not matter. The Skilfingers had provided excellent translators. They were used to this arrangement.

The northern kingdoms were perpetually at war with one another, their borders shifting back and forth a few miles every year. The territories changed hands so fast the cartographers could not keep up, and a map of the northern kingdoms could only show shaded areas where each kingdom's power was the strongest. Yet the wars had gone on so long these combats had become formalized and played out by very strict rules, and so any given kingdom was fighting only a month out of any year. The cost of keeping, paying, and feeding standing armies was extraordinary, and the Skilfingers defrayed the expense by hiring out their soldiers as mercenaries to any nation that required them.

That meant the Skilfinger warriors behind Croy were well-trained, well-disciplined, and carried the best arms available anywhere on the continent. Croy had no doubt they would be a match for an equal number of barbarians.

The best estimate he had, though, was that eight thousand barbarians had surrounded Ness, forming an enormous camp all around the city. Among them were perhaps seven hundred berserkers—and even a heavily-armored Skilfinger knight would have trouble standing against those mad warriors.

Sir Hew had been correct. He had been wise to think Helstrow the better choice for demonstrating their new-found power. What could be accomplished by attacking Ness was an open question.

Croy did not care.

Cythera was in danger, and that was all that mattered.

Hew had given him no trouble at all. Croy was the regent now, and for all intents and purposes he would be the king of Skrae for the next four years. Hew obeyed his every command without question. If the look on Hew's face sometimes betrayed his true feelings, Croy could learn not to meet the knight's eyes. Bethane, however, had proved less pliant. She had insisted on going with Croy when he marched toward Ness.

"It isn't safe," he'd told her.

"The only place I am safe is near you," she'd said.

He had stood firm. As regent, he could command even her, though he was required by law to couch his orders in terms of perfect courtesy and protocol. He sent her north with an honor guard of ten Skilfinger knights. She would winter in Skilfing Town—the capital of Skilfing—as a pampered guest of the king and his court there. Come spring, it remained to be seen where she would go. Or even if there was a place for her to go.

Croy and Hew marched southwest toward Ness, giving Helstrow a wide berth but otherwise taking the most direct route. It was slow going. They had plenty of horses for themselves and the Skilfinger knights, but that was only one tenth of their contingent. The rest were foot, retainers of the knights. Footmen could only march twenty miles a day. Less, sometimes much less, when they had to march through heavy snow. There was a reason armies did not move much during the winter. Croy pressed them for twenty-five miles a day whenever possible, knowing full well that would leave them exhausted and less effective when they arrived.

He called very few stops. Hew advised him over and over that he must give the men a day of rest or they would be in no shape to fight, yet still he pressed on. When he was only fifty miles from Ness, though, only two days' march away, he ordered the column to stop atop a barren hill overlooking wasted farmland.

He had heard a sound of distant thunder that rolled along the hills. In the distance, he saw a column of smoke splitting the sky in half.

"It could be anything," Hew told him, his voice for once sympathetic.

"It's Ness."

Hew sighed. "The barbarians could have put a village to the torch. It's impossible to say how far away that smoke is—it could be right down the road. It could be nothing. Perhaps they set fire to the manor house at Middleholt."

Croy watched the smoke rise into a perfectly placid sky.

"It's Ness," he said, again.

The whole city could be burning. The barbarians might have taken it, and razed it to the ground. Cythera could be dead, she could be—she could be—

He closed his eyes for a moment only, and prayed. He begged the Lady to let him see Cythera once more. If only for a moment before he died.

Then he opened his eyes again.

"There will be no day of rest," he announced.

Sir Hew did not argue. The translators called out the order to the captains, who relayed it to their serjeants, who passed it on to the men in words they could understand. There was probably a great deal of grumbling back there but Croy didn't have to listen to it. That was one advantage of being the man in charge.

"March, double time," Croy said.

Behind him, drums began to beat, and a fife made a good attempt at playing a rambunctious tune.

CHAPTER ONE HUNDRED AND FOUR

Mörget raced back into the camp, Balint at his heels, clucking at him not to exert himself and re-open his wound.

He had never felt healthier nor more vigorous in his life. He clutched in one hand the severed shard of Fangbreaker. In the other he held Dawnbringer, the blade naked and whole. A symbol, if one was even needed, that he was the stronger leader.

He would slay Mörgain in front of every warrior in the horde—after all, she had started their duel, and no man would stop him from finishing it—and then he would have no rivals. No one to challenge his supremacy.

Yet when he arrived at the camp, it was to find a third of the tents already taken down and packed away. Everywhere barbarians were on the move, bundled in thick furs as if they planned a long journey through the snow.

Hurlind lay drunk in the aisle between the encampments of two clans. The worthless scold stared up at Mörget with a bleary eye. Dried mead formed a crust around his mouth. "Hail the returning hero," he slurred, and pushed himself up on one elbow. "Survivor of a great ordeal. It's not every man who can take a spanking from his little sister, and hold his head high."

Mörget gave the old man a savage kick to the ribs. "You're no favorite of the Great Chieftain anymore. Just another warrior, barely able to lift a blade. If you can fight, then stand. If not, I'll take you on as my thrall." Mörget wanted nothing more than to slaughter the scold where he lay. But the law was clear—scolds, even the scolds of dead chieftains, could not be killed for words. Only for treachery or for boring their audience.

Balint bent over the old man and stared into his face. "Where is Mörget's sister? My master has unfinished business with her."

"She's there," Hurlind said, gesturing vaguely toward the center of the camp. "Gathering her warriors. She said you were dead, Mountainslayer."

Mörget kicked Hurlind again and hurried through the maze of tents. Even as he watched more of them came down. Their poles were separated into pieces, their hides shaken wildly to clear off accumulated ice, then folded and shoved into packs.

Mörget grabbed the first man he saw and threw him into the snow. "Put that tent back up," he commanded. The warrior just glared at him.

Enough. They would all obey him when he was named Great Chieftain. They would learn to fear him, one and all. He raced toward the thickest knot of activity, where horses were being loaded with gear and axes were being wiped down with animal fat to keep off the rust.

Mörget shoved his way through the milling warriors and thralls until he spied Mörgain sitting her horse in the very midst of the chaos.

She laughed bitterly to see him. "I like your new neck-lace," she said, pointing at the coarse thread that held his throat together. Balint had been an indifferent seamstress, though she had saved Mörget's life. "Perhaps I'll give you a matching belt, after I cut you in half."

"That might prove difficult, with a broken sword." Mörget held up the shard of Fangbreaker until it blazed in the sun.

For a moment all the activity in the camp stopped. Men dropped their burdens, tents remained erect as their owners leaned on their poles.

Everyone wanted to see what happened next.

Mörgain's horse whickered, perhaps sensing that anything—anything at all—could happen in the next moment. Mörgain patted the animal's neck.

Mörget lifted Dawnbringer and struck its blade against the shard of metal in his hand. Light burst from his Ancient Blade, light brighter than the reflection of the sun. "I would continue our conversation," he said.

The swordsmen of the west used the word conversation to describe the ringing back-and-forth of two blades engaged in combat. Every man listening got the joke. A few even chuckled.

Mörgain drew what remained of Fangbreaker. Though it was much shorter than Dawnbringer now, it was still broader and heavier. It looked more like a meat cleaver than a sword. But it was still more than capable of killing a man.

Especially one who had been mortally wounded the night before, and saved only by the ministrations of a clever dwarf.

Mörget took a step toward his sister. *If this is how it ends, let it end*, he thought. *Let her slay me, and I will accept my* wyrd *has run its course.*

Yet it seemed his doom had farther to take him.

With a look of supreme disgust, Mörgain put her broken sword back in its sheath. "Nothing would give me greater pleasure, brother. Yet I haven't the time. My clans have spoken. We head east, to winter in Helstrow. Where we should have been all along. That was the wish of the Great Chieftain, after all, until you tricked him into coming here for no profit."

"The Great Chieftain is dead," Mörget pointed out. "His wishes—"

"His wishes remain our course, because he has not been replaced. No man unites the clans now. No man speaks for us all."

"Call a conclave. Bring every chieftain forward. We will elect a new Great Chieftain here, and now."

There was a great cheering and acclaim from the gathered

warriors—yet it was not unanimous. More than a few of the chieftains only stood tight-lipped and glaring.

"I think not," Mörgain said. Her skull-painted face cracked in a wide grin. "You forget, my brother, that I am a chieftain myself. And a conclave cannot be called unless every chieftain agrees to attend. I refuse."

A chorus of hissing and calls of cowardice fell on Mörgain like a salvo of arrows—but not every man joined in. She turned and gestured at her thralls. They sluggishly returned to their work, breaking down tents and packing horses. They were making ready to leave at once.

And there was nothing Mörget could do to stop them.

Ah, but there was one thing. He could officially challenge her. He could name her a coward. He could call on his own chieftains to fight Mörgain and her clans. He could make war on her.

Civil war—while the Army of Free Men camped not thirty miles away, and Ness stood looming over them, unconquered. Mörg the Wise would have had a good laugh at the very idea. It would take a leader of surpassing folly to even consider it.

Mörget's *wyrd* thought it was exactly what he should do.

His sister looked down at him, waiting to see which way the wind would blow. She was ready come what may.

Mörget burned, his heart and his head already coming to blows inside him.

"You're a fool if you don't put that sword away," Balint whispered up at him. "No man leads a nation with his cock hanging out of his trousers."

She was right. Reason could make only one choice, and even bloodlust must bow to reason some of the time.

Mörget smiled down at Balint. Then he put Dawnbringer in its scabbard. He held on to the shard of Fangbreaker. It was his last badge of glory, the one thing Mörgain couldn't take from him.

"How many clans ride with my sister?" he shouted.

Nearly a third of the chieftains gathered before Ness gave their names. Two thousand warriors and thralls would march with them.

That still left plenty of men loyal to Mörget. Far more than he needed to take the Free City. "When I'm done here, I'll come for each of you. I won't rest until you pay for this betrayal," he said.

"You know where to find them. Come to Helstrow and we'll be waiting. That is, if you live through the winter," Mörgain said. Then she spurred her horse and rode off.

"Go," Mörget said, to the faithless chieftains who followed her. "Go hide from snow and wind behind a high wall, you cowards." He watched and shouted abuse until the last man had taken to his heels, heading east along the road. Then he turned his face away from them and started for where Hurlind lay in the snow.

His rage demanded bloodshed. If he could not avenge himself on his sister, he would turn instead on the last of his father's faithful retainers. He would kick Hurlind until he was given lawful provocation—and then he would carve the old man like a goose.

Before he could reach the scold, though, a peal of thunder rocked the earth and Mörget was thrown into the snow. Balint lay next to him, struggling to get up.

He looked at the walls of the city and saw a great pillar of smoke rising toward heaven. "What in the name of Mother Death just happened?" he demanded.

The dwarf looked where he pointed. "Perhaps they've decided if they can't hold their city, they'd rather burn it down."

"If I take Ness, only to find it a burned-out husk," he said to her, softly, "they will write songs about my folly. And I will never become Great Chieftain. You get that wall down."

"Work's going on apace, but you can't hurry a shit or a siege," Balint insisted.

"You can," he told her, "when the option is having your belly slit and being dragged behind a horse by your bowels." He grabbed her collar. The spikes dug into his hand until it bled. "You bring it down on the morrow. Use every man in this camp, force on them every pick, every shovel. Dig with your broken fingernails if you must. You bring that wall down before one more chieftain decides to follow my sister. Do it or I will use your defleshed skull as a codpiece."

The vulgarity of his oath seemed to get her attention. She ran toward the mouth of the tunnels, faster than he'd ever seen a dwarf move before.

CHAPTER ONE HUNDRED AND FIVE

Malden ordered Velmont to search for other survivors in the university cloister and organize teams of bucket-bearers to put out the fire. He picked Slag up in his arms and carried him away from the rubble. The dwarf's body was no great burden—dwarves were slender creatures to start with, and now, missing an arm, burned over so much of his body, Slag felt as light as a child.

The dwarf spoke no more as Malden staggered through the snow-clogged streets. Before they had gotten properly out of reach of the dizzying fumes of the fire, Slag had fallen unconscious in Malden's arms. It was quite likely he was already dead.

Malden did not have the heart to find out for sure.

He did not know how far he walked, carrying that slight burden. He was not aware of where he was, exactly, when Cythera found him. He heard her speaking, and saw her mouth move, but her words entered his brain and got lost there in the same maze that had confounded his own thoughts. He realized suddenly that she was trying to take Slag away from him. He resisted her, though he could not have said why.

Cythera gestured for him to follow her. She went to the door of the nearest house, the mansion of some great merchant. The door was boarded over but all the windows on the second floor had been smashed in—probably by thieves, back when there was still something to be looted in the Golden Slope. Malden started to climb up the side of the house but couldn't get far with Slag in his arms. Cythera shook her head. Then she lifted a hand and the boards across the door creaked and their nails glowed red hot, then dripped like candle wax. The boards clattered into the street.

Her witchcraft was weak, she had said. Her powers still untested. He wondered what marvels she would perform, when she had learned some more.

Inside the house was cold and empty and silent. They went into the kitchen and Cythera convinced Malden to lay Slag down on an oak table there. She pointed at the fire and a small flame leapt forth from the cold ashes. "Get fuel, or it'll go out again," she told him. She had to repeat the instruction three times.

Malden went and fetched the boards from where they lay in the street. He fed them to the fire. When they didn't catch right away, he found an expensive-looking chair in the front room and smashed it for kindling.

By the time he had the fire going properly, Cythera was already at work on Slag's broken body. She washed the soot and blood away from his many wounds and for the first time Malden saw just how badly Slag had been hurt. He had to look away. He couldn't breathe.

"It's . . . it's bad," Cythera told him. Her voice was thin and ready to break. "He lives, but his heart is fluttering like a bird in a snare. He has perhaps a few minutes left. He'll stop breathing soon, and then he'll convulse, and eventually he'll just . . . stop. Ah. Oh, Malden. It's happening. He's dying."

"Please. He's my friend. There must be something you can do. Maybe—maybe just make him comfortable. Take away his pain."

Cythera stared at Malden with desperate eyes. He didn't understand—she was wasting time, time Slag didn't have.

"You're a witch now. That has to count for something," he begged.

"It counts for a great deal. And it's why I can't—"

"Stop this! I can see in your eyes that you have the

power," he said. "Don't you care about Slag? How can you look at him like this and not help him?"

"I'm supposed to stay detached," Cythera said, but it sounded like she was trying to convince herself.

Malden had no idea what her words meant. He didn't care. "Don't you love me anymore? Do this for me, Cythera. Save him because you love me!"

"You have no idea what you're asking."

Her words were defiant but he knew he'd moved her. She would do it, he was sure of it. He opened his mouth, intending to renew his entreaties, but something in her countenance warned him not to speak. Eventually she broke his gaze.

"This is it. The moment mother foresaw, when I break my promise to her," she said. The words were not for Malden, so he did not question them. "I thought it would be easier to resist. But some temptations are bigger than us, aren't they?"

"Cythera," Malden moaned. "He's dying."

"Yes," she said. "Even Coruth couldn't save him now."

But then she began to incant, speaking words that didn't sound human at all. Malden smelled a sudden reek of brimstone, and red light played across the walls. He felt something move in the room behind him and he turned to look, expecting—well, he didn't know what to expect. There was nothing there, of course. He started to turn back to face Cythera and Slag but the air felt like it had frozen solid and he could barely move.

"Don't look at me," Cythera commanded, and he might as well have been made of marble. His neck wouldn't turn at all. He could only stare at the red-lit walls, and wonder what was going on.

"Cythera—" he tried, but she interrupted him.

"I'm going to save his life. But there will be a price to be paid."

"Anything," Malden told her. "Do you need gold? Rare medicinal herbs? The powder of crushed diamonds? Tell me and it'll be done."

"It's not your price to pay," she said, in a voice that was almost gentle. "Malden—is it wrong to heal? Is it ever wrong to heal?"

"I don't think so," he told her. "What is the price?"

She wouldn't answer his question.

"I can do it," she said. "I can."

She worked for nearly an hour. Malden stayed frozen in place the whole time. He heard . . . things, unguessable, unspeakable things moving about the room. He heard them whisper utter foulness to Cythera.

He heard her answer them back in kind.

As impossible as it seemed, as terrified as he was Malden started to drift off into a kind of doze before it was done. Yet when she finished, he snapped instantly awake and he realized he could move again. He spun around and found her slouched over the table, leaning close over Slag's body as if she was praying over the dwarf. Her back heaved as if she'd been drained completely of her vigor by the working.

"I had to call on certain . . . spirits. Creatures that haunt the ether, always looking to enter our world, to find any way out of their prison. It is forbidden to open a way for them." She was silent for a while. He heard her gasping for breath.

"Did you let them in?" Malden asked. He didn't care if she had, though he had begun to understand what she'd done. If there had been anything less than Slag's life at stake, it would have been unforgivable. The spirits she spoke of were demons, he was certain. Denizens of Sadu's pit of souls. The creatures Croy was oath-bound to fight against. The demons Acidtongue had been made to slay.

"No," she said, though it sounded like she wasn't entirely sure. "I needed their knowledge, not their physical forms. I was able to convince them to tell me what I needed to know without freeing them."

"Then you did the right thing," Malden assured her.

"It was difficult. The dwarves spurn all nature of magic," she said, her voice the whisper of a page in a book being turned by an index finger, nothing more. "The . . . spirits were loath to help. I didn't have the strength to convince them. So I compelled them. I compelled them, Malden. A witch does not compel. A witch bargains, cajoles, begs, tricks, cheats—never compels. Mother taught me that much. She didn't teach me this."

Malden understood only a little of what she was saying, but he knew she was distressed by what she'd done. He placed a hand on her back, intending to comfort her.

She flinched away from his touch.

Then she turned to face him. He saw that a streak of white had appeared amidst her sable hair.

He had seen practitioners of magic—sorcerers, not witches—deformed by congress with demons. Their faces and bodies had been distorted to perversions of the human shape. This was a very mild alteration, compared to some he'd seen. Yet he understood. These slight changes were only the beginning. The process was gradual, but irreversible. Every time she used this kind of power, the changes would become more salient.

"I had a father to teach me, as well," she said.

Malden remembered holding a dagger against her naked breast. He remembered Coruth's command, that Cythera must be slain if she chose the path of sorcery instead of the path of witchcraft. Her father's path, rather than her mother's.

He remembered the words Coruth had whispered to him, after she and her daughter fought off the barbarians scaling the wall. Coruth had tried to warn him that Cythera might follow her father's path. And tell him it was not too late, even now, to put that knife through her heart, to stop her from becoming like Hazoth.

"Cythera," he breathed.

"Do you still find me beautiful, Malden?" she asked. "Can you even look me in the eye?"

Her voice was so harsh Malden was fearful that maybe he couldn't—that maybe even meeting her gaze would kill him on the spot. He forced himself to take her by the shoulders and look into her face. He saw nothing diabolic there, nothing dangerous. She was still Cythera. Still the woman he loved. "You're as beautiful as ever," he said, and he meant it.

She gasped as if he'd utterly surprised her. Then she turned away and shook her head. "Soon I'll have to start wearing a veil," she told him. Veils were the traditional garb of sorcerers. Her father had worn one.

"No. Just promise me you'll never use that power again."

"What if it had been you lying on that table? Or Croy? I wouldn't have hesitated. I won't, when your time comes."

Malden looked past her, to see Slag lying in a peaceful sleep on the table. His burns were still pink and tender, the color of fresh scar tissue. Many of his hurts were gone altogether. His skin was pale white, the color of a corpse—but that was just the skin tone of a healthy dwarf.

Where his left arm had been, where there had been only ragged meat, there was now smooth flesh, free of scars or blemishes. It looked like he'd been born with only one arm.

"You did what you had to do," Malden said. "You did this because I asked you to."

"He's my friend, too," she told him. He tried to hold her but she pushed him away. "Look," she said.

Slag's eyes fluttered open. For a moment they remained unfocused, and Malden thought the dwarf would lapse back into unconsciousness. Then a weird vitality seemed to wash through him, all his muscles jumping at once, his eyes rolling wildly in their sockets. His lips pressed together, then opened again. He sat up and started to babble.

"The vessel, it's cast but—but I didn't have time to sound its impurities, it could shatter under the stress. And no time to make the projectile, I'll have to use—but the overpressure—wadding, maybe, perhaps a striking plate, except—except—the tunnels! We have to check the tunnels!"

CHAPTER ONE HUNDRED AND SIX

Malden looked to Cythera. She was drained, and worse than that, she was wrestling with something inside her he couldn't begin to comprehend. She couldn't meet his eye, couldn't so much as look at him. What had he done to her? What had he done to Slag? He had wanted to save Ness. Was it worth destroying everyone he loved?

"Lad! Come with me! We must check the tunnels—there was something—something," Slag said, bubbling with new strength. With desperation, too. "Something different. We need to go. We need to go now."

Malden reached for Cythera's arm.

"Go with him, Malden. Go do what you do best," she said.

"And what in the name of all that's good in the world is that?" he asked her.

"Go be smart. Be devious. Find the way to save us all," she told him.

"Lad! Come with me, now!" Slag insisted.

Malden went with the dwarf. What else could he do?

They hurried through the streets, Slag leading the way, still muttering to himself about dangers and fears and the rate at which burning gases expanded in a closed vessel. Malden heard none of it. He allowed himself to be led, and asked no questions.

"Make a big show of it," Slag said. Whatever foul magic Cythera had used to save his life seemed to be burning within him still, disordering his thoughts even as it filled him with boundless energy. "Maximize the surprise involved—only way to benefit from—they'll think twice, is what it's worth. My arm," he said, suddenly. "I'm missing a fucking arm."

Malden's thoughts came to an abrupt stop. He stood there in the cold air and stared in horror at the dwarf. Had Slag just noticed his arm was missing? Perhaps he had forgotten all about the explosion. Perhaps it had been a mistake to wake him.

"There was a great fire in your workshop," Malden explained. "Like an eruption of the pit. I pulled you out of there but you had already lost your arm. Cythera couldn't give you a new one."

Slag stared down at his shoulder for a while, as if he could find the arm there if he looked for it hard enough. Then he sighed, and some of his manic energy drained from him. "I remember, lad. I remember the light, the heat of it. This is what it cost me, eh?" Then he looked up at Malden with a wicked grin. "Good thing I have a spare. Come on, we're wasting time."

The entrance to Slag's counter-tunnel was in the cellar of a house on the western edge of the city, hard by the Ryewall. Once the cellar had been used for storing roots and preserved meat against winter's hunger, but all that food had been commandeered long since. Now the room was given over entirely to sacks of dirt, tailings from the tunnel below. If the barbarians broke through into the counter-tunnel and tried to use it to enter the city, the sacks could be toppled down into the tunnel mouth, sealing it instantly.

Slag took a lantern from a pile by the mouth and held it while Malden lit it. Then the two of them headed down the steep slope into the counter-tunnel. Its ceiling was so low Malden had to stoop, its walls rough as no effort had been made to smooth them. Tree roots reached out from those walls to snatch at Malden's cloak as they hurried along, squeezing past the hastily-placed timbers that kept the tunnel from collapsing under the weight of the earth above them.

The counter-tunnel was not particularly long. It didn't need to be. The barbarian sappers had already tunneled under the city wall, and were working, Slag had told Malden, on digging a series of parallel tunnels that would further weaken the stones above. As they came to the end of the counter-tunnel, Malden saw a number of bowls full of wine set upon the floor.

Ripples formed on the surface of each, then the wine stilled again. After a moment new ripples formed, and then stilled. The pattern repeated without cease. "They're digging right now," Malden said.

"Aye," Slag told him. The dwarf grabbed a pick from where it lay on the floor. "Day and night. They're in a hurry."

"Shouldn't our own diggers be working too, then?" Malden asked.

"No need. I sent them all home. We're ready, now." The dwarf took a step back, then ran at the far wall and struck it a mighty blow with his pick. Clods of dirt and small stones cascaded from the wall. Slag struck again, and again.

"It might help, lad," he said, breathing heavily, "if there were two of us at this."

Malden grabbed a mattock from the floor and struck at the wall as hard as he could. After a few more blows, he broke through. His mattock met nothing but air. They had breached the barbarian tunnels.

Together he and Slag worked quickly to clear an opening big enough to wriggle through. In the tunnel beyond Malden found he could stand up straight. "Their tunnel is bigger than ours," he said.

"The barbarians are bigger'n you," Slag pointed out. "There's also the fact that I was trying to *not* bring the wall down."

The timbers shoring up the barbarian tunnel were more slender than those Slag had used. They were propped up almost haphazardly. Shoddy workmanship—but then, as Slag had pointed out, this tunnel had not been built to last. The tunnel ran perpendicular to Slag's counter-tunnel, headed away in both directions into utter darkness. Slag looked both ways, then seemed to pick a direction at random. He handed Malden the lantern, then placed one finger across his lips for silence.

They moved quickly down the tunnel, all of Malden's senses alert and searching for any sign that they were about to stumble into the midst of a barbarian work party. He could just hear, faint and distant, the sound of heavy iron tools biting into the earth with a series of soft thuds. He knew from past experience that sound carried strangely underground, and was not reassured by the far-off quality of what he heard.

Had he not been paying such close attention, he might have missed the trap. Slag came very close to stumbling right into it. At the last moment, Malden grabbed the dwarf by the collar of his tunic and pulled him back.

Ahead of them stood an especially thin timber, propped up to hold a place where the ceiling sagged down toward them. At the base of the timber a web of thin copper wires stretched toward the walls, partially buried in the rough dirt of the floor. The wires were held at tension and bolted to the base of the timber.

Anyone who walked into one of those wires would yank

the timber out of alignment. Probably not by much, just an inch or so. Malden had no doubt that would be enough to bring the whole ceiling down on top of them.

He pointed out the wires and Slag nodded, a look of great consternation on his face. "Good eyes, lad," he whispered.

Malden just shrugged.

They headed farther down the tunnel, keeping an eye out for any more traps or dangers. After perhaps fifty feet, they came to where the tunnel ended at a junction with two more passages. The sound of men digging was much louder, there. Malden thought the work crew might be right around the corner. He could hear the barbarians talking amongst themselves in their guttural language. Then he heard someone else addressing the laborers.

"If you dug with half as much strength as you use pulling your tiny little manhoods, we'd be halfway to Helstrow by now," this other voice said. It used the language of Skrae, with a distinct dwarven accent.

Malden knew exactly who that voice belonged to. Judging by the look on Slag's face, he did, too.

"Keep at it," the voice said, "don't think you can take a break. Mountainslayer will personally eat the first man who shirks down here, don't forget it. I'm going to go drop my breeks and make some tailings. Don't let me catch any of you looking, neither."

Malden and Slag looked at each other. They were in perfect agreement. Malden blew out the flame of their lamp, leaving them in darkness.

A few moments later, he held his breath as he heard someone coming toward them. He saw her light—a low and guttering candle—paint the tunnel wall near him.

It was Balint. Malden should have guessed. The barbarians wouldn't know how to build trebuchets, or dig a sapping tunnel. Slag had even figured out they must have a dwarf working for them. What dwarf other than Balint would ever help such a monster as Mörget? There was something strange around her neck, though, like a ruff but made of iron. A badge of office? Jewelry that Mörget had given the dwarf as a gift for her service? Malden couldn't figure it out.

She didn't see them until it was too late. Slag grabbed one of her braids and yanked her off her feet so she fell on her back on the tunnel floor. Her eyes opened wide and her mouth began to form the syllables of a cry for help.

The law said that Slag could not use violence against anyone, not even a fellow dwarf. Malden was happy to do it for him. He used Acidtongue's pommel to knock her unconscious.

The law was *very* clear on what penalty Malden faced for assaulting a dwarf. It said Malden should be roasted alive for striking her like that. Of course, Malden *was* the only law within a hundred miles, and he had struck down capital punishment in Ness.

He picked Balint up and carried her back to the cellar and the city beyond, Slag following close behind. By that point she was starting to come around again.

Out in the street, Slag picked up a handful of snow and smeared it across her face. It was enough to rouse her instantly.

She looked up at Malden, first. And smiled merrily.

"Thank the ancients it's you," she said.

Malden's eyes went wide. "You're happy to see me?" he asked. "Do you even know how much trouble you're in?"

"Not as much as I was. Mörget had me in thrall."

"That's your excuse? For building trebuchets so he could bombard the city? For trying to break through our wall?"

"If I didn't do those things he would have cut me into morsels and eaten me raw," Balint insisted. "I only stayed alive by doing his bidding. He was going to kill me eventually anyway. He kills everything he ought to preserve. That boy would bugger to death a horse he was riding on at the time, just to get his jollies. You've rescued me from that, and I'm grateful."

"You might find me just as dangerous," Malden said, putting a hand on the hilt of his sword.

Balint laughed. "Unlikely."

"I have every reason to slaughter you!" Malden rasped. "You've played at evil for the last time."

"Evil?" Balint shrugged. "What have I done, but it's not the same as you?"

It was Malden's turn to laugh. "You aided my enemies in a time of war."

"Indeed," she told him. "I also goaded him to kill his father and drive off his sister. I kept him burning for Skrae's blood. And with good reason. I've never done aught but my duty to my own king. As long as the barbarians tarry down here in Skrae, they won't turn their bloody eyes toward the dwarven kingdom. I've been protecting my people, at no small danger to my own beautiful arse."

"Utter pother and nonsense," Malden cursed. "You're a villain pure and simple, and you live to do bloody mischief, you're a—"

"Enough, you two! The tunnels," Slag insisted, waving his one hand in frustration. "Balint—tell me fucking true. How long until they're finished?"

The female dwarf had no reason to tell the truth—but perhaps no reason to lie, either. "Oh, they're done now. I was just adding a few flourishes for a more pleasing aesthetic effect. I'm a bloody artist, I am. The wall comes down at dawn. Mörget insisted on that."

Cold fear gripped Malden's heart and he thought he might lose consciousness. That soon? "How can we stop it?"

It was Slag who answered. "You can't, lad. I saw enough down there to know it's truth she's telling."

Malden spat out the bile that had seeped up into his mouth. "So that's it? We're finished?"

"Aye," Balint crowed.

"Maybe so," Slag said. He turned to look at Malden. "You want to just give up, then? Fucking surrender and ask for terms?"

"From Mörget? He'll offer nothing," Malden said. He knew it was true. He'd spent enough time with Mörget to know the barbarian would slay every man, woman and child in Ness, just for having given him such troubles already.

"Then we get back to work. Nothing's changed," Slag said. The look on his face betrayed him, but he remained adamant. "Nothing's fucking changed. You going to kill her now?" he asked.

Malden studied Balint's face. There was no fear there—as

if she already knew he couldn't kill her. That he wouldn't. Was he really that predictable? "I wouldn't kill the child-murderer. I wouldn't kill the priest of the Lady, or even Pritchard Hood. No. I don't kill anyone except in self-defense."

"Good," Slag said. "Because I can use her."

"On your secret project?" Malden asked. "Why would she help with that?"

"Because she's an arsing dwarf, that's why."

"Fuck you," Balint said. For once it seemed the limit of her crudity.

It was Slag's turn to smile. "Oh, milady, you'll sing a different tune when you're in on the game. I know our kind. You won't be able to resist when you see what I'm building. It's just that clever."

Malden stared at the two of them. "You seriously believe she'll work nicely with you?" he asked.

"Oh, I do, lad," Slag said. There was something funny in his eye. A certain twinkle. Balint must have seen it, too, because she started giving the one-armed dwarf a shrewd look that on a human face would have meant only one thing. If Malden didn't know better, he'd think—

—never mind. It didn't concern him. "Take her, then. Er, lead her where you will. I have a million and one things I need to attend to, if tomorrow's the day we face the enemy."

CHAPTER ONE HUNDRED AND SEVEN

In her bed, Coruth struggled for every breath. Her hair was full of yellow-edged leaves and one of her arms was made of wrinkled wood. She lived. Cythera was relatively certain that she would survive. Yet she had so over-extended herself, pushed herself so far past her limits, that she could not have defended herself against a pesky fly, much less a horde of barbarians.

Probably for the best, Cythera thought. When she told her mother what she'd done, Coruth would want to kill her.

Cythera licked her lips and forced herself to keep her hands at her sides. It still had to be done. She owed her mother than much. "I've done . . ." she said, and found she couldn't go on. It was past human endurance to have to make this confession.

Then again, she was a witch now. A witch and something more. "I've done something you'll find unforgivable," she said. She forced herself not to lower her eyes.

In the bed Coruth's mouth opened a little wider, and Cythera expected her to start cursing, to castigate her daughter most severely. She deserved it, after all. Yet no sound came from those dry lips.

"I used sorcery," Cythera said, forcing herself not to falter over the words. To speak them clearly, out loud. A witch accepted her responsibilities. She acknowledged when she'd made a mistake, and she took what was coming to her. "I know better than to make excuses to you. But it was for the right reason, I am sure of it. It was to save a friend."

Coruth's eyes couldn't quite focus, but they moved in their sockets.

Cythera nodded as if her mother had spoken, because she knew exactly what she would have said. "You're right," she agreed. "I am still clutching to my attachments. I should renounce the bonds of my prior life. That was part of my initiation—to force me to let go of old desires and old bonds. Slag was going to die, and I couldn't just watch it happen. But I know I should have. If it was his time, then it wasn't my right to stop what was meant to happen. There may be some reason why he was supposed to die. This project he's working on, the thing that nearly killed him, by all accounts it's some miraculous weapon. By saving him maybe I'm introducing something terrible to the world, something that will cause untold suffering. And I let that happen because I cared for him. Perhaps I cared too much."

Coruth closed her mouth. Her body shifted in the bed as if she were struggling to sit up, or perhaps to speak. She lacked the strength to do either.

"A witch can't afford to favor one life over hundreds, maybe thousands of others. That's why I can't be Malden's lover anymore. I know this—you taught me well. I can only say I've learned from my mistake. I paid for what I did." She reached up and touched her hair. The white streaks would always be there. They would be a permanent reminder of what power cost. "You said that when . . . when I did it, Malden would never look me in the eye again. But you were wrong, mother! He looked right into me, right down to my soul, and he saw no corruption there. I made a bad mistake. But not as bad as the one you saw in my future. Your training was enough—it gave me the discipline to use only a little sorcery, just enough to do a good thing."

She closed her eyes.

"Mother, I promise now, on my life, on my vows as a witch. I promise I will never make this mistake again. I've learned my lesson and I assure you I know just how badly I've transgressed. Witchcraft may not be as powerful as sorcery, but it's clean. It is the only right way to use magic. I know this in my bones. I will die before I make contact with the pit again."

She opened her eyes again and found Coruth staring right at her. She couldn't help herself—she flinched backwards, away from that gaze.

"Some," Coruth said, and then swallowed and squinted as if just saying the word had caused her unbearable pain. "Some demons," she went on, forcing the words out, "are smaller than others."

Cythera reeled backwards as surely as if she'd been slapped. "No," she said, "no. I opened a way between the worlds, yes. But only a tiny crack—not enough to let anything come through. I watched like a hawk for it. I bound the demons I drew power from. There is no way anything could have come through—mother, I would never allow a

demon to come into this world! Even in my moment of
weakness, even when I was stupid enough to do this thing,
I was strong enough to make sure that didn't happen!"

Coruth's chin bobbed up and down. She was nodding.

"That's true," she wheezed. "It . . . didn't. Nothing came
through."

Relief flooded through Cythera's veins. If she'd failed,
if something had come into the world she would never have
been able to forgive herself. She turned to leave the room,
to let Coruth rest peacefully. If she stayed, she knew, her
mother would feel forced to admonish her further.

"Not . . . this time," Coruth said, and Cythera's shoulders
slumped as she stepped out of the room.

CHAPTER ONE HUNDRED AND EIGHT

On the march, it is far too easy to slip into a kind of
trance. At first every mile is marked. But there are so
many, and each when conquered seems so little, so in time
there is only the automatic motion, the necessary action bred
into the bone. Croy kept his horse on the road, and kept his
pace, and saw little while his mind roamed freely. In his
inner vision he saw Cythera, and what might become of her.
What might already have happened, and that was all.

Yet it is the nature of a warrior to be silent much of the
time, but always ready. When something happens to break
the routine, response is instant.

Ahead on the road a horse reared, and another screamed
in panic. Croy fought to keep his own seat. He shot looks
around in every direction, trying to see what had happened
to break the road's spell. At first he saw only his own retinue.

The Skilfinger knights around him broke ranks to spread out, not waiting for the order to protect the flanks. Drums beat to arms, and Sir Hew galloped forward to stand his horse next to Croy, waving behind him for his standard-bearer to bring up the colors of Skrae.

Then Croy saw the threat, and he drew Ghostcutter from its sheath in a practiced, effortless motion.

On every side of them, massed in neat ranks and pike squares, an army of men on foot came across the fields. There were thousands of them. Moving as one they encircled the Skilfinger column and dropped to one knee, setting their polearms as if to receive a cavalry charge. Croy very nearly ordered such a charge, thinking he'd been caught by an ambush of barbarians.

These soldiers wore no furs, however, instead wrapping themselves in blankets and mantles of cheap homespun. They didn't carry axes or swords, but instead armed themselves with bill hooks and glaives. Their serjeants held mismatched halberds, while in the midst of the pike squares men with longbows drew and held.

They carried no flags, nor wore any kind of badges or insignia. And Croy could not see a single knight or captain among their ranks. Who in the Lady's name were they?

In the distance someone shouted. Croy peered over the iron blades of the hooks and polearms facing him and saw one mounted man moving through the ambuscade, one man alone on a horse. The homespun soldiers parted to make room for him like waves parting before the prow of a ship.

When the mounted man drew closer, Croy saw he was dressed in a full coat of plate that gleamed brighter than the snow. The visor of his helmet was down, but atop the helm he wore a simple golden coronet. Croy knew that crown well enough.

"Tarness," he shouted, "what is this? Stand aside and let us pass."

"Sir Croy," the Burgrave of the Free City of Ness called back, "I had heard your body was not found at Easthull. I am glad to see you live."

Croy had no time for pleasantries. "Move your men

aside," he repeated. He glanced warily at the pike square nearest the road on his left side. If they pressed an attack now he would have a hard time fending them off. His left arm was still too weak to hold a shield. "I have important business to attend to."

Tarness walked his horse a bit closer. Behind him, sticking up from his saddle, a lance bobbed in the cold air. It bore no pennon, though it was painted in Tarness' colors. "There was a time, Croy, when you swore an oath of fealty to me," the Burgrave said. "Now you give *me* a command. Is it possible you've forgotten who I am?"

Sir Hew pushed his horse forward, Chillbrand lifted to point at the Burgrave. "Your lord gave you an order, man. He is Sir Croy no longer. He is Croy, Regent of Skrae, and your master."

"Perhaps," Tarness answered. "If this land we stand on can still be called Skrae. There are those who would say it is not."

Croy's eyes narrowed. He had heard from his scouts of the Burgrave's Army of Free Men. He had assumed that like himself they fought for the preservation of Skrae's monarchy.

"According to the charter of Ness, this land is mine, to work and profit from as I see fit," Tarness went on. "It is under my protection. None may pass over these roads unless I permit it."

"A charter," Sir Hew insisted, "signed by a king of Skrae at Helstrow. With the express understanding that royal authority could not be arrogated by any subject."

"Yes, a king—at Helstrow. There is no longer a king, at Helstrow or anywhere else. I assume Bethane is queen now, and she named you regent, but I also assume she was never properly crowned by a priest of the Lady. I also assume, since Helstrow is in the hands of the barbarians, that she is not sitting on a proper throne right now."

"Both those things are true," Croy admitted.

"You see how these things so quickly grow complicated."

Sir Hew lifted Chillbrand as if to signal an attack, but Croy stopped him with one weary gesture.

"What do you want of us?" Croy asked of Tarness.

"To know your intention, first."

Croy nodded. Very well. If the man was getting to play at insurrection, Croy would play along—to a point. "We come to liberate Ness from the barbarians. Will you stand against that goal?"

"Hardly, since it is my own. We march for the same purpose."

Croy sighed. By law he could demand that Tarness fall in with his company and assist him. He was the ranking commander on the field. Yet he sensed that if he tried to enforce that demand he would be met with more obstruction. Tarness was playing a deep game, here. Liberating Ness was only the first move. He was already thinking of the next, and the next. Which was only to be expected from the Burgrave. Croy was one of the few people in the world who knew the secret—that it was the soul of Juring Tarness, inside the crown, who spoke to him. Juring Tarness had been a master at games of strategy, both on and off the battlefield.

Croy had to start thinking strategically, himself. The knight he had been would have called an attack and bulled his way through these so-called Free Men. The regent he was must find another way.

"Let us be allies, then," Croy said, "and like two oxen pulling a plow, double our strength. Yes?"

Tarness laughed. "Milord, you think as I do."

Croy nodded. Whatever it took to get the road cleared, even if it would cause problems later on. There were plenty more miles to cover before they reached Ness. He fumed with impatience while the Burgrave moved his men away from the road, clearing a path for the Skilfinger mercenaries. It seemed to take all day.

While the Free Men moved out, the Burgrave brought his horse close enough to Croy's that they could talk quietly, man to man. "I must admit," he said, "I am glad to see you here. The battle ahead will go hard enough even for our combined strength."

"The Lady will aid us, if this is Her wish," Croy said, uninterested in the other man's small talk.

"Of course. Already she has smiled on me. When I heard an army of Skilfingers marched on Skrae, I did not expect you to come this far west. I thought for sure you would go after Helstrow first."

Croy glanced at Sir Hew. His fellow Ancient Blade refused to even turn his way, though he must have heard what the Burgrave said.

"I have my reasons to want Ness secured," Croy said.

"Yes, I know," Tarness agreed. "Reasons of the heart."

Croy stiffened in his saddle. Was he really that transparent? Or that besotted? "You speak of—"

"Of Malden, your friend and bosom companion. I for one should remember the exploits of the knight and the thief. The adventures you two unlikely comrades have shared! You look to save your friend."

"I . . . do," Croy said. Better the Burgrave think he had come to rescue a friend than a betrothed, perhaps.

"I've just two days ago had a report from a source inside the city. You'll be glad to hear that Malden lives," Tarness told him. "More than that—he's raised himself high in station. They call him Lord Mayor of Ness, now, and he commands the city in my absence."

Croy could scarcely credit it. His first thought, in fact, was not one of surprise. It was simply: *In the Lady's name, he's always been a brazen burglar, but now he's gone and stolen an entire city!*

"I was as surprised to hear it as you look just now. Considering I had another man in charge of the place when I left. Still, better one of my citizens is running the place than the barbarian, eh?"

Tarness leaned in close, pleased to be able to share such juicy gossip. His tone was positively prurient as he went on. "I'm told Malden holds out against the foe with the aid of an army of thieves and whores. One can only imagine the debauchery that must rule inside those walls. They say he's even made his headquarters in a bawdy house, where he lies abed of days with his witch consort, though they remain unmarried."

"His witch consort?" Croy asked, and he couldn't help

but laugh. "My good lord Burgrave, I think these stories must have grown in the telling. She is a formidable woman, but Coruth is far too old to be taking up with the likes of Malden." He couldn't even picture it, the two of them rutting in bed. Why—

"I speak not of Coruth but of her daughter," the Burgrave said, with a laugh of his own.

Something inside Croy's head popped like a soap bubble. For a moment he could neither hear nor see nor think. Something impossible had happened, and he was unable just then to even understand the simple words.

When the moment passed, and he could think again, he decided he must have misunderstood. "I'm sorry," he said. "Could you say again that part about who his consort is? I do believe I misheard you."

Tarness lifted the visor of his helm. His face was leering and spiteful—or perhaps that was just Croy's imagination, too.

"He desports himself most shamelessly with the woman called Cythera," the Burgrave clarified. "I believe you know her, do you not?"

CHAPTER ONE HUNDRED AND NINE

There was no time to think on all that had happened, no time to think at all. Malden ran from house to house, bashing at the doors, rousing the people inside. "To arms! To arms!" he shouted, and whenever he found a man with two working legs he sent them forth, to carry the message, to spread the word. "At dawn we fight," he told them. "At dawn there will be barbarians in Ryewall! To arms!"

"The priests say we can hold them back," a boy with a withered leg told him.

"And so we shall," Malden insisted, clapping the boy on the back.

"They say all it will take is giving Him His blood."

Malden turned to say something but the boy was already gone.

He hurried to the arsenal, and threw open the great doors. Already a crowd had gathered, perching on the ruins of the university cloister, milling in Market Square, wanting to be the first to get their pick of weaponry. Malden had worried his people would be too afraid to take up polearms and crossbows when the time came. It seemed he'd underestimated their patriotism—or perhaps their terror. They looked ready to fight. They looked ready to kill anyone who dared invade their home.

He watched them file in and out of the big building, each man and women brandishing a rusty longaxe or a glaive with a rattling blade as they emerged. The crowd behind them cheered, intent on getting their own means of defending themselves and their families.

They would fight.

"For the bloodgod!" one newly-armed man shouted, and a great hurrah went up. "I'll shed blood in Sadu's name!" another called.

As long as they were ready, Malden didn't care whose holy name they praised. He hurried next across the bridge to the Royal Ditch, to summon the harlots there, and make sure he could count on their bows. "Up on the walls—up to Westwall, and Swampwall. Stay away from Ryewall," he told Herwig, and Elody, and all the madams. "It's going to come down."

"Just like that?" Elody asked, her eyes bright with fear. "They'll magic it down?"

Malden shook his head. "Don't ask me how it's done. It's dwarven trickery, not magic, though. The one thing we can count on is that it'll come at dawn."

One of the girls, a thin waif with dark circles around her eyes, whispered something to another, who nodded meaningfully.

"What are you saying?" Malden asked, pointing at the girl.

Herwig glared at her until she came forward.

The girl looked at her own feet, not Malden's eyes. "Just, if it please you, Lord Mayor—we can count on one other thing."

Malden sighed. "The bloodgod?"

The girl nodded and simpered. "If He's given the proper sacrifice, we're told He will smile on us. The *proper* sacrifice is all—"

"Hush, you little twit," Herwig chided. "Pay no mind, Malden. There's those among us who know better."

Malden frowned, not fully understanding. It sounded like the priests of Sadu had been hard at work, spreading some mischief. Maybe they had called for human sacrifice at last. He should try to stop that, but he hadn't time at the moment to winkle out the mystery. He hurried on, through the eastern edge of the Stink. He used the rooftops to make his way quickly through that district, where criers were out calling all to arms. Many citizens, it seemed, had congregated in Godstone Square, perhaps looking for someone to tell them where to go. A priest was there, handing out loaves—surely the last of the food. Fair enough, Malden thought. Better to go into battle and die on a full stomach. He headed onward to the work yards of the Smoke, where he'd had the guilds working night and day on defensive engines. There had been diagrams of such in Rus Galenius' *Manual*, improbable constructions of wood designed to slow, if not stop, an invading army. Great logs studded with spikes and mounted on wheels, to act as mobile barricades. Leather bellows that could squirt flaming oil across an invader's path and force them back. Mantlets, giant wheeled shields behind which crossbowmen could shelter while they reloaded their weapons. "Get these moving toward Ryewall," Malden called. "I don't care if they aren't finished, just shift them."

A former journeyman in the wheelwright's guild saluted Malden and promised he'd have the engines in place on time if he had to drag them himself. "Sadu helps those who help themselves," he said, and gave Malden a knowing wink.

Malden had been about to race away, but he stopped himself. "I get the sense you're saying more than you're saying, if you catch me right."

"Less said the better," the journeyman said, and chuckled. "Just know, Lord Mayor—we all appreciate what you've done for us. And what you're going to do, on the morrow."

Malden was more confused than ever. "You're welcome, then," he said. "I hope tomorrow you'll feel the same way." Riddles! Too many riddles. There was so much left to do.

And so little of it that could make any difference. The barbarians wouldn't be stopped by a rabble of townsfolk, no matter how desperate they were. Mörget wouldn't stop until everyone was dead, everyone—

No. Malden would not give in to despair. Slag had been right. You had to keep fighting, or give in. And if Malden decided to give in now he would just go hide in some quiet place and shiver in fear and wait to be slaughtered. Keeping busy at least kept him from unmanning himself.

And who knew? Perhaps the bloodgod *would* come to their aid, at the last minute. Perhaps he would open up the pit and a legion of demons would come boiling out, all teeth and claws and nightmarish shapes to save the city.

Malden laughed to himself as he hurried across the rooftops, down to the Ashes and the headquarters of Cutbill's guild of thieves. He laughed because he'd half begun to believe it himself. The faith of the people was infectious, it seemed.

When he reached the burned-out tavern above Cutbill's lair, he dropped to the street and stepped inside the ruin, looking for 'Levenfingers or Lockjaw. One of the oldsters should always be guarding the entrance, but neither of them was present.

It didn't matter. Since there were no more watchmen in Ness, nor any bailiff to raid the place, security on the lair was of minimal importance. Malden hoped that the old men were out enjoying themselves, maybe having one last drink or enjoying the caresses of one last wench before the desperate moment came. He hurried down through the trap door into the lair and through the empty common room, headed for Cutbill's office. Velmont should be there, collecting last-minute reports from Malden's thieves.

The Helstrovian was inside, as expected, which was at least something. Velmont sat in the chair behind Cutbill's old desk, counting coins into a sack.

"It's coming tomorrow, at dawn," Malden said. "Send word around. I want every thief in the city on the rooftops before Ryewall. Make sure they have plenty of arrows, and—and—"

There were a *lot* of coins on the desk. And they were all gold.

Velmont hurriedly shoved them into his purse as if he didn't want Malden to take them away from him. Odd.

"Where did you get those?" Malden asked.

"One last job," the Helstrovian said, with a shrug. "Surely you don't begrudge it, boss. A man must get coin in this world where he can."

"I'd be a sorry kind of thief if I disagreed," Malden said. "Enjoy your newfound wealth while you're able. Just make sure you get those archers in place before you go looking for ways to spend it."

"They'll be at it, sure enow," Velmont said.

Something was wrong. The city was about to be overrun—sacked by the barbarians—but Velmont seemed calmer than he'd been in weeks. Almost like he knew he wouldn't be around to see the end happen.

So many coins in that sack. So much gold. "You aren't planning to run out on me now, are you?" Malden asked, laughing to make it sound like a joke.

"Perish the thought," Velmont said. He rose from the chair and went to a side table to fetch a bottle of wine. "Quite the adventure we've had, eh? Not what I thought I was getting into, when I signed on." He pulled the cork with his teeth.

"Hopefully it's been sufficiently lucrative that you don't question your decision," Malden told him.

Velmont grinned broadly and poured a cup of wine. He handed it to Malden, then started pouring a second cup for himself.

"I'd love to stay and drink with you, believe me," Malden said, sipping from his cup, "but I'm afraid there's no time."

"Certes they're a moment for one mickle toast," Velmont said. "Just swear one oath with me, is all, and be on your way."

Malden sighed but raised his cup and touched its rim to Velmont's. "And what oath will that be? To coin? To . . . loyalty?"

"To honor among thieves," Velmont said, tilting his head to one side. "The most valuable commodity in this sorry world, eh?"

Malden laughed. "Because it is the rarest," he agreed. And drained his cup.

Something rattled around at its bottom. A whitish lump of something half-dissolved. It slid forward on the dregs and touched Malden's lips. Instantly they went numb.

Malden dropped the cup. He tried to grab the hilt of Acidtongue. His arm felt like a piece of rope. He could barely feel his hand at all.

"You . . . bass . . . yuh basst . . ." he slurred.

A tapestry hanging across one wall twitched aside, and half a dozen priests of the bloodgod stormed into the room.

CHAPTER ONE HUNDRED AND TEN

"Get that iron off him," Velmont commanded. His eyes stayed on Malden's face. Malden tried to fight off the priests as they took Acidtongue from his belt, but he could barely slap at their hands. Already he was weak as a kitten in a sack.

"P-p-poison," he said, forcing the word out.

"Now that'd be folly pure, ain't it?" Velmont said. "Killing you now, when these fine gentlemen have such plans for you?" The Helstrovian chuckled. "They'd hardly forgive me. No, I just done you a favor, boss."

Malden tried to take a step toward Velmont but his legs felt like springs and he stumbled forward onto his knees.

"What I put in that cup's only a bit o' deadener. To take away the pain, like. Now when they stick you, you'll feel nary a thing."

Malden grabbed at the edge of the desk but his fingers were ten pieces of soft wood. Behind him two priests came forward to haul him upright and back onto his feet.

"M-money," Malden said.

"Aye, boss, they pay well, this lot. Enough to get me out o' this pest-hole, and set up real nice aught where else. They're e'en gonna help with that. Got me a boat, just a mickle skiff down in Eastpool, gonna send me out to sea while the barbarians is distracted tomorrow."

Malden sagged against the priests holding him, but one of them pulled up on his collar and he got back on his feet. For the first time he looked at his captors. They were dressed in red, the color of their god, but he was surprised by how young they were. He'd never seen any of them before. Apparently Hargrove had been busy recruiting new acolytes. Malden wished he'd paid more attention to the growing priesthood—or stamped them out altogether when he had the chance.

"Bl-bl-bl," he drooled. The drug left his mind untouched, but his body was feeling further and further away.

"Blood," one of the priests said, for him. "*His* blood. In olden times, when the people faced certain peril, only one thing could save them—a sacrifice of proper magnitude. When the danger is the greatest, only the blood of kings will suffice. Your blood should be close enough. Did not Sadu pick you, of all men, to bring back the old religion? Has he not worked through you, lo, these many weeks? Your sanctified blood will anoint the Godstone and finish His holy work. You're going to be a martyr, Lord Mayor. You'll be remembered forever in the prayers of the faithful."

Cold dread washed through Malden, fighting the drug.

It wasn't enough to give him back the strength to fight, but it bolstered his tongue.

"Trai . . . tor," he said, and spat in Velmont's face.

The Helstrovian wiped the spittle away with his hand. He did not look particularly offended. After a moment he smiled sadly. "You had your chance, boss. When Mörg offered up safe conduct, you could've jumped. Well, if this bunch is right, you'll have one more go at savin' your people, won'tcha? That's what you wanted, ain't it?" Velmont tied his bag of coin to his belt. It was so heavy it pulled down one side of his tunic, but he didn't seem to mind the weight.

The Helstrovian went to the wall behind Cutbill's desk and lifted aside the tapestry that hung there. "Fare thee well, boss. Can't say it weren't a pleasure, workin' for you." He gave Malden a mock salute, then disappeared behind the tapestry. A passage back there led back up into the Stink, many blocks away. Malden had used it often.

The priests walked Malden out through the common room, and between them they managed to lift him up through the trap door that led back to the Ashes. Outside the burnt-down tavern a wagon was waiting, drawn by a spavined horse with ribs protruding so far from its chest it looked like a skeleton. Malden was thrown into the back and held down by two of the priests while a third perched on the front of the wagon to drive.

Malden could barely move his head to look around. It didn't matter. He knew where they were headed. When he'd seen the crowd gathering around the Godstone, he'd thought they just wanted bread. Now he understood—they were waiting for the great spectacle of a human sacrifice.

And there was no way to stop it. Malden could as easily have fought off Mörget and the entire horde of barbarians single-handed as he could push away the men holding his arms. One of them wore Acidtongue at his own belt, now— did they intend to use it as the sacrificial blade? Malden knew if he'd had a little strength he could grab its hilt, pull it away from the man, slaughter them all before they knew what was happening. But he didn't have that strength.

He could only look up at the cold stars and wonder how

it had come to this. He'd never wanted to be Lord Mayor. He'd only wanted two things, ever, in his entire life. To have enough money to live comfortably, and to be a husband to Cythera.

He reflected that it was not the bloodgod who'd brought things to this pass. One of the old names of the Lady was *Fama*. It was she who raised men from one station to another, whether they wanted to rise or not. She who, in her other role, as *Fortuna*, brought them crashing back down to earth again.

Sadu didn't bother with such cruel games. He only brought justice—more often than not, the utterly equal justice of death.

The wagon bounced on over the cobbles, Malden rocking back and forth with its motion, unable to brace himself. He barely felt the jars and bumps, and was only peripherally aware that at some point the wagon stopped. This was it, then. They must have arrived at the Godstone.

Yet he couldn't hear the roaring of the crowd, or the chants for blood, that he would have expected. He glanced from side to side with sluggish eyes and saw the wrong buildings on either side of him. The wagon had stopped somewhere in the Smoke, well short of its destination.

"You," the driver of the wagon called. "Old man. Please clear the way. We are on sacred business, and can't be delayed."

One of the priests holding Malden let go of him and stood up in the bed of the wagon. "What is this botheration?" he asked.

A crossbow bolt suddenly appeared, sticking out of his left eye. The wickedly barbed point protruded from the back of the priest's head, along with a thin spurt of blood.

Malden watched the man fall. It seemed to take a very, very long time.

He heard a groan of pain and looked forward, as best he could, to see the driver of the wagon tumble toward the street. The third priest, the one wearing Acidtongue, grabbed for the side of the wagon in panic. The wagon rocked as someone else jumped into the bed. The last of the priests drew Acidtongue clumsily from its sheath and held it out, point forward. Malden could see its point trembling as the priest's hand shook.

A drop of acid spilled from the blade and fell to the bed of the wagon, mere inches from Malden's face. He tried desperately to turn his head away, to avoid the next drip, but he could barely twitch to the side.

His head rolled—and he saw who it was who'd killed the other two priests. Who now stood in the wagon, facing down Acidtongue.

It was Cutbill. The old guildmaster of thieves, dressed like a peasant in a shapeless russet tunic.

Cutbill grabbed the priest by his baldric. The priest tried to bring Acidtongue up to defend himself but he was too slow. Cutbill launched his head forward, connecting his forehead viciously with the priest's nose. Cartilage snapped with a sickening crunch and blood splattered down the front of the priest's tunic, turning its red fabric black in the moonlight. The sword fell uselessly to the bed of the wagon in a pool of its own acid.

Cutbill had a knife in his hand, no bigger than the belt knife he might use to cut and eat his food. He struck with it three times, perforating the priest's neck in three precise, almost surgical cuts. The priest fell backwards, out of the wagon, without a sound. Malden had no doubt the man was dead before he hit the cobbles.

Then Cutbill grabbed Malden and hauled him out of the wagon. He pushed him toward a disused horse trough that had frozen over in the night. With his bloody knife, Cutbill smashed up the ice and shoved Malden's face into the bitterly cold water.

The effect was immediate. The cold shocked Malden's system—left him feeling still weak as an infant but at least able to gasp for breath and look around him. He saw the wagon standing exactly where it had stopped, the starveling horse waiting patiently for a command that would never come. He saw the deserted streets all around them. Saw the three bodies lying on the cobbles.

"How . . . did," Malden said, but lacked the strength to

finish his thought. *How did you know they would do this? How did you know where to find me?* Those were only his most pressing questions.

Cutbill, though, never gave away his secrets. Rather than answering, he grabbed Malden's face and slapped him mercilessly. "Fight it, son," the guildmaster told him. "You're going to need to walk in a moment. After that, you'll need to run."

Malden forced his left hand to clench into a fist. It didn't quite make it, but he felt the blood surging through his fingers. He tried again. Cutbill nodded and went back to the wagon. When he returned he had Acidtongue, its scabbard, and Malden's sword belt. He helped Malden strap it back on.

"Not . . . your usual . . . style," Malden forced himself to say. He'd never actually imagined Cutbill capable of leaving his various lairs and bolt-holes. Certainly never thought the guildmaster of thieves capable of such a daring— and savage—rescue.

"In fact this was exactly my style, once upon a time," Cutbill assured him. "In a less decorous era. These days I find it more to my advantage to plot and scheme from the shadows, yes. But I've done my share of desperate things in the past, when plans fell apart. I need you still, Malden. I'm not done with you, not quite yet. I still need a hero to save my city tomorrow."

"Too bad you only . . . have me," Malden joked.

"You know I hate false modesty. You're exactly the man for the job. If only because no one else is here to do it. Bend this knee," Cutbill said. "Farther. Does it pain you to bend like that?"

Malden shook his head. "Nothing hurts."

"It will. When the drug wears off, it's going to hurt a lot. Now. Bend the other knee. Good. Again."

CHAPTER ONE HUNDRED AND ELEVEN

An hour before dawn, the snow burned a deep blue. Fires burned low in the barbarian camp, untended now by men who expected to be inside walls and warm in a little space of time. Mörget dropped to his knees before the wall of Ness, and spread his hands wide, for that was how the men of the east prayed.

O mother, O Death, come today for my enemies, he beseeched, silently, for no man of the east prayed aloud when another could hear. *O my mother, come for my men too, my warriors, who I would slay myself to please you, until their blood painted this world. Come for the little people of the west, and conquer their little gods. Come for the innocent. Come for the women. Come for the children, and even the little babes.*

Slake this thirst inside me with hot blood.

Or come for me, if that is my doom.

But come, and reap, and take many souls into your arms.

No one was there to ask him what he begged for. Hurlind the scold was passed out drunk in his tent. Balint the dwarf was gone, spirited away in her own tunnels by hands unseen. Mörgain was riding for Helstrow, well beyond Mörget's reach. Mörg the Wise, Mörg the Merciful, Mörg the Great Chieftain was dead by his son's red hand. The chieftains who remained, their reavers and their warriors, their thralls and their berserkers, did not dare approach a man communing with his *wyrd.*

Mörget was alone. No one remained to share in his glory.

Which meant it would all be his.

Everything was in readiness, and everything was planned for. The berserkers would be first and already they danced before the wall of the city, danced wildly working their blood up, danced and sang with great ululating shrieks and shouts, with atonal, wordless chants to drive themselves mad. When the wall came down they would rush inside and slaughter indiscriminately anyone they found. After them the clans would pour through, a river of iron to wash away any defenders that remained. Mörget would be in amongst them, with axe and Dawnbringer, and he would reap a great harvest.

Or so it had been planned. Yet destiny, or doom, whichever it might be, was known to laugh at men who schemed, and so it was to be that day.

The sign, the portent of what was truly to come, was a ring of steel against iron, and it was repeated not once but a hundred times even before Mörget looked up from his prayer. Behind him at the edge of the camp horses screamed and men cried out in pain. Mörget jumped to his feet and grabbed his weapons.

He was not expecting this, but still it brought a smile to his face. He hurried past surprised-looking chieftains standing outside their tents, past thralls holding the ropes that would bring down the wall of Ness. He hurried to where men held weapons in their hands, and pushed into their ranks so he could see what gift his mother had brought him.

An armored man on a horse nearly put a lance-tip through Mörget's chest as he looked around him. Mörget was fast enough to spin out of the way and bury his axe deep in the haunch of the horse as it passed. The animal faltered and went down, and the knight on its back had to jump down into the snow.

Mörget did not recognize the armor the man wore, nor the way he braided his mustache. This was no man of Skrae. He found this fact deeply intriguing.

The knight got to his feet while Mörget waited. The barbarian could have struck his enemy down a dozen times, but he wanted to see what this new foeman would bring to bear. The knight had a long, tapering shield across his left arm, and his right hand came up with a flail, three spiked steel balls whirling over his head. If they found purchase on Mörget's flesh they would tear away skin and muscle and crush his bones. With an ease and a grace that came from a hundred such encounters, Mörget stepped inside the knight's reach and thrust Dawnbringer into the air. The Ancient Blade burst with light as it fouled the chains holding those deadly orbs, clattered as they wrapped around and around Mörget's foible.

Mörget's axe came round and bit through the wooden shield that came up to meet it. The boards groaned and split and the steel rim of the shield twanged as it snapped away. The shield fell to pieces and the arm underneath it steamed with blood.

The knight let go of his flail—trapped and useless, now— and punched Mörget hard in the face with a steel gauntlet. Mörget's head spun round to the side and spittle launched from his lips as his entire skull rang with the impact.

He shook off the blow and brought his head back around to see the knight dancing backwards, reaching for a long dagger at his waist.

"Very good," Mörget laughed. "You're very good," he said, in the same moment that he flicked Dawnbringer to the side to free it of the entwined flail. The knight did not reply as he brought his knife around, the blade held diagonally across his chest to ward off Mörget's next blow.

Mörget feinted with his axe, and the knight drove hard with his knife to parry. That left his chest open, so Mörget impaled him on Dawnbringer. The blade lit up inside the knight's body and red light glowed from inside the dying man's ribcage.

Mörget spun around, even as he pulled his sword free of the corpse. All around him more horses were circling, the knights on their backs lashing out left and right with morningstars and cavalry spears, cutting down thralls and warriors.

Who were these knights? From whence had they come? They were nearly as vicious and well-trained as Mörget's own warriors, and they knew how to use their horses to their advantage. They were a real threat, for once, and Mörget's blood sang with excitement. A real battle!

Then, behind the horses, he saw a pike square advancing toward him. Each was made of a score of men, each man armed with a ten foot pole with an iron spike at its end. Five men stood shoulder to shoulder with no break between them, while another five walked sideways to their right and left, and a final five brought up the rear, walking backwards, trusting the men in front to lead them. Simple weapons, simple tactics, but Mörget knew how dangerous pike squares could be. The length of the pikes made it impossible to get at the men directly, while they could jab outward with impunity.

Of course, the tactic assumed that when presented with such a wall of spikes, any sane warrior would retreat, knowing he was beaten. In civilized lands pike squares could drive a whole flank back, or break a main charge, or even hold their own against cavalry. But Mörget was not civilized. And he was not altogether sane.

Howling a war curse, he ran straight into the midst of the pikes. One spike lodged in his neck but he tore free of it and pushed in closer. His axe swung in a wide vertical arc that sliced through the wooden hafts of the pikes until their severed ends bounced and drummed around his feet.

Dawnbringer took the head of one pikeman, and suddenly there was a gap in the square, and just as suddenly Mörget was inside it, looking at the unsuspecting backs of the men in the rear. One of them glanced over his shoulder and dropped his weapon in terror.

The square tried to turn in on itself, but the pikes were useless in close quarters. The pikemen were as likely to stick each other as Mörget. The barbarian's axe and sword flashed left, smashed right, came round, circled, cutting everywhere, slashing and stabbing and thrusting and lunging until twenty dead men fell against Mörget and threatened to knock him off his feet. He jumped over the falling bodies before they'd even stopped breathing and looked up to see four more pike squares coming toward him, even as the knights on horseback kept charging through the camp, slaughtering men who were still half asleep.

"Well played," Mörget said, addressing the unseen commander of this ambush.

Yet one quick sortie of overwhelming power did not a rout make. Mörget had his own gambit to try. This assault of mixed foot and cavalry was deadly, but only on open ground. If he could get the clans inside the city wall before they were cut to pieces, he could build a defensive barricade and hold off his enemies forever with arrows.

He dashed toward the city wall, just as the first limb of the sun crested the horizon, shouting, "The ropes! The ropes! Bring down the wall now!"

O mother, he prayed, *O Mother Death you have blessed me this day!*

CHAPTER ONE HUNDRED AND TWELVE

As soon as Malden could stand on his own two feet, Cutbill disappeared into the shadows without so much as a parting word of advice. Perhaps, Malden thought, that suggested the guildmaster of thieves had such confidence in him that Cutbill thought he no longer needed guidance.

Or perhaps Cutbill went to make his own exit from the city, just like Velmont, while the getting was still good.

Malden clenched his hands, released them again. His fingertips burned as the blood rushed into them. Cutbill had warned him that there would be pain when—

"Gaah!" Malden shouted, unable to stop himself. A violent cramp had run up and down his whole left side, as feeling returned to his trunk. He felt a vein in his temple curl and spit venom like a snake, and he cried out again.

The agony was enough to drive him to his knees.

Unfortunately, he didn't have time for pain just then. His cry had drawn attention from the nearby streets. A man with a torch came hurrying around the corner, leading a half dozen curious citizens. One of the six was dressed all in red, like a priest.

If the priests caught him now, he knew better than to expect them to apologize for seizing him and threatening him with human sacrifice.

"Blast," Malden said, looking around for a convenient shadow to hide in. But the torch-bearer was already shouting that he'd found the Lord Mayor. Malden glanced over at the wagon that had brought him this far, and the three dead bodies lying around it. He looked intently at the horse, still standing there waiting patiently in its traces.

The horse turned its head to look back at him with impassive eyes.

Malden knew how to ride, barely. Though he'd never mounted a horse before without someone there to give him a leg up. It didn't matter, he decided. There was no time to get the animal unhooked from the cart.

So instead he looked up. It was his natural instinct when being pursued to climb. He ran at a half-timbered wall that offered so many hand- and foot-holds it might as well have been a ladder and leapt to catch a particularly thick beam.

The drug Velmont had given him was still at work in his blood, however. His leap was more of a lop-sided hop, and when his fingers latched onto the side of the house he was barely able to cling to it without falling.

Looking back, he saw his pursuers were only seconds away. "Hold, damn you," he grunted at his own hands. They'd never failed him before. He managed to swing one arm up and grab the ledge of a second story window. Cramps ran up both his ankles and made him gasp for breath. When the muscles there relaxed again, he swung his right leg up to get purchase on the top of the door frame.

"Lord Mayor!" someone shouted below. "Please—your people need you! We need you at the Godstone!"

"He's slaughtered this crew," someone else said, in a hollow voice. A woman screamed. "They were Sadu's ministers—what has he done?"

"Please," a third voice shouted. "Think of us! Think of our safety!"

Malden didn't have the breath to waste on a reply. Pain wracked his arms but he managed to pull himself up onto the shingles of the house's roof. He lay there gasping for a moment, staring up at the sky, while the entreaties continued from below.

The sky was a peculiar shade of purple. He turned his head and saw orange clouds on the horizon. *No—no, it can't come so soon.* But he could not deny the evidence of his senses. Dawn was about to break.

He had to get to Ryewall, as quickly as possible, to lead the counter-attack.

Malden rolled over onto his side, then painfully rose to his feet. He was halfway across the city, and he could barely trust his legs. What if he had a cramp in the middle of leaping from one rooftop to another?

There wasn't anything he could do about that, though. He would have to take his chances.

Moving as quickly as he dared on feet still half-numb, he scurried over a roof-ridge and down the other side. The street beyond was blessedly narrow, and he managed to hurl himself across and roll along the shingles on the far side. Bits of wood, brittle from the cold, broke away underneath him and pattered down into the road, but he managed to get his footing. Ahead of him lay a long row of rooftops, the houses all attached to one another. He kept low as he ran from eave to eave, even as cries went up all around him.

"His blood! He demands His blood!" they all said.

Malden scowled but kept running. There was no time to convince the people of Ness that he was worth more to them now alive than dead.

Up ahead lay a broad street—Crispfat Lane, where a dozen butchers had their shops. The gap between the roof-tops was too wide to jump, even if he'd been in a condition to do so. Malden ran to the edge and looked down.

The snowy street was almost deserted—but not quite enough. He saw women holding candles peering into every alley, every alcove. No doubt looking for the appointed sacrifice of their god. The priests must have put out a general hue and cry to find Malden. The damned fools didn't seem to understand that every able-bodied citizen of Ness was needed to repel the invaders—these women looked strong enough to hold polearms.

There was nothing for it. Malden would have to scramble down into the street and up the houses on the far side. If the searchers tried to stop him, he would have to fight them off. He hurried down a gutter pipe as quietly as he could, praying the dark of night would be his ally as it had so many times before.

Halfway down a searing pain burst through his stomach, and his hands turned to spasmodic claws. He lost his grip as he screamed in agony and fell the last ten feet into a snowdrift. For a while he could do nothing but curl around his midsection and blink sweat out of his eyes.

The pain felt like it would never let him go. He could not move, could not even think as the agony wracked his body. It was all he could do to keep breathing. As the snow melted on his face and hands, paining him still further, he tried to force it away, tried to unclench his closed eyelids.

Eventually it worked.

When he looked up a small crowd had gathered to peer down at him by candlelight. "Lord Mayor," one woman said, "you've come to your senses. If you'll just come along with us, now. We want no trouble."

Malden rose carefully, the pain in his middle still making it impossible for him to stand up straight. He reached for Acidtongue's hilt with a hand that barely obeyed his command.

It would have gotten ugly, just then, if Slag hadn't come tearing down the street, screaming, "Make way! Make way or get fucking crushed, you pissants!"

CHAPTER ONE HUNDRED AND THIRTEEN

The crowd of devout citizens gasped and ran as a massive wagon covered by a tarpaulin came rumbling down the hill toward them. A dozen men were pushing against it from the front, trying to slow its headlong descent and mostly failing.

Running ahead of the wagon Slag carried a long brass staff topped by a hook that looked like the head of a snake. Meanwhile, sitting atop the wagon's burden, Balint waved a cloth back and forth, cheering and shouting curses.

"You'll all be flatter than a spinster's tit if you don't scarper right now!" she cackled. She looked like she'd never had more fun in her life.

"I am well pleased to see you," Malden said, as Slag hurried toward him. "I take it this is your secret project."

"It'll be the world's most expensive heap of scrap if we take this hill too fast, lad," Slag explained. "Help us!"

Malden hurried toward the wagon. He recognized the men straining against it as workers from Slag's shop. Some had burned faces and hands wrapped in bandages, but they seemed less concerned with their own hurts than with slowing the progress of the wagon. Malden put his own shoulder against the wagon's boards, and was shocked to feel how heavy its cargo must be. "What is this made of, Slag? Twice-refined lead?"

"Bronze, mostly. Put your fucking back in it, boys!"

They heaved and struggled and strained. The wagon roared as it rolled over the cobbles. The wheels screamed and the axles spat sparks. Somehow they managed to avoid crashing at the bottom of the hill. It was far easier moving it through the relatively level streets beyond, even with no dray animals. Suddenly Slag called a halt, and Malden looked up for the first time.

Directly before him was Ryewall.

High above, his thieves and whores were busy taking random shots at targets on the other side. Loophole and 'Levenfingers moved along the ramparts of Westwall and Swampwall, shouting orders like they were born serjeants, calling out targets. When he saw Malden, Loophole gave a cheery wave—even as a barbarian arrow shot past his ear, inches from skewering his head.

"It's begun, lad," the oldster called down. "You'd best join me up here."

Malden grabbed Slag's shoulder—the one still attached to an arm. "Are you ready?" he asked.

"As close as I fucking can be," the dwarf told him.

Malden glanced at Balint. "She gave you no trouble?"

A twitching smile passed across Slag's face as he tried to maintain a sober countenance. "Oh, she distracted me a bit from what I was doing. But after the—well, after some initial, ah, fractiousness, we, ah, we got along right well. She had some excellent ideas, actually, about brisance and containment." He glanced away from Malden's feet. "Very imaginative lass, our Balint."

Malden laughed and slapped the dwarf on the back. "What exactly should I expect from this thing?" he asked, changing the subject. "Are you going to shoot a giant arrow at the barbarians, or will it throw a flaming rock like a catapult?"

"Neither. It'll either explode when I set it off, and make a much bigger bang that we did at the cloisters," Slag confessed, "or, it will actually work. In which case—" Slag's face grew dark with evil excitement, "—it'll put the fear of fucking dwarves into those stinking cock-suckers."

"Do your worst, when I give the signal," Malden said. Then he hurried up the steep, narrow stairs that led to the top of Westwall.

It was only then he saw what he was really up against. The barbarians had massed and armed themselves, and he looked out over a sea of iron and shaved heads and eyes burning with hatred and bloodlust. The warriors out there filled the land as far as he could see. Off in the distance it looked like some of them were fighting each other, which he couldn't quite understand. Maybe they were just running through practice drills—or perhaps they'd grown so tired of waiting to kill that they'd started hacking at one another for something to do.

Then again, perhaps—

No. Malden's luck couldn't be that good. So far everything that could possibly go wrong had, and the idea of something actually working in his favor felt wholly out of the equation.

Yet soon he couldn't deny the evidence of his own senses.

"Look," one of the archers said, pointing at a line of flags in the distance. Over where the barbarians were fighting a rearguard action. "Those are the Burgrave's colors!"

Malden's eyes weren't as good as hers, but he squinted and strained and—yes. He saw it. The Army of Free Men had come at last to relieve the city.

Now that it was almost surely too late. Directly below him, hundreds of berserkers danced and howled. Foam flecked their lips and cheeks and their eyes were wide with insanity. The Burgrave had plenty of men but they were poorly trained, poorly armed—no match at all for the reavers and berserkers out there. Tarness could do no more than pick away at the barbarian horde. And he most certainly could not break through in time to save Ryewall from coming down, or the berserkers from overrunning the city.

A stroke of good luck, but good luck too late, Malden thought. He would have to stick to the plan he'd already made.

Malden signaled to the archers around him—Elody's whores, women he'd known for years. They looked at him with trusting eyes. They were counting on him, he realized. Expecting a miracle. He truly hoped he had one left in stock. "Don't waste shots on the berserkers, unless you think you can actually kill a few. They don't feel pain or wounds. When they come through the—"

Down below he heard Mörget's voice. The barbarian shouted, "Pull, you weaklings! Pull or die!"

Under Malden's feet, the very stones of the wall began to shake.

"Get back, get back from Ryewall," he shouted, again and again. Soon he couldn't even hear his own voice. The noise of the wall was just too loud.

It started as a low creaking, like an unoiled hinge being ripped from its nails. The noise grew to an unearthly moan, accompanied by the percussion of stones falling from a great height. As Malden watched in horror the Ryewall began to shimmy, its ramparts swaying up and down as if they were made of water on a foaming sea.

"Pull!" Mörget screamed again, and *his* voice carried. "Again! Pull!"

Below and behind Malden, Slag tore the tarpaulin off his secret weapon.

"That's it?" Malden demanded.

It didn't look like much. Just a metal tube ten feet long and two across, dull yellow in color. Bands of steel wrapped around its length like the hoops of a barrel. One end was open, and Balint stuffed handfuls of nails and broken weapons and old horseshoes down its mouth. Slag busied himself at a small charcoal fire, a little ways off. It looked like he was just trying to get warm.

"This is what you've been working on? The thing that was going to turn them back?" Malden demanded. "It looks like a giant pestle. Do you need me to drive the barbarians into the world's largest mortar?"

"Pull!" Mörget roared.

And Ryewall fell.

CHAPTER ONE HUNDRED AND FOURTEEN

Croy brought Ghostcutter around and disemboweled a gray-bearded reaver, then ducked as an axe whistled over his head. He had lost his horse at some point—he barely remembered when—and had been wading through the melee ever since, cutting down any man who came before him. The clatter of glancing blows on his armor and helm drowned out the thoughts in his head. The strength in his good arm saw him through.

He laid about him left and right, barely looking at the men he killed. If they wore furs or had shaved heads it was enough.

Ghostcutter lifted and fell, swung out and took lives on the backswing. He dodged under blows that would have cut through his armor like rotten silk, rolled away whenever they knocked him to the ground, leapt back to his feet. Wounds didn't matter. The fatigue of the long march south didn't matter. Anger—if nothing else—could sustain him. Rage.

Cythera, he kept thinking. Just her name. Her face swam before his eyes, that beloved face now distorted by betrayal. He had trusted her. He had trusted in her pledge, her faith, her constancy. Cythera, he thought as he stabbed a man in the kidneys. Her name formed on his lips and he slashed through the tendons of a barbarian's neck. Cythera.

Malden. Malden, whom he had put in charge of Cythera's protection. Malden, whom he had asked—pleaded with—to preserve her chastity. What had he been thinking? The man was a thief! Malden never saw anything that belonged to someone else, save that he wanted to steal it. Croy slashed open the belly of a reaver and was washed in hot blood. Of course Malden had stolen the one prize in all of Skrae worth having! "Malden!" he screamed.

Three men came at him, all at once, with axes and maces. They howled like wolves as they piled on to him, but Croy stabbed one through the stomach and bashed in the face of another with his pommel on the return swing. The third raised his mace to crush Croy's skull but before the blow could connect a knight on horseback came galloping through and cut the barbarian's throat nearly to the spine.

In the breaking light of dawn, Croy looked up and saw Sir Hew come trotting back around to salute him. He forced himself to focus, to hear what his brother Ancient Blade had to say. "It's going hard for the Free Men, but they're holding their lines," Hew said. "The Skilfingers are a wonder. Worth ten times what we paid. And still no berserkers have engaged us—do you think Mörget's holding them in reserve?"

Croy gasped for breath and wiped Ghostcutter on the fur of a fallen barbarian. He knew he should say something— give some order, perhaps, or ask for a more detailed report. He only resented the interruption, however. Free of enemies for a moment, his brain started to work again.

Images of Cythera cluttered his thoughts. Cythera, with Malden writhing atop her, strewn across a whore's bed—

It was almost a welcome distraction when the wall of Ness collapsed.

The Burgrave came racing past them, his lance pointed up in the air. "Not my damned city, you don't!" he cried, and behind him a hundred Free Men with bill hooks cried out as they rallied behind their leader.

Sir Hew stared toward Ness. "Sappers, would be my guess," he said, sounding shocked. "If they can get inside the city—"

"We'll have to besiege Ness ourselves," Croy replied, nodding. That would be next to impossible, with winter growing colder and the snow piling deeper every day. They couldn't feed the Skilfinger mercenaries for another week, not and besiege the city at the same time.

"Give me an order," Hew demanded.

Croy shook his head. "Press the attack. Hurt them as much as we can before they get inside." He thought he knew now why Mörget had held his berserkers in reserve. Once those battle-mad warriors were inside the wall, no force inside the Free City could hold against them. They would slaughter the citizens of Ness indiscriminately, hacking and slashing until the streets were slick with blood.

Once that slaughter began, there would not be a single thing Croy—or the Burgrave, or Hew, or anyone else—could do to stop it.

CHAPTER ONE HUNDRED AND FIFTEEN

When Ryewall collapsed Malden was thrown from his feet. He was luckier than some of his archers, who were tossed off the wall altogether. Dust filled the sky and stones bounced off nearby rooftops, smashing chimney pots or shattering on the cobbles with great thuds. When the dust started to clear and Malden was able to stand again, he looked across a great gap in the wall, wide enough to march an army through.

Which was exactly what Mörget had in mind. "For Mother Death!" the chieftain called, and six thousand gruff voices answered with a cheer that made Malden's teeth rattle in his head. Below him the berserkers bit their shields and screamed and started running toward the gap, their axes flashing all around them, ready to kill without discernment. They made no attempt at formation as they came through the wall, stumbling over each other in their rage, their red-stained faces burning with blood.

Once they were inside, once they passed the wall, there would be no stopping the orgy of death they wreaked. Malden shouted for his archers to slaughter them, but the whores and thieves around him seemed too stunned to lift their bows.

Luckily the dwarves kept their heads.

"She's charged!" Balint called, and raced away from Slag's engine, as if terrified that it was going to erupt in fire at any second.

The berserkers scrambled over the pile of rubble that was the sole remnant of Ryewall. They leapt and cried like birds of prey as they came.

With perfect calmness, Slag reached into his fire with a pair of tongs. He brought out a piece of wire glowing red hot. He fixed this to the serpent head of his brass staff.

He seemed completely unaware that a horde of deadly berserkers was bearing down on him, only seconds away.

Malden could only watch in terror as that human flood came boiling toward his friend. Had Cythera sacrificed so much, had Slag lost his arm, had all of Malden's desperate hopes and Cutbill's schemes and the fears of an entire city come down to this? To a dwarf playing with a piece of hot wire?

Malden could just make out a tiny hole bored into the closed end of the bronze tube. He watched, not knowing what to think, as Slag carefully inserted his wire into the hole—and then dropped his staff and ran as fast as his short legs could possibly carry him.

"Go, go, go!" Mörget shouted. It sounded like he was right below Malden's feet.

Then there was a sound that Malden had never heard before. A sudden, horrible noise, louder than a lightning strike, that ran through Malden's body and threatened to crack his bones.

The noise alone was enough to strike a man dead.

But the noise was only a side effect of what Slag had wrought upon the world. Immense gouts of smoke and sparks burst from the mouth of the engine. The force it unleashed drove the engine backward, sent it flying into the front of a house directly across from the ruins of Ryewall. It smashed through plaster and beams and set the whole building ablaze.

In the gap, the berserkers froze in place as they were buffeted by the explosion. They seemed transfixed as a thousand whizzing noises shot past them, a million trails of sparks and fire. Iron tacks, horse brasses, broken and twisted pieces of door latches, soup spoons and farthing coins, andirons, candle snuffers, leather punches, signet rings and steel spurs—any metal scrap that Slag could find at the last moment, dozens of pounds of the stuff, countless pieces— came flying out of the mouth of the tube so fast and with so much force that they cut through flesh, shredded tissue, shattered bone into fragments. Lines of blood appeared on every berserker face and hand. Severed limbs tumbled through the air, as time itself slowed to a crawl. Whole bodies were taken to pieces as thoroughly—if not as neatly— as if they'd been worked on by a master butcher. Hair caught flame. Shields went spinning away like wagon wheels. Iron axes fell from broken, bloodied hands.

Those few berserkers who survived the blast stopped in their tracks. Their mouths hung open, their eyes wide, but no longer with the fury of battle. For the first time in the history of the eastern clans, someone had discovered a way to break the berserker trance.

Not howling, not foaming at the mouth any longer, but

crying for mercy, the berserkers turned and ran as fast as they might for the safety of their own camp. Not a single one of them made it through the wall.

CHAPTER ONE HUNDRED AND SIXTEEN

"What in the Lady's name was that?" Hew asked. Croy had no answer. He'd heard that noise like the sky had split open, seen the gout of baleful fire that lanced straight out from the breach in the wall. What could create such a tongue of deadly flame he could not imagine.

What he did know was that it had changed everything.

A melee battle like this was always a scene of chaos, of commanders shouting to know what was going on, of soldiers running back and forth, operating under orders that had been countermanded though they did not know it, of whole formations wheeling the wrong way because it was impossible, in the thick of things, to get a proper view on the proceedings. A good commander learned to take the temperature of a battle, to rely not on hard facts but intuition and respond accordingly. Croy had developed almost a sixth sense for such things.

A moment before he'd been convinced that Skrae had already lost, that the Army of Free Men was about to break and rout. That he was helpless and should retreat himself, if honor would have allowed it.

Now there was a different smell in the air. A smell at once hopeful and terrifying. It seemed that Croy still had a chance.

Some great miracle of magic and fire had burst from the walls of Ness, some work of sorcery perhaps, or witchcraft or . . . or divine favor or . . . it didn't matter. All that mattered was that he must, absolutely must, take advantage of the change before things settled and went back to how they'd been. "Press, and don't let up," Croy commanded. "Get our footmen over to the left—it's mostly thralls over there. Thralls who will surrender quickly, and open a wedge. We can split the horde in half, let the Free Men take one part, and—"

"Was that sorcery, do you think? A demon set loose?" Hew asked, softly.

Croy trudged over to him across the frozen ground and smacked the knight's greave with the flat of his blade. The impact seemed to shock Hew back to his senses.

"Press the fucking attack," Croy said.

It was not a word he used often. It had the desired effect. Hew rode forward to relay the command. Croy stomped after him. The steel armor he wore weighed him down, made his movements sluggish. He longed to be out of it. He longed to go running into the fight, to lose himself in swordwork.

Yet suddenly the barbarians were all moving away from him. Running toward the city. Did they run to get inside the walls? Yet it looked like they were being pushed toward one of the intact sections of wall, not toward the gap they'd made. Whatever infernal force had been set loose in that gap had cast terror into the hearts of the barbarians. They were not alone in their fear. Even the Skilfinger knights seemed loath to get close to the fires that still burned near the city. Croy waved Ghostcutter at them. "Push them up against the wall so they have nowhere to retreat! Press the attack!"

He heard his command repeated in the Skilfinger tongue. His translators were still alive, then. Good.

"Onward!" he shouted, and all around him went up a ragged cheer. He ran as fast as he could toward the main force of barbarians, heedless of how many casualties he took, heedless of his own safety.

He arrived just in time to find Mörget coming toward him, leading a host of reavers. The giant barbarian had an axe in one hand and Dawnbringer in the other, and he showed no sign of fear at all.

Very good. Here, at last, was an enemy that wouldn't run away.

Yet before Croy could reach Mörget, Sir Hew came riding past again, Chillbrand swinging low to touch as many barbarians as it could reach. Hew made no attempt to cut them, he just tapped his magic blade against their exposed skin wherever it presented itself. Their faces turned blue and they dropped their weapons to hug themselves for warmth as the Ancient Blade's magic stole all the heat from their bodies. Chillbrand flashed down to touch Mörget, but the chieftain was too fast for Hew. He ducked low and rolled between the legs of Hew's steed, disemboweling the beast before he rolled out the other side.

Hew was an old and seasoned warrior. He'd lost plenty of horses in his time, and knew how not to be thrown. Half sliding, half jumping, he landed on the frozen ground on one knee, his shield already coming up as Mörget advanced on him.

"You're not the one," Mörget growled.

Sir Hew started to rise, even as Mörget hammered at his shield with Dawnbringer. The Ancient Blade burst with light, again, again, again.

Hew pushed forward with the shield, perhaps trying to knock Mörget down. He might as well have tried to bull his way through a hill. Mörget's axe came down and split the side of Hew's vambrace wide open. There was blood on the blade when it came back up, and Hew's shield arm fell limp at his side. Croy raced forward to help his old friend, but he could only watch in horror as Mörget twisted around at the waist, all the strength of a rushing river in his axe arm.

Hew raised Chillbrand to ward off the blow. Axe and sword met with a horrible clang that made Croy's teeth hurt, even from a half dozen yards away.

The axe cut through Chillbrand's frost-rimed iron, barely slowing down as it shattered the Ancient Blade.

Mörget boomed out a gruesome laugh. "Another one!"

"Try this one," Croy screamed, and drove Ghostcutter deep into the barbarian's side. While Mörget exulted, he had closed the distance between them.

CHAPTER ONE HUNDRED AND SEVENTEEN

Slag crowed and danced and shouted up to Malden where he stood on the wall, "Lad! Lad! Did you fucking see that?"

"I did," Malden called back. He turned to the far side of the wall and peered down. The barbarians had surged away from the gap in the wall. Terror gripped them—many had even dropped their weapons. Yet behind them were thousands more, confused, perhaps even frightened by all the noise and smoke, but who had seen nothing of what Slag's weapon could do. Still they pressed onwards toward Ness. Still they continued the attack.

He looked all around for Mörget, because he knew that once the huge barbarian had time to realize what had happened he would instantly begin rallying his troops for another attack. Even fire and destruction would not stop that man.

This wasn't over. This was just beginning.

Cold fright gripped Malden's bowels and he worried he might soil himself. They'd driven back the first wave, that was true. Slag had made that happen. Yet now there was an enormous gaping hole in the wall. Malden had no way to fight an effective battle without the wall to protect them.

Ness had a hope in the opposing army—though not much of one. Who was it out there, fighting the barbarians from the rear? Was it the Burgrave and his Army of Free Men? There was no way that rabble could defeat Mörget once he regrouped. They might be making some small dent in the rearguard but they could never hope to overcome the main force of easterners.

Malden rubbed at his face. It was bitterly cold up on the

wall where the wind stung every bit of exposed flesh, but still his face was wet. Greasy, sick-smelling sweat rolled down inside the collar of his tunic and pooled in the small of his back. He had to do something. Something!

He hurried down the wall and ran over to where Slag stood, still holding his snake-headed staff.

"Come to congratulate me?" the dwarf asked.

Balint was inspecting the broken wall, picking up chunks of masonry and debris and then casting them away again. Malden grabbed her arm and pulled her over to where Slag stood. "You two are the finest engineers this world has ever known, surely. And you deserve a grand reward already. But I must ask you to continue your labors. Get your weapon ready to be used once more. Once the barbarians have a chance to find their scattered wits, we'll need to strike them again. And again."

The two dwarves looked up at him with open mouths and wide eyes.

"I know I ask much of you, but—"

Malden stopped. He knew what they were going to say. So badly did he not want to hear it that he held up a hand to keep them from speaking.

He looked up at the weapon, the giant brass tube that Slag had made. It had rolled back into a house across the street, shattering the façade and half burying itself in fallen timbers and bricks.

It had also shattered itself. Long cracks ran up and down its length, and its mouth was splayed wide, the bright metal curled backwards on itself like a flower of brass. Smoke dribbled from that opening still.

It was clear to anyone, even one of so little learning as Malden, that it would never work again. It had done what it could, but in the process it had destroyed itself.

"That . . . was it," Malden said. "Wasn't it? There was only one volley in it."

"I did warn you, lad," Slag said, in a very small voice.

Malden closed his eyes. Was this the end? "Then we must all hope," he said, "that Tarness is as great a general as he thinks he is."

CHAPTER ONE HUNDRED AND EIGHTEEN

Mörget shouted in pain and for a moment froze in place, unable to continue his attack. It gave Hew time to scuttle away on his back like a crab, and that gave Croy room to dance around and face Mörget directly. He knew better than to think his blow had killed the barbarian, though he was certain he'd pierced vital organs.

It had not been a particularly virtuous attack. He'd struck out blindly to save Hew—but even Mörget deserved a better death than a sneak attack to his unprotected side. Croy stepped back, flicking blood away from Ghostcutter's blade, while the giant barbarian bent around his wound and watched his blood drip on the ground.

There was a way these things should be done. When two great swordsmen met in single combat, it was called a conversation, because the swords ringing against each other could sound like they were arguing in something approaching human speech. But also because any such fight should properly begin with words.

Each side must state his case—explain, in detail, why he had the right to win the contest. Why fate should favor him. It was an old ritual, but it served one perfectly functional purpose as well. The banter before the exchange of blows could drive one man or the other to anger or fear or resignation to death. Many conversations ended before swords even met or blood was drawn. Croy was a master of every aspect of the swordsman's art and he knew how to taunt and accuse just as well as he knew how to parry and feint and lunge.

"'My sword is my soul,'" Croy said. The creed of the Ancient Blades. "You don't have a soul, do you,

Mountainslayer?" he asked. "You defile Dawnbringer by touching it."

"A soul?" Mörget asked. He looked as if he would be happy to discuss fine points of philosophy rather than continue the fight. As if his wound didn't pain him at all. Perhaps Mörget had learned something about dismissing pain while he had been a berserker. "Perhaps I do not. But I am possessed by a *wyrd*."

Croy had no idea what that meant. He did know he was fighting one-armed against a giant of a man who could fight with two weapons at once. "Have you any honor?" he asked. "Face me, blade to blade. Like a knight. Prove to me you have the right to carry Dawnbringer. Or die, and let me take it from you. That's one of the vows we take as Ancient Blades. If we fail to live up to the sword's worth, it will be taken from us. Given to someone more virtuous."

"Come and get it, then. For I have no virtue at all," Mörget said. "I'm too honest for such lies as honor and valor. All I know is strength and glory."

Croy tried to laugh. All that came out of his mouth was a dry rasping rattle. "To the end you are a barbarian. Uncultured, and unknowing of the ways of true honor. You never deserved to hold Dawnbringer. Look, even now you hold it the same way you hold your axe. Like a laborer holding a tool. A true warrior fights with sword alone."

Mörget smiled, showing enormous teeth like the pegs on the neck of a lute. He bowed, slightly. Then he made a great show of dropping his axe.

Croy spared a quick look around him. Reavers surrounded him on all sides, but they were holding back—either because they knew Mörget would want to fight Croy alone, or because the Skilfinger knights were constantly harrying them to keep them away from the regent of Skrae.

Fate had conspired to bring the two of them together like this. At long last. From the moment Croy had realized Mörget still lived—when he struck down Sir Orne and broke Bloodquaffer, while Croy carried the sleeping king away from Helstrow—he had known this moment would come.

Justice, honor and the Lady were all on his side.

Against them Mörget had an enormous reserve of strength and a shocking brutality of nature. This wasn't going to be easy.

"I called you brother, once," Croy said, taking a step sideways, toward Mörget's less defensible left. "That was a mistake."

"I took your hand in friendship, once," Mörget replied, not bothering to follow Croy's footwork. "It was the smartest thing I ever did. Look where it got me!"

"It's about to get you killed," Croy said.

Mörget looked as if he was framing a reply.

Croy didn't wait to hear it. He leapt inward, striking low at Mörget's thigh. Ghostcutter rang like a bell when Dawnbringer came down to block its cut. Light flashed up from Mörget's blade.

"Fie!" Croy cursed, blinking furiously. The light had dazzled him momentarily—but even in that split second Mörget had plenty of time to counter-attack.

Yet the barbarian did not take the advantage. "You could be the enemy I've sought," Mörget said. "The man my *wyrd* has been chasing all this time. Yet I see you've been wounded, and have not yet had time to heal. Should we postpone this fight for another day?"

Croy spun around, Ghostcutter whistling over his head. Dawnbringer came up and batted it away with little effort. At least this time Croy kept enough of his wits about him not to look into the blade as it flared with light.

He tried to follow through with a slash down the center of Mörget's chest, but Dawnbringer moved so quickly he couldn't follow it and parried the strike. Croy took a half step backward, then spun Ghostcutter around and around in a series of quick, shallow cuts that would never kill Mörget but might make him bleed.

Dawnbringer rang and flared, rang and flared, rang and flared once more. Not once did Ghostcutter break through that flurry of iron.

Staggering backwards, Croy sucked wildly for breath. He didn't have the stamina for this. It was possible—just possible—that a man with boundless energy could wear

Mörget down, given enough time. Croy's limbs, though, were already gripped by fatigue and his armor had never felt heavier.

"You've made your choice, then," Mörget said. "I'll give you time to pray, if you like. Before I cut you in half. Perhaps I was wrong. Perhaps yours is not the strength my father spoke of, either. Perhaps—"

With everything he had left, Croy brought Ghostcutter around in one unstoppable cut, the kind of furious strike that could carve a man like a goose. It was the most deadly attack he knew how to make, and desperation pushed it harder than any blow he'd ever swung before.

Dawnbringer came down hard, and the two blades met with a sickening crunch.

Burning light erupted all along the length of Dawnbringer's forte. Ghostcutter grew hot in Croy's hands as the cold iron of its blade took the energy of the blow and lost its near-magical temper. Silver flaked away from the sword's trailing edge.

Neither man could move. The swords had cut into each other, locking together as if they had fused into one piece of iron. For a moment everything was frozen, time itself having stopped to wait and see what happened next.

Then Mörget wrapped both hands around the hilt of Dawnbringer. He twisted from the hip, his massive arms flexing until the veins popped out on his forearms and Croy could see his pulse beating.

There was a noise like great mill wheels grinding against one another, and then a soul-sickening snap. Dawnbringer gave out one last feeble burst of light.

Both swords exploded into shards that spun and hung in the air and flashed with reflected sunlight when they hit the snow. Both men stood where they'd been, holding only the hilts of now-useless weapons.

"My soul," Croy whispered. "My sword—"

"I see, now," Mörget said. He raised his free hand high as if beseeching the heavens. His eyes weren't looking at Croy but at a dead man. "I see it, father. *This* is my *wyrd*. My destiny. To destroy not men, but their swords. To be the last of the Ancient Blades, and their ending. This is what drove me, and now—"

Croy threw himself forward. The hilt in his hand ended in a good inch and a half of broken metal, jagged and sharp. Ghostcutter would perform one last service in the name of Skrae.

He punched the inch and a half in through Mörget's left eye. He ground it in until he felt bone split.

Mörget dropped the ruin of Dawnbringer and squealed in fury and pain. Then he brought up one massive fist and slammed Croy away from him, smashing the knight along the jaw so that Croy's head spun round and up and white light burst in his head, white light that faded to black.

The blow laid Croy out on the iron-flecked snow, unable to stand, unable to focus his eyes. Skilfinger knights came and dragged him away, slapped his face and shouted his name until he could see again, see and hear the sounds of the battle. It raged still all around him.

"Mörget," he said. "Mörget—does he still live? Did you see his body?"

But the Skilfingers didn't know his language, and none of his translators were nearby.

CHAPTER ONE HUNDRED AND NINETEEN

Smoke from the explosion of Slag's weapon hung in the air, great choking clouds of it. Malden hurried forward into the gap in the city wall, his ankles twisting this way and that as he clambered over piles of broken stone and the bodies of dead berserkers. He heard movement up ahead of him and he drew Acidtongue from its sheath. There was no telling what lay out there, beyond the wall.

Behind him a mob of armed citizens had formed. They muttered and moaned amongst themselves, terrified as he was, as desperate to learn how things stood beyond the wall. Ready for whatever came through, or as ready as they could be.

At least this time they weren't calling for his blood. They weren't demanding he sacrifice himself at the Godstone for the good of the city.

Malden trod on the shield of a dead berserker and it crackled under his foot. It had been so peppered with flying debris that the wood fell apart like hard cheese. Up ahead, in the dim smoke, something moved fast across his field of vision.

He lowered himself to a defensive crouch. He remembered the ill-fitting suit of armor he'd worn when he spoke to Mörg from atop the wall. As painful as it had been to wear, he would have been glad of its protection now.

Moving forward, he lifted his free hand and waved it behind him, ushering the mob forward, after him. He didn't bother to look back to see if they complied. Another step, into the smoke. Another, Acidtongue's point bobbing in the air as Malden sought for something to strike.

When the reaver came for him he still wasn't ready. The man was huge, a wall of muscle, his face red with blood, his axe raised high. He looked even more terrified than Malden felt, but the thief knew that fear could make a man more dangerous than a lion.

The axe came down before Malden could even react, its wicked pointed blade slicing through the air. Malden tried to dodge to the side but the blow was just too fast, just too brutal. Malden winced, expecting to be cut in two.

Instead the axe struck a stone near Malden's feet, smashing it to powder.

"Where are you, you western bastard?" the reaver demanded. "I can smell you! I can taste your blood already!"

It was only then that Malden realized the reaver was blind. A sword stroke had cut across his face, ruining his eyes. Other wounds marred his arms and chest. The man must have been wounded in the fighting outside, then wandered in through the gap in the wall without even realizing where he was.

Malden felt pity well up in his chest for the barbarian, despite the fact the man had just tried to kill him. It was no kind of world for a blind man. "Surrender," he said, almost pleading with the reaver. "Give in, and you'll be spared, I promise—"

"Die, you fucker!" someone shouted, from behind Malden and high over his head.

One after another five arrows pierced the reaver's body. The barbarian winced and staggered backwards under the blows, then sank to his knees and gasped out his last.

Malden turned and looked up at his archers atop the wall. They waved cheerily down at him, and he raised Acidtongue in a half-hearted salute. A bead of vitriol rolled down the blade and stung his fingers, but he made a point of not flinching.

He turned back to the gap and moved forward into the smoke, as carefully as he could. Soon he was as blind as the man he'd just watched die. His throat burned with the stink of brimstone and he would not have been surprised if he walked out of the cloud straight into the pit itself.

When he did emerge it was to find a scene not wholly dissimilar. Bodies littered the ground before him, bodies torn to rags of flesh and dropped without ceremony. Directly ahead an army of men—Free Men, but also knights on horseback—pressed an attack, driving home lances and pike heads as barbarians screamed and died. The horde was pushed up against the city wall with nowhere to run, hemmed in on two sides by advancing troops.

"In Sadu's name," Malden said. "Are we winning?"

He could scarcely believe it. Yet he had the evidence of his own eyes to prove it.

Barbarians were cut down in waves. Some tried throwing away their weapons and shields but the Free Men ran them through anyway. The pikemen had to stop from time to time to shove the amassed bodies out of their path just so they could continue their advance.

"They're giving way," someone said from behind Malden's shoulder. He turned and saw a hundred citizens of Ness—his own paltry troops—gathering to watch. "Ness is saved!" He could see the bloodthirst on their faces. The joy they took in this spectacle. He couldn't blame them, in all fairness. How long had they lived in terror of the barbarian throng? How long had they been expecting that horde to come sweeping through their houses, murdering and savaging? Now they had their revenge. "This is your victory, Lord Mayor! Sadu be praised!"

But for Malden, the vision was utterly sickening. Barbarians were being put to death out there by the hundreds. The soldiers were executing them. They weren't even trying to fight back. Where was Mörget to rally them? Where was Mörgain? The mounted knights cried out and drove a wedge between two masses of pikemen, as if they were afraid the footmen would have all the fun without them.

"Look! There!" someone called. "It's Sir Croy!"

Malden felt like the wind had been knocked out of him. Or perhaps like he was seeing a ghost. But there, yes—right there—was the knight-errant, limping along in his armor, clutching his side. His colors, black and silver, were instantly recognizable, but even at a distance Malden knew that face. An empty scabbard bounced against his thigh. Where was Ghostcutter? Malden couldn't remember the last time he'd seen Croy without it.

More to the point—Croy was here? Croy had come to Ness?

At least, Malden thought, Croy would put an end to this slaughter. He would drag his men back from the brink of madness and keep them from butchering every single barbarian on the field. Any minute now, Malden was certain, Croy would raise his voice and call out to give quarter, to end the bloodshed. Surely honor demanded it.

Someone brought Croy a horse. Someone else helped him climb up into its saddle. It seemed to take forever, and all the while the wholesale murder continued. The barbarians tried to surrender en masse, lifting their arms high, their weapons piled in glittering heaps at their feet. It made no difference. The knights and pikemen might have been slaughtering wild animals out there.

"Come now, Croy," Malden whispered. "For honor's sake."

Croy stood up in his saddle. His hand reached for a sword that wasn't there. Instead he lifted one armored fist.

"No quarter!" he shouted.

The civilized armies took that as a sign to cheer and redouble their attacks, even as the barbarians howled for peace, for mercy, for justice.

Malden staggered back to the gap in the wall. Alone he slunk back inside the comforting embrace of his city. Slag came running up through the smoke and grabbed at the hem of his tunic with his one remaining hand.

"What is it, lad? What did you see?"

"We won," Malden told him. He very much wanted to go sit down somewhere.

CHAPTER ONE HUNDRED AND TWENTY

The Lemon Garden was far enough from Ryewall that Malden could not hear the sounds of the work crews busily repairing the fallen wall. Nor could he smell the bodies that lay beyond it, all that remained of the barbarian horde, unburied save by snow. In his private room upstairs he had a cheerful fire going, and while there was nothing to eat there was plenty of wine to be had, or ale if his guests preferred it.

He made no apologies for asking them to attend upon him in a bawdy house. Nor did they express offense, at least

not openly. Elody led them to Malden's door and curtseyed
deeply, as if she was unsure what the proper show of honor
would be for three such distinguished guests. None of their
station had ever visited her humble place of business before—
typically, had they required the services she provided, they
would have gone instead to Herwig's House of Sighs.

The soldiers who accompanied these three were of a
different lot in life, and were happy enough to be entertained
in the courtyard.

For a while, none of the four men spoke or even looked
each other in the eye. Sir Croy wouldn't even sit down. He
stood by the door as if guarding it. Such duty was, of course,
far beneath him now—Malden had heard of Croy's elevation.
Somewhere he had found a circlet of silver that he wore
upon his brow to indicate that he had become the Regent of
Skrae. Ostentation had never been Croy's style, but he had
to ensure that he looked at least the equal to Ommen Tarness,
the Burgrave, who wore his own coronet everywhere.

Sir Hew, Captain of the Queen's Guard, wore only the
colors of his sovereign. His left arm was in a sling tied
around his waist, but still he seemed the best pleased of the
three to be there. While Tarness and Croy stared daggers at
each other, he gladly took a cup of hot mulled wine.

"Just what these aching bones need," he said, and drained
the cup in a single draught. Malden poured him another.

"I understand you were wounded by Mörget in the battle,"
Malden said. "Few men can make that claim. Few living
men, anyway."

Hew favored him with a warm smile. "I'll heal. I dare
say none of us came out of this unscathed. Though some
certainly profited. Didn't they, my Lord Mayor?"

Malden returned his smile, but said nothing.

The three visitors intended to strip him of that title, one
way or another. The Burgrave wanted his city back. Having
ruled it for eight hundred years, he seemed to think it
belonged to him. Croy and Hew wanted Ness as a staging
ground—a fortress they could hold through the winter, until
spring cleared the roads and they could mount an attack on
Helstrow, and take it back from Mörgain.

So far Malden had managed to keep them all out. He had refused to unseal the gates until he was given guarantees of safety for himself and his people—as well as certain other considerations. Chief among them, the right to worship whichever god they pleased, a right to be added to the city's charter in perpetuity. For himself and his thieves he'd asked immunity from prosecution for the murder of Pritchard Hood, the burglary of the entire Golden Slope, the seizure of the arsenal, and so many more crimes.

Hew and Tarness had been happy to accept these terms, and each had sent messengers indicating that anything else Malden desired would be made his. In response, Malden had allowed the three and a small number of bodyguards inside the wall so they could discuss terms.

Of course, all this politesse was just for show. The gates might be sealed, but until the gap in the Ryewall was repaired it would be simple enough for either army to storm the city. Malden had forestalled that kind of drastic measure in a way that should make Cutbill proud. Rather than threaten two armies he could not beat, he had held out the promise of a reward they both desperately wanted.

"Perhaps," Hew went on, "you might profit further. I see you wear Acidtongue, still." The knight nodded at the sword on Malden's belt. "I'm sure you haven't forgotten how you fared when you tried to use it against me."

Malden laughed in good humor. "Forgotten that? Hardly. I sometimes wonder if I feel winter's chill, these days, or simply remember the touch of Chillbrand."

It was not lost on anyone in the room that neither Hew nor Croy had a sword on their own hips.

"Perhaps you would do me the signal honor of training you in your weapon's proper use?" Hew asked. "I've seen your potential. You're as fast as the wind. It would only take a little practice to make a first rate swordsman of you. And as an Ancient Blade, you would be entitled to all manner of privileges. Houses, lands, perhaps a manor of your own to profit by. Why, Malden, you could become quite the gentleman, in time."

Malden tried to catch Croy's eye, to determine how much

of that would have the backing of a royal decree. It was well within Croy's power to appoint Malden to any knighthood or lordship he saw fit. There were very few limits now as to what Croy could do now—at least until Bethane reached her majority.

What Croy might be thinking at that moment, however, remained a mystery. The knight-turned-regent's face might have been chiseled from marble for all it revealed.

Hew cleared his throat and smiled when Malden turned to face him again. "I suppose what I'm saying is that you've proved yourself a hero, and a man all Skrae can be proud of. I'd like to repay you for your impressive work. Yet before any of that reward can be granted, I do require that you open the gates to our Skilfinger friends. And, of course—"

"Yes?" Malden asked. The bait was wriggling. The fish were biting.

"We'd like to speak with your dwarf."

There it was. They'd taken the hook.

Slag had invented something terrible and strange. A new weapon, one that could change the way wars were fought. One that could change the world. Whichever army came into possession of the secret formula would be nigh invincible.

"It would be a terrible shame if his knowledge were to fall into the wrong hands," Hew said. "Hands, to be blunt about it, which would only divide this land further. Can I call upon your patriotism, now? Can I ask you to aid me, in one simple, effortless way, to save your country, as you have already saved your city?"

The Burgrave snorted in derision. "His city? It isn't his city."

"It's not yours, either," Hew said, his eyes suddenly very sharp. "Not right now."

"It belongs to no one. And to everyone," Tarness replied. "To every free man. Give me the dwarf, Malden. Open the gates to my army."

Malden sat down on the bed. He meant to suggest nothing by his choice of perch, but he saw Croy's chin jerk round as if he'd violated some holy taboo. For a moment no one spoke, yet every one must have been wondering the same thing. What had just passed through Croy's mind?

Sir Hew broke the silence by clearing his throat. "He seems to offer you nothing in return," he said, tilting his head toward the Burgrave.

"Is that correct?" Malden asked.

"It is, in fact. I offer you nothing, Malden. I don't owe you anything. You protected this city because you were one of its citizens. Any man of Ness would have done the same."

"Hmm," Malden said.

"So I offer you nothing, save freedom. Freedom not just for yourself. For every man willing to reach out and grasp it."

"Tread carefully, Tarness." Sir Hew rose to his feet. "You're talking mutiny. Insurrection."

"I am talking of rights. Not just rights granted by some antiquated charter signed by a king long dead." The Burgrave frowned and looked upward. "I speak of rights every man has, by virtue of being born."

Malden drank some wine. He waited to hear if there was anything else. Any further offers, any further appeals. There were none. The three of them had said what they'd come to say.

And so there it was. Malden must choose, it seemed, between one ruler or another. He could allow the Burgrave to return to Castle Hill (he would have to rebuild his palace, but that was a minor detail) and restore Ness to what it had once been. Or he could turn the city over to Hew and Croy and declare for the kingdom, and become a lord in his own right.

Or—and the thought made Malden smile despite himself—he could refuse both entreaties. He could keep the gates sealed. He could stay on as Lord Mayor. Oh, they wouldn't like it. The Burgrave and the Regent would want to take Ness at any cost. But Malden could buy them off. He could turn Slag over to one or the other and in return he could have Ness as his very own fief.

The people would stand behind him. They loved the Burgrave in their way—just as they always had, loved him just as much as they hated him. And they were all Skraelings, and loyal to the flag and queen Bethane—as loyal as free people in a free city that didn't pay taxes could ever be. The Lord Mayor, though, was their hero. He had saved Ness in its darkest time. He had worked miracles with nothing, and he had delivered them from certain death.

It would be a hard fought thing, but he could stay exactly where he was.

And in truth that had a certain appeal. He had been born the lowliest of Ness's citizens. The son of a whore, and then a thief. Now he was a great man and well beloved and he held all the power of the city in his hands. As much as every day of his reign had been misery and toil, beset by endless problems (very few of which had gone away—the city was still starving and his thieves were still restless with nothing to steal), for a moment, for just one moment, he had become more than what he'd been born into. He'd been respected, and adored. And he had possessed power, which, it seemed, was the closest thing to freedom a man had in this world.

In the process he'd lost Cythera. He'd nearly lost Slag. Velmont had betrayed him and Cutbill had used him to his own nefarious ends. But everywhere he went in the city, people had smiled and lifted their hands and been glad to see him.

"Perhaps," Malden said, "you'd be kind enough to let me sleep on this decision," he said, patting the bedclothes by way of jest.

He did not expect what came next.

"No, damn you," Croy said, storming across the room. He leaned over Malden and for a moment their eyes locked. "You'll give us your answer now."

Malden heard the words. They did not register within his brain, however, because Croy had communicated something far more important with a look.

He knows, Malden thought.

He knows about what Cythera and I had.

He glanced down at the bed on which he sat. The same bed where he and Cythera had played at being man and wife for a few precious, irrecoverable nights.

Croy growled, low in his throat, like a barbarian.

Ah. Well. That changed everything, didn't it?

"Very well," Malden said, and rose carefully from the bed. Croy did not take a step back, so Malden had to snake around him. "Very well. You need a decision now. I understand you must be very impatient, after having been through so much." He went over to the table where the wine bottle stood. A broad casement window above the table looked out on the dwindling sunlight of afternoon.

Malden was a thief. He thought, still, like a thief.

When he had entered the room, he'd made sure that window was unlatched. Just in case.

"Here is what I have to say, then."

The three of them leaned close to hear it.

"Work it out between yourselves, you bastards." He threw one foot up on the table and vaulted out the window, which flung open under his weight. Three faces rushed to watch him as he scrambled up to the roof of the Lemon Garden, then danced away across the rooftops.

EPILOGUE

He'd made his decision. He'd been forced to pick between responsibility and death. Like a good thief, he'd picked the third option no one else had seen: he had picked freedom.

A little boat awaited him at the Ditchside Stair. It was, in point of fact, the same boat Velmont had intended to use to escape from the city. Malden had not been able to ascertain what had happened to the Helstrovian thief—but he had it on good authority that Velmont didn't need the boat anymore. Cutbill had seen to that.

Slag was already aboard. The dwarf had fitted himself

with a new wooden arm to replace the one he'd lost. He waved merrily as Malden approached, his real hand grasping the painter that held the boat to the dock. Balint sat at the rudder, looking bored and anxious to be gone. Malden had one more stop to make before he left, however.

Cutbill sat on a stool in a tiny cookshop nearby, little more than a stall with a counter where fishermen could sit and eat fish stew before they set out for their catch. The guildmaster of thieves had a wide-brimmed hat pulled low over his eyes.

"Half the city is looking for you," Cutbill said. "It seems you left a bit of business unresolved."

"Hardly. I did what I set out to do—I kept the city safe from the barbarians."

"Ah, but responsibility never actually ends," Cutbill said. "I should know. A problem solved is simply the first step toward discovering the next problem. Still, I imagine our wise and just rulers will handle things just fine without you. Tell me, was it difficult to give up all that power?"

Malden shrugged. "You should know that, too."

Cutbill nodded. "Yet now here you are, running away like a thief again."

"Croy will kill me the very first second he gets the chance," Malden admitted. "He knows I've been swiving his betrothed. How she might have felt about things makes no difference to him."

"The Burgrave might have protected you," Cutbill suggested.

"Tarness? From the second he was forced to acknowledge my existence he's always wanted to kill me for one reason or another. Now he's got even more cause—I stole his city."

"So you're running because your life is in danger."

Yes, Malden thought. *Isn't that reason enough?*

Except that it wasn't.

Malden looked up at the ruins of Castle Hill. "If I stayed it would mean more trouble for Ness, and she's been through enough lately. If I gave preference to one army, the other wouldn't just go away. The one who lost out would besiege the city—again—and only further this misery. If they both take the city, they'll have to work together to put it back together again. For a while, at least, they'll have to pretend to like each other. And as long as that fragile peace lasts, the people of Ness won't suffer and die for ideals they never understood, much less believed in."

Cutbill nodded. "Well played."

Malden sighed. "The people won't see it that way. Some of them will call me a coward. Some of the same people who called me a hero yesterday. I admit it will bother me."

"I never thought the love of the people was what you desired," Cutbill said. "It's too fickle a commodity to be relied on, anyway."

"Is that why you always work in the shadows?" Malden asked.

"Power must often be its own reward."

"Power," Malden repeated. "Power. I thought if I had power it would make me free. It's completely the opposite though, isn't it? The more power you have the more chains there are that bind you. To have power over others, you must at the same time give them power over you. Freedom and power are incompatible."

Cutbill shook his head. "I'll miss you, Malden. It was nice having someone so devious around. Someone whose brain ran along the same tracks as mine." He held out one hand. "Do me the honor of taking this, will you? It will mark you as a friend of mine, to anyone who knows what it means."

Malden took the badge that Cutbill offered. It was a small enamel pin, painted to show a heart transfixed by a key. Cutbill's personal symbol, in essence his coat of arms.

"No offense meant, but I intend to go somewhere they've never heard of you," Malden said. "And then go a bit farther still."

Cutbill smiled. "You'll have to go very, very far away, then. I have friends in many places. You'll know them when you meet them. If you ever need their help on your travels, show that badge to them."

Malden sighed. "I thank you. You know, I never did get my revenge on you for trying to have me killed."

"Do you expect an apology, now?"

"I suppose not," Malden said.

He headed down to the boat, then. Between himself and the dwarves it was easy enough to get it underway. Eastpool was frozen over, but everywhere the boat went the ice broke up before its prow and then re-froze just behind its stern.

"Malden, ask your witchy slut if she can un-freeze my arse, too," Balint said. "It feels like a block of ice from sitting so long on this leaky tub."

Malden made no reply. Balint's barbs could not touch him now.

They passed the Isle of Horses on their way toward the sea. A figure dressed in a black robe stood on the shore, watching them. Cythera wore a veil now, too, whether she needed it or not. She'd made her choices.

Yet Malden did not want to accept it was truly over. He waved to her, beckoned her to join him. To come with him, wherever he went. He knew she would not. It would mean giving up all her magic, both witchcraft and sorcery. It would mean leaving her mother behind, Coruth who was still in the shape of a tree as she recovered from her exertions.

"Come anyway. I promise it won't be boring," he whispered, to the wind.

She only watched him go, and did not so much as lift a hand in farewell.

By the time she dwindled behind him until he could no longer see her, the boat was running fast on open water that was kept liquid by the current rather than by her spells. Malden felt saltwater on his cheeks.

"You're not fucking weeping, are you lad?" Slag asked. Balint looked up with hungry eyes, hunting fodder for her mockery.

"It's just the spray from the sea," Malden replied.

And thus it was, that Malden the Thief, Malden the Lord Mayor, left the Free City of Ness. And how it was he came to wear at his belt the sword called Acidtongue, very last of the Ancient Blades.

THE END